PRAISE FOR *S*.

T0266375

"A thrilling and elegantly wrought de
our decisions, and our irrepressible .
Treiber is a writer of enormous talents, and *Spirit Walk* will leave you
breathless until the final page."

—JONATHAN EVISON,
author of *The Revised Fundamentals of Caregiving* and *West of Here*

"At once gritty and lyrical, *Spirit Walk* is a haunting tale of the modern
American West. Out of the explosive violence, hard living, and stark
beauty of the Arizona borderlands, Jay Treiber has woven a gripping
story of remembrance and redemption, beautifully painting the place
and giving voice to its people. I can't stop thinking about it."

—JENNIFER CARRELL,
author of *Haunt Me Still* and *Interred with Their Bones*

"There's a wonderful sense of authenticity and place here, as well as a
credible and engaging set of characters. It's a book that on one level is a
strong page-turner, with a plot that takes us into a trip of discovery as
the best of mysteries do, but also explores in good Faulknerian fashion
the burden of guilt and pain that discovery of the truths about the past
brings with it. Add to that just a taste of Tony Hillerman's recognition
of the other kinds of mystery that always hang over the Southwest's
past (and present), and Jay Treiber has given us a rich, well written,
multi-layered book to satisfy wide reading appetites."

—ROBERT HOUSTON, author of *Bisbee 17*

"The borderland setting of *Spirit Walk* only appears empty. This landscape is inhabited by commingled cultures, crisscrossed jurisdictions,
and colliding values—where a rancher wouldn't leave a bottle cap, traf-
fickers litter bodies. Depicting an episode of violence as confound-
ing in memory as the day it erupted, Jay Treiber shows the corrosive
costs of the drug trade—and of burying the past. In the vein of Philip
Caputo's *Crossers*."

—CHARLIE QUIMBY, author of *Monument Road*

Spirit Walk

by Jay Treiber

TORREY HOUSE PRESS, LLC

SALT LAKE CITY • TORREY

First Torrey House Press Edition, May 2014
Copyright © 2014 by Jay Treiber

Published by Torrey House Press, LLC
Salt Lake City, Utah
www.torreyhouse.com

International Standard Book Number: 978-1-937226-29-9
Library of Congress Control Number: 2014930122

Author photo by Egnecia Stafford
Cover and interior design by Rick Whipple, Sky Island Studio

FSC
www.fsc.org
MIX
Paper from
responsible sources
FSC® C011935

Spirit Walk

by Jay Treiber

*In dedication
to the memory
of my father,
Tom Treiber
1940 - 2004*

One

A hoarse wind had piled up from the south and by afternoon blew strong enough to make the wires on that particular stretch of fence hum. Kevin noted their faint music as he looked down at the kid, maybe half an hour dead, his jacket sleeves tangled in the barbs as if he had tried to climb his way out of oncoming death. The boy's hazel eyes had clouded, and with his slack body hanging from the strands, he appeared for all the world like a scarecrow on permanent vigil over his charge of jack wood and cedar trees. His hat had fallen to the wayside, and a lock of his sand colored hair lifted with the late fall breeze. The neck wound had emptied down the front of his shirt, the blood gone tacky and smelling, Kevin thought, the same way an old penny tastes on the tongue.

A tapping noise lifted Kevin away from the grip of that long-ago moment. He turned his head to find Julie, the student aid, rapping lightly on the doorframe to his office. "Dr. McNally?" she said, smiling. "Are you okay?"

He pushed his fingers back through his hair and swiveled his chair around to face her.

"The lady in the Indian dress came by again." Julie shifted a leg, fidgeted with the pen she held. "Your stalker?"

Olivia Hallot had phoned the office earlier and said she'd be on campus sometime that day. He'd successfully ducked her all afternoon, but now that he was back from his last class, it looked like she would finally corner him.

Kevin shook his head, looked to the computer screen where he'd been pretending to vet emails. "She's not a stalker, Julie. She's an old friend."

"I think she might be lost on campus somewhere. What should I tell her if she comes by again?"

Kevin struggled to call up a response. "You don't have to worry about her, Julie. I'll handle it."

The girl backed out of the office a step. "Okay," she said, lingering a moment before stepping away, her heel clicks fading down the hallway.

1

Alone now, Kevin closed his eyes and pressed his palms hard against his forehead. "Shit," he said, shaking his head. "It's not her fault." Olivia had come unbidden, and like the bad memories, could not be ignored.

Those memories caught Kevin off guard frequently now, the triggers that prompted them multiplying by the day. The nightmares could not be helped, but the daytime memories brought a distinct kind of discomfort, as though he had lost the refuge of his waking hours when the old hurt could be pushed away with the sunlight.

Perhaps it was Olivia's presence or the breeze that swayed the branches on the planted mesquites outside his window that had brought him back to a place in his mind he did not usually go. As if caught in some kernel of compressed time and space, he found himself in that long ago November morning on the Escrobarra Ridge. The dirt smell of grama and bunch grass rode on a soft wind and the grackles spoke from the tops of the oaks. The sky had begun to whiten in the east, and young Kevin wore the easiness of seventeen years like a light jacket.

The hunt that Friday morning had started with the customary excitement. He'd parked his truck at one of the usual spots, and with him as always was Armando Luna—they had hunted deer and *javelina* together these last five years. An hour before, Kevin had stopped in Douglas at a ramshackle duplex apartment. Luna had emerged half-dressed, rheumy-eyed with sleep and offering no excuses or apologies.

"Shit, Mondy," Kevin said. "You told me you'd be ready."

"I am ready," Luna said. "Just give me a minute."

Mondy was broad and thick at the belly and chest, built like a middle linebacker, and despite his 250 pounds walked light on his small feet. Kevin stood in the doorway as Mondy clambered in and out of rooms. A young woman's voice came from the bedroom, and Kevin recognized it immediately as that of Jolene Sanders, who'd been two years ahead of him in school. Jolene had wavy nut-brown hair to her belt loops and blue eyes. She was stone-cold beautiful and Kevin stood livid and jealous that she now lay in Armando Luna's bed. He could not for the life of him determine why. Kevin could hear their voices, a soft love-clucking behind the bedroom door, until Mondy stepped out with his rifle and gear and smiled at Kevin quick and smug as he passed him in the doorway.

They took Geronimo Trail east twenty miles to the Magoffin Ranch road, where they unlocked and passed through the gate, then bounced Kevin's old three-quarter-ton truck to the head of Baker Canyon. They hooked south a mile on a track that quit at a windmill, water tank, and a scattering of salt licks at the base of the Escrobarra. Shot with runs of granite rim rock and dense stands of jack pine, juniper and oak, the ridge occupied a six-mile length of the twenty-five mile Peloncillo mountain range. It started on the Arizona side, doglegged two miles into New Mexico, then tapered into a gentle slope across the Mexican border at the point where the two states and Sonora intersected.

Mondy tried to convince Kevin to park at a different spot, another half-mile up canyon, but Kevin, as usual, ignored him. They stepped out into the chilly near-dawn and gathered their essentials from the truck bed—rifles, binoculars, canteens, a single daypack in which they carried emergency items, and a lunch of left-over roast beef and tortillas.

"We're pretty close to the border," Mondy pointed out. *"Muy cercanos."*

"¿Qué importa?" Kevin asked. *How does it matter?*

Mondy shrugged, moved to the other side of the truck bed. "You bring extra ammo?"

Kevin winced at the question but offered no response. He lifted his right foot to the back bumper and tightened his bootlace, allowing the question to hang between them, then looked up at the ridgeline where they would soon break trail. "That's not a question, Mondy," he said. "You're just making noise."

"I just wanted to know how many shells you had, that's all."

Kevin looked at him. "Eleven."

"I've seen you miss that many times."

"I've seen *you* miss that many times."

"Everybody misses."

Mondy's concern over extra ammo, in Kevin's estimation, was due to his own lack of talent in marksmanship. In the last five seasons, Kevin had watched him miss a number of game animals, the bullet flying several feet over the intended target's back. Mondy was twenty-three, six years Kevin's senior, but age gave the big Indian no advantage.

"I brought extra," Mondy said, finally. "But I guess you didn't."

"Kiss my ass," Kevin came back.

"*Andale pues,*" Mondy said, forcing a chuckle. "I'm just shitting you, man. Eleven shells. A good shot like you only needs one. You're a good kid. I think you got potential."

For the next half hour they negotiated their usual route over the high saddle to the north, picking through a thatch of cat claw then up over the shale slide and finally to the rim rock at the top, where they squeezed through a small gap, just wide enough for an average-sized man to pass. Mondy turned sideways, hitched up his gut, and inched through while Kevin, smiling on the other side, held his rifle and pack. When Mondy finally grunted his way out, he glared at Kevin's grin.

"Are you saying something?"

Kevin shook his head, motioned toward the gap. "It's plain to see the damn thing's shrunk since last year."

Mondy gave a quick nod. "Good kid. I knew you had potential."

"You got potential, too," Kevin said. "I mean, by Christmas you could weigh…I don't know…"

Mondy squared another hard look at Kevin. "I got two words for you," he said. "Jolene. Sanders."

"Okay," Kevin said. "It's all in the interest of your health, anyway."

"Well, quit being interested in my health."

When they finally crested the bald saddle, the sun was just touching the top of the ridge five-hundred yards opposite them. Mondy was winded, but Kevin knew, despite the labored breathing, that the big Indian would light a cigarette. So proud of his O'odham heritage, Armando Luna often introduced himself as Armando White Moon—especially to women—and, despite Kevin's derisive laughter, donned a beaded headband, Concho-spangled vest, and knee-high moccasins to drink at a bar, looking more Apache than Papago. Kevin always carped at him about his smoking, pointing out that Indians in movies weren't fat and didn't smoke cigarettes. Mondy fished one from his breast pocket and stropped at his Bic lighter until his muttered curses, it seemed, finally brought the thing to flame. He drew in the smoke and looked at Kevin.

"Smoke 'em up," he whispered. "You want one?"

Kevin shook his head. Though he sometimes smoked, the thought of it seemed distasteful when hunting. The wind, gentle on their faces for now, rode out of the ever-whitening east, and the scent of the smoke would not be picked up by any game in front of them. Mondy puffed on his cigarette, and they stood some moments taking in the old familiar canyon. Though Kevin had looked on it from this vantage point many times, the waxing dawn light seemed to wash it anew. Opposite them, several runs of limestone rim rock descended like ribs halfway into the canyon, where in its lower side grew generous sprinklings of Emory oak, mountain mahogany, and mesquite. The south end seemed bare but for the brown tobosa grass, yet a pair of binoculars would betray a forest of ocotillo cactus, its crazy tendril-like limbs as impenetrable as chain mail.

For the two hunters on the saddle, the canyon pulsed with life. Each picked a clump of nearby broom grass and sat. They raised their binoculars to their eyes simultaneously, as if on cue. Others they'd hunted with had noticed this idiosyncrasy in the pair—Kevin's father found it especially hilarious—but the two seemed impassive to any ridicule and seemed altogether unaware of the quirk.

"*Venado*," Mondy said almost immediately.

"*¿Donde?*"

"*Abajo*," Mondy said. "Low in the canyon, *debajo del árbol grande—el verde*."

"Shit, Mondy, there's a thousand green trees in that canyon."

Though their tones were flush with the excitement that comes with sighting game, still they whispered.

"Where?" Kevin asked again.

"Big tree, man, right down toward the bottom."

Kevin was reminded of the futility in following Mondy's spoken directions. He glanced over and tracked the line of Mondy's binoculars where it ended slightly north, up canyon, at a clutch of juniper trees.

He raised his glasses and almost at once picked the all-but-transparent forms of the two animals out of the grain of the slope. The camouflage, the uncanny cryptic coloration, of the Couse Whitetail always stunned him. Even in the open, these tiny, mouse-colored deer—a big buck weighing little more than a hundred pounds—were difficult to see with even the best optics.

The two deer, feeding, picked their way into a mesquite where now only the hind end of the smaller one could be seen.

"Doe and a fawn?" Kevin asked.

"I don't know. The bigger one—I looked for horns. *¿No hay, pues?*"

"Doe and a fawn, I think."

"The one was big," Mondy said. "Big chest, like a buck. But I think you're right."

"Yeah," Kevin allowed. "Like a buck, but bald."

They sat the canyon an hour longer and glassed up seven more deer, three doe-fawn pairs and a small fork-horned buck high in the canyon under a mature oak, on whose acorns the young deer fed. The buck was too small for either of them to consider.

"I think I see three points on one side," Mondy offered hopefully.

"He's a piss-ant two point," Kevin assured. "A dink. You're welcome to go after him, if you want."

Mondy sighed and lowered his glasses, touched his chin philosophically. "No," he said, "I think I'll let him grow up."

"Good," Kevin said. "Fat as you are, little bastard look like a jackrabbit when you dragged him down the mountain. Be shameful and tacky, downright untoward."

Mondy sighed again. "Have I given you an ass-kicking yet today? Because you're in definite need." He paused, and Kevin knew what was coming.

Mondy reached for his rifle, shouldered it, and with some effort found the deer in his telescopic sight. *"Untoward,"* Mondy said, peering through his scope. "I bet you got that word from me."

"I read it somewhere."

"Most fancy words," Mondy said, "you get from me. You use my words all the time and don't even know it."

Kevin didn't deny this. Armando Luna had an admirable vocabulary, though along with his penchant for big words he bore an embarrassing tendency toward malapropisms. During a heated conversation on evolution, of all things, with Kevin's mother, Mondy had used the word *relative* when he meant *relevant* half a dozen times. And though Teresa McNally was perfectly aware of the misuse, she was gracious enough to not so much as smirk. At the hands of her son, however, Mondy suffered greatly for such language errors. Luna never failed to use *conscrew* when he meant *construe*, which Kevin first corrected then derided, and he could speak no more than two or three sentences with his nouns and verbs in perfect agreement.

"If I could hit him from here," Mondy suggested, his rifle still trained on the small buck across the canyon, "it would make it worth it—bragging rights, man."

"Hell, Mondy, that's over five-hundred yards."

"Yeah, you're right," Mondy said, lowering the rifle and stroking the butt almost affectionately. "A little too far for my .243."

"Shit, you couldn't hit that deer with a .338."

"There you go, disrespecting your elders again. I'm pretty sure it's about ass-kicking time."

"I've never seen you hit anything over two-hundred yards but the one time, and that was an accident."

"Details," Mondy said. "You *gabacho* white eyes, so concerned with fucking details. You know, you're being kind of a little punk today."

Kevin was quiet a moment. "How'd you meet Jolene?"

Mondy shouldered his rifle, looked through the scope again. "You know, here and there. I don't even remember anymore."

Kevin looked at the ground.

Mondy lowered the rifle, looked over at him. "Opportunities come around," he said. "You'll see."

They had planned to hunt south as usual but lingered in this first good canyon just past an hour. The cue to get up and move on was usually given by Kevin, and the older man had always conceded this, an unspoken custom of their friendship. For some reason, today, Kevin wanted to take in this canyon a little longer.

And now, over three decades later, as he sat in his air-conditioned office, where he normally worried over the petty vagaries of the English department he headed, his mind had suddenly traversed those many years and dropped him onto a hillside a hundred miles south. He glanced out his office window, which neatly framed Sentinel Peak near the Tucson Mountains. Pima College was a nice place, but he found himself longing for the excitement that attended the sharp morning air and dawn light of that canyon in the Escrobarra, where he could go tomorrow and still find deer.

Even with his back to the door, Kevin could feel Julie's presence behind him. He swiveled in his chair, reminding himself to look the girl in the eye and not let his gaze drop below her neckline. Julie had been the office work aid for the past seven weeks, hired that fall by Norma, the department secretary, though Kevin would not have hired the girl simply for the way she dressed. She never wore a top that didn't sport a bit of cleavage nor a skirt that didn't allow the distraction of her young legs.

"Yes, Julie?"

"Norma just called. That lady was over in Student Services earlier asking for you."

Kevin glanced again toward the window.

The girl tilted her head, squinted. "Seems like she's lost. Are you sure she's not crazy or something?"

"No," Kevin said. "She's not crazy."

"They told her your office hours, but she didn't come here. Norma saw her sitting at the campus Starbucks drinking coffee. Do you even know her very well?"

"I know her quite well," Kevin said. "And she's not lost."

Two

Olivia Hallot sat in a corner booth, a cup of black dark roast steaming in front of her. Kevin knew she had spotted him immediately, but she didn't let on as she continued to survey the young people moiling about over afternoon snacks of scones and bear claws. Except for the obviously dyed auburn-red hair, Olivia didn't look much different from when he'd seen her last three years before.

"Hi darling," she said as he sat down across from her.

"Hi, Oli."

She reached out and took his hand. "You're just as cute as the last time I saw you—cuter, even."

Though the compliment had been genuine, Kevin knew it wasn't true. At fifty, he was beginning to show his age, and women (especially younger ones) had begun to respond to him with the kind of distance usually reserved for respectable middle-aged men.

"Thanks, Oli. You look great, too."

"Oh, nonsense," she said, waving off the compliment. "I'm a fat old squaw woman—a happy one, though."

They both laughed. There was a long pause.

"Well," Olivia said finally. "I's on my way to Douglas and my sister Dotty ast me to drop by the college here and pick up my niece for the long weekend. Thought I'd look you up, see what you were up to."

"Well, I'm glad for it," Kevin lied. "I know a good place to eat dinner."

Tucson had no shortage of great Mexican restaurants, but the best were on the old south side, family-owned businesses that had been passed down through several generations. They went to Mi Nidito on South 4th Avenue, a place that served, among a cadre of great food, the best taco buffet in town. As he and Olivia sat down with their full plates, Kevin held an outside hope that she had just breezed in to say hello and did not harbor some ulterior motive. They chatted a quarter hour, the usual exchanges about relatives and mutual relations between two people who had not seen each other in a long while.

Kevin finally spoke up after a pause in the conversation. "You got any other business in Douglas?"

Olivia shrugged. "Something I been thinking about for a while. Meaning to do."

Kevin nodded. He had a dark guess about what she referred to. He ventured a sort of ruse, though he knew she would detect it immediately. "Hubert's estate?" Her uncle Hubert had died in Douglas the year before, and Olivia had had legal trouble with the will.

Olivia shook her head, intent on picking at the lettuce on her plate. Finally, she looked up at him. "I'm going back to the Escrobarra."

Kevin felt a sudden flush in his chest, like something draining from him, as though someone had pulled the stopper from a full sink. He'd dreaded this confrontation for years.

Olivia spoke. "I know what you went through up there, Kevin. I wouldn't ask you to do this if it wasn't what O.D. wanted."

"Oh, Oli, please!" He pushed himself back from the table.

"You know you need this, Kev."

"I know I don't, Oli—I *do* not." Kevin's voice rose. He looked about the dining area, though no one seemed to be listening. He lowered his voice. "I've had nothing to do with hunting or shooting in thirty years. I don't believe in guns anymore."

"Oh, I see them all the time," Oli came back. "They're as common as ghosts and UFO's."

"Okay, so you're a rhetorician? You know what I mean."

"I'm not talking about hunting, or guns," Oli said. "I'm talking about going back to the site and doing what O.D. asked."

"I haven't even been to Douglas in a decade." His parents had moved away nine years before, so even six years later, when his father, Thomas, had died of a heart attack, he didn't have to go within thirty miles of that valley. But Oli was at the funeral, and for the two days she'd spent in the guest room at his parents' house she did not mention the subject. It was only as she stood at his parents' front door, ready to leave, that she spoke of it: "With Tom gone, it's just you now," she said.

Kevin had nodded at her characteristically cryptic phrasing. He knew well what she referred to. The failing O.D. was Thomas McNally's life-long friend and had charged both Kevin and his father with the task, a deathbed request that Olivia had held onto with a bulldog's grip.

After O.D. had refused the chemical therapy, had grown so emaciated as to look mummified, he'd called them to his house and asked them jointly, father and son—something a person agrees to do under the circumstances but then avoids, like someone who hides from debt collectors for unpaid bills. For a decade now his wife, Olivia, had been that debt collector.

A thought struck Kevin. "You brought the ashes, didn't you?"

Olivia had just taken a bite and finished chewing before she spoke. "Trunk of my car."

"Jesus." Kevin no longer cared if anyone in the restaurant heard him.

"I talked to your mom, Kevin. You need to do this."

"Oh, yes. I should have known. My meddling mother."

"You need to bring your devils out into the open. Not just for you but for me—for all of us. We need a kind of spiritual settling."

"I'm not a very spiritual person."

"That's bullshit. Don't believe in guns! When did you get so full of shit?"

Kevin was two feet from the table now, his body folded into a kind of childlike pout. O.D. had been like family to him; still, there were places both physically and consciously he would not go. That afternoon in the Peloncillos on Escrobarra Ridge was one of those places. He could live with the nightmares, even the flashbacks, but he wasn't going back to that ridge.

"You blame yourself," Olivia said boldly. "What happened wasn't your fault."

"Good part of it was. I got people killed, Oli."

"Bullshit," she said. "You were a boy. You need to go back to that ridge. O.D. knew that."

Kevin was thrown into silence.

"That day has pressed its shape on you. You wear it around, Kevin, like a mourner's coat, and you don't even know it."

"Oh, that really makes sense. Jesus, Oli, you sound just like him."

"Like who?"

"You know who."

Olivia sat up from her food and squared herself to him, a fighter about to deliver a knock-out blow. "You need to do it for *him*, especially him."

Kevin looked at his watch and let out a long breath. He became aware that he was slightly rocking his upper body.

Olivia touched his forearm, then the side of his face. "Settle down, honey."

Kevin felt the impulse to cry. "I am settled down, Oli, and I want to keep it that way. I adjusted myself to that incident a long time ago. I've put myself right with it, and my life is moving along well."

Olivia took both his hands. "Kevin, you haven't put yourself right with it."

He pulled away, looked toward people drinking at the adjoining bar but saw none of them. He dropped his shoulders, shook his head. His eyes loaded up. "God, Oli. Don't do this to me."

"You can't just keep it shut down, dear. You got to let it out—if just to stretch itself and get some sunlight. So you can live your life."

"I am living my life!"

"Not all the way."

Kevin saw other diners glance in their direction, whispering to one another. "I knew my damned mother would put you up to this."

"But she didn't, Kevin. This was my idea. Yes, she wants it for you, but after what happened last time, she wouldn't dare try."

Kevin looked at his full plate and felt nauseous.

"You're like one of my own, sweetheart. You know that."

Kevin reached for her hand and squeezed it. "I've got a long weekend," he said. "No classes Tuesday, either. I'll think about it."

"Good," Oli said. "You should do more than just think about it."

"Where would we do it?"

"Got it planned. I know the perfect place," Oli said, putting down her fork. "There's a good Forest Service trail now to that first long, deep canyon—the one where all the ocotillo bloom so pretty at the bottom. You remember?"

But Kevin didn't answer, caught in sudden surprise of the crystalline memory that had taken him.

"You know the one."

"Yes," he said, immersed now in the clear image of that mass of ocotillo crowned with orange blossoms. "I know the one."

Three

The ocotillo become all but invisible to anyone who lives in the southeastern corner of Arizona. From a distance, their shape is subtle, their limbs twisting from the ground like the legs of an upended octopus. But for anyone who leaves a roadway, walks over a rise or into a canyon, they become a formidable presence, any dense stand of them almost impossible to negotiate. Even these many years later, Kevin's skin remembered their thorns. Tangled and gray, the ocotillos on that November morning were not in bloom.

Two canyons north of where they'd started their hunt, Kevin and Mondy cut the tracks of a large cat. They had encountered the prints—three of them, pressed deep in the mud along the bank of a rock spring—half an hour before, shortly after lunch, and still they could not agree on what kind of animal had made them. In the midday hours they tended to work lower in the canyons, hoping to push up bedded game, and had crossed the spring bottom when Mondy stopped and raised one hand. He stared down at the ground. The prints were undoubtedly feline, but Kevin found no reason for it to be any other than a lion, perhaps a mature tom. Armando Luna, though, would not be moved, his argument planted as the mountain they stood on. "This is Pete's track, man. I know for sure." Old Pete, *El Tigre*, a black jaguar the Mexicans sometimes called *El Sombro*, came from the south at intervals over the last ten years to ravage game and livestock, international borders and paid-for cattle and colts be damned.

"It's probably just a cougar," Kevin said.

Mondy was patient. "Cougar track is smaller and more square."

"How do you know that?" Kevin regretted the question the moment it came. Tracking was Mondy's one solid skill.

Mondy looked off toward the valley, the grassy flat stark under the afternoon light. "We've had this argument before."

Two hours later, John Monahan squatted on his haunches before the same set of tracks. Forty-six years old, he was a third-generation area rancher, and his outfit encompassed a good part of the San Bernardino

Valley along the New Mexico border. The Monahan family had hunted big cats as long as they had ranched and had gained national attention for their prowess.

Local lore had it that John harbored a personal vendetta against the cat in question. For the last five years, Pete walked on only three paws, for which the rancher himself, as the story went, could take personal credit. Having woken one morning to the sound of a screaming filly, Monahan, in bedclothes and slippers, caught the old tom—a surreal silhouette of black—just as he was dragging the mare's dead week-old colt out of the corral. The rancher had picked up the Mini 14 instead of the .270—the two rifles stood side-by-side in the entry-room closet—and the cat, no more than a hundred feet from the house, had slowed for the dragging of the colt. The telescopic sight of the deer rifle would have gathered enough dawn light for a good shot, but Monahan had instead blazed out 22 caliber bullets, emptying the entire clip, never able see the pins on the open sights of the little carbine well enough to fire a killing round. And it was only after sunrise that he had found the few spots of blood. He'd fed the dogs, saddled the good mule, and set out knowing full well he'd waste a day—though he had to try—as Pete, lame though he was, would fly like a spirit back into Mexico. Kevin, though, had never heard this story from Monahan himself—nor was he inclined to enquire about it now, as he and Mondy watched the rancher examine the tracks.

John looked up where the sun had moved toward the horizon and stood a fist and a half above the Perilla Hills. "It'll be getting on dark in an hour or two." It took only a beat for him to make his decision. "My dogs're about used up today. And Pete's not going anywhere, not too fast, anyway—we'll wait till morning."

"It's him then," Mondy said.

Monahan thought before answering. "Magoffins over in Guadalupe canyon are missing two colts." He nodded down at the tracks. "And a three-footed animal could have made those. I think it's him."

Mondy might have glanced at Kevin, some sign of his triumph, but he didn't.

"Your dad and O.D. come with you?" Monahan asked Kevin.

"They were drawn for the December hunt," Mondy answered, sensing that he and Kevin might be in trouble with the rancher. "We came alone today. I told this kid to start further north, more toward Cottonwood, but he didn't listen."

"Well," Monahan said, his pauses uncomfortably long. "I'm not sure it's good idea for anybody to be out here, especially near the border—damn dope runners sometimes get out this way." He shook his head, looked sideways from under his winter Stetson at Kevin. "I don't know that I'd even be out this way but that I have to look after my cows."

At six o'clock the next morning, horse trailer in tow, they crossed the cattle guard and pulled up to the main house of the Cinder Knoll ranch. Thomas McNally, Kevin's father, and his long-time hunting partner, O.D. Hallot, had come with them, unable to resist the chance of getting a glimpse of the big cat. The two men had ridden comfortably in the front of the King Cab Ford, while Kevin and Mondy had been stuffed into the back along with rifles, glasses, scopes, and ammo. Kevin and his friend had by turns accused each other of farting, hogging precious space, and stealing the last bit of coffee in the thermos, until O.D. had spoken up.

"Tom, slow this thing down to about forty."

"Why's that?"

"It'll give these guys a better chance of survival when I throw their sorry asses out."

The last half hour of the drive had been quiet.

A single flood lamp burned by the Quonset hut and corrals. John Monahan was loading four bridled and saddled mules into a well-used stock trailer. The last one had spooked slightly at the lights of the truck and Monahan had since calmed the animal and slapped it on the rump and it clumped into the trailer with the rest.

"Gentlemen," was his greeting when the last of them, Kevin, had emerged from the truck.

They shook hands all around and had to speak above the dogs. Kevin counted six, who bayed from their pens for the excitement of the hunt. Tom gestured at the stock trailer. "Looks like we have more animals than people. I brought my two geldings."

"No," Monahan said, "Amanda's got a deer tag. I just loaded up that damn sorrel mule she likes so much."

Amanda Monahan, the rancher's petite fifteen-year-old daughter, with whom Kevin had a speaking acquaintance at school. A cold tingle moiled at the bottom of his belly as he tried to recall whether he'd combed his hair and how well he'd brushed his teeth that morning. The girl was two years behind him (he a senior and she a sophomore) and had blossomed the last six months. Their slim relationship was based on a single conversation they'd had a year before about James Harriot's *All Creatures* series which both had read.

The girl had slipped unnoticed into the cab of her father's pickup, where she fired the ignition, grinding the diesel engine to a start, an impatient signal that she wanted to get this enterprise under way.

"Well," Monahan said. "Looks like we'll get out of here before noon, anyhow."

To Kevin's chagrin, though, his father had asked the rancher if the two-hundred-fifty pound Armando Luna could ride in his truck and the girl in the king cab to make better use of space. The passenger switch decided, Kevin's heart rate rose, and he hated himself for it. He'd thought about arguing for another plan but knew it would only cause his clueless father confusion, making the situation worse.

Mondy, rifle slung in the crook of his elbow, stood at the passenger door of Monahan's truck and waited as the girl slid out, smiled up at him bright and quick, then headed for the king cab. She swung open the passenger's side door and greeted Kevin with a nonchalant "Hi," and enough of a smile to raise a dimple in her right cheek, then tossed her braided rope of honey-colored hair and deftly scooted her slight rear end behind the front seat and between rifles.

The thirty-minute drive to the Escrobarra was uncomfortable, the two teenagers silent and squeezed as far as possible into their respective corners.

"You hear that, Tom?" O.D. said suddenly.

"Hear what?"

"Why, them smooching noises coming from the back seat."

Hallot's mocking tone was lost on Kevin's father. "What the hell noises are you talking about?"

"That kissing." Hallot was delighted, reveling in the stew of confusion and discomfort he'd created. "I think them two kids is making out in the back seat."

"Oh, okay," Tom said, getting it.

"For Christ's sake O.D." Kevin said, his face ablaze. "Quit it."

But Hallot was unable to resist. "Don't worry, Kev, I won't look."

Kevin saw his father's eyes sweep him in the rearview mirror. And he knew well the smile he couldn't quite see—the one that came when his old man was finally enlightened and included.

"Please, Dad, make him stop."

A look, not even a glance, really, from Tom to O.D., mouth turned down and a slight wag of the head. It was a code between them Kevin had learned to read, and now understood he would be hectored no more. Still the humiliation of it stood thick as cedar smoke between him and the girl. This was one of many of O.D. Hallot's capers that Kevin would find, even after three decades, hard to forgive.

They took the Starvation road south through Three-Mile Flat then made the winding climb up the first bald ridge on the southwest side of the Escrobarra, parking the trucks and trailers at an ancient and dilapidated corrals and loading shoot, hewn of rough-cut lumber. Monahan climbed out of his Chevy and clanked open the tailgate. The dogs jumped in pairs from their pens and scooted around the horse trailer, greedily taking in their freedom. They milled about, licking at themselves and one another and whining as they snuffed the morning ground. All were Blue Tick but for one heeler mix, a house pet named Bonny whose nose was reputedly as good or better than any of the full-breed hounds.

The party mounted up and broke trail, moving some five hundred yards along a fence line, then cut a good game path and began the long climb up the ridge to the cat track. Kevin was unsettled as he rode an unfamiliar and belligerent roan mule named Sally. The less experienced Mondy rode Turk, Kevin's gentle one-eyed gelding he'd had since childhood. Sally's rough, jaunting gait made him feel like a sack of rocks in the saddle, and he muttered and cussed under his breath.

The dogs had scattered, some of them fanning out and flanking the group, others trotting along some fifty yards ahead, snouts low and working to pick up a scent in the brush and grama grass. Out on point now, as the trail had gone gentle after the first steep climb, Monahan raised his bay mule to a molly trot, and Amanda, just behind him, followed course.

When they crested the first rise to a narrow brush-choked canyon, Monahan stopped his mule and raised his binoculars, only looking a moment before turning to his daughter and motioning her to halt. He raised the glasses again, and again only glanced, then signaled Amanda off her mule. Kevin, closest to them, dismounted, pulling his rifle from the saddle scabbard and creeping up quietly to sit beside John.

"That little clearing," the rancher whispered, pointing down canyon some two hundred yards at a grassy patch in the chaparral.

The two bucks, both respectable, stood dead still, their shiny nostrils curling out steam into the dawn light. Amanda, having already chambered a shell, had slung off her fanny pack and bunched it into a rifle rest and now lay prone, aiming at the deer. The muzzle blast from her 6-millimeter caught Kevin full force, like a wave on the side of his body. The larger buck dropped from the field of Kevin's scope, attempted vainly to stand, then crumpled into death throes.

"That took care of him," the rancher said, his voice, though quiet, rife with pride and excitement. "Good shot, Mandi."

Kevin had framed the other deer, now at a dead run, in his scope, and pressed his finger down on the trigger when John spoke up.

"Don't shoot," he said.

And now he could hear his father behind him, just above a whisper. "Hold fire, Kevin, don't shoot."

And now he was conscious, lifted from primal impulse into something like reason: not being able to recover a wounded animal was the most shameful of errors, and Kevin, even at his age, had already a profound sense of this code. He was to remember, many years later, even beyond the imprinted images of high desert landscape, even beyond the smells and sounds—of gun oil, and the metallic *snick* of a chambered shell—this code: you cannot call a bullet back, the trajectory fixed and damage done with the pulling of the trigger.

Kevin offered to drop down canyon with the girl and help recover the buck while the rest continued up ridge to the track site. Normally, the entire hunting party would have gone to inspect Amanda's kill, but today old Pete's trail was cooling fast. John had expressed some worry about leaving his daughter alone, and Kevin told him he would see her to the vehicles.

"Why don't you two just unhitch the trailer, drive that deer back to the house, then come back with the truck."

Kevin agreed. They would meet up later that day, two miles higher at a designated horse gate. John knew they had started far enough north to be out of the way of any recent smuggling activity. The teenagers stood more in danger of being thrown by one of those cantankerous mules than anything else.

It took the two little time to find the fallen animal. Amanda, excited and proud, pushing her red mule, Dunk, through brush and over rocks which Sally seemed reluctant to negotiate. The little heeler mix, Bonny, bounced along happily at Dunk's heels.

"Slow down," Kevin said. "Sally doesn't love me like Dunk loves you."

This earned him a sweet, green-eyed glance and quick smile over the girl's shoulder. Amanda's beauty, in large measure, could be credited to the genes of her stunning Hispanic mother, Yolanda. The woman's pairing with the fair-skinned John had resulted in a lovely combination of blonde hair and Latin features. Both Kevin and the girl spoke fluent Spanish, but for some reason felt comfortable—in the limited exchanges they had had, at least—speaking only English.

When they'd reached the clearing where the deer lay, Amanda lifted her right leg over the saddle horn and hopped from the mule with no more thought than a cat. She picked up the buck's head by the antlers for general appraisal and looked up at Kevin as he sat on Sally. Kevin noticed the dimple on her left cheek was more pronounced than that on the right.

"Good buck," he said. "Hell of a shot, too. I'm damn jealous. I wish I'd have done it, but I didn't." This was true, as this three-by-three buck was bigger and more mature than the one he had taken the year before.

"You'll get your chance," the girl said. Another smile.

Kevin had offered to help field dress, hang, skin, and bone out the deer, but by the time he'd mentioned it, the girl had already snapped open her buck knife, made the long incision in the belly, pulled out the stomach and liver, and was elbow deep in the opened animal. Kevin was even more envious and painfully attracted, his turmoil made worse by the girl's ambiguous signals. She told him, and he believed her, that she could take care of the animal by herself and that he should catch up with the men, but Kevin lingered, watching her field dress the deer. "I told your dad I'd stay with you."

Bonny licked at the entrails and Amanda shooed her away. The dog moved off some ten yards and lay panting in a patch of sun. The girl stood up from her work, cut a glance Kevin's way. "No need," she said.

Kevin felt a slight pinch of rejection, not so much in her words but in that glance. He struggled for something to say.

Finally: "That damn dog doesn't hang with the rest," more a question than a statement, and the second ill-placed use of the word "damn" was embarrassing, but the girl pretended to take no notice of it. She'd rolled the sleeves of her canvas camouflage shirt up to the elbows, and the blood had come to that point but no further, a trick Kevin could never manage.

Done with the gutting, Amanda drew a cotton rope from her fanny pack, tossed it over a mesquite limb, passed it through the deer's opened hocks, and tied it off then dallied the other end to her saddle horn. "Bonny's kind of a loner," she said, "but she'll stay on a cat trail just as well as the others."

This, Kevin did not believe. If so, the dog would have gone with the others.

The girl clicked her tongue and Dunk stepped forward, raising the carcass to where the nose was about a foot from the ground. Amanda half hitched the dallied end of the rope around her hand, walked to the mesquite, keeping the rope taut, and tied it off around the trunk in no more than forty-five seconds.

"What if the others strike a trail?" Kevin asked.

From her pack, Amanda had taken out a sharpening steel, over which she stropped her knife blade with half a dozen quick, chirping passes. She looked up at Kevin, squinting for the sunlight at his back. "She'll hear them baying and catch up after a while."

Kevin didn't believe this either but didn't want to say it. He wanted to stay longer, but knew, and understood the girl knew, his lingering was useless toward any purpose either of them could think of. The embarrassment of Hallot's earlier teasing still hung on the air about them, and Kevin suddenly became anxious to leave. "You're taking the deer home?"

"I think so," the girl said. "Then I'll come back."

But she glanced toward the ground when she said this, a signal, to Kevin's thinking, that she was not comfortable spending too much time alone with him. He both wanted her to stay and wanted her to go, those conflicted feelings pulling at him. This was a moment, in years to come, he would recall and regret many times.

He nodded, clicked his mule to a start and turned to go, when the girl called out to him.

"Hey, Kevin."

He had never heard her use his name before and was surprised by the strange warmth it sent through his chest. He stopped his mule and waited, the girl's pauses as unnervingly long as her father's.

"Tell my dad not to worry," she said. "I'll catch up."

"I don't think anybody's worried for you, Mandi."

She smiled, brightest one of the day, perhaps for the sound of her name on Kevin's voice, perhaps for the comment itself. "Why's that?" she asked.

Kevin nudged Sally to a start and turned her up canyon. "Looks like you can take care of yourself."

Four

Kevin rolled in from Tucson just after eight o'clock Thursday morning and stopped at the same Circle K which had stood at the west edge of Douglas some thirty-five years now. The woman behind the counter, Yesenia Romero, was the same clerk hired the day the place opened for business. He could tell that Yesi, though she didn't let on, recognized him. For how many times as a youngster had he purchased beer and cheap wine illegally across that very counter? He put down his Danish and coffee and the woman did not look up at him.

"How you doing, kiddo?"

"I'm okay, Yesi." He said this as though that interim span of time had been a week instead of thirty years. "I'm in Tucson now."

"S'what Oli tells me. *Me dicen que estás muy bien.*"

"*Gracias a Dios.*" he said. "I'm still here, still walking around."

"*¿Qué más se puede esperar?*" she said. *What more can you expect?*

When Kevin pulled out of the Circle K, he noted the beautiful morning, his mood elevated now that he'd made the decision to come here. He'd driven Pan American Avenue no more than a block, when he caught a flickering in his rearview mirror—police lights, that of a Border Patrol cruiser, in fact. It took him a moment to realize those lights were meant for him. Having lived in southern Arizona most of his life, Kevin had been stopped by Border Patrol a half dozen times, but never for more than a routine check. This part of the state bore a number of rotating checkpoints, and anyone who lived close to the Mexican border was accustomed to the dark green uniforms of these federal agents.

The young man who stepped up to his vehicle was blue-eyed and square-bodied with a buzz haircut and a slight paunch and seemed interchangeable with every Border Patrol agent he'd ever seen.

"Good morning, sir," he said through Kevin's open window. But after that, the agent seemed at a loss. Kevin recognized the same confusion he'd seen in his students' faces over the years when they tried to pretend they understood something—Derrida's concept of relative truth or Edmund Wilson's views on Faulkner.

22

"Can I help you out with anything?" Kevin asked.

"Well," the officer said. "I just need to see some identification."

"Okay," Kevin said, opening his wallet, which he'd pulled out as soon as he'd seen the flashing lights.

The agent took his driver's license, said thank you, and walked slowly back to his vehicle, peering down at the document cupped in his hand as though he'd picked up some interesting artifact, a pot shard or arrow head.

His back still turned to Kevin, the agent reached through his window and picked up a hand radio. As he spoke into the receiver, he moved his arms, and Kevin sensed something in the movement, sheepishness perhaps, like an adolescent explaining a dented fender to his parents.

When the officer came back to Kevin's SUV, he hesitated before handing Kevin the license.

"Is everything okay?" Kevin asked.

"Oh, yes," the agent said. "We, um, received a call on a vehicle like this—just routine. You're okay."

"You sure?"

The agent nodded, looked toward downtown, then back at Kevin. "Sorry for the inconvenience, sir. Have a nice day."

The incident left Kevin perplexed, though the recondite agendas of law enforcement, especially the Border Patrol, had always been a mystery and of little interest to him. He checked into the Frontera Motel a little while later, after driving around town for a bit. Outwardly, Douglas had changed little. The buildings that lined G Avenue, though ramshackle, looked generally the same. The government brick had endured well over a hundred years. Most of the structures were stucco, and patches of that brick showed through the less maintained edifices. The better part of the downtown had been built in the crib-row, parapet façade urban architecture of the early twentieth century, so that the building-lined street looked almost like a time capsule of 1915 small-town America, flecked unselfconsciously with elements of its southwest border-region environment. Touches of green, red, and white, the colors of the Mexican flag, had found their way subtly into the grain of the townscape. The sign heralding La Frontera Bar and Grill sported letters alternating those colors, the Modern Look discount clothing wore them in proud, foot-wide swaths across the awning, the barber pole at the door of Albert Garcia's shop bore a green stripe along with the usual white and red.

Kevin noted that all but a few of the old prominent business-es—Ortega's Shoes, Thompson Jewelers, Douglas Drug—had been absorbed in the last few years by "big boxes"—Wal Mart, Target, and Ace Hardware had lumbered into even this remotest of regions. There seemed a gut-it-out toughness to the faces of the old survivors. "Good for you guys," he said aloud. "Good for you."

He made a jaunt by the high school to discover the cinder-block structure had recently had two wings added, a hopeful sign. He remembered his Senior English class, how Mr. Roth began every class session by writing a quote on the board—often Shakespeare, some-times Milton or Donne. The kids in the 10:00 a.m. class had tittered one morning at the words, "No man is an island," whereby the middle-aged teacher smiled and raised an index finger, his signature gesture. "You may poke fun now, you guys, but such words tend to burrow into the mind and stay. You'll come to appreciate them in later years." And this was true for Kevin McNally, for whom works like *Hamlet* and *Paradise Lost*, rather than fading quickly from the consciousness, took root and grew. In April of the spring semester, he had read ahead of the class in *Macbeth*, encountering the bloody king's dark solilo-quy: *Tomorrow and Tomorrow and Tomorrow/creeps by this petty pace from day to day...* The words in the passage were astoundingly apt, the very shape of Kevin's dark feelings at the time; even then he'd had a sense that the tome in his lap—the *Riverside Shakespeare*, now growing august and dusty on his office bookshelf—somehow spoke his future.

"Things have changed more than you think," Olivia Hallot told him. They'd met for breakfast at the Corazón Hotel. The building had originally been a colossal mission, the oldest standing structure in the state. Sometime shortly after the turn of the twentieth century, an architect had recast the place into a hotel, and thus it stayed. No record of the original architect or when it was built was known to ex-ist, so there hung a mystery about the place, which for many was the defining feature of the county. Kevin had been struck immediately by the familiar smells of the dining area, the cooking chorizo and eggs, ham and sausage that cloyed into the room from the kitchen—while Olivia Hallot claimed that some things had changed, the smells of the old diner had not.

He sunk his fork into his red-eye gravy and biscuits. "I haven't seen much of it. High school's bigger."

"That's from a bond-issue vote," Olivia said. "The money source has changed. And it's no longer Phelps Dodge." P.D., as locals tended to call it, had been a copper mining conglomerate that had fairly owned Cochise County for over a century. The company had folded up twenty-nine years before, leaving the cities it had built around it stranded. Douglas's proximity to Mexico and the quaint uniqueness of Bisbee had kept them alive. Much of the new money source Olivia had mentioned came from black-market smuggling along the border.

The suggestion, however faint, of the illegal drug trade killed the conversation for the moment, and they looked self-consciously down at their food as they ate. "Well," Kevin said finally. "It's good to see this old place again."

Olivia nodded and looked around the room, though they both knew Kevin had meant the town, the valley, the spirit of home and birthplace. "It's good to see that it's survived." The old high ceiling and dark, early-American woodwork of the dining area had been meticulously maintained.

"I found an article in the library I think you need to look at. On microfilm."

"Oh yeah?" Kevin said. He forked in another mouthful of biscuits and gravy.

"I didn't print it out—just took a look. It's from November of '76." Olivia had not looked up from her food.

Kevin stopped chewing, swallowed with some effort.

Olivia raised her head finally, caught his eye. "Xavier Zaragoza wrote it—after the state police had put things together. Not much to it but the basic facts, but the article kind of pushed that incident back out into the open for me. Made me look at things again—try to remember."

Kevin had put down his fork, though he had not been conscious of it.

Olivia looked down at her plate. "I'm working hard to not upset you, but I think it would help you to look at it before we actually went out there," she said. A pair of busboys rattled dishes into tubs and a waitress whisked by their table with a tray full of food. "I know you're only trying to help, Oli," Kevin said. "And I appreciate it."

Olivia nodded. "Your mom sure looks forward to seeing you," she said.

Kevin smiled. "And I her."

"She and Tracy are staying at the Gilbert's guest house for the weekend. There's room for you, too."

"Well," Kevin said. "I think it's more convenient for everyone that I stay at the motel. I brought work with me."

Olivia measured him a moment, went back to her food. "She's glad you finally called. It'd been a while."

"My work is fairly consuming."

They ate quietly, knowing Kevin's work was the least of his preoccupations. The divorce two years before had been an emotional hit, though the warning signs had appeared for a decade, and Kevin had ignored them. His daughters, both in college, had known well before their mother had even phoned an attorney. The youngest, Cinda, was attending Pima at the time of the break-up, and showed up in Kevin's office the afternoon of the day her mother, Janice, had announced her intentions to him.

"Dad," the girl said, shaking her head now for the third time. "There *is* no other man. You need to start seeing the you-and-mom thing better."

His daughter had stood but obviously had one more bit of wisdom for her father. "You and mom were together for a long time, but she finally understands that you guys have finished with your thing. Time to take another road. You need to understand that, too."

For the next eighteen months, Kevin endured the usual distress that attends such trauma. His alcohol consumption increased, and though he had quit smoking twelve years before, he briefly picked up the habit again, so that often he found himself lecturing on Barth or Updike hoarse from the twenty cigarettes and dozen scotch-rocks he'd consumed the night before. The dating aspect compounded the difficulties. Most women within ten years of his age were already attached, and those available were most often at least twenty-five years his junior.

Then Jessica stepped into his life. The young Ph.D. had been newly hired in the science department fall semester about a year after the divorce. Though just three years clear of thirty, she was brilliant and mature, a bookish blond girl with a quiet beauty, whose sexiness, as one came to know her, unfurled like a flag. She'd minored in English as an undergrad and loved twentieth-century American lit, Kevin's specialty. They'd been together three months now and had announced their love to each other a few weeks before. And so Kevin's life had begun to settle. He'd stopped the smoking and tried to drink no more than three scotches at a sitting, which was most nights of the week. The comforting sting of alcohol on his blood was harder to let go of than the cigarettes.

He lay in his bed at the Frontera Motel regretting he had not brought Jessica with him. He'd planned to read a while and nap, but he could not bring himself to engage in Tobias Wolf's latest book, *Our Story Begins*. His better sense, though, told him that he'd made the right decision not to drag Jessica into the old hurt with him, not now, when the relationship was so fresh.

His mind kept tracking back to a face he'd seen two hours before, after breakfast. The face belonged to an old Hispanic man whom Kevin had noticed as he left the restaurant at The Corazón. He'd only caught a glimpse of the man, who wore shoulder-length gray hair, but Kevin couldn't shake the feeling he'd seen him somewhere before. He'd written it off as déjà vu, simply a trick of the brain. But the man's face had planted itself between him and the page he struggled to read.

Before he met his mother and sister for dinner, Kevin, despite what he'd told Olivia earlier, had decided to stop at the city library. He wanted to make the first move, visit in on his past before it paid a visit to him.

Five

In 1976, Kevin was a senior in high school, and Jimmy Holguin was just a name in a missing persons police report. Kevin knew nothing of the man until 2001, when he stumbled onto the name in an archived article in the *Douglas Daily Dispatch* when researching for his Ph.D. dissertation. Holguin had been born in Agua Prieta, Sonora, Douglas's sister city on the border, but had lived on the Arizona side after the age of fifteen. In early November 1976, Jimmy Holguin set off a chain of events which would culminate in violent crisis on a Sunday afternoon on the Escrobarra ten days later. He had, in essence, ghost authored the life-defining moment of Kevin McNally's young life.

The son of a fourth-generation Sonora ranching family, Holguin had decided early on that he would break from the family tradition of abject poverty. The most expedient way to do this, of course, was to mule contraband to the north side of the border. After seventeen years in the drug smuggling business, Holguin had established himself, but he made some dangerous decisions that ultimately sealed his fate. The last night of his life, his two partners asked him to join them for drinks at a small table in a tavern called Club Las Vegas in the red-light district of Agua Prieta, Sonora.

The girls working the bar that night took an interest as soon as the three men walked in. The men were well dressed and ordered *Presidente* and *Dos Eqes* chasers, and they surveyed the girls with a passing interest, glancing at smooth legs and exposed cleavages, returning the girls' smiles with a slight nod of their heads. None of the men cared who paid for the drinks, and the money was not an issue. One of them was *muy guapo*, quite good looking, and the girl named Dora, who had celebrated her twenty-fourth birthday the day before, gave a look around to the others, most of whom were seated along the bar, which said: "Stay away. He's mine."

Isedro Leon, the handsome one, had been listening to his friend Jimmy Holguin talk for the last ten minutes, but now was only half hearing as the little auburn-haired girl at the bar with blue eyes and a scatter of freckles across her nose leered intently at him.

"By middle of March, latest, I could have the rest," Jimmy was telling Leon. "At ten percent interest," he said, looking down at his beer bottle as he ciphered out the figures, "it will be eighty-two five. I know that isn't the same amount of return you would expect, but it's the best I could do."

Isedro waved his hand as one would shoo away a fly, a gesture that said it was of no consequence, that everything was all right. He glanced over at the girl, still staring at him. The jukebox played an old *corrido* that Leon recognized from his teenage years, and he felt nostalgic, sentimental enough to take the girl up on her implied offer, even though he knew it would cost him plenty. "If you have fifty right now, it's fine," he said to Jimmy. "I wouldn't have had that money in circulation, anyway."

The third man, Juan Carlos Roscon, had not said ten words the entire evening. He was a big, squarely built man with *Indio* features, a large heavy-skinned face, thick hair and a tuft of wispy mustache and goatee. His upper arms were the thickness of most people's thighs and bore a tangle of green-ink prison tattoos from a coiled snake to the Virgin of Guadalupe. Juan Carlos was the homeliest of the three and paid the most attention to the girls.

"I still can't believe it," Jimmy said to Isedro. "We had just crossed and were going down that arroyo with all the trees, and shit, there they were, man, six *migra* with their pistols pointed right at us."

"I thought you said there were five."

"I remember it better now, and I'm sure there were six."

"Sometimes you have to run," Leon said.

"I can still hear the bullets, too, man, shit." Holguin made a popping-whistling noise between his teeth and lower lip. "We couldn't run with the backpacks on." Jimmy went quiet, pondered the bottom of his brandy glass. "I was scared, Ise, you know?"

"Shit," Leon said. "You remember that time with Ochoa, don't you? When I didn't even know I had pissed my pants until I got out of the truck?"

Jimmy nodded, still fixed on the brandy glass. "I just want you to believe me."

"Hey," Leon said. "Look at me Jimmy." He pushed his face closer to Holguin's and jabbed the table with his index finger for emphasis. "You are my best friend. I never question you, even in my heart. What you say is implicitly the truth for me."

Jimmy smiled at Ise's words. Leon could take on such a comforting, almost fatherly, tone so quickly. Jimmy put out his hand, and Leon hauled back and clapped his fist around Jimmy's, loud enough to draw notice. Both men's eyes had teared up.

"*Hermanos*," Ise said, his hand tight around Jimmy's.

"*Hermanos*," Jimmy came back, Ise working his hand so hard his whole upper body shook.

Dora had kept her eye on the handsome man with the gray at his temples and goatee. He had not looked her way in several minutes and seemed more interested in his friend than in her now. She would probably have to make a move soon if she was to have any chance. She lifted her small Naugahide purse, hung from her shoulder on a faux gold chain, and assessed its contents: a little over a thousand pesos and a half gram of cola, about half the money needed for two hours of crib space and enough coke for one more night. Dora snatched out her compact, snapped it open, and quickly checked the makeup around her eyes. For the past year, she'd saved up for the blue-tinted contacts, and she felt sure they made her the prettiest girl in the club.

When she climbed off the barstool and stepped up to their table, both Holguin and Rascon were annoyed, but neither man was surprised. In the fifteen years Jimmy had partnered with Isedro, he'd seen this sort of thing dozens of times: they're at a bar and some lady asks Ise to dance, or if she could talk to him a minute, or how his sister or mother or brother was, or did he have any cola, or was he going to the *quinceañera* reception later on, or could she have a ride home. Anything to get closer to him, because, clearly, Isedro had it—the looks, the money, and something more. It wasn't just the fancy words he used sometimes but the way he looked at you and the way he phrased what you were thinking already, as though to reach inside with a warm hand and gently touch the middle of you. Jimmy Holguin was one of the few who understood it was at that moment that one should be most afraid. A few times, and Jimmy had been there to witness, that warmth meant he (sometimes she) had maybe ten, fifteen seconds to live.

"*¿Qué ondas, mija?*," Jimmy said to her. The girl stood between Rascon and Jimmy, directly across from Isedro.

"Hello," she said, awkwardly trying her English. She had known immediately the men were American.

Ise sat back in his chair, linked his hands behind his head as he looked up at the girl. "*¿Le puedo ayudar?*" he asked her, may I help you, and his two companions jeered his politeness.

"*Hay, ¿Le puedo ayudar?,*" Jimmy mocked gently.

Dora waited for the chuckling to die. "*¿Podemos hablar?*" she answered in kind, *Can we talk?*

"Hey," Jimmy said, getting Ise's attention, and speaking English the first time that evening. "Let this be my treat."

"Oh, bullshit," Leon said, the English feeling strange, incongruous to the sounds one hears in a Sonora red-light cantina. He nodded toward the girl, now blank-faced amid the garble of Anglo-Saxon schwas and diphthongs. "You pick up the tab on this kind of shit for your little brother, not your partner."

"Just thought I'd offer," Jimmy said. "She looks like she wants to give you a discount, anyway."

"Discount?" Rascon said, breaking a ten-minute silence. "Free, is more like it."

Isedro spoke again to the girl. "*Siéntate,*" he said, gesturing at the empty fourth chair.

She moved her head slightly toward the bar. "*Pa' allá,*" she said, as though she would have it no other way.

Ise rose and followed her to the bar where she regained what seemed to be a familiar perch on the barstool, and he stepped up close. Her perfume was a midline knock-off but smelled expensive on her young skin.

"*¿Presidente?*" he asked.

"*¿Por qué no?*" she said.

Ise held up two fingers, and the bartender was quick to respond, the snifters and smell of brandy at their elbows within seconds. The girl took only a sip before she had out her handbag. She removed a threadbare cotton change purse that still bore the semblance of some design in blue ink and drew out ten one-hundred peso bills rolled into a neat tube. "That's half for the room," she told him.

"No, no, *mija,*" Ise said. "I can pay for the room myself."

"You don't understand," she said, pushing the money into view of the bartender who managed the room transactions. "It is my proof that this is not just business."

She smiled at him, and he saw she was young, not much over twenty. "*Bueno,*" he said. "I see now."

The girl lifted her brandy snifter and threw back its contents like a dose of medicine.

"*Hijuela,*" Leon remarked.

She slapped her hand down and looked at the bartender. "*La llave,*" she said, *the key.*

Two hours later, a little before 1:00 a.m., Isedro and the girl stepped back into the bar. Her hands were linked around his elbow as though he'd been her steady the last six months. Holguin and Rascon had been inspired in kind but neither transaction had taken over thirty minutes, and the girls with whom they had consorted sat along the bar with their friends, no more interested in either of the men than they had been before.

Leon, ready for a drink, stopped at the bar and ordered a house tequila and a Dos Equis, then, with the girl still attached, stepped up to his two friends. He emptied the tequila glass and chugged back half the beer.

"*¿Listos?*" he said. *Are we ready?*

Jimmy and Juan Carlos glanced at each other. "We're still doing it tonight?" Juan Carlos asked in English.

"*Simón, pues,*" he said. "Don't you think, Jimmy?"

Holguin shrugged. "Why not?" he said. "Just as long we don't wake up my grandmother."

"You think we can be quiet enough?" Juan Carlos asked.

"I think so," Jimmy said. "It's pretty far from the ranch house, and she doesn't hear good anyway."

Jimmy had to use the bathroom before they left, and when he had gone from the table, Rascon rose quickly and approached Isedro. "*Por favor,*" he said to Dora, who reluctantly gave up Ise's elbow and stepped over to the bar to give them a moment's privacy.

"The chick's going with us, man?"

"Why not?"

"You know what we gotta do. We can't have her around for that."

"She'll wait in the car. No big deal. We'll say, 'Jimmy's grandmother wasn't feeling well, or she needed his help, so Jimmy had to stay out there tonight.' Right? No problem."

"But it's an unnecessary risk."

"How good would life be if you didn't take unnecessary risks."

Damn good, Rascon thought, but didn't dare say it.

When Jimmy came out of the bathroom, the three others were waiting for him at the door. They had come there in Jimmy's GMC Suburban, and when they climbed in with their extra passenger, it was late and the clubs in the red light square had quieted. A few neon signs and lighted windows still glowed out into the plaza, where in its center stood a small and solitary police station, about the size and construct of a San Francisco toll booth, which most nights sat empty. A thin strain of *Tejano* music, from an indeterminate direction, leaked from a jukebox somewhere, and weaved into the music was the faint sound of men's laughter and the smell of cooking masa, torillas, and chile meat as the late-night restaurants were serving the empty-bellied drunks who, this time of night, stumbled around for that *something more* all humans seek.

Jimmy and Juan Carlos sat in the front seat, and Isedro and Dora in the back where she was free to run her hand along his thigh. As she pressed herself up against his left side, she could feel the steel lump of his nine millimeter under his leather coat. She'd done business with men carrying guns before.

They took *Calle 14* south until it intersected with *Avenida Industrial*, a main street that headed out of town. Isedro and Juan Carlos had been born US citizens on the Douglas side of the line. Jimmy had been born in Cananea, Mexico, a town about forty miles south, within three years of the other two.

"How far is it?" Juan Carlos asked.

"Not far," Isedro answered from the back seat. "What, about three miles out of town, Jimmy?"

"Yeah," Jimmy said, "about three or four miles—just before the hills start."

"Do you still run cattle?" Juan Carlos asked, renewing Leon's admiration of him for working so deftly at putting Jimmy at ease. The guy may have been quiet, but when things got tight, when it came down to the wire, he always came through.

"No, not since my grandfather died. Two horses and my grand-mother, and sometimes my niece, and that's it."

"*¿A dónde vamos?*" Dora asked Ise. *Where are we going?*

"*Un ranchito,*" he answered.

"*¿Por qué? ¿Más pisto?*"

"*El Jimmy necesita hablar con su abuela.*" *Jimmy needs to talk to his grandmother.* "Right, Jimmy?" he said into the front seat.

"*Sí*" Jimmy came back.

They arrived at the small, disheveled ranch, lighted only by the headlights and what appeared to be a single lantern or candle burning from within. The shakewood shingles of the main house had rotted and all but fallen off. Two clapboard out buildings and small barn had never seen paint and stood at a slant as though to topple with the slightest nudge. The small rough-hewn ocotillo corrals held two plug bay geldings that shied at the headlights, which Jimmy immediately snapped off as they parked in front of the house.

"What's that light inside?" Leon asked. "I thought you said she'd be asleep."

"She is. She just burns a candle at night to keep the evil spirits away."

Isedro kissed the girl and told her firmly she must stay in the car, that they would be back in less than an hour. He fished in his pocket and found the gram vial of coke and left it with her.

"Remember," he told her. "Stay in the car," at which she nodded reluctant assent and looked down at the vial in her palm.

Jimmy brought a flashlight out from under the seat, and the three men walked past the ranch house to the ramshackle barn where, after some searching, Jimmy found two shovels and a digging bar. He led them about a hundred yards back of the house to a lone mesquite tree, the ground around it trampled bare and flaked with dried manure from generations of starving cattle. Once at the tree, Jimmy oriented himself a moment, then counted out ten paces to the west. "*Esto es,*" he said, *This is it.*

Isedro, not shy of hard work, broke the ground with the digging bar and the other two used the shovels. The hole they dug was about five feet in diameter and after three feet and half an hour's work they came to the strong box, twenty inches long and ten wide and deep, wrapped in a burlap sack.

Jimmy dropped to his belly and drew out the box and unwrapped it. The lock had long since broken and he opened it immediately and shined the light on several rows of bundled, new hundred-dollar bills. "It's all there, Ise. You can count it if you want."

"No," Leon said behind him. "I don't need to count it."

When Jimmy rose, Isedro had the nine millimeter pointed at his forehead.

"Sorry man," Rascon said, sincerely remorseful that he had to be part of this.

"Where's all my dope, Jimmy?" Isedro asked.

"Ise, I don't know what you're talking about." Jimmy held out his hands as one would in a hopeless attempt to stop a flood or avalanche.

"You've been taking *mordiditas* out of our business for fifteen years and you don't know what I'm talking about?" He stepped up close to Jimmy, then, pressed the gun into his gut and grabbed him behind the head by a handful of hair.

"Ise, man," Jimmy said, his voice breaking. "Think about this. Think about what you're doing."

"*Mi hermano*," he said, the affection in his voice genuine. "You don't know how long I've thought about this." He shook Jimmy's head, almost playfully. "Remember our days in Hermosillo, when we first met." He drew Jimmy close then, whispering in his ear, "When we were young, all the money and good food and dope, all the women we wanted until we got sick of having them. Remember when we would drive for days, no destination, no worries. There are things we lose in youth that we can't call back. Do you ever think about things like that, Jimmy?"

"Oh, Ise," Jimmy said, his frantic thoughts broken mid-sentence by his sobbing. He gave way to weeping, loud inconsolable moans with no more dignity than a ten-year-old. Finally, he recovered himself enough to speak. "It's in the house, Ise. All of it. My grandmother sleeps on it under her mattress. But please, man, it was like a savings account. I was going to split it even with you." Jimmy was breathing hard now, though hopeful he'd at least scratched the surface of empathy. "Man, I made some trades, some investments. There's ten times more than I ever took."

"Oh, my sweet Jimmy," Isedro said in his ear, then kissed him on the cheek. "*Adios.*"

The report of the pistol, pressed as it was into Jimmy's belly, was so muffled as to be perverse. Jimmy yelped, took a step backward, and fell into the hole where he lay moaning. He had dropped the flashlight beside the hole and Isedro picked it up and shined it down on him.

"Don't feel bad, Jimmy," Isedro said. "I would have shot you whether you lied or told the truth."

Isedro looked over at Juan Carlos. "Bury him," he told the big man.

"Fuck, man," Juan Carlos said. "Finish him."

"No," Leon said. "He needs time to think about this."

Juan Carlos handed him the shovel. "You'll have to do it, man. I can't."

Ise gave him the light, but Juan Carlos snapped it off. "We don't need to see this."

Isedro had tossed in several shovelfuls of dirt which, in between the moans, he heard strike Jimmy's clothing, when the sound of footsteps caused both men to wheel around. Juan Carlos caught the girl's face and blue-tinted eyes in the flashlight.

"*¿Qué pasó?*" she said.

Jimmy screamed, something the way a calf bawls, then fell off into an eerie whimpering.

"*¿Quién es?*" she asked, *who is it.*

"*Vete al carro,*" Isedro told her, *go back to the car.*

It was perhaps the tone of her new lover's voice or the nagging portent that had burned at her gut since the men had left the Suburban, but Dora suddenly arrived at her better senses. Without ceremony or hesitation, she chucked off both her pumps, turned on her bare heel, and bolted toward the thicket at the edge of the pasture. She had only covered about twenty yards before Isedro closed the distance and caught her by the hair. He dragged her back to the hole.

"I told you to stay in the car, *mija.*" His tone was fatherly, almost gentle.

The girl shrieked and clawed and tried to bite whatever of his flesh she could find. In her purse, she carried a medium-sized locking knife, but when she tried to get at it, Isedro yanked the purse from her shoulder, breaking the chain, and flung it into the darkness.

By the time he got her back to the hole she was begging for her life.

"Damn, Isedro," Juan Carlos said. "I told you."

Isedro reached under his jacket and drew out the nine millimeter.

"Shit Ise, don't kill her."

"What do you suggest?"

Juan Carlos had no answer.

The girl was on the ground just shy of the hole now, sitting with her legs folded under her, eyes down and rocking back and forth. "*Por favor, Ise. No me mates. Por favor.*" She sounded like a child pleading with her father not to be punished. Under the beam of the flashlight she looked up a flickering moment at her attackers, all the joy and love and sorrow and regrets of her young life seeming to pass from her eyes to theirs.

Isedro put the gun to the top of her head and fired. She dropped straight forward. Her arms at her sides, she looked like a subject prostrate before a king.

Isedro lifted her by the shoulders backward and tumbled her into the hole on top of Jimmy who groaned more loudly than he had the last few minutes.

"She should have stayed in the car," Isedro said.

"Would you please finish Jimmy," Juan Carlos pleaded. "Man, I can't do this. I gotta get some sleep at night."

"Shine the light," Isedro instructed. Jimmy's head and shoulders were still exposed and visible under the light beam. His eyes were tightly closed, and he seemed to have shut out everything but the pain. Isedro took careful aim at the base of Jimmy's skull and pulled the trigger.

It took the two men only a few minutes to bury the bodies. They found the back door leading into the kitchen unlocked and lit a kerosene lantern. The first room they came to seemed to be that of a child, the bed no longer than five feet, and the floor strewn with toys and rag dolls. Isedro walked up to the bed, which appeared to have someone in it, and pulled back the covers only to discover a large stuffed bear.

When they walked out of the child's bedroom, the old woman,

dressed in a cotton night gown, was standing in the doorway of her own.

"*Dios mío*," she said, her hands on her chest. "*¿Quiénes son?*"

"*Amigos de Jimmy*," Isedro answered back.

"*¿Qué quieren?*" *What do you want?* She was shaking, her lower lip trembling.

Ise gestured at the big chair in the living room. "*Siéntese usted, señora.*" He took the woman by the elbow and politely helped her to the chair. As soon as she was seated, he reached under his jacket and pulled out the pistol, drawing a startled shriek from the old woman. She had her hands to her face and her eyes had gone wet. In the kitchen, a few paces away, was a cooking timer and a rosary, both of which Isedro took from the counter and set on the coffee table in front of the woman.

Isedro picked up the timer, set it for five minutes, and handed the rosary beads to the woman. He looked over at Rascon, who still held the lantern, and spoke to him in English. "Wait outside a few minutes, Juan Carlos."

"This is fucked up, man."

"Go ahead," Leon said gently. "I'll be five minutes. We have a lot of work to do tonight."

Rascon, incredulous, shook his head. "It's gone bad, man. I don't know."

For a moment, Isedro did not acknowledge the statement or even look at him. He stepped over and stood before the woman quietly crying in the chair. Staring down at her, he addressed Rascon. "Do you think we can turn it around now? You can't call it back halfway through, man."

Leon looked at the woman as he might his own grandmother, then went to one knee before her and addressed her politely in Spanish: "Madam, I will allow you five minutes at prayer. I will put the kitchen timer behind you so you are unable to see it. And I assure you, you will feel no pain. I admire you for succumbing so gracefully to your fate."

He looked up at Juan Carlos. "Please," he said. "Five minutes."

Rascon waited outside for what felt like an hour when the kitchen timer sounded and the shot immediately after. When he stepped back inside, the old woman and the chair she sat in had been covered with a large flannel quilt decorated with the red silhouettes of running horses.

He followed the faint lantern light into the largest bedroom where he found Isedro lifting the mattress from the bed. Packed into the frame were many kilo bundles of cocaine and heroin.

"Jesus," Juan Carlos said.

"There's more somewhere. Horse. Eighty or ninety kilos—uncut."

"You're fucking kidding me." Juan Carlos pointed to the bundles in the bed frame. "This is coke?"

Isedro nodded. "About two-hundred keys."

Juan Carlos shook his head. "Unbelievable."

"Like I told you, he'd been siphoning off me since the beginning." Isedro was rummaging around the room now. He stepped over to the vanity and pulled open the drawers. In the lower three he found what he was looking for, the kilo bags so heavy the drawer bottoms had collapsed from their weight. Juan Carlos marveled as Ise laid the plastic bags out on the floor.

In the dim, greenish light of the kerosene lamp the men stood, hands on hips, surveying their bounty.

"You want to do this all in one run?" Rascon asked.

"We've got to. Jimmy wasn't bullshitting about the border patrol. Those fuckers are all over the place. Nobody's getting through the port either, man, so we can't spread it out between the cops, and I don't trust anybody anymore. We need to do this in one shot. Walk it across ourselves. I know a hook-up guy who'll pay full on delivery."

"It's gonna take a lot of guys."

"Five, maybe six kids, plus you and me. Pay them a couple grand apiece. It'll take a few days to round them up, find the connection, but we can get it done inside a week—ten days max."

"Where do you think we can cross?"

"They know about that brushy wash. It'll have to be further east, man, at the Escrobarra."

"Shit, that's a hard hike." Rascon kicked at one of the bundles. "We'll have to carry seventy—eighty pounds apiece."

Isedro reached over and patted him on his large belly. "You think you can make it, *panzón?*"

"For that much money? Hell yes."

"You'll probably end up with a couple million. You invest some of it and don't piss it all away on party and women, you shouldn't have to take any more hikes."

"You thinking about retiring, Ise?"

Leon looked genuinely pained. "When you have to pop your best friend, and his grandmother, it's time to hang it up."

Rascon thought hard before he spoke. "What was the girl's name?"

"I don't remember," Leon said. He was working his jaw, the way he did when he was upset. "I don't want to remember. Don't bring her up again."

Juan Carlos didn't speak for a moment. "So, we'll probably do it next week sometime?"

Isedro nodded. "I know a little road. We'll hike two, maybe three miles. We can take Jimmy's truck and my Dodge out there—just leave Jimmy's rig at the drop. They're working on Highway 2 right now, but I know a ranch road that goes out there."

"You know what," Rascon said. "I just remembered something—I think hunting season starts next week."

"Well," Leon said, the same slate-colored cast in his eyes Juan Carlos had come to fear. "Hunters can be taken out, too."

Six

The old Douglas Library had changed little, and Kevin was glad for it. Masoned of reclaimed government brick in 1906, the structure resembled the one-room schoolhouses of its time. Inside was cavernous and ramshackle and the rafters creaked with any kind of wind. Susan Marline Murray, great-granddaughter of the place's original librarian, had come back from her big city library post to reclaim a legacy and head the place that, in the interim decades, had idled into disrepair. For the last eight years, Murray had waged an all-but-private battle to thwart the many efforts to modernize and upgrade, some to even raze the place and put up a stucco modular. So when Kevin walked in the door that afternoon, inventory stood at some ten-thousand books, periodicals, and magazines, four microfilm scanners, and two eight-year-old computers.

Examining the stacks and leafing through magazines no more sophisticated than *Time* and *Newsweek*, Kevin had procrastinated an hour before he went to the microfilm. It wasn't a matter of locating the thing—he knew exactly the date it was published. He scanned the edition from the November eleventh, then the thirteenth. The font in the title head of *The Douglas Dispatch* hadn't changed in thirty years. Xavier Zaragoza, a local whom Kevin had known all his life, had been head reporter for thirty-five years, and his articles tended to worry over local issues of the time, school-funding crises, labor strikes at Phelps Dodge, that the state Department of Corrections had slated a prison to be built in the area within a few years.

Kevin found a tactile comfort in the mechanics of old-fashioned devices. He turned the film crank at a measured speed. Images from his youth, some of them faces of those long dead, conveyed past the screen like specters in a dream. And, finally, the front page from the November thirteenth issue, as if of its volition, slowed to a stop before his eyes. The top read The Douglas Daily Dispatch. The lead story was just below, but he could not will his brain to cipher the words in the headline.

The clicks of a woman's plastic heels turned him from the screen and he found Susan Murray, her hands politely coupled, standing at a safe distance behind him. A slim, handsome woman just shy of forty, clad in a sweater and jeans, she didn't look anything like a typical librarian.

She nodded at the scanner. "You like antiques," she said.

"I do," Kevin allowed.

"You're Kevin, aren't you." She ventured two steps and put forth her hand. He took it and smiled at her.

"I'm surprised you remember me." Kevin had known Susan when she was a teenager, a passing friend of his youngest sister's, a bright, spirited girl with wild blond hair. He pointed at his own head. "Dyed it gray."

Susan ran her fingers down a length of her hair, now a deep, natural auburn, touched at the edges with strands of a lighter color. "Dyed mine brown."

They chuckled, a bit uneasily. Susan gestured at the stacks. "Once more to the books, I see."

Kevin smiled. "Never left them."

"Well, then, that makes us kindred spirits, doesn't it?" She tipped her chin at the scanner. "Copies are a dime a page."

Kevin gave his head a jerk, "Steep," he joked. Copies in big cities were at least fifty cents.

Susan folded her arms across her chest, nodded toward the dim light on the screen. "Find what you were after?"

Kevin glanced back at the monitor, careful not to read any of the words there. "I hope so. Part of it, maybe."

He stepped onto the front porch of the Gilberts' house on 9th street just after 6:00 p.m. and was thankful when Olivia Hallot answered the door and took the bottle of Merlot from his hand and welcomed him inside. His mother and sister, Tracy, had not yet arrived. He'd put on his least faded pair of blue jeans and sported a crisply new ivory-colored shirt, wanting for all the world to look his best for his mother and sister, neither of whom he had seen since the blowup two years before.

"You bring me back," Patty Gilbert was telling him. Kevin was on the couch and Patty sat curled in the love seat across from him. Approaching seventy years old, she wore a flower-print dress rife with tiger lilies. She was working on her second glass of wine and waxing sentimental. "You and Johnny used to cut up so when you guys were together. Something about you two was a recipe for trouble."

Kevin nodded. "J and I made some mischief."

"Funny," Patty said, smiling, "it wasn't so cute back then."

"Little distance softens things." Kevin felt his face darken at the glib remark and was grateful when Jack Gilbert stepped into the room and handed him a scotch. He and John Jr. had been buddies since childhood and through high school, one of those friendships in which the parties meet again in adulthood only to discover they'd all along had little in common. John Jr. now ran the sand and gravel company which the Gilberts had bought from Kevin's father almost twenty years before. The business had made a comfortable living for the McNallys in the Douglas area, but the Gilberts had expanded the company with outlets in most major cities in the state. Johnny now lived in Scottsdale and was by most standards quite well off.

Kevin's father had sold the company for a reasonable amount, though Kevin couldn't recall exactly how much—well over a million dollars. At the time Thomas had unloaded it, Kevin was certainly of an age he could have competently picked up the mantle, but the old man had long realized his son seemed slated for something other than managing which diesel-belching trucks delivered what tons of mixed concrete to which addresses. By the age of thirty-five—the business having been sold, inherited bonds matured, and stocks peaking—Kevin could have quit teaching and lived reasonably well—like Hemingway, he might have written books while living on family money. But Dr. McNally had long since come to terms with his lack of talent in such things; his place was before the chalkboard espousing the work of others.

Tracy McNally, this evening, made as much eye contact with her brother as possible. Kevin sensed she wanted the old closeness they had felt as kids. They had spent many hours over the phone when he and Janice had divorced, and when Kevin finally told her there was someone new in his life, Tracy was surprised it had taken so long.

They sat now at the Gilbert's dining room table, chatting amiably. "That's great, Trace," Kevin said to her. She had been telling him about her recent move to Silver City, New Mexico, and the excellent middle school where she taught social studies. "I'm glad things have worked out so well for you."

Tracy remarked that Kevin had come to look more and more like their father as he aged, the shadow of Thomas McNally whispered into the features and expressions of his son's face. Her throat tightened and her eyes loaded more than once during their conversation. Their mother sat with Patty on the loveseat across from them, and though she'd chimed in once in a while, she allowed the siblings their long-needed talk. Olivia and John Sr. clattered about in the kitchen. Not once did any of them bring up the subject which had, when last they met, run their visit aground and ended in such bitter argument.

Two hours later, having finished dinner, Teresa touched on the sore subject. "Kevin, I'm bringing one of your poems to read on Tuesday." For several beats, none of them spoke. No one all evening had brought up Tuesday's trip to the Peloncillos.

"Oh great."

"You gave it to me," Teresa said, more intrepid now that the subject had been broached. "I figure I own it and can do whatever I want with it."

"Most of my creative work is pretty crappy."

"You always say that about your poetry."

"And it's the truth. It's all crap."

"*No me puedes decir lo que pienso*," Teresa said.

"*Piensa lo que quieras*," Kevin came back.

"Okay," Tracy interrupted, holding up both hands. "This quits here. We're not going to end this like last time. No Spanish, either." Though both Tracy and their younger sister, Linda, understood Spanish, neither one was comfortable speaking it.

Kevin found himself up and in the kitchen unscrewing the cap on the bottle of Johnny Walker. John Gilbert was fumbling about as though to clean up, obviously uncomfortable with where the conversation had gone. "I'm sorry," Kevin said, pointing at the bottle of scotch in his hand. "I shouldn't just help myself."

"Oh," John said with a wave of his hand. "It's perfectly all right. Go right ahead."

When Kevin reentered the dining room, Olivia and Patty had fled the tension at the table and now sat in the living room. His mother and sister were whispering vehemently at each other in an attempt to keep from breaking into an all-out shouting match. They stopped as soon as they saw him. Kevin sat back down, both women staring at him.

"Kev," Tracy said. "Going up there is the reason we're all here. It just feels weird to avoid talking about it."

"Look Kevin," his mother broke in, impatient with the kid gloves. "For over thirty years you've pretended like this thing never happened."

Angry, Kevin made to stand, but Tracy put her hand on his shoulder. "Kevin, settle down." She looked at Teresa. "Mother, please."

"I'm just saying, Kevin," Teresa persisted. "We need to come together. To acknowledge and talk about this thing—those we lost."

"Mother," Kevin said, no longer conscious of the volume of his voice. "You think I haven't obsessed over this?"

"We all have," Teresa said.

Kevin killed his drink, at least a double, the bits of residual ice already melted. "You don't think I've owned those deaths the last three decades?" John Gilbert, gentleman that he was, put another scotch at Kevin's elbow.

"There's the problem," Teresa said. "You blame yourself when it wasn't your fault."

"Like hell it wasn't."

Teresa, rather dramatically, swept her arm to indicate everything around them. "What do you think this is?" she asked. "A Hollywood set, where the hero always rises to the occasion?"

"You know better than that," Kevin said. "You couldn't know what I've gone through."

"Yes I could," Teresa said. "Remember, I was there, too."

Kevin jabbed his chest with his finger. "*I* was the one who wandered off. *I* started the whole goddamn mess. *I'm* the one who froze up under pressure."

"Oh, Kevin," Teresa said. "You were young and there was a lot of miscommunication. If you'd tried to do any more than you had, you'd probably be dead."

Silence. Tracy put her hand on Kevin's back. "We need to go on Tuesday," she told him. "Okay?"

"I'm here, aren't I?" Kevin's voice caught, just a little, with these words. He peered down at his whiskey glass, surprised that it was empty, that a fresh drink stood beside it, that he had no recollection of drinking the first one.

Olivia Hallot stepped out of the kitchen with a deep pan of rum cake in one hand and a handful of forks in the other. "I don't know about you guys, but I'm tired of waiting for my dessert."

All laughed. The levity was well overdue.

"Ghost of O.D.'s telling us to eat," Teresa said.

Two bites into his dessert, Kevin fell asleep in his chair. Teresa shook him awake and offered a ride back to the motel, but the Gilberts would have none of it, insisting he stay in one of the extra bedrooms for the night.

Three hours later, Kevin woke in the dark room, a rectangle of dim street light outlining unfamiliar curtains, and was for a moment panicked as he put together where he was. He'd stayed in the room many times—all of his and John Jr.'s rowdy nights, the times it was unwise to drive the five miles back to the ranch. The room smelled the same, a sort of warm musty odor.

Kevin tried to will himself back to sleep but after half an hour abandoned the effort. He snapped on the bedside light and reached for his jeans in a heap beside the bed. From the back pocket, he withdrew the folded three sheets of paper he'd printed out at the library. The half-inch headline read: **BLOODBATH AT THE BORDER: 14 DEAD.**

Seven

Kevin had come to understand how one often sees the folly in seemingly casual actions, and he had spent countless miserable hours agonizing over a number of ill-advised decisions he'd made that long-ago weekend. Leaving Amanda Monahan to tend her deer that day was one of them. For the last half hour, he had coaxed the temperamental bitch mule up a rocky trail to what he thought was the agreed-upon horse gate. The whole way there, he'd measured each word he and Amanda had exchanged and found himself embarrassed and confused. Even then he'd regretted every decision—not helping her with the deer, what he'd chosen to say to her, the fact that he didn't stay longer—all of it like a tickle in the back of his throat. When he found the horse gate, he sat leaning against one of the stay posts, hoping she would come riding up on Dunk. He had just opened the plastic on his second ham sandwich, when he spotted Bonny trotting toward him through the grass about a hundred yards down canyon. She'd apparently left her master and followed him and Sally.

"What are you doing here, huh?"

The dog lowered her head, waggling her body submissively at the affection in his voice. She sidled up to him and he scratched her neck. "Where's Mandi, huh? Is she behind you?"

Kevin stood and looked down canyon the way he had come. No movement. He took another bite of his sandwich and reached down and scratched the dog's head. "I bet she lost you taking that deer back to the trucks," he said, half to the dog, half to himself.

The dog was whimpering then, sitting expectantly before him, her tail sweeping the ground, the same way his Lab at home acted when she needed outside. "What's wrong with you?" he said. He tossed the remaining corner of sandwich on the ground in front of her. She seemed surprised at the gesture, nosing at the bread and meat a moment before licking it up and swallowing it. Still, the expectant look, the whimpering, the wagging tail.

Kevin held out his hands. "I don't have any more, see?" She took a hop backward, a sort of buck, and yipped at him. The dog wanted him to follow her. He'd heard the baying from the hounds earlier and was inexperienced enough in lion hunting that he didn't know quite what to make of it. It could have been the dogs sounded like that when they pushed up a jackrabbit, and Amanda hadn't been around for him to ask. But now he suspected the baying had meant something more and that Bonny wanted to join in the hunt. Amanda was probably with the rest of the party, and he'd be left out.

"Okay, Bonny," he said, untying his mule and mounting up. "Let's see what you're so worried about."

Though she took him a bit further south than where he'd heard the other dogs, he followed her, about a quarter mile through the bottom of a short, rocky canyon. It was there in the sandy bottom that he spotted the tracks. He dismounted and called back the dog, who quickly complied. Kevin didn't need Armando Luna's skill to realize the prints had been made by a big three-footed animal.

"Damn," he said to Bonny. "Maybe they're on him, you think?"

But this didn't make sense—the baying he'd heard was at least a mile further north, and there was no way the rest of the party could have come this direction. He squatted down to his haunches and with a small twig poked the edge of the most well-formed of the tracks. It was about the size of a medium-sized pancake. "It's gotta be him," he said.

Bonny's patience was running out. She bucked backward a few hops and yapped at him, eyes bright and ears pointed forward. "Okay," he said to her. "Hold on." A moment's apprehension, verging on panic, ran over him—the same feeling he'd had at nine when he became separated from his parents and sisters one Saturday evening at a crowded county fair. He was comforted at the sight of the old bald ridge north of him where he knew the trucks were parked.

"Okay," he said. "We'll go a little more."

The dog worked the bottom of the canyon some two-hundred yards, then broke from the wash to move uphill toward a low yucca-clustered saddle. Surprisingly, old Sally never balked, climbing from the relative comfort of the sandy bottom to the rock-and-brush-tangled hillside. This belligerent mule rose to the occasion when it came to chasing cats.

Once he'd topped the saddle, Kevin recognized the long shallow basin he'd glassed so many times. Just a few hundred yards this side of the New Mexico border, and about two miles north of Sonora, the half-mile flat was crowded with stands of Emory oak and cedar with several breaks speckled with bunches of bear grass. Knowing the basin was a good place for the old tom to cross, Kevin negotiated Sally into a clearing just below the saddle, climbed off and tied her and called back the dog then sat to glass a few minutes. He worked the brush hard, knowing a cat, even a black one, if hiding, would be difficult to spot.

After fifteen minutes, the big black cat stepped into view, though it took several moments for the stunning fact of it to take hold in Kevin's mind. A rush from his heart climbed from his chest and whirred between his ears, and his hands shook so he could hardly steady the binoculars. His first thought had been "cow"—until he made out the yard of tail that followed the animal.

Some thousand yards away, the jaguar sat like a housecat on its haunches, the black fur and powerful muscle beneath so distinct under the afternoon sun as to appear unreal. Kevin didn't think about his rifle, still sheathed in its saddle scabbard, and could only sit paralyzed, unhinged at the animal he'd only heard stories about.

Without taking his eyes off the black speck, which he knew now to be Pete, Kevin managed to open his fanny pack and set up his tripod, then mount his binoculars on it and not lose the animal. He'd done this all in a frenetic thirty seconds.

Pete was walking now, two-hundred pounds, at least, his head the size and somewhat the shape of the deep cast-iron skillet O.D. cooked camp eggs on. The limp was definite and pronounced—the left hind foot—and Kevin wondered at how an animal so impeded and so stark in shape and color could have for so long escaped his many pursuers.

The old cat stopped then, and looked straight up at the hillside where Kevin sat. He'd spotted the mule. For a solid five minutes he stared, the little dog all the while tensed to give chase, her growls like a small motor.

"Hold on, girl," he told her. "Hold on."

Pete suddenly appeared to make up his mind, turned and scurried east, belly low to the ground, not quite at a dead run. He disappeared in a series of blinking black flashes as he moved between the trees and into a brushy draw that was fed from the far ridge just this side of the

New Mexico border.

Kevin didn't think about the time—it was already late afternoon—or whether he would cross a state border or have to spend the night without food or bedroll. He, like the little dog, acted only on impulse, swinging up onto the mule and hissing down, "Let's get, Bonny. Let's get that old devil."

But after he'd ridden down and found the tracks at the bottom, he'd gotten a little more firmly fixed in his senses. Bonny had become harder to bring to heel, and he'd had to call her back half a dozen times before she'd heeded, and he'd yanked her by the collar, hard. "You stay," he told her. "You heel."

He was thinking now, finally. Inexperienced though he was, Kevin had gained enough sense to know treeing the tom was probably out of the question with just one dog. Old Pete could take Bonny out with one fell swat, and the whole thing wasn't worth killing someone else's dog over.

Standing beside Sally now, he glassed the ridge some four hundred yards ahead of him. He tended to work the hillside with his binoculars from left to right, scanning from bottom to top, then from top down. He'd traversed about half the ridge when the old tom limped into his field of view.

Kevin didn't hesitate this time, quickly lifting his Winchester from the scabbard, sitting and jacking in a shell. Pete was moving through the brush now on the shadowed half of the hill in no apparent hurry. Kevin could feel his breathing, deliberating the rise and fall of his chest, working it in rhythm with the crosshairs in his scope. The way his gun was sighted in, the one-hundred-thirty grained bullet would drop fifteen to twenty inches at the estimated range.

Pete passed into an opening, still moving slowly, and Kevin caught his breath, his finger giving perhaps a quarter pound more pressure on the trigger, but he did not shoot, and the cat moved again into the junipers. Kevin was unsure why he was not able to shoot, and would only determine the underlying reason some ten years later in a conversation with someone, that no one—including himself, including Armando Luna, and even John Monahan—genuinely wanted to kill the old black cat.

He watched the patch of alligator juniper in his scope until the cat emerged again, undoubtedly too far this time. Pete lumbered up into a clearing above the trees then gained the top of the ridge, his black figure sharpened by the graying eastern sky behind him as he disappeared over the other side.

It was perhaps five o'clock, but Kevin gave no mind to this. He mounted up, to Bonny's delight, and began the climb up the ridge and through the saddle. Sally was easily raised to a canter as she found a good game trail that led to the saddle.

"You love me when it comes to chasing cats, don't you, old bitch?"

When they'd crested the ridge, Kevin stopped his mule and called Bonny back. Staying mounted, he made a quick sweep with his glasses of the canyon below. He worked to calm himself as he knew the chance of a reasonable shot at the cat was high in the next half hour.

They moved down the lee side of the hill at a fair pace, Bonny all the way indicating a strong trail, and Kevin on ready with his palm on the rifle butt. They bottomed out again, and again gained the top of the next ridge—still, no Pete.

"You still have him?" he asked the dog. "You still on his scent?"

It was heavy dusk when they'd reached the four-strand barbed wire fence that marked the New Mexico state line, and Kevin realized then that a decision had been made without his having to think about it. The little heeler dog had never lost old Pete's trail, but the old tom had picked up his pace, and it was clear they would not catch him before dark. There was a good chance, though, that Kevin could find the cat at dawn and with some luck could marshal a decent shot at him. Opportunities of a lifetime happened only once, and Kevin, young though he was, understood this intuitively.

Under the waning light, he looked back the way he had come but could no longer see the bald ridge where they had parked the trucks. The new moon, he remembered, had just begun and would offer only a crevice of reflected light to find the way back. Then his being able to find the vehicles and get there before the rest decided to leave was dubious at best. No, the decision had been made for him to spend the night.

He had water enough in the half-gallon canteen tied to Sally's saddle horn, and the mule had watered three times at various tanks that day. He was surprised to find a plastic bag filled with about a half pound of homemade jerky in one of the side bags, the saliva under his tongue gathering as he opened the bag, the smell of the peppered venison rising to meet his nostrils. Bonny sat at his feet, apparently resigned that the chase was over for the day.

"Hey there mutt," Kevin said to her. "I guess there's enough here for both of us."

Kevin knew they would worry, mount a search, be livid when they finally reconnected, but he also knew this transgression to be forgivable, a small fault when one backed up a step or two and really looked at it.

Two hours later and four miles west of where Kevin was camped, the men began to wait, then to worry. They'd gotten back to the trucks and trailers just before 6:00 o'clock expecting to find both kids, but neither was anywhere in sight. Amanda's deer had been boned, the meat cut into strips and packed in a large pillowcase, the hide and head bundled in the truck next to the meat, but the girl was not around. The men discussed the possibilities, then waited in silence. Mild concern turned to worry and they mounted up and began a quarter mile circle around the perimeter of the parked vehicles, calling out the kids' names the whole while.

After two hours of this, they quit their calling. Under a thin slice of just-risen moon, they sat their mounts in silence. The horses and mules under them, exhausted and footsore, snuffled and clomped their hooves in the dirt. By turns the last hour, each animal had barn soured, jerking its head and making feints toward the trucks.

The click of O.D.'s pin light broke the silence as he held it to his watch. "Eight-thirty," he said to no one in particular. "I'm just about sure them kids is onto that tom cat. That good mix bitch probably hit a strong scent and those two just took after her." He'd arrived at this theory two hours before and had mentioned it a half dozen times since.

Monahan shook his head. "I don't know," he said. "Could be. I just can't see Mandi going off like that. She's not done that sort of thing before."

"I can see Kevin doing it," Mondy spoke up.

"Me too," Tom said.

They were quiet a moment, and all understood it was the rancher's turn to speak. "Well," he said finally, "she likes old Kev well enough to follow him, I guess."

Another silence, this one quite uncomfortable, while all waited for John to speak again, which he did: "I sure don't know what I'll tell her mother, though."

"Amen to that," Tom said.

Though the men talked a few minutes about what next to do, three of them had already decided that to look and call any more that night was futile. They would return home, where they would alert the sheriff's office and spend a sleepless several hours before they came back next morning, perhaps with a Cochise County deputy or two, maybe some search volunteers.

But Mondy had stayed silent as the decision was hatched. He had set his mind far earlier to the course he would take when he had strapped his bedroll behind the gelding's saddle.

When the rest realized his intent, Tom spoke up. "You ready to pay me for that old horse if you end up busting a leg on him kicking around in this dark?"

"You think I wouldn't?"

"Look, Mondy," Tom said. "Those kids are perfectly capable of surviving a night alone in the hills."

"And they've got that jerky and plenty of water," John added. "That boy had on a lined chore jacket and Mandi has a down coat. Even if it hard freezes again tonight, they'll be fine."

But Luna was unmoved. "You guys got people to go back to," he said. "I don't. Not really. If I go back to Douglas, I'll just end up at the Red Barn getting drunk. I don't want to do that."

"Now us and the sheriff's department'll have three fools to worry about out here," O.D. said.

Mondy brought old Turk around and started him toward the east. "I'm an Indian, remember."

"A fat Indian," O.D. pointed out.

"Can you see *your* dick to pee lately?" Luna came back.

"Okay," Tom broke in. "If you want to stay out here, it's your own damn foolish decision. But if you don't find those kids before ten o'clock tomorrow, meet us back at the holding corral and tell us what's going on."

"Will do," Mondy said. "Thanks for the use of old Turk here, Tom."

"Mind where he steps, like I told you."

About an hour later, Mondy had picked his way to his intended destination. He'd made a cold camp, for no reason other than he felt no need for a fire, on a grassy saddle overlooking a long tree-crowded basin he and Kevin had hunted a number of times before. Though he was playing a hunch, the decision to go there had been driven by reason as well. If old Pete was on the prowl in the area, that basin served as a good gateway to both New Mexico and Sonora.

Mondy ate the extra burrito he'd saved and for a long while sat on the saddle overlooking the basin. He could see only the edge of the next small ridge opposite him and the general shape of the Escrobarra beyond that. Before he made his bed, he lit a cigarette, drew on it a few times then crushed it out before it was half burnt. He was thinking of a prayer, one based in his Catholicism, but the words came to him in the old language, and he began to say it. Perhaps his aim was some effect he'd only intuited at the moment, perhaps to give the prayer a kind of resonance and subtlety it deserved. Kevin McNally was his best friend, and his worry for the boy struck as deep, he felt, as that of anyone involved. Suddenly, he was visited by a passing regret that he'd not thought to go back to the trucks for a set of radios, as they surely would have come in handy.

When he'd finished, he looked out into the night. "I'll find you," he said. The stars were especially bright. "I won't leave this ridge without you."

Eight

Kevin McNally was thirteen the first time he saw Armando Luna. Armando's black hair, almost purple under certain light, was bound in a ponytail and quit just past his shoulder blades. He wore a vest and knee-high moccasins, both adorned with quarter-sized silver conchos and a Bisbee Blue rock the size of a quail's egg on his chubby pinky finger. While the young man's bulk and wide shoulders made him appear quite tall, a fair measurement would have put him about an inch shy of six feet. Kevin, along with his father, was selling raffle tickets for a guided elk hunt at the Cochise County Fair's Round Mountain Outdoorsman booth when Luna stepped up to their counter. Young Armando Luna had come to the Sulfer Springs Valley a few weeks before from Sil Nakaya on the O'odham reservation. Earlier, at the archery booth, he had purchased a half-dozen fletched cedar arrows, which he tapped against his palm as he talked with Kevin's father. The arrows, along with the outfit, completed what Kevin recognized to be a very well-studied look.

"That bull was a five-point, but he'd go three-fifty," Armando was telling Tom McNally, who even at thirty-eight already looked hard and worn out.

"Not possible," Tom said flatly. "Bull elk would have to be a six-point to score that."

The Indian lifted his right hand and placed his finger against the side of his chest. "Caught him right here with a 200-grain Nossler bullet from a Winchester 300—between the fourth and fifth ribs. Bull went about three feet—from his belly to the ground."

McNally just shook his head.

"I got a picture," Luna said. "I'll bring it and show you sometime."

"I'd like to see it."

"I'll bring it," Armando assured.

"And I'll look at it," McNally came back.

Armando registered membership and paid yearly club dues that afternoon, which pleased Tom McNally but put away none of his doubts about the verity of the several tall stories he'd heard that day. A few weeks later, at the monthly club meeting in the McNallys' large, comfortable home, Armando paused only a moment to thank Teresa when she let him in, before stepping up to Tom in his easy chair and handing him a dog-eared, coffee-stained Polaroid photograph. Kevin could not see the photo but noted the look on his father's face. Tom squinted at the photo, looked up at Luna, and nodded an approval any hunter would recognize.

"Good bull," he said. "Hell of a bull, in fact."

Tom handed the snapshot to O.D. Hallot, who was working on his fourth Coors. Hallot shook his head and curled his lower lip.

"He's a five-point alright, and he won't go no 350, but he's a good measure over 300 all day."

McNally nodded. Same squint. "That's about what I figured."

Teresa stepped in from the kitchen and handed a beer to Luna, who tipped the yellow can, glanced at the label, popped the top, and tilted back a quick swallow. "Coors," he said. "My flavor." Armando scanned the walls, pausing on the better mounts—the heavy-antlered Kaibab mule deer, the Boone and Crockett antelope, the desert big-horn ram. "Nice place," he said. "You got some good mounts. I think I'll like coming to meetings here."

It was perhaps his graceless charm, the way his outrageous stories were so often cut with measures of truth that endeared Armando Luna to the McNallys and their circle. That November, Luna hunted whitetail with Kevin, Thomas, and O.D. Hallot. The afternoon before opening day, they drove to the west edge of the Peloncillos and made camp south of Starvation Canyon in a cedar flat rich in grama grass and adult oak. Tom and O.D. pitched a rumpled, slouching canvas tent bereft of half its ribs and made a wide fire of deadfall cedar. Hallot threw a stick of butter in a Dutch oven and fried a wedge-thick, three-pound sirloin along with some onion and new potato. After dinner, Kevin chose the truck cab to sleep, and Mondy rolled his sleeping bag out on raw ground some thirty yards from camp.

In the yellow shroud of a Coleman lantern, Luna carefully made his bed, kicking down clumps of grass, removing sticks and pebbles, until he had cleared out a suitable space.

"Hell, Indian," Hallot remarked, forking a chunk of steak into his mouth. "This ain't the Regency. You should've brought your feather bed."

"Good sleep, good hunt," Mondy came back, which brought only derisive laughter from the two men.

Satisfied the bed was ready, Mondy removed from his daypack an apple-sized, hollowed-out gourd stopped with a small cork. He held the gourd to his ear and shook it as though its content told secrets, then unstopped it. He began to sing: low tones at first, rising to a pitched falsetto, bringing more laughter from the men and Kevin, who sat with them at the dying fire.

"What the hell is that son of a bitch singing?" Hallot asked, grinding a piece of steak in his jaw and chasing it back with a swallow of Coors.

Kevin listened carefully to the song. "I don't know," the boy said, finally. "It's not Spanish."

"Your mother sounds like that sometimes—when she's talking to her sisters," Thomas remarked.

Kevin shook his head. "No, that's Basque Spanish, Daddy." He gestured at Luna. "Those words are altogether different. Probably Papago."

Hallot belched. "That silly bastard don't know real Papago."

The conversation was cut by another high-pitched keen. Struggling to control himself, Tom McNally shook his head. "Son of a bitch is probably faking it," he said, just before he and O.D. were taken by another fit of chuckling.

Even if Mondy was aware of the jeering, he was unmoved by it. He squared himself against the yellow light and raised the gourd, cupping it in his palms above his head as in an offering to the gods. *Hay-yay-yay-yay...he-ya-ya-ya-ya-heeee...*

O.D. and Thomas were beside themselves now. But as they laughed, Kevin heard a shape and consistency in the words and knew they could only be real. On the playground all his school life he'd heard children fake Spanish. Tones and syllables gave an impression of the language, but their spurious words lacked continuity, no two utterances exactly alike.

His song finished, Luna knelt and sprinkled a powder-like substance from the gourd, as one would pepper a steak, onto the ground beside his bedroll.

"God," Tom said. "Whose idea was it to bring that dipshit with us?"

"Yours," O.D. pointed out.

"Well I guess I was eat up with the dumbass at the time," Tom said. "A moment of temporary insanity."

"Well," Hallot mused. "The insanity part may be temporary, but I figure the dumbass part to be permanent."

"Have I told you to kiss my ass yet today?"

Hallot drew down his brow in mock contemplation. "I don't believe so," he allowed.

"Well, kiss my ass."

Kevin left the fire, fingers pushed into his jean pockets, and walked up to Luna, who had just finished a circle of the powder around his sleeping bag.

"What is that stuff?" Kevin asked.

"For a good hunt." Mondy didn't look up at him. Since their first encounter, they had spoken no more than twenty words together. The breech in their ages was wide at the time, Kevin's thirteen to Mondy's nineteen. A few years later, doing research in college, Kevin determined that Mondy's performance was an odd derivation of the Yaqui Deer Dance, the rite observed not so much for the sake of good hunting but as an appeal to the "Flower World," a version of Heaven. Traditionally, the dance was done by men wearing crowns made from deer antler. Armando Luna had modified the ritual dance and some of the words in the song to meet his own ends. That the ceremony was not O'odham seemed to bother him not at all.

"Why'd you put it around your bedroll?"

"It's ground-up whitetail antler—spiritual significance."

Kevin stared at him.

"The circle is sacred," Mondy said, meeting the boy's eyes as best he could in the dull light. "It keeps the good spirits in and the bad spirits out. It also helps my dreams."

"I think you make things up," Kevin said.

Mondy laughed. "Well," he said. "Kind of. I just retool some Indian traditions to my liking. Bet I don't go to Hell for it, though."

Kevin shrugged.

Mondy laughed again and shook his head. "We'll see," he said. "We'll see."

Next morning, to Kevin's surprise, Mondy tapped on the truck window to wake him. Tom and O.D. stood in the early morning dark warming their hands against a mature fire, the smell of coffee, bacon, and peach cobbler from Hallot's Dutch oven rich on the air. Kevin tumbled out of the truck cab rubbing his arms for the cold, pulled on his chore jacket, and stomped into his boots. Mondy handed him black coffee in a tin cup, the only one in camp.

"Coffee gets cold in that," Mondy pointed out. "Better drink it quick."

Kevin sipped the coffee, still hot, and tongued at the grounds as they hit his teeth, not surprised to have gotten the bottom of the pot.

"I had good dreams last night," Mondy told him, low enough that the men by the fire would not hear. "I'll take a buck today."

They agreed to split in twos, Kevin and Mondy taking the higher north end of Silver Creek ridge, while the men stayed low and glassed mesquite and ocotillo hillsides. Tom and O.D. would drive the Jimmy along those lower cuts and the boys would take the Ford. They would meet at a water tank at the head of the canyon about noon.

The east sky had just begun to lighten when Kevin and Mondy made the ten-minute loop back within sight the house and outbuildings of the Snure Ranch, then began the rough climb up the Jeep trail to the top of a ridge that ran in a low-pitch off Starvation Peak. Kevin had warned Mondy twice not to drive too fast and was ignored. Just as they hit the stretch where the road flattened out toward the top, they were taken by the unmistakable sway and grind of a flat tire on gravel road.

Kevin climbed out first and kicked the deflated tire hard enough to jam his toe. "Shit, fuck, puke," he said, trying out a particular arrangement of oaths he'd learned from O.D.

Mondy stepped from the truck to examine the ruined tire, but seemed more taken by the boy's ire.

"I told you not to drive so fast," Kevin said. "This'll put us half an hour late."

Mondy was staring at him. "You're a feisty little shit when you get mad."

"I wanted a chance to kill a deer today," Kevin said. "We'll be too late working that canyon."

"I didn't dream a deer for you today."

Kevin kicked at the tire again. "Did you dream *that* fucking thing?"

Mondy laughed. "Your logic is good, but I think you need to learn more respect for your elders."

Kevin went silent.

"Listen, man," Mondy said, opening the driver's door and pulling a lug wrench from under the seat, "I've already changed more flat tires than you will for the rest of your rich-boy life. This is a ten-minute job. We'll be up there in plenty of time." He stepped around the nose of the truck, and in a single, quick movement bent and cracked the first lug.

He glanced up at Kevin as he worked. "You need to learn to relax and be patient, let things happen the way they're supposed to. You white-eyes spend too much time fighting the current. You need to just go with it, man."

This was a thesis Kevin was to contemplate, in various forms and manifestations, the next thirty years of his life, a sort of maxim he could never escape. It wasn't the fatalism that was so striking, but the way Armando Luna, as he would come to realize, had fixed his life so solidly in it. He had not met anyone before or since who so willingly succumbed to any perceived will outside his own.

They topped the ridge to the first long canyon by 7:00 a.m.—no more than fifteen minutes later than planned—and agreed to split, Mondy working the ridge fifty yards higher, Kevin traversing the lower, brush-choked arroyos, stopping at clear points to glass. He picked carefully over rocks and around the cat's claw, creeping along the angled ridge, willing his footfalls and body weight lighter. To turn an ankle or roll a rock out underfoot could end the hunt or even worse. Kevin stepped past a cluster of prickly pear and gained the top of a small limestone outcropping. He looked down into the throat of the valley. From here, one could see almost the whole of the Peloncillos as they chained north into bare, rocky peaks past Rodeo and out toward Lordsburg. To the south, the mountains peaked again at Robinson's Bunk then trailed out low into Mexico. Fifteen miles west, across the Bernardino Valley, stood the majestic Chiricahuas, Round Mountain Peak haloed in a ring of thin clouds. Through the late fall and winter months, this pitch of morning light cut the mountains into magnificent relief, canyons five miles distant seeming close enough to touch, and Kevin's heart surged for thinking of their mysteries and possibilities. On some school days, the image of those canyons stole between him and classroom work, spiriting him away from the tedious smells of graphite, paper, and chalk. Never was he happier than when seated on a rock in the Peloncillos in this particular slant of morning light, the air absent of all man-made smells and sounds, and Jackwood Canyon across the valley opening before him like the gates of Heaven itself.

Forty-five minutes after they'd split, Kevin glassed up a buck some four- hundred yards down canyon. He saw the deer as it stepped out from behind a manzanita bush, unmistakably a buck—a mature one. On his rear end, Kevin shinnied twenty feet downslope to a fallen log, over which he laid his .270, but as soon as he'd found the deer in the scope he knew, sensed really, that the shot was too far. *Don't panic,* he told himself. The wind was steady in his face and immediately he determined a way to get closer. He pulled in three good breaths and raised his binoculars. There were two now, both bucks, the one he'd seen first the biggest. He could feel his heartbeat and wished he had some way to steady it. Years later, he realized that the rise in heart rate, the adrenaline, the tapping of something primal was the very reason he was on the mountain.

Kevin had raised his binoculars again when the spaniel-like bark of Mondy's .243 rolled down canyon from a rim rock above him, the small caliber bullet splitting the air. The larger buck crow-hopped when the bullet, at the end of its long arc (too long for such a rifle), hit him in the hip, the buck's companion flagging his tail and making a headlong burst into the brush. The wounded deer recovered himself and limped, head bobbing, straight downslope, disappearing into the dry wash below.

"Shit," Kevin said aloud. "You stupid son of a bitch." He heard Mondy picking through the mahogany and cholla as he made his way downhill.

"Hey, kid," Mondy called. "Where are you?"

Kevin didn't answer.

"Yo, Kevin."

"Here," he said finally.

When Mondy found him, Kevin did not stand or even look up.

"Did you see that buck?" Mondy asked. "What a beauty."

"I saw the buck."

"Think I may have hit him?"

"You did," Kevin said. "You shouldn't have taken the shot."

Mondy stood a moment, staring down canyon. He nodded. "Maybe not," he said. "But does it do us any good to contemplate that now?"

They had crossed the canyon and made their way up to a game trail just above the spot where Kevin had last seen the wounded deer. They worked the area slowly, alert to any noise or movement out of keeping with the landscape or time of day. When they came to within a few yards of the spot, Kevin pointed.

"He was standing right there when you shot."

Mondy stepped over, knelt and pushed his face close to the ground. "Blood," he said. "Not much. Two little pinpoints." He looked back up at Kevin, a question on his face, and spoke just above a whisper. "You said he went straight downslope?"

Kevin nodded.

"Okay," Mondy said. "He's in that brush below us."

Kevin was quick to disagree. "He could have gone down the wash with the other one. He wasn't hit hard enough to kill him."

Mondy shook his head. "No," he said gently. "He would have taken this game trail and side-hilled. Besides, you never know what hard enough is." He gestured to the dry wash fifty yards below. "He's down there somewhere, dead or alive."

Though Kevin doubted this assessment, he'd agreed to work through the brush to the bottom while Luna waited, ready above him, in case he moved the wounded animal out onto the open hillside. Kevin had gone less than twenty yards when he came to the buck, stone dead, where he had fallen without struggle just below an agave cactus.

"What'd I tell you," Mondy said after Kevin had called him down.

The bullet, too small to penetrate the thick bone at the hip, had deflected and tumbled into the chest cavity, killing the deer almost immediately. For Kevin, the buck's death had been a mystery until they'd field dressed the animal.

"Maybe it's closer than I thought," Kevin said, raising his glasses to look again at the rim rock from which Luna had shot. "I just can't believe it."

"Four-seventy-five, five hundred, maybe," Mondy said. "Little bullet will reach that far—an ill-advised shot, but it will reach. Besides, I told you about my dream." He spoke as if the whole episode should have been a forgone conclusion instead of hoopla and bad judgment.

"It was an irresponsible shot, at least. And you didn't even know for sure you hit him."

"You're right," Luna said patiently. "But I would have checked for blood like I always do."

And for a moment, Kevin was put to thinking he might be wrong. Though seldom guilty of a rush to judgment, Kevin may have, this one time, misread someone.

Mondy looked at him as though he'd somehow tapped Kevin's thoughts. "Sometimes you have to think about a situation," he told him in Spanish. "Sit around in it for a while then look back on it, retell the story before you find out the truth."

"*No comprendo,*" Kevin said.

"*Mentiroso,*" Mondy came back, *liar.*

Kevin sensed Armando Luna might be right in some way he didn't understand, perhaps a tucked-away truism he would come to know and use later in life. They sat eating lunch, admiring the buck, whose antlers, they later found out, would score just over ninety-five Boone and Crocket points. They ate tamales from the twenty dozen Kevin's mother had made for the hunting and coming holidays.

"*¿Me haces un favor?*" Mondy asked suddenly.

"*¿Mande?*"

"*Tu padre,*" Luna went on. "Your old man—I don't want him to know there was any doubt."

"How do you mean?"

"*Andale pues.* I mean we tell the story of this deer the right way to your dad and his pot-bellied friend."

"You mean lie? Hell no, we'll just tell it the way it happened."

Luna said nothing, made no gesture either way. "Getting the story right is important," he finally said. "As important as anything else."

They'd met the two men at the water tank and windmill two hours later than planned. Tom and O.D. had come up empty for their half day's effort, and having eaten lunch already, sat drowsily in the Jimmy when Kevin and Mondy pulled up in the Ford. The two men had not expected success from the other pair, figuring they were late just because they were kids.

There was some talk of what everyone had done that morning, the routes taken, the effort put forth, the number of deer seen. The flat tire was mentioned, and all agreed that it needed to be fixed before they used two vehicles again. Tom, with his usual concern for such things, walked to the truck bed to examine the flat tire and found the buck lying there. He was stunned into silence.

"Oh yeah," Mondy said, his tone and timing as surprisingly dead on as his shot several hours before. "I took a pretty good buck this morning. You guys ought to have a look."

They'd hunted, the four of them together, the rest of the afternoon without success, then made back for camp when it fell too dark to see. O.D. baked two small chickens in his Dutch oven that night and drank several Coors as he stood over the fire. Occasionally, he glanced up at the young Armando Luna and shook his head. When the fire had gone to coals and they had made their beds, O.D. finally spoke.

"Hey Indian," he said, slumped by the fire, the perpetual yellow can wrapped in his palm.

Luna was just climbing into his bag. "*Sî, senor,*" he said.

O.D. tossed an oak knot on the coals to bank. "How about dreaming me up a buck tonight."

Nine

Kevin had snapped off the bed lamp thirty minutes before. He was tempted get up and slip into the kitchen, where he'd last seen the bottle of scotch. The end days of his marriage had haunted his thoughts most of the last half hour—they seemed liquid and incoherent as he'd tried to put a timeline on events. The only moment he could clearly place was the evening he'd packed up his things and pulled out of the drive, how he'd fought to keep from glancing into the rearview mirror.

He and Janice had been polite, civil, as he'd gotten his belongings together. When he asked if she'd seen his elk hide slippers, a long-ago Christmas gift from her parents, she sat down on a corner of the bed, which for some months they had no longer shared. He recognized the stricken look. She pressed her small hands palms-down onto the teal quilt, leaned forward, almost as though to push herself off, and began to cry.

And what could he do but go about this business. The rummaging through the upper shelves of closets, and finally a pile of sundries in black plastic trash bags at the front door. He and Janice had never really talked about "The Shooting Incident," not like they should have. It had been the catalyst of the rift between them, what had now been, essentially, a five-year silence. Kevin loaded up the trash bags, ready to drive to a motel, and Janice walked to the front door, leaned against the jamb. He looked up at her over the top of his car.

"How are you going to get well, Kevin?" She asked this as though they lay in the intimacy of some long-ago bed. "This is not because I'm bitter. I want to know for you."

He drove away, intending not to look back, but he knew better, she knew better, and the memory of her standing there was one of the many that circled, like buzzards, in his sleeplessness. He'd regretted a dozen times staying with the Gilberts, and that he'd lost his nerve to read the newspaper article, which would probably have told him little and helped him not at all.

He got out of bed about five o'clock when he'd finally heard John Gilbert stirring in the kitchen. Kevin had coffee with John, thanked him, then left for his motel room where he read, puttered about, and tried to nap before he checked out and met his sister for lunch at El Texano. Like so many others in that town, the place was almost a still shot of itself thirty years before. The same cash register, the plastic red and white checkered tablecloths, the utilitarian dishes and utensils. Even the food, Kevin was told, was good now as it was then. He and Tracy had just sat down when Rick Elsie, an old friend, stepped into the little restaurant.

"*Palabras*," he said, reaching to shake Kevin's hand when recognition rose in his eyes.

Kevin had not heard that nickname in many years. His face darkened, stunned into a moment of silence.

Ricky, hands on his hips now, nodding his head—a characteristic gesture—took the shape of that boy thirty years before. "You look great, man."

"Thanks," Kevin said. "You, too." A lie, as the man before him was jowled and rheumy-eyed with a gut that obscured his belt buckle. But Ricky had been a good friend, had hung with him and Mondy even in the most dicey of times.

"Jeez it's good to see you, Kevin—wow."

"You, too, man." Kevin was standing now, realizing, regrettably, that he knew at least half the people in the restaurant. Tracy stood up, hugged Ricky and kissed him on the cheek. He sat with them a few minutes, and when he was about to leave, asked them to join him and his wife for drinks at Dawson's that night.

"Sure," Kevin said. "I can do that." He glanced at Tracy, her face clouded. "I'll think about it, at least."

He showed up alone just after seven. He'd napped two hours at his motel room, then phoned his sister, tried to talk her into coming out with him, and she had politely declined. Drinking had been a problem several times in his life, especially when he felt emotionally fragile, and Tracy knew this well.

The smell of the old tavern had not changed. It had once adjoined a Mexican restaurant, and the ghostly presence of green chile and enchilada sauce hung about the air. Dale Ackerman and Lester Johns were matched over the same shabby pool table with the same burred felt from three decades before, names tooled into the backs of their belts as though no one in this county might otherwise know who they were. The only change was both men had more gut and less hair.

Dale eyed Kevin over the pool cue he clutched. Kevin always thought it strange when someone didn't recognize him right away. He'd lost little hair and his weight had shifted no more than ten pounds since high school. People who had been acquaintances, friends, spouses for many years tended not to realize the changes in one another brought by age. Perhaps it was because he had been away that he was difficult to recognize. He was glad for it, though. He'd left at eighteen, wanting nothing more than to be shut of this place, but for some circumstance or another—none of them pleasant—he had been forever drawn back.

Dale Ackerman continued to study Kevin, who worked hard to avoid his gaze.

Dale bellied up, one barstool between them. The bartender, a hard-edged woman about sixty, tipped her chin up at him.

"Two Coors, Joanne," Dale said to her, then glanced over at Kevin.

Kevin dropped his head, looked over toward the entrance, wishing for all the world Ricky would show up and save him from this. "Hey, Joanne," he said. "I'll get those two Coors."

Dale was aiming a hard stare at him, his expression lingering somewhere between confusion and hostility. "Do I know you, mister?"

Kevin turned to him, the half-light catching the edge of his face, and Dale squinted.

"Go back to '76," Kevin said. "Picture center field."

Dale cocked his head. "Kevin McNally?"

Kevin smiled, offered his hand.

"Jesus," Dale said. "Kevin McNally. I can't believe it."

Lester walked up, shook Kevin's hand. "You know, I thought that was you, but I just wasn't sure. You didn't look quite old and ugly enough, to tell you the truth." The three chuckled.

Kevin finished two beers with them at the bar. The warm tinge of alcohol in his belly welcomed a bit of nostalgia, and they chatted of old times. All three had been on the varsity baseball team together. Douglas High had done well both years, though the three of them had spent most of both seasons on the bench. What had seemed miserable and inglorious then was now embroidered with age, distance, and a touch of humor.

"You left right out of high school, didn't you?" Lester said.

Kevin nodded.

"I remember," Lester added. "Some bad stuff happened, huh?"

Kevin nodded again, looked toward the door, hoped these two had the social wherewithal to recognize a cue. He was thankful when Dale slapped him lightly on the back. "Glad to know you're doing good, Kevin."

Ricky and his wife, Sheryl, came in after eight, apologetic for being late. They had two teenagers at home and had to review house rules before going out.

"You know kids," Sheryl said. "You make a rule, they break it." She wore a flattering blouse and skirt, and had gained some weight. She and Ricky had been together since the eighth grade.

Dale and Lester, having forgotten a half-finished game, joined them. They were drunker, more raucous, the bar beginning to crowd up. Kevin recognized most everyone there, including Sandy Alden, a girl he'd dated in high school. They made eye contact almost immediately, but she pretended not to recognize him.

Lester punched up some songs on the jukebox and let out a ridiculous "Yeeeehawwww," when the first one kicked on. Ricky shook his head, looked at Kevin. "Can you believe those assholes," he said. "Like they never left eighteen."

Kevin was working on his fifth beer, and the alcohol felt good. "None of us has, in some ways."

At one point Kevin glanced at his watch, surprised to see it was after ten. A three-man country band had started to play. The place had become too noisy for intelligible conversation. Dale and Lester had commenced—as usual, Kevin was told—to make abject fools of themselves. They were shaking their beers and spraying each other with the foam.

More and more faces from that other life approached Kevin. Mary Jacobs, without ceremony, walked right up and hugged him. Brothers Billy and John Bartmoth recognized him immediately. John bought Kevin a beer, and handed him his card—Custom Ironwork Gates, in case he was ever in the market.

"You're a *pro-fessor?*" Andy Romero said for the second time, just in case he hadn't heard right. "*¿De veras?*"

Kevin smiled and nodded, tickled at the drunk man's incredulity.

Andy shook his head. "Wow, man. I never would have thought."

That Kevin spoke Spanish had surprised and impressed people in his professional life, but the home crowd had fallen comfortably into step. No one looked like a gringo more than Kevin McNally, and yet every Hispanic he encountered that night greeted him in their native tongue.

Kevin couldn't have named the time of night or how many beers he'd had when Lester Johns appeared before him amid the noise and smoke and faces. Kevin would not, the next morning, be able to recount exactly what the man had said to him. In a moment both men were on the floor, Lester's face bloodied, the knuckles of Kevin's right hand feeling as though he'd crashed it against a wall.

He could hear Ricky's voice, then a woman shouting, hands on his shirt tail and a man's arm cinched around his neck, and finally his friend's words became clear. "Calm down, man. You hear me? Calm down." Kevin bared his teeth and kicked at the man on the floor. Lester started and curled tighter into his fetal curve.

"You say that shit again, asshole. Go ahead. Say that shit about him again."

"Kevin," Ricky barked in his ear.

"He talks shit again, Ricky, I'll stomp a mud hole in that motherfucker."

"He says that shit again, *I'll* fuck him up." Ricky addressed the man on the floor. "You hear what I'm saying, Lester. You're not talking like that, you hear."

Lester, still tight as a ball, nodded quickly. "I won't," he said. "I didn't mean nothing, but I won't, I swear."

"Out," the bartender shouted for the tenth time. Kevin and Ricky listed out the door and leaned against a random pickup truck, the latter cupping the former's face in his hands, and Kevin weeping as though his heart would break.

"Don't listen to that shit," Ricky said to him. "You were there. You're the only one who knows what happened on that mountain, and none of these other fuckers know jack. You know that, man. You put that here." He placed the flat of his hand over the middle of Kevin's chest.

Kevin shook his head, resisting his friend like a despondent three-year-old might its mother. "No—I don't, Ricky. I don't know shit. It's all blurry, just a fucking bad dream I can't remember." It was difficult to tell if his slurred speech was due to upset or alcohol.

Ricky shook him. "Listen to me," he said. "You listen to me. Look here," Ricky said, putting his finger to the bridge of his nose. "Look at my eyes."

Kevin looked up.

"You know you're a good man, and you understand better than anyone," Ricky put his hand on Kevin's chest again. "Right here, man. You know."

Ten

Kevin's first look in the mirror almost caused him to vomit, for shame mostly. His left eye was swollen almost shut, the edges around the cheek and brow beginning to darken. He had no idea how it had happened during the fight, not having felt any pain until he had woken that morning. It took him some time to muster the nerve to come out and join Tracy and his mother at the kitchen table. John, in his bathrobe, poured a cup of coffee and sat it in front of him.

"That eye looks bad," his sister finally said.

Kevin touched at it. His sister and mother glanced at each other.

"What are you going to do?" His mother asked, tearing the crust off a piece of toast.

"I'm going somewhere today, meeting someone."

His mother looked at her plate, and Kevin could tell she was doing her best not to pry. "That's good," she said. "Is this someone we know?"

"Xavier Zaragoza, at the *Dispatch*. Someone told me he's there on Saturday."

Again, Tracy and his mother gave each other an involuntary look, and Kevin was annoyed.

He groaned, flopped his hands on the table. "What the hell should I do then, Mother? What? I don't have a set of instructions. I'm just groping here."

"Oh, honey, I know. We're not second guessing you. We're just worried." Teresa looked all of her sixty-eight years this morning, her eyes heavy for worry, the flesh under them and along her jaw line loose and sallow.

John Gilbert had slipped away unnoticed, and Kevin was struck again by the man's stealth and tact in such matters. "I just feel like I need to do something, anything, but sit here and stew—everybody watch how black my eye gets, avoiding the subject of my stupidity."

"Kevin," Tracy said. "This is not stupidity, this is crisis. And we're all wondering what the hell to do. You're the one defusing the bomb, and all we can do is stand here and watch."

Kevin smiled. "Nice metaphor."

Tracy tilted her head. He'd always poked fun at her metaphors. "Bite me," she said, restraining a smile.

"Honestly," their mother said. "Is this going to turn into a round of 'bite me's?'"

John Gilbert laughed from the kitchen. "Sorry," he said. "Didn't mean to eavesdrop."

Kevin and Tracy looked at each other, giggled.

"Look," his mother said. "I think you should do *something—anything* before, like Tracy says, you blow up on us, but Jesus," she made a gesture at his eye, "when you came back last night—my god, we've hit a rough spot here. You don't get in fights like that, Kevin, or you never have, anyway. Some idiot says something, and it triggers that. It's scary. You're lucky you're not in jail. This weekend was supposed to be something good for us—now it's running toward disaster."

"Okay, look, Mother, I know I stepped in it last night, but all I can do is move on and do what I think I need to do. I'm just going over to the paper, talk to Xavier, that's all. For me, to figure this thing out—I need to fill in some blanks. I know you were there—that day on the Escrobarra, but you weren't in my skin through the thing, and I have to figure out what was going on inside my own self before I can go any further."

"I'm concerned about the guilt—you drinking too much, the whole damn thing." Teresa said, as though the thought of it were something she'd been harboring. "I mean, you've packed it around for so long."

"Mother," Kevin said. "I would hope you think this is progress. I'm at least talking about it."

"Maybe," she came back. "But damn scary progress."

"Well," Kevin said. "Today I've chosen to do something. And I've decided what that something will be. No drinking. No festering guilt."

His mother nodded but did not look up at him.

"Today's a start," Tracy said. She looked across at their mother. "We'll call it that."

"It happened in Mexico, and it was a long time ago." The old reporter seemed annoyed at the question. "I just remember scared people and dead bodies."

It had been ten o'clock that morning before Kevin worked up the nerve to walk into the office. *The Dispatch*, Kevin noted, had gone as digital as it could afford. The place had six computers and an adjoining print shop. In a town whose population had not changed in a hundred years, this represented progress. Zaragoza, a crusty old jade of seventy, with a lazy right eye that had seen two tours early in the Vietnam conflict, scarcely glanced at Kevin as he ambled past the Dutch door and sat down at his desk.

"Honestly, Kevin, the only document I know of is that old piece on microfilm. I lost the notes I took along with my memory, along with my hair." He ran his hand back over the naked pate of his head, linked his fingers behind his neck.

"Sure," Kevin said. "I understand." A chair stood in the corner close to him, but Kevin did not feel invited to sit. Xavier had an air about him that would make any adult feel like a school boy.

"I know how fucked up it can be," the old man said. "From my own experience, I know."

Kevin nodded.

"You might try the Mexican Consulate," Xavier said. "That shit happened on their side of the line. Of course, it's probably buried under all the other drug bullshit that was going down then, that's going down now. It's all related, part of the evolution of decay in that country."

"This is a personal thing," Kevin said.

"I can see," Xavier said, glancing up at Kevin's face.

Kevin put his fingers to his brow above the eye. "Oh," he said. "A fight last night. Stupid."

Xavier nodded. "I heard."

An uncomfortable quiet, Xavier glancing at his computer. He cleared his throat.

"When people die, it's always a personal thing. I know there's one old guy in town that was there, but he's eighty-some years old, World War Two vet, probably has trouble remembering his own name—Benny Conchillo, you may know him, maybe remember him. Had a ranch nearby in Mexico at the time of those shootings."

Kevin's belly froze at the mention of the name. The shape of Conchillo's face, the sound of his voice, rose to his mind. It came to him now, the man he'd seen in the restaurant at the Corazón. He wondered now if the old man had recognized him. That Conchillo, seemingly ancient years ago, was still alive, stunned Kevin. The old reporter talked a full minute without Kevin hearing a word. "I'm sorry," Kevin said. "You were saying?"

Xavier shook his head. "Nothing really. Just thinking like a reporter, that simple information will solve everything—it won't." He put his hands on his lap, looked down at them. "You know, kid, I understand how heavy you must wear this thing. I know myself—after two divorces, three estranged children..." He tipped his chin up, indicating the room. "An office where people don't want to work with me anymore—I understand, man. But yours was just a little skirmish in a big war, and everybody but those closely involved have forgotten about it."

"I understand," Kevin said.

"I don't think you do." Xavier swiveled to face his computer, tapped the space bar. The screen glowed to life. He turned his good eye half over his shoulder. "You won't be able to do this all the way by yourself—it's bigger than you, believe me. I tried, and I learned, finally, but only after it was too late. Take my advice and don't make that same mistake. Get some help for the emotional bullshit, or you might end up some old fucker like me."

Kevin opened the Dutch door, ready to leave. "Thank you," he said.

"Don't thank me," Xavier said. "I didn't really do shit for you, but I know, kind of, what you're going through, man. I can tell you this: that fucking drug shit in Mexico right now is a coiled snake. You shouldn't poke at it too much, or you'll have new problems. You've got your own shit to worry about right now. Take care of that."

Eleven

It wasn't until morning that Kevin recognized error in his judgment—spending the night in the hills had possibly worried a lot of people. He'd woken just as dawn broke, sat up from his blankets. The dog came to him and he petted her. He'd gathered up his things and saddled the mule when he spotted his horse, Turk, skylined in a saddle about half a mile west of him. Through his binoculars, he found the horse and Mondy peering back at him beside it. Mondy waved, Kevin waved and they both mounted up and rode down slope where they met at a clearing in the basin. The heeler dog had been resistant until Kevin tied a cotton rope to her collar and fairly dragged her downhill for the first hundred yards.

Kevin knew something was wrong when he saw Mondy's face. "What?" Kevin said to him. "I've been chasing Pete. There's good tracks just over this ridge. I can show you."

Luna shook his head. "Amanda," he said.

"What about her?"

"We thought she was with you."

"I thought she'd gone back to the trucks."

"She wasn't there when we got back last night," Mondy said.

Silence as they turned the fact over in their minds.

"Shit, Mondy, I left her with that deer yesterday. I figured she'd just take him back to the truck."

"You think she could have gotten lost?"

"Hell, I don't know," Kevin said, looking off at the rugged chain of hills to the west. "I don't know her that well. She seems to know her way around this country, though."

The sky had begun to whiten toward sunrise. "You know what?" Mondy said. "Where she killed that deer was a pretty rough pack back to the trucks. She might have ridden a couple ridges over and caught the main road and gone over to Three-Mile Flat and waited for us to come out. Shit, I wish I'd borrowed John's radio. We'd know for sure."

A sudden guilt moved through Kevin. "The others left for home last night?"

"Yep."

"Probably come back with Russ Billman and that moron, Banks."

"Probably."

Russell Billman was the sheriff's deputy usually assigned to any rural detail—roadkill cattle obstructing traffic, shot-up windmills and water tanks, search and rescue, the decomposing bodies of migrant workers, or the remnant corpses of drug-smuggling operations gone bad. Simon Banks, despised by area teenagers for taking such relish in busting drag racers and breaking up campfire beer parties, was the twenty-three-year-old rookie, born and raised in Chicago, who'd been assigned to partner with Billman the last year.

"You think Tom'll kick my ass?" Kevin asked.

"No. But you deserve it," Mondy said. He looked to the top of the ridge. "Can you see pretty well from up there? We could at least take a look around."

Bonny was happy when they turned and started back up. This meant more chasing the big black cat, and the little blue tick mix could scarcely keep herself from a full run as they made their way to the camp site from the night before.

"Damn right," Mondy said when they came to the border fence. He quickly dismounted and looked down at the cat tracks about ten paces from where Kevin had camped. The clearest print was just this side of the barbed wire fence that marked the New Mexico border; old Pete had paused there a moment before he'd shinnied under the bottom strand. "Damn right," Mondy said again. "That's the old boy himself."

"It's what I told you. I saw him clearly."

"Well, I don't blame you for coming after him, especially if you got a look at him, like you say." Mondy looked toward New Mexico, where, two miles east, the Escrobarra bent and tapered off into Mexico, and Kevin knew what he was thinking. "What time is it?" Mondy asked.

"I don't know," Kevin said. "I didn't bring a watch."

"I didn't either, but I'd guess it's before seven. I told your dad I'd meet them back at the corrals between ten and eleven—let them know what's going on."

Both stood silently, looking down at the track, as the urgency of their dilemma became clear. Bonny whimpered and twisted on her tether until Kevin yanked at the rope and spoke to her sharply.

"Old Sally munched the hell out of grass all night," Kevin finally said. "And that dog there ate a good quarter pound of jerky."

"Turk, too. He ate a lot. And I know there's a wet tank a little east of here. There'll be water and nobody's too hungry."

They'd arrived at a decision, though neither spoke it. "Shit, he'll be pissed, man," Mondy said. "Probably shoot me and kick your ass out of the house. Of course it would all be worth it if we brought back that old black *diablo* laid over the saddle."

"I don't know," Kevin said. "The old man can surprise you sometimes. Besides, we could go after that cat a little more and still be at the corrals before noon at least."

"Well," Mondy said. "We're not legal in New Mexico."

"Hell, I don't even know if we're legal here. I don't know of any hunting permit for a jaguar."

"I wonder what happened to Mandi," Mondy said.

"She may have done just like you said."

"Just wish I knew for sure." Mondy wrapped his hands between barbs around the top strand of the fence. "It'd be pretty damn shitty of me to show up late if that kid was missing."

"You know, Mondy, she might have seen old Pete, too, yesterday. Decided to go after him herself."

Mondy shook his head. "Doesn't seem like something a girl would do."

"She's not a normal kind of girl."

Mondy nodded. "Well," he said. "Let's get this fence down."

They didn't have time to look for a horse gate, and there were gloves, fence tools, stays, and staples in Sally's side bags. It took them ten minutes to take down the four strands of wire from three posts. Mondy pressed the strands down with the crook of his boot heel as Kevin led first Turk then Sally across, cajoling each animal softly when it balked, and after a feint and slight rearing-up from Sally, all were safely across. They restrung the fence with their extra stays and packed up, all done inside twenty minutes.

Bonny was already strong on Pete's trail, head pointed forward and loins tensed as she restrained the urge to break into a dead run. She broke from the bottom to a cattle trail that negotiated the most tenable way to higher ground. Bovine trails always, like streams, found the path of least resistance, and it appeared, if Bonny's nose was right, that Pete had been in agreement with the cattle. They crested the low part of the ridge, leaving the cattle trail, and started the long ascent of the more rugged parts of the Escrobarra.

At the base of a rim rock choked with a tangled stretch of oak and manzanita, Mondy stopped Turk and called Kevin back.

"Check this out," he said, climbing from his horse.

Kevin called the dog to heel and backtracked the fifty yards to his friend, who was picking something up from the ground. It was a tuft of black fur the size of a match book. Kevin and Mondy stared at each other in disbelief. For the two hunters, the find was akin to a pair of prospectors encountering a gold nugget of the same size. The big cat was in some way the embodiment of the collected rural mythology of the region. A close encounter with Pete was next to spiritual, like touching the sandals of one of the twelve apostles.

"The son of a bitch has to be close."

Mondy nodded and pointed uphill. "Maybe just over the top on the other side."

Kevin checked the sun. "About eight-fifteen" he said. "What kind of thunder stick you got?"

"I borrowed O.D.'s .308."

"That's enough gun. Maybe we'll get lucky."

Mondy nodded. "I'd give us another hour and a half if we want to get back to the corrals anywhere close to noon."

The climb to the top of the ridgeline was brushier and more difficult than they'd apprehended. The other side was steep and had shale slides; if they wanted to move on, they'd have to find another place to cross. They dismounted and climbed to a small point of rocks where they could see the main part of the Escrobarra. A canyon whose opposite side stood three hundred yards away cut back to the west, and they realized Pete could have gone any one of ten different directions. Bonny hopped up onto the rocks with them and panted happily as Mondy scratched her head.

"This is a hell of a dog, man."

"Agreed." Kevin gave Mondy a look when he lit a cigarette. "I wish you'd run out of those damn things."

Mondy ignored the comment and gestured to the opposite side of the canyon. "Maybe we'll get lucky and he'll cross right there."

"That would work," Kevin said.

They'd glassed about ten minutes when Mondy gasped. Kevin glanced at Mondy's binoculars, determining the line of sight, and put his own to his eyes. Pete appeared, limping slowly south.

"*Abajo*," Mondy said, chasing his breath, "*en los arbols.*"

"I see him."

"He's about a hundred yards below that rock slide."

"I got him, Mondy."

Mondy lifted his rifle and chambered a shell. "How far?"

"Five hundred. Don't shoot, Mondy."

Mondy lowered the rifle and lifted his binoculars. He looked for a long moment. "Thanks for the check, Kevin."

"No problem. I was shaking, man."

"Me, too. Five hundred and moving. I'm glad I didn't shoot."

The big cat had disappeared amid the thick pool of oaks and junipers in the canyon's heart.

"He wasn't moving very fast," Mondy said.

"No, he wasn't."

A few seconds passed as they took this in. "How long do you think it would take us to get to the west side of that canyon?" Kevin asked.

"Ten—fifteen minutes."

"If we could be up there when he came out of that brushy bottom, we'd have a hell of a shot."

Kevin tethered Bonny again, one end of the rope on her collar, the other knotted to his saddle horn. He and Mondy agreed they'd be slowed for the rope tangling in the brush, but they didn't want her running ahead and destroying their chances. Their route to the top of the canyon on the other side was a gentle, ten-minute ride. Just before they crested at a good vantage point, Mondy stopped and turned to Kevin.

"We've been nice and quiet, man," he said, his voice just above a whisper. "We got a really good chance."

They left their mounts and the dog tied to a mesquite and crept light-footed uphill and over the other side with their rifles at ready. They were careful not to skyline in full view and came out amid a group of junipers in order to break up the semblance of upright human form. They'd just gained an open view of the trees in the bottom when Mondy spotted Pete, ten yards clear of the trees and stark black against the grama grass, about two hundred yards away. The old cat had long since seen them and now stood ghost-still, watching.

Mondy and Kevin sat and chambered shells, aiming, each struggling to stay his heart and breathing.

"*Fuego, pues*," Mondy said. "Go ahead and shoot, man."

"I'm too rattled," Kevin said. "I can't keep the ex on him. You shoot."

Mondy's rifle cracked beside him and a puff of dirt rose over the cat's back—the bullet had gone high. Pete bolted up canyon faster than Kevin could have imagined a three-legged animal to run.

"You missed," Kevin said.

Mondy chambered another shell and sighted his rifle. "Where'd he go?"

"Up the canyon," Kevin said. "You missed."

Mondy lifted his rifle, jacked out the shell. "I had trouble pulling the trigger. I don't know, man."

"We'll go down and check for blood, but I'm sure he's not hit."

"Good," Mondy said, as the fact of his failure settled in. "That was a pretty easy shot for me. Damn, I wonder what happened."

Kevin shook his head. "Mondy, I've seen you miss shots like that a number of times."

"I've seen you miss, too."

"Agreed," Kevin said. "Everybody misses." They both smiled at the quip.

Mondy lifted his binoculars on the outside hope he might see the cat. "I think you could have made that shot," he said. "What happened to you?"

"I was too twittered. I can almost guarantee I would have missed, or tagged the son of a bitch in a bad place."

They sat the ridge another five minutes, then dropped back over the top to get their mounts and the dog, picking their way down the steep slope to the bottom where they found the place Pete had stood— no blood. The canyon up which Pete had run was fairly short with a low, easy saddle at the end, and it took little discussion to decide they would top out to look at the other side.

"You know," Mondy said as they made their way uphill, "he'd be more inclined to hide. There's no pack of hounds chasing him, and he might just figure he can give us the slip."

"Agreed," Kevin said. "He's probably not far."

When they dropped over the low saddle, they could see the whole south end of the Escrobarra tapering off into Mexico.

Kevin glanced at the sun. "It's probably about nine o'clock or so. We'll look here a few minutes, then we'd better get headed back." Kevin measured his words. "We've had our chance."

Mondy nodded. "We did, at that," he said. The ignominy of their failure had taken a firmer hold. Kevin thought about the likely punishment from his father, the long climb toward redemption, and Mondy had already begun to build the story he would tell.

They'd glassed about ten minutes when Mondy shifted his seating. "What the hell?" He was looking off at the brushy swells well into Mexico.

"What do you see?"

"I don't know," Mondy said. "Looks like a moose."

"Well that makes sense, considering how many of those bastards there are in Mexico."

"Would you give your smart-assed comments a rest for once and just have a look?"

Mondy directed him to a mesquite-ringed dirt tank in the flat about three miles south. Immediately, he sighted the animal—big, but neither cow nor horse. It stood in the shadow of a tall mesquite. Kevin suddenly felt the thump of his heart. He knew which animal this was but wouldn't say it. It had to step clear of the shadows and he had to be sure. When Kevin could see it wore a saddle, he spoke its name: "Dunk."

"The girl's mule?" Mondy said.

"Yes."

"You sure?"

"Yes."

Mondy adjusted his binoculars. "Yeah, I think I see now. It looks like it has a saddle on. Kind of like a moose's hump."

Kevin refused to acknowledge the last comment.

"How the hell did he get clear down there?" Mondy asked. "Do you think he threw the girl?"

Kevin thought a moment. "No," he said. "She rode before she could walk. And that mule loves to have her on his back."

"What do you think, then?"

"I think she's probably down there, shaded up somewhere." Kevin was doubtful even as the words left him.

"Why? You think she's chasing old Pete, too?"

"Don't know."

Kevin lowered his binoculars. "We can have it both ways," he said.

"How do you mean?"

"I can go down there and find Mandi, and you can meet the others back at the corrals."

"There's where your wisdom's wrong, kid. You can never have it both ways, and we're not splitting up."

"Wrong wisdom is a contradiction in terms."

"You and your fucking logic. Mistaken wisdom…whatever."

They raised their glasses again, watching the mule. The situation had become more complex, and their dilemma lay like a weight in Kevin's chest. He felt his blood quicken with all the grim scenarios his mind almost allowed him to imagine.

Mondy finally shook his head. "We either both go down there together or both go back together."

"I just don't want to leave her down there," Kevin said. "I've got a bad feeling. I left her before."

Mondy was silent for a long time. "Don't get yourself twisted up over this. You didn't do anything wrong."

"I just think I need to go down there, Mondy."

"Well," Mondy said. "You're not doing it by yourself."

They mounted up and found a cattle trail that switched backed down a gentle ridge to the bottom. The fence that marked the Mexican border was strung of deadfall mesquite and they easily cleared it, Kevin dismounting and folding down a weak ten-yard stretch with his boot.

"You know," Mondy said after they'd crossed. "There's something that smacks of destiny in this. It's kind of like what my grandma called a Spirit Walk. You may be finding your way to *Himdag*."

"You mean like a 'Vision Quest'?"

"Exactly."

"But isn't that a Navajo thing? You're O'odham. Besides, the journey is supposed to be done alone."

Mondy sighed and shook his head. "Details, man," he said. "You white eyes and your obsession with minutiae."

Twelve

The kitchen smelled of fetid meat, and the coffee Ben Conchillo had poured into mismatched cups was a day old and burnt, heated from a questionably washed saucepan left on the stove, apparently from last night's dinner of *tacos de cabeza*.

The old man pursed his lips, blowing at the gray slick on the surface of his coffee.

Kevin lifted his cup, sipped, repressed a grimace. "*Está bien,*" he said.

"It tastes like shit," the old man said. "But it's all I got."

"Well," Kevin said in Spanish, "something is better than nothing, true?"

The old man shrugged. "Depends on what that something is and how bad you want it."

"I suppose," Kevin said.

"I remember you," Conchillo said. "You look older now."

Kevin nodded, looked down into his coffee cup. The old man looked the same, neither older nor younger, just as tattered and scarred up as he was thirty-two years ago.

"You were just a kid." A gray tabby cat had padded into the kitchen, mewed once and the old man scooped it up by its belly onto his lap. He pulled gently on one of its ears with thumb and forefinger then looked full on at Kevin for the first time since he'd arrived at his front gate earlier that morning.

Kevin had driven by the house twice, mostly because it was for all intents not a house, more like an augmented lean-to garage. It sat between two more accomplished places next to an alleyway. A coat of sandpaper-brown paint had been tossed over it, spatters left on the windows and tiny front porch. It stood three blocks north of the border. These were the same rows of houses they were a century ago, those living there little different from their forebearers.

The Consulate's office had been no help, neither providing this address nor releasing any information regarding Ben Conchillo's involvement in the 1976 incident in Mexico. Kevin had found the place the old-fashioned way, by looking in the phone book. As far as he remembered, the old man had little truck in the shootings, though he recalled being at the Conchillo's ranch shortly before and that he may have been around sometime in the aftermath. Kevin had sat in his car, wondering what the hell he was doing there in the first place. Perhaps because everyone else had given their version piecemeal over the years, perhaps because he had nowhere else to look.

As he'd fretted in his car, the old man himself had stepped around from the north side of the shanty into his side yard, and Kevin recognized him at once. He gathered his garden hose into a coil of loops with the same precision Kevin had watched men gather in cow ropes many times. Kevin became conscious then of the newness of his SUV, thrown into sharpened relief by the neighborhood around him.

He had thought at first the old man had not recognized him, for when Kevin had introduced himself, Conchillo only looked at him, blinking his rheumy, cataract eyes no differently, Kevin thought, than a person would regard a door-to-door salesman. The man finished the hose in a tight coil then hung it on a stay hook screwed to the frame of the house, made of a welded-together arrangement of horseshoes. He motioned to the front of the house. "Come on," he said. "The coffee inside might still be drinkable."

"Do you know who I am, Senor Conchillo?"

The old man's only answer was to let the screen door slap closed behind him, and Kevin followed him inside.

Now, Conchillo worked the cat's fur, clucking softly, *cálmate, Gordo…qué pasó, manito, qué pasó.* "You look like someone trying to find something," he said, finally.

"I don't know. I can't put words to it." These were the first whole sentences, Kevin realized, he had spoken in English.

Conchillo smiled, his face a cross hatch of fissures. "I know how it is," he said. "You want things finished."

"I'm not sure what you mean," Kevin said.

"Do you want revenge? To hunt someone down? Kill someone?"

"No."

"Good. Anyone to hunt down is probably dead already. Like everyone I know. I'm the only one left."

"*Lo siento.*"

Conchillo nodded, put a hand on the table. It looked like a hunk of clay. "Maybe there's nothing to finish. Maybe this is as good as you can expect."

"I hope not."

The old man chuckled. "I don't like John Wayne movies—or Louis L'Amour novels. They've fucked things up worse than tract homes."

"*¿Perdón?* I don't understand."

Conchillo shook his head as though Kevin would never be capable of understanding. He went back to the cat, slit-eyed and blissful, as he worked its ribs with his fingers. "I had a friend, once, who had a bad back, and he hurt all the time, sometimes so bad he couldn't get out of bed. Went to a hundred doctors. Nothing they could do, they told him. I'd see my friend stand or turn to walk and his face would grab with the pain, and I'd ask him, 'What will you do about this thing,' and he tells me, 'I'm going to carry it, pack it all the way to the place I finally stop.'"

Kevin shook his head politely. "*Qué malo*," he said. "I'm sorry for your friend." The story swung in his mind, somewhere between parable and an old man's arbitrary ramblings.

Conchillo nodded, a length of silence between them.

"It was November at your ranch by the Peloncillos in Sonora. 1976."

"Sure," the old man said. "I remember. I told you that. "

"I don't."

"Remember?"

"Yes, I don't remember—all of it, at least."

Conchillo's brows arched, he scratched at the white stubble on his cheek. "It's hard to remember some things." The old man kneaded the cat's fur. He shifted his feet, his worn-out green slippers now flat on the scarred and yellowed linoleum floor. Kevin realized he was waiting for him to continue.

"I was there, I know this," he went on. "But after it happened I didn't want to think about it. I wanted to throw a cover over it, the way a child tries to hide a mess it's made."

The old man's hands stopped, resting on the cat. "That eye looks bad."

Kevin raised his hand but didn't quite touch it. "A fight last night."

"I knew that. This is a small town."

Kevin's gut tightened, a touch of shame. Here he was, fifty, a respected professional—in a bar fight.

"You think you are culpable for this mess? To clean it up yourself?" the old man asked in Spanish.

Kevin answered in kind. "I'm not sure what mess you mean."

"I mean from that time near my ranch, not last night. I know you're to blame for that. If you weren't Tom McNally's son you'd be in jail."

"Hell yes," Kevin said in English. "I think I'm to blame, in part, at least."

"Then you make impossible things for yourself." Conchillo stubbornly held to the Spanish. "What mountain would you flatten next with just your two hands?"

Kevin felt stymied, his argument dispatched by a man, he was certain, who had no more than a fifth-grade education.

"Let me ask you, then," Conchillo said, "what good would it do for me to remember, even if I could?"

Kevin's breathing had shallowed, his throat tightening, a momentary impulse to slap his hand hard on the table, turn the damn thing over on the old bastard and his fat cat. "I don't know," he said, finally.

Conchillo lifted the cat from his lap and put it on the floor. "Do you remember what you were looking for that time in the Peloncillos?" The old man looked at him as though Kevin already knew the answer.

"I remember making a kid's mistake, chasing after something I shouldn't have. Something forbidden—sacred."

"Something forbidden," the old man repeated. "Do you think you should have done different?"

"You know," Kevin said, "I think I'm wasting your time, sir." He lifted his shoulders, about to stand.

"One time I knocked my daughter unconscious," Conchillo said.

Kevin was stopped cold by the statement.

"Ever been to Monument Valley?" the old man asked.

Kevin stared, his attitude toward the old man softened by what he took to be dementia.

"It looks like God kicked over a bucket of rocks and dirt then took a piss on it. His piss is kind of red colored, if you ever wondered."

Kevin, perplexed, willed himself to leave, but he didn't move.

The old man chuckled softly. "Laugh," he said. "It's a good joke."

"I'm sorry," Kevin said. "I don't have much of a sense of humor right now."

"Too bad," Conchillo said. He looked down at his hands, his expression now serious. "She was nine years old at the time. I was stretching a run of fence between two T-posts with a come-along and she was at my side like always, wanting to help me with my work. I was grouchy that morning, cussing the breeze on the back of my neck and even the birds talking in the trees. That strand of barbed wire popped like a fiddle string. When I flinched, I caught her in the face with my elbow, busted her nose. She fell on a rock—like the damn thing'd been laid there for her. And I thought I'd killed her. Cussed myself for being a grouchy, impatient bastard, cussed the rock, cussed God for putting it there." The old man shook his head. "She was limp, and I'm telling myself, 'I should have done this, I shouldn't have done that—if only...' The truth is I was a cranky rancher who had to be that way to get the work done and she was a little girl who loved her father. She's almost sixty now. Comes down from Tucson every couple weeks to check in on me."

"Your mistake was more reasonable than mine," Kevin told him in Spanish.

"You know what you sound like?" Conchillo said, English now. "You sound like a man looking to be pardoned. But there's nobody there, no big boss somewhere waiting behind his big desk to do it." The old man lifted his cup slightly, shook the dribble of coffee in it. "Maybe that big boss is you."

When Kevin left, he'd started back for the Gilbert's house but passed Ninth Street where they lived and kept driving. The First Baptist Church, banks, chain convenience stores slipped by as he drove north. He paused at the stop sign at Fifteenth and Airport Road, glanced east toward the Perilla Hills. Beyond them stood the Peloncillos, awaiting his arrival. The Mexican Consulate's office and county archives might give him a stack of reports detailing the whole matter, people could account scene by scene what had happened, lay a kind hand on his shoulder, say, "You were only a boy," but it would do no good.

He turned and drove east.

Thirteen

The evening of November 9th, 1976, Russell Billman perched on a barstool at St. Elmo's in Bisbee for two hours. He'd stationed his six-four, two-hundred-twenty-pound frame at the dark end of the place, close enough to smell the nearby men's room, and was working on his third pitcher of beer when the phone behind the bar rang. He would turn fifty in a month, and after a few beers had started to hate himself for it—half a century of life come to little more than loneliness and frustration and bad habits he couldn't climb clear of. Having been sober three years, he'd fallen back into the drinking six months before, and for the life of him, he couldn't pinpoint why.

It started harmlessly enough, even though his girlfriend Rachael, who was at work at the time, would have stopped him. His partner, Si, had brought over a six pack of St. Pauli Girl to celebrate an important bust they'd made, offered up one of the cold bottles, and Russ just lifted it out of the kid's hand, a reflex so impressed in him it felt no less natural than stretching his back after a long night's sleep. And he drank only two, sipping them slowly while the young officer quickly finished the remaining four. When that pleasant, stinging warmth found the bottom of his belly, and the alcohol hit his blood, he wondered what had given him such an absurd idea in the first place to deny himself this particular pleasure.

Rachael had smelled it immediately when she'd gotten home, clicking on the bedroom light and shaking him awake. "You've been drinking," she said.

He shaded his eyes against the glare and held up two fingers. "That's all," he said.

"That's enough," she shot back.

He'd only understood later how inane he had been to qualify himself, that his defense was ridiculous and a surer sign than the drinking itself that he had made a backward plunge into the murky world of denial. In a month, he was drinking twenty or more beers a night. Within three months, Rachael had moved out.

Russ had just drawn a beer from his pitcher when Donny, the bartender, picked up the phone, and Russ knew immediately it was for him. Ron Jessum calling from home, and Russ had to cover his free ear in order to hear him on the receiver over Silver Wings blaring on the jukebox behind him. Jessum, recently elected sheriff, was a young and ambitious man of more a political than ideological bent. He deigned to keep Russ on as a lieutenant deputy during his administration, despite Billman's age and reputation for being fiercely independent.

"Ron?" Russ said into the receiver, fighting to sound sober. "I'm not on call tonight."

"I know, Russ. I'm sorry. You don't have to go out tonight but I need to explain the situation."

Two lost kids and a pair of terrified mothers. The last call he'd had similar to this involved two teenagers, also a boy and girl, but it turned out they'd gone to Kino Bay on a lark and came back dirty and broke a few days later. Russ knew these two kids, though, and such a scenario seemed unlikely. He was surprised that the girl, Amanda, John Monahan's daughter, with whom he was vaguely familiar and thought of as a little girl, was already fifteen.

Kevin McNally he knew well. The boy's parents had split for a while ten years before, his father taking a job in Las Cruces, and Teresa staying behind with Kevin and his sisters to live at her parent's chile and alfalfa farm in the Sulphur Springs Valley. Russ had started seeing Teresa about a month after the break up. He had all but taken up residence with her and the kids in the two-bedroom mobile out back of her parent's farm when the relationship ended with a call in the night from Tom. Russ could tell from Teresa's expression and her end of the hushed conversation that she had buried the better part of her love with her marriage.

Eventually, Tom found out about the relationship but held no bitter feelings—he had taken a lover in New Mexico and was magnanimous enough to see the balance in the situation. Still, things were quite uncomfortable between Russ Billman and the McNallys.

Billman had had no recent encounters with Amanda Monahan because the kid never got into trouble. Kevin, on the other hand, was a bit more fractious, having been caught with beer in hand at more than one keg party in the boonies. A good kid in all, built like a corner post with a square-shouldered, Celtic physique, he played center field for the varsity baseball team and, now in his senior year, vied academically for the top of his class and any number of first-rate college scholarships. The boy, though, had inherited one or both parents' audacity, so whenever Russ and Simon Banks, his new partner, little older than the kids whose parties they busted up, drove up in the county-issue, sheriff-brown Dodge pickup, flashing lights scattering kids like flushed quail, Kevin McNally made no effort to hide his cup of draft, and in fact would stride up to Russ, shake his hand and offer him a beer. Russ had given the kid a break on three separate occasions the last year, but if Kevin McNally was up to similar nonsense now, the time had arrived for a sit-down with the parents and a come-clean session with the kid.

Russ woke up at 4:25 the next morning, five minutes before his alarm clock had been set to go off. It was his normal time to wake, though the night before he had drunk more than usual, thinking he wouldn't be at work the next day. Regrettably, in the months since he had started again, he'd learned this hard lesson more than once. So he was heavy headed when Si tapped on his door at 5:15.

It took an hour and fifteen minutes to get to the Cinder Knoll Ranch, and both deputies knew the drive well. The department's efforts to thwart the spate of smuggling activities from a year ago had taken them out to border area ranches a score of times in the last year. When they'd crossed the cattle guard and pulled up to the front of the main house, it was a good thirty minutes before first light. At the sound of the vehicle and the first sign of headlights, the two mothers had stepped out into the yellow light of the front porch, both wearing chore jackets and dressed to ride. The women were anxious and their greetings to the two officers were curt and nervous. Yolanda Monahan, an unadorned woman who seldom wore make up and made no attempt to cover the twists of gray in her hair, seemed to have aged ten years overnight. Teresa McNally seemed more calm. Russ's heart rate rose whenever he saw her, reminded anew how stunning she was— pale blue-green eyes, like Montana river pools, amid olive-colored Spanish skin and dark hair.

Russ stood in the yellow bug-bulb light of the front porch trying to wrangle a coherent dialogue with the two women as his young partner stood quietly by, his hands respectfully folded just below the waist like a praying churchgoer.

"Okay, ladies," Russ said, finally, holding out his hands for silence. "We need to calm down here." He turned to Yolanda Monahan. "And, in all likelihood your daughter is with Kevin."

The woman shifted her rear end on the porch rail where she leaned. "I don't know if that makes me feel any better."

Both fathers, along with Olivia and O.D. Hallot, had stepped out of the house. Russ learned later that all of them had spent a restless night at the ranch. The black jaguar they called Pete was back in the area.

"You think that cat is any kind of danger to them?" Russ, who knew little of hunting, asked.

"No," the rancher said, "they've got a good dog with them, and we're thinking they may have went after old Pete, and got too far back, so they spent the night."

The legality of hunting a jaguar occurred to Russ, and he hesitated to ask. "You know," he said, "I don't usually get mixed up in Game and Fish matters. But if we don't find those kids by this afternoon, Search and Rescue crew is poised to respond, and once they get in it Brady Jenkins is bound to find out about this jaguar deal."

"No law against chasing him," John responded.

"I don't know that for sure," Russ came back. "I'll take you on your word." In order to kill endangered species, such as the American Jaguar, one had to procure documentation from the state showing the animal was a threat to one's livelihood. Old Pete had been that to many people a long time, and John Monahan wasn't the only rancher in the area with reason to kill the big cat.

Russ offered to trail in county quarter horses for him and Si, but John insisted he had two mules better equipped for the job. All mounts had been saddled and loaded into the stock trailers well before the officers had arrived, and they soon set off for the southeast stretch of the Escrobarra.

The eastern sky had just gained a thin whiteness when they parked, and by the time they unloaded mounts and gathered up hand radios, optics, and weaponry, the dawn had bled out enough light to see a few hundred yards through binoculars.

Russ, with some effort, had managed to pull together the group to finalize plans for the search. These people's worry, along with the fact of their fierce, prideful independence, made them inattentive, if not outright contemptuous, of his authority. The men, particularly, appeared somewhat deferential, especially Tom McNally and O.D. Hallot. The two had been involved in helping the sheriff's department break up a furious bar fight one night at the Red Barn Tavern in Douglas. The place had been, and still was, a notorious honky-tonk.

On the night of this fight, five years before, the labor union for Phelps Dodge Copper Company had been on strike six months, and a birthday party had brought some twenty company scabs together in one place—the Red Barn. A number of the toughest union members had hatched a plan before any of the scabs had arrived. By eight o'clock, some eighteen out-of-work miners sat stonily at one end of the bar while the new Phelps Dodge employees, some of them not from the area, milled about apprehensively at the other. O.D. and Tom were associated with neither group but stumbled in inadvertently just before the confrontation exploded into a blur of swinging fists, wielded pool cues, and flying beer glasses.

Russ and his then partner, John Beal, arrived seconds after the fight had started on a tip delivered from one of the frightened wives of a union member. Russ was tough in a fight and quick for his size, and after he had promptly subdued three brawlers, breaking one man's nose, he and Beal, with the help of Thomas and O.D., had managed to bring the room to heel. The sheriff's department made nine arrests that evening, and the episode had left an impression on O.D. and Thomas. They had confidence in Billman's toughness and prowess as a law officer.

"I'm not waiting here," Teresa said resolutely for the third time.

"Someone has to," Russ said.

Teresa stepped up to Russ and squared herself to him, her teal-colored eyes feral looking in their urgency. She pointed to the stock trailer. "I'm getting on my horse and going to find my son." She tilted her chin toward Simon. "Make that kid there stay."

Finally, it was O.D. who volunteered. When the party left, he had with him a Cobra radio, the keys to the sheriff's department vehicle, four ham sandwiches, two Ding Dongs, his Ruger Seven-Millimeter

Magnum, which he'd dubbed Old Death and Destruction, and three boxes of high velocity ammunition, "for varmints." He was to wait until eleven o'clock for Mondy to return, as planned, then radio the search party with news.

True to his sedentary nature, O.D. was happy to stay. He'd enough food to keep him busy, and, as with anywhere he ventured, from the doctor's waiting room to a shopping foray in the Tucson Mall with his wife, he'd brought a book with him. Along about five-ish he'd be ready for a Coors, but he'd worry about that time when it arrived. The book he was whittling at now was about some ranch kid who'd made friends with a wolf, and 7:10 a.m. found him just enough light to start a new chapter and peel the shrink wrap off his first ham sandwich. O.D. had liked the novel the first few chapters, even if it was "written by a pencil-necked candy ass who lived in England and ate boiled bean sprouts and tofu for breakfast." In this chapter of the book, though, he'd run into a hitch he just couldn't get around.

It was an elk hunting scene where a young boy had taken his first bull. The fact that the kid was sick with guilt and repulsed at himself for the act didn't bother O.D. so much; some kids weren't wired for that business. What O.D. didn't like was the feeling of the author standing in the shadows, pumping the skillfully rendered scene with the fetid smell of his own moral superiority. It would be one thing for the writer to revile hunting, but to represent the act with such eager realism was like a teacher showing a porn loop to a group of adolescents as a lesson in depravity, then proclaiming "good people" are above any titillation the acts on screen might provoke.

But O.D. figured he might be missing something. He, after all, was not an educated man. Perhaps some deep hidden meaning in the scene eluded his grasp. But he suspected not. So he read on just for spite, turned the pages, alert to the least opportunity to cuss the sanctimonious little peckerwood.

About 9:30, having polished off three ham sandwiches and both Ding Dongs, O.D. began to glass for the Indian, figuring he would top one of the ridges within the next few minutes. Ten o'clock came and went, and Mondy had not appeared.

Three miles away, on a rocky crest with good visibility, the other six members of the party, sitting in various attitudes, were intensively glassing the surrounding countryside. They'd cut a single set of mule tracks, which all had silently interpreted as a bad sign. If the two kids were together when they started, they hadn't been several miles from the corrals. Even more, the kids' mules, Sally and Dunk, had roughly the same size and shape of hoof, and John could not be sure which animal had left the tracks.

Just as they'd encountered the prints, though, all began calling out *Kevin-Mandi, Kevin-Mandi*, a grim replay of the night before. All six at once would stop their calling, lower their heads, and listen for the least hint of human voice against the quiet hum of the high desert.

It was 10:15 now and no voice had come. They followed the mule tracks east another mile and came to the fence marking the state border. They found signs of a camp, the boy's boot prints, and dog scat, probably Bonny's. That the dog was not with Mandi was even more troubling.

"What kind of foot gear did your daughter have on?" Russ asked the Monahans.

Yolanda turned a miserable glace her husband's way. "Do you remember what she wore?"

John shook his head regretfully. "Probly those Red Wings, but she owns several pair of boots."

"Well," Russ said, the pause running out several unintended beats. To finish his sentence became unnecessary and even painful. The two kids were probably not together, not swept up in some adolescent whim, as all had hoped. Other difficulties began to take form: the fact that ten feet east was out of the officers' jurisdiction, the question of the progress of the search itself. Would they split up, stay together, cross a state line? When and where and how could Search and Rescue become involved?

Tom plucked the Cobra radio from his belt clicked the talk button.

"Go Tomcat," O.D. answered.

"What you got?"

"Indigestion from the green chilies on them sandwiches—but no Indian, no kids—not yet anyhow. What you got?"

"Set of mule tracks and Kevin's boot prints. No sign of Mandi."

A long silence from O.D.'s end. "Damn," he said. "I thought for sure them two was together."

"Us too," Tom said. "Keep an eye open for the Indian and we'll keep going."

"Will do," O.D. said. Then, uncharacteristically, "You do the looking on your end—I'll do the praying on mine."

Russ had called the Hidalgo County sheriff's department before he'd left his house that morning. He'd gotten a dispatcher who'd connected him with a lieutenant, and though the officer said he would contact the first available deputy in Animus, he understandably didn't share the same sense of urgency. It would probably be twenty-four hours before he got any kind of response, and another few hours before any New Mexico officer made it out there.

Tom and John began almost at once to unfasten the four strands of barbed wire with fence tools, legalities be damned.

Young Simon was taken aback, removing his hat and mopping his sweaty brow with his shirt sleeve. The kid wore his light-colored hair a bit longer than regulation permitted, his brown locks falling in a curl just below his ears. He shot Russ a pleading expression. "Man, Russ, I don't know about this. That's state property."

"It actually belongs to the rancher who put it up," Russ told him. "State won't usually string border fence. But if you don't like it, just look the other way, deputy."

"You can't order me to do that."

"You're right, but I can ask."

"What are *you* going to do?"

"Go with them."

"Man, Russ," Simon shook his head. "I don't know about this."

It was decided that rather than cross, Simon would stay and ride the fence line south looking for any sign of the missing kids.

In fifteen minutes the fence was back up, Si was three hundred yards south, riding the state line on a low ridge, and the other five searchers had ridden over a high saddle a stone's throw past the border. Again they all sat, each working a different area with his or her glasses. Had they been two ridges south, one of them (probably Tom, who was the most skilled with binoculars) would have picked out the slow-moving figures of Kevin and Mondy making their way across a mesquite flat two miles into Mexico.

Tom had sat this saddle before, had stood on the ridge to the south overlooking Mexico, driven by the desire to spot a lazy old buck lacking the spunk to live in the hills, or perhaps an errant black bear nosing around the flats for succulent prickly pear fruit. Today his mind was not on finding animals but lingered on a photo in his hunting album. In the picture, ten-year-old Kevin was caught just as the wind had blown his cap from his head. The look on the boy's face, a combination of surprise and (for some reason) fear, Tom had always thought comic. Today, though, the picture did not seem funny and he could not rid himself of the image of the child's fine blonde hair in its neat crew cut just as the hat lifted off. That still shot of the boy burned behind his eyes and made his heart seem light in his chest.

In the past, Thomas McNally had been moved by the desire to find the gray shape of a deer or the dark glint of a javelina's bristles. Today—with every minute of his unspoken love—he searched for his son.

Fourteen

Forty-eight hours before Thomas McNally was to go in search of his son, five young men stepped into the living room of Isedro Leon's house on 9th and Airport Road in Douglas. None of them had been inside so nice a residence before. Two of the young men had lived their lives in the parts of Mexican pueblos where most houses had no running water, gas, or electricity, where chicken coops and rabbit hutches were made from stolen grocery carts and the walls of houses built from discarded plywood, where a third of neighborhood children didn't live past their second birthdays, and for those who did the want of all things tightened like a hunger in the belly, where the contemplation of the ethics of any act—cutting the throat of a pet dog for food, clubbing to death a betraying friend—came far behind the art of survival. Because the three other boys had been born a few hundred yards north of the border, they were American citizens, all the children of itinerate, drug-addicted women who had dragged their surviving progeny through the most squalid side of every town either side of the border, from San Diego to El Paso. These three were the most dangerous of the five, and Isedro Leon knew it.

Twenty minutes before, the young men had passed through the front entryway of the house between the two roaring granite lions and were confronted in the foyer by the three-by-five oil painting of an African pride taking down a zebra; the simple, tacky symbolism had been lost on them. Ise had sat the boys down, served them drinks and a couple fat lines of good coke, the yellow flaky stuff that hangs like a favorite old song in the head. The boys had been polite and cordial enough, but all were high strung by nature and emanated a general mean-spirited cockiness.

Paco and Miguel were brothers two years apart who'd been born in a tarpaper shack in Los Mochis, Mexico. Paco, the younger, had just turned seventeen. His thick dark hair had been freshly shaved two days before and the suggestion of his hairline widow-peaked almost between his eyebrows, giving his face the look of a dog who'd been chained too long. He was the youngest and the least polite of the boys—he didn't know enough to kiss up to his new boss, and

Isedro forgave him this immediately. Experience had taught Ise that he could better trust the less seasoned mules. Nineteen-year-old Miguel, as though to balance out his brother, wore his dark hair long and tied in a ponytail. He flashed a quicksilver smile, nodding to Ise's every word, the kind of young man about whom people would remark what a good kid he was. By various means and circumstances, he had killed a dozen people, one of them his best friend, whom he'd cut to pieces with a straight razor at the age of twelve.

The other three were friends, all of them somewhere within their twentieth year, who had attended Douglas High together for a time. Billy Rojas and Ralph Garcia were distant cousins by marriage, but no longer remembered the filial connection. They'd been busted on a small-scale sting two years before and had done ten months together in Florence State Prison. Billy wore a skillfully rendered blue-ink prison tat of the face of Jesus on his right shoulder, and Ralph, to match, had one of the Virgin of Guadalupe on his left. The meanest and most dangerous of the five was a white kid they called Chingo.

Ise had thought a long time before deciding to take on this particular mule. "Cueball" was another of the boy's handles, as his hair was so blond that it shone almost white in the sunlight. He'd done two years in Maricopa in Phoenix, had been released a month before, and was a good six feet, two-hundred pounds, his upper arms seventeen inches around from pumping state prison iron. A proliferation of tattoos covered his body—a foot-long snake on his right forearm, a spider nestled in its web on his left bicep, a neat line of three blue teardrops, presumably for each person he'd killed, descending the left cheek of his face. He spoke border Spanish as well as any of the other four and was not at all self-conscious about being the only white guy of the group. This boy had more guile than all the others together. Rumor on the street named three killings to his credit, and Ise didn't doubt this for a minute.

Chingo finished his Jack and Coke and rattled the ice in the glass for Rowena, Isedro's girlfriend of a month, to fetch him another, gazing unapologetically at the girl's ass as she walked away. Ise decided to ignore the gesture, knowing this cocky kid would find out who's boss soon enough. If not, then he could very likely wind up buried in a nameless grave like Jimmy did three days before.

"Seventy-five pounds," the white kid was saying. "That's a lot of weight, you know what I'm saying, Billy?"

Bill shrugged and put back a shot of Cuervo. "We can do it," he said. "I've done it before. Three grand is good money."

Chingo looked skeptically into his new drink, his jaw working as the coke kicked in. "How long did you say?" He addressed Ise, though he didn't look up at him.

Ise measured out a long silence. He stood and walked to the bar, where Rowena cleaned glasses. "*La comida,*" he said to her, whereby she unceremoniously stepped from behind the bar and left the room.

Ise poured a neat Jack Daniels and swirled it in the bottom of the glass. "From seven in the morning until about noon," he said, finally looking up at the white kid. "We camp the night before, a couple miles from the drop point, have a good time, make our connection the next day. Three-thousand dollars for half a day's work. You can pull out if you want, man." Isedro spread his arms, as if to say "who cares?", the drink held precariously between thumb and forefinger. "But if the law shows up down there, I know who to go looking for."

The kid didn't even twitch. He turned down the corners of his mouth and nodded. "It's cool. *Verdad*, Billy?" he said with a quick glance to the other American boys.

"*Si, pues,*" Billy affirmed, then opened another concerning issue. "You know, I'm pretty sure it's hunting season right now. We might have some company down there."

Isedro glanced at Juan Carlos, who sat, arms folded and still as a Buddha statue. "Me and J.C. talked about that," he said. "This weekend is the only time our connection can make it. Otherwise, we wait a couple months."

The Los Mochis brothers, neither of whom were fluent in English, occasionally looked over at J.C. who would vet their confusion in quiet Spanish. The good cocaine had found its way into everyone's blood and the mood in the room had softened. Isedro had put an album on the turn table, The Eagles' *Greatest Hits*, and the mid-day light of late fall shot the room with an amber glow, so that now the puffy velour cushions of the divan, the glass coffee tables, the miniature Bulgarian chandeliers, the tacky burnt-orange carpet, and even the harmonizing voices in "Tequila Sunrise" had a sort of poetry to them. And lions were everywhere: wrought in the brass door knocker when they'd first walked up, stenciled into the glasses they held, drawn in half a dozen portraits of various mediums—a meticulously rendered four-by-four pastel of a heavily maned, roaring male stood over the couch. It was Chingo, the cue ball, who finally made the connection.

"Man, Ise, I like the way you take your symbolism seriously," he said. "No shit, man. It's cool."

Isedro nodded at the compliment, which he sensed was not false flattery. Rowena had brought out hot wings and ranch dip, but the boys had barely touched the food, the smell and even the idea of it good, appropriate, though the coke made it impossible to eat more than a bite or two.

"*Entonces,*" Chingo asked over the music and general glow of the room. "*¿Quién es el otro vato?*" *Who is the other guy?*

"*El* Philip Waylon," Juan Carlos said, glancing at Ise. "He's my buddy."

"Philip Waylon," the white kid said. "Your friend sounds like a gringo." The comment prompted a good laugh.

"He is a gringo," J.C. came back. "A big fucking gringo."

"*La migra también,*" Ise added offhandedly, silencing the room but for Don Henley's soft voice pillowing out "*oooo—whoooooo, witchyy woooman, see howww highhh she flyyyyyyayyyyys...*"

Each of the boys in his own way considered whether he had heard right. Finally, Billy spoke. "You mean a cop?"

Isedro stood and pointed at the turn table. "'Witchy Woman,' my favorite song." He smiled, shook his head, feigned a sort of reverie. He moved to the bar and poured another Jack, waiting several strategic beats as he mouthed the words to the song, before supplying Billy's question with an answer: "I mean a mother fucker who dresses in a green suit five days a week, catches evil drug dealers and wetbacks, then puts on a pair of hiking boots once every few months and makes a lot of extra money helping us out."

"Why?" Chingo asked. The question covered all intents, that of J.C. and Ise for cosigning him as a mule, and that of the border patrol officer who led a dangerous double life.

"Lots of reasons," Juan Carlos said.

Isedro held up a finger in the back-of-the-hand style of the Mexican. "Reason number one: he'll die a rich man if he takes a bullet tomorrow." A second finger. "The fucker is big and strong and can shoot straight and would take out his mother to not get caught. Third: he's a green suit, so he knows where every fucking migra and sheriff's deputy between New Mexico and Nogales is stationed at all times, and we've never seen one fucking cop anywhere in any run we've ever done with him. *Verdad*, J.C.?"

"*Es verdad*," Juan Carlos answered back with a nod. On his end of the couch, J.C. had gotten comfortable, sipping on his second Seven and Seven. His wife, Rosemary, and their three kids were visiting her sister in Tucson and he was free to stay out with the boys tonight. A good family man, Juan Carlos was usually home by six, ate dinner with wife and kids by seven, read pretty bedtime stories to his two small daughters, and fell asleep in front of the television before the ten o'clock news. He was active in the church and attended mass regularly, and on some Saturday evenings when the confessional door slid open, he passed all but a few crucial sins of his life to the priest for absolution. Juan Carlos Rascon knew he would account for these sins one day in Purgatory, but he would shoulder that burden when it came.

"Fuck," Billy said. "Doing a crime with a cop. That fucking freaks me out."

"You can take off if you want," Ise said, pointing at the door. "Leave now, and I've never seen you before in my life."

"No," Billy said. "This is too fucking good. I'm in."

Ise looked to each boy and each affirmed his commitment and the album started again at "Tequila Sunrise." Rowena cleared away the food, barely touched, and the men did lines of coke and drank into the night.

That Saturday, late morning, the day after Kevin McNally and Armando Luna found the original jaguar track, Ise and Juan Carlos met the five boys at Rulfo's, an upscale bar in Agua Prieta, Sonora, where they drank Presidente and ate fresh oysters and crab legs. Afterward, they traveled east six kilometers to a spot in the foothills near Jimmy Holguin's ranch. Silently, the seven men emerged from Jimmy's GMC and Ise's Chevrolet, shovels in hand, and made their way up a brushy arroyo a hundred meters to a place where a six-by-six patch of ground had been recently cut. The men dug no more than five minutes when Paco said, "*Andale Pues*," as his shovelhead bumped the top layer of quilos.

The five boys had never seen so much dope, especially horse and coke, in one place before, and muttered in amazement as they loaded the cargo into the two vehicles. They set out east on Highway 2 and turned off north after five kilometers, before coming to the road construction. They hooked onto an obscured gravel road that meandered generally east. After about twenty kilometers, Ise slowed his Chevy and turned north onto another dirt track that would eventually wind its rough way through rocky arroyos and into a long, remote mesquite flat a mile from the base of the Guadalupe Mountains on the Mexico side. They made camp at a grove of cottonwood and ash trees, and just after three, after they'd passed around a bottle of Old Crow and drank Coronas and the fire was down enough to cook *asada* steaks, Juan Carlos, binoculars hanging from his neck, walked up to Isedro, who sat comfortably in his fold out canvas chair. The urgency on J.C.'s face was clear.

"*¿Mande?*" Isedro asked.

"A *ver*," Juan Carlos said, motioning him to follow.

The five boys looked on. "What's up?" Chingo asked.

"Nothing, man. Just stay here and cook steaks. Me and Ise'll take care of it."

They walked down the wash and clear of the trees where a view of the mountains opened up, the slanting afternoon light cutting the rugged peaks, rim rock, and saddles in sharper edges. J.C. handed Ise his glasses and pointed to a bald ridge in the Peloncillos about a mile and a half to the north on the U.S. side of the border.

"Look about three ridges away, right in the middle of that brown hillside, toward the top," he said.

Isedro raised the binoculars and saw them immediately. From that distance, they were tiny specs, but he could tell what they were, parked side by side in the solitary grove of scrub oaks in the saddle.

"Do you see what I'm talking about?"

Ise nodded. "It looks like trucks and horse trailers?"

"Hunters?"

"Maybe. They gather cattle this time of year. Could be a rancher."

"Fuck, man," J.C. said. "They're right close to the drop point."

Ise shook his head. "Shit, I knew it was going too good. Something had to go fucked up on us."

"Could you call on the radio for him to meet us at another place?"

"*No, hombre, no tenemos otro lugar.* It's the only place he can get to. I couldn't reach him out here, anyway."

"What do we do?"

Ise shook his head. "I don't know, man. I need to think."

When they returned to the fire, the boys had put on the asada steaks and had drunk all but a twelve pack of the Coronas.

"Shit, you fuckers drink fast," J.C. remarked.

"Don't drink anymore," Ise said, resuming his place on the lawn chair. "We may have a job for some of you tonight."

"What job?" Billy asked. The look on his face was serious. He was squatting beside the grill and the steaks had already begun to sizzle. He had the least hubris of the five boys and in their short partnership had become the unspoken leader.

Isedro had understood this even before the boys did, and he'd made up his mind that he would charge Billy with the job. He pushed his sunglasses up above his eyebrows and looked over at the kid. "Reconnaissance."

Isedro let the kid choose one other person to go with him, though Ise knew already who it would be—Chingo, of course. He agreed to pay them an extra two hundred apiece and wanted them there and back fast. They'd taken the boys to the spot outside the trees and shown them the trucks and trailers. They let them take the binoculars but no flashlights, and after debating hard with himself, Isedro gave them each a Ruger Mini 14—a small semi-automatic carbine-type rifle.

"We don't want to hear any fucking shots," J.C. told them. "Not one. Don't even get stupid and try for a rabbit or nothing."

"I want you there fucking fast," Ise reiterated. "Jog when you can, and walk like a mother fucker when you can't. You should get there about half an hour, maybe less, before dark."

The boys were listening well enough, but were clearly delighted by the heft of the rifles they held and they nodded a quick assent to every instruction.

"You're looking for camping shit, right?" Ise said. "Anything—a lantern, a cooler, a put-out fire. If you don't see anything like that then they'll probably leave tonight; tomorrow we make our connection, and everything's cool."

"What if they're camped?" Chingo asked. He slapped the butt of his rifle. "Can we take them out?"

Ise lifted his hand and pointed his finger, like the barrel of a pistol, at the kid's nose about a foot from his face. "Don't you even fucking think about it."

Fifteen

It was after midnight and Kevin lay in one of the spare bedrooms at the Gilbert's house, unable, again, to sleep, and it was everything he could do not to go to the liquor cabinet and pour himself a tall scotch. He had dialed Jessica's phone number for the third time in half an hour and was sure he would get her voicemail again—*Hi, this is Jess, can't get with you now, but leave a message, Ciao*—when, finally, she picked up. He could tell she was out with friends, and a momentary collusion of irritation and jealousy hurried through him until, chagrined, he put his free hand over his now ripened left eye. She was standing too close to what Kevin could tell, by the song selection mostly, was the blaring juke box at the Bay Horse Tavern on Grant Road. She'd tried to speak over Miley Cyrus' "Who Owns My Heart" until she'd moved into the billiards room where Kevin could hear men's voices and the click of playing balls.

She was telling him about her evening with Cat and Gloria. "We were all so pissed off, we left the meeting early and came straight here."

"Might as well," Kevin said. "Senior administration already has it bagged and tagged. You're usually just wasting time and oxygen."

Then a silence, which Kevin hated with cell phones. One was made to think half the time the connection had been lost. Finally, Jess spoke. "You sound a little strained, babe. Everything okay?"

Though she knew of this incident from his youth, that he'd visited a dozen therapists over the years, he'd downplayed the significance of this trip to Douglas, probably because he didn't have an honest read on it himself. "It's kind of a long story," he said.

"Where are you at right now?" she asked, no question now of the fear in her voice.

"At the Gilbert's."

"You sound like you've been drinking."

"I had a couple of scotches earlier, before dinner." Silence from the other end. "Okay, four scotches. Big ones."

"Jesus, Kevin," Jess said. "What's going on?"

He could tell she'd stepped outside.

"I got in a fight last night. In a bar. And, yes, I'm a fucking idiot."

"What the hell? Jesus Christ, Kevin, you got to talk to me. You got to talk to me now. This is not you. This is—scary."

It took him a few minutes to convince her not to get in her car and start driving south, and Kevin knew had she not been drinking she would have. After a couple of meandering false starts and too much back story, he told her about Ackerman and what he'd said that touched a nerve, his blurred recollection of the fight, his swollen-shut left eye. He told her about his visit to the newspaper, then to the consulate's office, then to Conchillo's house. She stayed silent on the line, offering the occasional yes, or *uh-huh*, to let him know that she was there and listening.

"Honestly, Kevin," she said. "This scares me. You need some help—somehow, somewhere."

"That's what I'm doing," he said. "I thought, at least."

Another long silence. "I remember Conchillo," Jessica said. "I remember your telling me about him."

"Yeah," Kevin said. "He talked to me that time there in the mountains. We stayed at his ranch. I just don't remember what he said. It was decades ago."

"Do you think you need to? I mean, should you spend the energy on that?"

"I'm not sure, Jess. I just don't know right now."

"I have the impulse to go to you, Kevin. To go down there tomorrow—first thing. I feel like you're capable of doing something...I don't know, but I've got a bad feeling."

"No, no, Jess," he broke in. "I can honestly say I'm okay. And it's not that I don't want you here, but something tells me no. I mean, it's kind of like not being able to go with your kid his first day of school."

"Okay," she said. "I'll honor that."

"Jess..."

"Yeah, babe."

"I went there today."

"Where?"

"The Escrobarra."

"Oh, Kevin. Are you sure that was a good idea?"

"I don't know. But I went. I drove out past the old transfer station and just kept driving. I'd forgotten how stunning the country is. I went out past Art Thomason's old place. The road gets narrow and snakes up through those lower canyons. The oaks were in full leaf and the afternoon light sat pretty on them. I can't explain it, Jess, but it was a kind of warm feeling. I pulled over at the foot of Cottonwood Canyon by Sycamore Ranch, right back where we always used to hunt. I just sat in my car. I didn't know how long I'd been there, but when I looked at my watch, it was almost two hours later. Then I drove up to this place along the road, this place where—a young man was killed in that deal. He was tangled up in a barbed wire fence. That image keeps on popping up in my head, kind of out of nowhere. I thought about calling you. I don't know if it was a good thing or not. I looked up toward the ridge line and finally got the nerve to look down lower where everything happened. Do you think that was okay?"

Quiet again on the other end, and Kevin could hear in it that she was crying. "Jess," he said. "Honey."

"I don't know, Kevin," she said, finally, "if it's good or bad or what, but I am scared as hell. What about the old man?"

"What about him?"

"Did he tell you something important? I mean, after your visit you actually went out there."

"I don't know that it was because of him."

"Kevin, honey, I just get a bad feeling, like something dark—I don't know. I'm just scared, that's all. There's all kinds of drug shit going on down there now. And I feel so helpless just sitting around up here."

"Jess, I'm going to handle this. I need to handle it, I think."

"Maybe you could go back to that old man," she said. "You've mentioned him a number of times. Maybe he could help you."

"Maybe."

"Also. I want you to get help again when you get back. I mean immediately. I'm sorry, but I question your emotional state. And digging around about drug-related incidents is nothing but dangerous."

Kevin promised her, and they talked another hour, their conversation drifting into the mutually familiar: work, the Tobias Wolff book Kevin was reading, his relationship with his mother. Kevin had not met another person with whom he could so easily disclose the stuff of his life, and he longed for her to be there with him. At one point he heard her say goodnight to Cat and Gloria as they filed out of the bar.

"You're still outside?" he asked.

"I'm sitting on that little bench out here by the front door. It's pretty warm out—Tucson, baby."

Kevin urged her home to get some sleep and when they finished their conversation, it was 2:00 a.m. He felt the fatigue set in then and switched off the bed lamp. When he closed his eyes an image came, surprising and of its own accord, drudged up intact and crystalline as the moment it happened so long ago: old Conchillo holds the stub of a pencil, the white calluses of his work-fat fingers awkward around the implement. On the blank side of a brown paper grocery sack, the old man is making a sketch—a maze, a labyrinth, about the diameter of a basketball. Ready to enter it is a stick figure man. Conchillo taps his index finger against the sketch and looks at Kevin, who cannot determine if this is memory, imagination, a dream or all three, but he is there and listening. And he is not afraid.

Sixteen

Amanda Monahan always felt perfectly suited to the outdoors, except when she had to pee. She'd gotten back to the trucks with her deer just before noon and packed the meat in an ice chest and tucked the head and hide neatly in a corner her father's truck's bed. Bonny had run off somewhere on the ride back and Amanda had tried calling her to no avail. She would have headed back to the house but now waited for Bonny and felt the dog would show up sometime soon. The little heeler mix was something of a loner, and it wasn't unlike her to go off by herself—but after four hours, two of which Amanda had napped in the truck, she had begun to worry. Now she needed to pee.

Secretly, she'd hoped that Kevin would return shortly behind her, but she'd hours before given up that notion. Since the eighth grade she'd had crush on this boy, and she was pretty sure he had no idea, so there was no way he was going to catch even a glint of her little white ass on the off chance that he (or, God forbid, his father or O.D. Hallot) was situated just right on one of the surrounding ridges. She chose a steep bar ditch about fifty yards from the truck, skittered down the bank, and stood a short while surveying the territory she'd chosen for this short bit of business, finally judging there was no way anyone could see her from any ridge. It struck her as an unspeakable injustice that a female had to bare her naked butt just to take a piss, especially for a girl who, at fifteen, had already ridden rough stock in women's rodeo, who had team roped with her dad since she was twelve, who'd taken five trophy class Coues Whitetail bucks—more than most men could rack up in a lifetime of hunting. No flower patterns, frilly fringes or honeysuckle scent for *her* bedroom—horse posters and head mounts, coiled up heeling ropes, a trophy case full of gold-studded buckles, and the smell of leather and equine were more her style.

Her parents of late had noted with some surprise that she'd recently become quite a baseball fan. In the spring the family lived mostly in their house in Douglas, and Amanda, along with her two best friends, Didi Price and Janine Bartell, was able to attend most of the Douglas High varsity games, which usually started just after school.

Amanda had been discrete about her infatuation, and it wasn't until the third game they'd been to that Janine noticed her staring out into center field. When Amanda turned to her friend, the girl's mouth was agape enough, it seemed, to catch flies and she was tying her reddish hair back with a rubber band. She leaned forward and looked across at DiDi.

"Oh...my...God," Janine said. "Mandi is hotting on Kevin McNally."

Amanda, between them, knew that to deny it would be futile and only bring on an even heavier drubbing of ridicule. So she steeled herself, resigned to the inevitable deluge—DiDi Price, the biggest smart ass at Douglas High, was surely cooking up some sharp remark.

"I don't know, Janine," Didi said offhandedly, "She may change her mind once she finds out it's only a plastic cup under those pants and not the real deal."

Though caustic, her friends were, if anything, loyal, and word of her crush had never found its way to Kevin. Sometimes she wished it had—she often got the feeling the attraction was mutual. Her pride and her reserved nature, though, kept her from approaching him. They'd talked a few times about books they had both read but she couldn't describe Kevin McNally as even a casual friend, let alone a close one.

So now, as she hitched up and zipped her pants, Amanda hoped for damn sure Kevin was nowhere within a mile. She glanced at the embankment she had used to slide down into the ravine and judged it too steep to climb back up. In fact, the banks were unscalable for about a hundred yards, as far down the culvert as she could see.

She walked the sandy bottom and came to a bend in the wash when she saw them. At first they seemed to be hiding, but when it became inevitable she would pass within five feet of where they were crouched, they stepped clear of a juniper bush and stood shoulder to shoulder, staring at her about ten steps away. Each of the two young men wore a football jersey, denim bell-bottom jeans and hiking boots, and each held an open-sight Mini 14, though Amanda would have known they were bad news had they not been armed at all.

She turned in her tracks and in three steps was at a dead run. She heard them closing on her, neither of them speaking a word in their labored breathing. If she could find a way out of the wash, she'd have them beat. In her estimation, no coyote or dope runner could traverse brush like she could.

She'd just hooked both hands around the low-hanging branch of a mesquite and had gotten a solid foothold, when one of them caught her by the root of her long braid and yanked her straight back to the ground.

"Run from me, you fucking bitch," he said, his boots straddling her head, the business end of the Mini 14 pointed at her left eye.

And in an instant Amanda became aware of herself fighting. With the chuff of her hand she shoved the rifle barrel, driving the butt straight back and hard into the boy's nose. In three quick movements she wrested the carbine away and gained her knees, when the other boy, the Mexican boy, tried to slug her, missing her face with a wild right cross but grabbing the barrel of the Mini 14 with the other hand. With the boy now off balance, Amanda had his face within reach and felt her left ring finger sink deep into his eye socket just before a white light flashed through her brain.

She felt her limbs go limp, useless, like she sometimes felt in bad dreams, and her back floated on a cushion of air. And the boys' voices sounded strangely distant, like those of characters on a television show. Her vision slowly began to return along with her senses, as she pieced together her situation. One of the boys, the big Anglo boy, held the rifle on her. His nose was bleeding. The other, the Mexican, a hand over his right eye, rocked his upper body back and forth for the pain.

"Shit, Chingo," he was saying. "Cap that fucking bitch."

"They said no gunshots, dude."

"They couldn't hear fucking gun shots from here, man. Look what the bitch did to my eye."

"Look at my nose. If you got a knife, I'll cut her throat, but no shots, man."

The Mexican boy, Mandi sensed, had begun to soften as his pain subsided. He stood a few moments, no longer rocking, and slowly lowered his hand from his eye. His longish black hair was feathered back like John Travolta's in *Welcome Back, Kotter*.

"Look," he said. "Is my eye still there?"

The white boy glanced over. "It's still there, fool. Just a scratch." The boy's accent was a somewhat forced combination of inner-city black and border Latino. "*Puedo matarla*," he said. "I can still take her out. She's dazed, man, I could kill her easy with a big rock."

"No," the other said. "Don't cap her, man."

"What the fuck do we do with her, then?"

"We take her with us."

Neither spoke for a few moments, and the white boy finally shook his head, his shoulders tensing as he tightened his hold on the rifle. "Fuck, man," he said, pushing the barrel down within two inches of Amanda's face. "I think we got to take her out, man."

"Don't shoot her," the Hispanic boy said. "Come on man, *cálmate, hombre.*"

Amanda had not moved, the fear tightening in her belly until she felt she would vomit. She lay still, her arms splayed in the sand of the dry wash, palms out, and she had not moved so much as a finger. Amanda had been surprised at how quickly she had prepared herself to die, and conversely the extent to which she was willing to go to insure she lived, how she would offer anything, the money in her trust fund, her best mule, her own body, that she might live to see her mother again. She sensed now her best tactic was not to fight but to tap the thin current of humanity she sensed in each of the boys. They were, after all, not much older than herself—maybe they listened to some of the same music, watched the same TV shows, perhaps even wept at the end of *Rocky* as she had.

The white boy was speaking again—*Fuck, man.* Suddenly, she knew he was afraid, just like her.

"Ise will kill us, Billy," he said. "And he'll feed us our balls first. This wasn't in the plan, man."

"It'll be worse, Chingo," Billy said, pointing at the girl, "if we waste her without his permission. I've heard about Isedro Leon, man. Besides, they'd find her right here, dude, even if we tried to bury her and shit, and then every fucking cop in the country would be out here, and then we could never make our connection."

"They'd look for her anyway," Chingo said impatiently. "They'll have a fucking chopper out here."

"Not as fast as they'll hunt for us if we cap her, man. They'll think she's lost or ran away or something, send a few people out. That'll give us some time."

"We could bury her deep, man," Chingo offered. "Put her far enough down the fucking dogs won't smell her."

Billy shook his head, turned to the white boy. "Do you see a fucking shovel, man? It would take too long, anyway. We'd have to tell Ise what we were doing. He'd fucking shit, man."

"He'll freak when we bring her back."

"Then he can cap her himself," Billy said. He turned to Amanda. He put his hands on his knees and leaned down close to her face. The white of his eye, outside the pupil, was blood red, and it made her wince to look at it. "Listen to me, bitch," he said. "Can you sit up?"

Amanda nodded.

"Don't nod your fucking head, bitch, talk to me."

"Yes," she shot back, surprisingly sullen.

"You're going on a little trip, alright? A little vacation, okay?"

She nodded again. "Okay," she answered.

"But if you scream or try to get away, we'll kill you. You understand that?"

"Oh, yes," she said. "Yes, I understand that."

Billy took her under the arm, almost gently, to help her stand. But he'd led her about three steps down the wash when her knees hollowed under her and she collapsed to the sand, vomiting the little contents of her stomach.

"Shit man," she heard Chingo say behind her. "She's fucked up. She won't make it all the way back."

Billy knelt and looked into her face. "Hey," he said. "What's your name?"

"Mandi," she said. "Amanda." The sound of her name on her own breath was oddly disconsolate, she having said it and heard it in so many other happy contexts.

"Okay, Mandi," the boy named Billy said to her, seeming nice, calmed. He pointed up the embankment toward the trucks and trailers. "Do you have a horse up there?"

Amanda had to call together her scattered thoughts until the image of the brown mule formed in her mind. "Dunk," she said, grateful to be alive. "I've got Dunk."

It took the boys a clumsy quarter hour, with Amanda's listless instruction, to finally saddle the animal and hoist the trembling girl onto its back. Every few minutes, Mandi was taken by another fit of violent dry heaves, almost falling from the mule at one point. Chingo asked why she was throwing up so much; Billy explained somewhat knowledgably that she had a concussion. Before they'd set out, the boys had argued and negotiated how they would proceed so as not to be tracked, finally striking on a satisfactory plan. They followed the trail the party had made earlier that morning, then broke off into a thick vein of mesquite and mountain mahogany where they could descend the hillside and gain an easy ridge to the bottom.

The boys took turns riding the mule behind Amanda, who kept the animal at a slow pace so as not to leave the walker behind. After a half mile on the familiar back of old Dunk, Mandi's retching subsided. No one spoke, and Mandi arrived at the grim reason why—one could more easily kill a person with whom he'd had little personal contact, and though she had her life for the moment, she countenanced the fact that she would probably, at some point, be shot and left in the desert.

She glanced toward the western sky. Some hundred yards away, a pair of grackles sat perched atop a dead mesquite, their slight, dark bodies cast against the sunset, which painted the dusk air with a sullen umber wash. Amanda Monahan wondered if she would live to see next morning's light.

Seventeen

Ramirez says the dismembered girl had been in her mid to late teens. The bodies of all five victims will be taken to the forensics lab in Hermosillo where experts say...

Kevin tried to track the text on the computer screen, its dim glow the only light in the room, but his mind kept running off the page, digressing back into his own meandering thoughts. As he'd suspected, he'd found only a few references to the drug problems of the 1970s but no specific information on the hour that had so distempered the last three decades of his life. The incident he looked at now had happened only two weeks ago. After talking with Jessica, he'd dropped off to sleep—then, on the heels of a nightmare, came wide awake again. He'd sneaked to the liquor cabinet, poured himself a full tumbler of neat scotch, then crept back to the bedroom and punched on his laptop. The alcohol had made a warm sting in his belly and was beginning to find his blood; he was having trouble distinguishing past and present. The piece he read now touched too close, and he resisted a full-blown anxiety attack, sipping at the scotch and rubbing his temples.

The photo in the web article showed a young, stocky Mexican police officer wearing a ball cap, the whisper of a sad black mustache gracing his upper lip. He was caught in the still shot looking exhausted and staring off at some point outside the frame of the picture. The dead from this particular incident—covered in sundry sheets, tarps, bits of clothing—lay in a row between two mangled vehicles, like broken piano keys. The ads for cars and male enhancement products posted in the margins of the web page were maddeningly incongruous, and Kevin found himself overwhelmed by the whole prospect, ashamed at his continued pain over something so diminished in scale against such a devastating backdrop. Old Xavier was right. A small skirmish in a big war.

And in a moment, as if dropping into sleep, ten minutes of Kevin's young life on that Sunday afternoon slid into memory—fractured, dreamlike, moving in some state of blurred consciousness.

Strange, the clarity of the senses in the midst of trauma. The sound of voices was vivid—he picked out his father's from all the rest of the shouting. Then, only gunfire. The shots died and shouting again, some of it Spanish. He recalled the sudden, bizarre impulse to laugh, as a kid will when at a complete loss. From the rock he hid behind he could see the northern sky, clear and blue, the cut of the rocky foothills under the cast of fall light, and he wondered if this was really happening, if the director might raise the megaphone and say *Cut! Okay, Kevin I love it, baby, but try to act a little more scared—and, please, don't laugh on this take.*

The bullets cut the air no more than a foot above his head nicking the brush behind him, leaving a wake of scooped air, almost palpable. Just as a real fistfight featured less poise and heroic grace than in the movies, so it was with a gunfight. Like a boxing match on TV, time passed between the frantic flurries of blows, as fighters rested, negotiated strategy, talked to each other.

This is bullshit, a man's voice shouted. *You guys just get out of here, and everything's cool.*

Another voice, distant but distinct. O.D., mad, maybe scared. *You play hell, you son of a bitch.*

A strange listlessness pervaded the air on the unseasonably warm afternoon. The wrong sort of weather for being shot at. The running footfalls he heard a few yards away were perhaps the most frightening aspect. He could also hear Mondy's breathing beside him and smell his sweat and Kevin shook himself free of the dream, the memory, the altered state. His breathing and heart rate accelerated. The alcohol weighted his limbs, and he was unsure whether he had fallen asleep.

Someone was tapping on the bedroom door and tried the lock again for the third or fourth time. The knocking came again with more force, then whispering and then he recognized the voices of his mother, sister, perhaps Mrs. Gilbert, low and urgent, then footfalls moving back down the hallway.

"Kevin," his mother said behind the door.

"I'm alright."

"You didn't sound alright a minute ago."

"I'm okay, Mother."

"Let me in."

"I said I'm okay."

"Unlock this door—now."

Kevin found the floor with his right foot. His body felt heavy as he fumbled forward. When he turned the lock, his mother opened the door just a crack. He was struck, surprised by the slackened features of a woman approaching seventy.

She shook her head. "Honey, you were shouting."

"I was?"

She nodded. "You were cussing. It woke everyone up."

For a moment, he didn't believe her, was tempted to question her senses. Maybe the shouting had come from someone else. "I might have been dreaming," he said.

His mother widened the opening with the back of her hand, stepped in and let out a breath. She looked around the room then up at him, waved her hand in front of her face. "You reek," she said. "Why are you drinking scotch at three in the morning?"

"Couldn't sleep."

Teresa crossed her arms over her chest, stared at him a few beats too long for his comfort. She sat down at the foot of the bed. "Drinking instead of sleeping doesn't seem like a great idea," she said. "Kevin, you've hardly slept in two days."

Kevin shrugged, drove his fingers into his tangled hair. "Christ," he said. "I don't know what's happening to me."

Teresa moved her hands to her face, palms pressed to her forehead. "God I wish I knew what to do, how to help."

"I wish I knew."

His mother drew a breath, released it. "Kevin, I want you to know, to understand, that you can overcome this."

Kevin nodded, ran his fingers again back through his hair. "It's just that it was so long ago, and I'd counted it over, done with."

Teresa shook her head. "Listen," she said, and Kevin could tell by the arc of her voice she was close to tears. With her arms folded across her nightgown and bed-wrangled hair she looked frail, elderly. "This all seems like such a wreck right now, but I have to think it's progress."

Kevin nodded.

"Just because you'd covered it up doesn't mean it somehow magically vanished. It has to be dug out, and I'm sorry for that."

He sat down beside her, put his hands in his lap. "I don't know, Mother." He tried to sound sober, cover his scotch-crippled tongue. "I just know I'm having a lot of trouble living with myself right now."

"You don't need to be miserable and guilty."

"I know that," he said. "Consciously, at least, I know that. But, my god, Mother, it's still all banging around inside of me, and I just don't know what to do."

Teresa put a hand on his knee. "Oh, honey, I wish like hell I did, that I could make it go away."

"I know that I can't keep blaming myself if I want to live my life. All the damned counselors and shrinks over the years, and I feel like it's come to shit. It may even have hurt. I don't know. I do know something has to give, because I can't do this anymore."

They contemplated the dark side of the room.

"You'll find it," Teresa said. "You'll come to the place. You just need to wait for it. A sign, maybe some kind of help, but you'll reconnoiter some way."

"I wish I was that confident."

Teresa smiled.

"For the longest time," Kevin said, "I wanted that part of my memory to go away. And now I know I need it back. It's like a damned bum tooth or a splinter that needs out."

His mother chuckled softly. "And I can't help you. The mother can stand beside the child, but then it comes down to the work between the dentist and his victim."

They laughed at the image, ridiculous and skewed by exhaustion, alcohol, the mysterious despair of three o'clock in the morning.

Kevin drew a breath. "Mother—I know who died and who didn't, but that's all. A big chunk of me was left out there. I know you were there, too, but you were a long way from where things were happening. Some of those things happened only in my frame. Those are the ones that won't come out—my devils. Those are the ones I need to call into the open."

Even before his mother left the room, he had decided. They hugged and said good night. The atmosphere of their parting was hopeful, and she gripped his hand almost happily before she went back to bed. The old man would be up by this hour, as old men always were. Ranchers, especially early risers, welcomed any kind of company with their morning coffee. Kevin dressed, downed the last of his scotch, eased closed the front door, and started his car.

Eighteen

The mule they'd seen from the U.S. side of the border was Dunk. Tired and ready to go home, he had ambled out toward them as they rode up to the water tank. Kevin called the girl's name at once when he'd confirmed the animal and the saddle it bore. No answer. He and Mondy looked at each other.

"What the hell," Kevin said.

Mondy shook his head, motioned toward the tank. "Let's look at tracks."

The footprints had been made by three different people, two of them probably men, but Kevin and Mondy could determine little more. The party may have left the mule sometime after the border fence and taken the long dry wash that ran toward the southeast on foot. Kevin put Bonny on what he thought was the trail, but after trying to follow the prints for a distance, they determined tracking them would be futile, the ground in that area a crosshatched chaos of every kind of track imaginable, both human and animal. Bonny, in fact, had several times hopped out of the wash and trotted in confused circles. It was apparently a popular crossing point for migrant workers and smugglers, and the dog's olfactory sense had been overloaded.

It was close to noon. Surely by now people were hunting for them, but their dilemma hinged on whom they felt most responsible for—the concerned searchers or fifteen-year-old Amanda Monahan. For all they knew, she was with the worried search party on the other side of the border.

"Well, what the hell do we do?" Kevin asked.

"Your guess," Mondy said.

They stood on the levy of the water tank, which someone had bulldozed together no more than a year before, the track marks of the machine still visible. Mondy took the saddle off of Dunk and the mule contentedly snuffled at tufts of green bunchgrass.

Kevin nodded down at the animal. "We'll tether him back with us."

"No doubt," Mondy said. "I sure hope that girl's with them."

They sat down on the dirt levy and, knowing nothing else to do, exercised their hunter's impulse to glass, first the ridges west of them, then out at the long flat that some miles south ascended into the foothills of the Sierra Madres. Highway 2, which skirted the Mexico side of the border, was under construction. They could see the site about a mile south, clutches of heavy equipment and turned earth scattered over a two-mile stretch, but no workers, as it was a weekend. Mexico road contractors seldom worked Saturdays, and certainly never on Sunday.

After a rough night's sleep on hard ground, they were tired and loath to pick up at the mid-day hours and start back. They found the shade of a desert willow and had high ground enough to see three horizons. Mondy, head back and Adam's apple moving in rhythm to his breathing, snored loudly. Bonny quit her whimpering and dozed, her head in Kevin's lap.

About to nod off himself, Kevin spotted something on a ridge a mile and a half northeast in the lower side of the Pelocillos that took his interest.

He nudged Mondy awake. "Check this out," he said.

He'd seen the two vehicles, black trucks of some sort, as they'd started up a semblance of Jeep trail at the foot of a long jackknifed canyon on the Mexican side. The trucks were about a quarter of the way up the ridge, and Kevin caught glimpses of them, riding close together, as they moved in and out of the trees. As he'd woken Mondy, they'd dropped out of sight, though he could hear the faint groan of their engines on the easterly breeze.

"I still don't see what you're looking at," Mondy said.

"Listen, you can hear them."

Mondy tilted his head and concentrated. "That could be the wind," he said. "I think you're hallucinating. I know there's an old ranch road up there, but I don't see any rigs." As he raised his glasses again, the two vehicles cleared a stand of jackwoods and crawled into plain sight.

"There they are," Mondy said. "About two-thirds up. They look like maybe Suburban four-wheel-drives."

"I see them," Kevin said.

"They're on that old road, alright."

"What do you think they're doing up there?"

"Probly dumping off *mojados*."

"Bullshit," Kevin said. "They wouldn't climb clear up into the mountains when they could drop people off here in the flats."

"Disrespectful as usual, but you make a good point." Mondy lowered his glasses. "I know the rancher who owns those sections up there. Old Conchillo. He used to live by us on the res near Sil before he moved back here to Mexico. He's a mean old bastard. If he catches them up there he'll shoot shit out of all of them."

The vehicles had disappeared again in the trees of the canyon, but the sound of their engines was distinct.

"Where do you think that road goes?" Kevin asked.

Mondy put down his glasses. "It's been a long time since I been up there," he said. "I was a little kid hunting with my uncle. I know it forks off all over the mountain on this side of the border. One fork goes real close, like within a mile or two, of those corrals we started at yesterday. But, like I say, I don't use that road no more because of Conchillo. Mean old bastard."

"Who the hell is he?" Kevin asked, and settled back for what he knew would be a long story full of made-up bullshit.

"You'll just laugh at me, accuse me of embellishing."

"No guarantees," Kevin said.

Mondy sighed. "No respect," he said. "I don't know why I even expect it anymore."

Mondy had been twelve years old at the time, so memory was a little shadowy. For years, the children in the Three Points area had been terrified of Ben Conchillo, who even that many years ago seemed a very old man. He was one of three bastard sons born to an infamous *curandera* named Mocha Villalobos, and he lived alone outside Sil Nakaya, high on a rocky ridge in the Santa Rosa Mountains. All one could see of his house from town was the occasional glint of his tin roof and the wisps of smoke from his wood-burning stove in the wintertime.

His being alone, save for one dog named *Feo* ("ugly" in Spanish) was no accident, for legend had it that some years before he had lured his wife and six children high into the mountains where he shut them in a cave, blocking the entrance with large stones and mesquite logs so that they could never escape. On cold winter nights, some claimed, if one were to venture high enough into the Santa Rosas, he would hear the mother crying and the children screaming for food. It was said that Conchillo once had many dogs but had grown tired of their barking at night and had eaten all but Feo because he never barked. The old man was said to live on rats and skunks that Feo caught and brought home to him.

Conchillo liked to be alone—he didn't even like birds and wild animals around. If anything came close to his house, it would be shot and eaten, even, some claimed, if it were human.

Mondy, in the throes of his story, moved his hands about as he spoke: "A lady who lived by us, Señora Noamavas, had this little fucking dog, the kind with the smashed-in face—a Pekinese—and everybody liked it. A real friendly little dog who liked to play with the kids. So one day this dog, Chica was her name, wandered off and got too close to the old man's house. The fucker killed the dog and ate half of it and brought the other half back and laid it on the old woman's doorstep. He'd skinned it out except for the head and neck so she could see it was her little smashed-face dog. Old Conchillo pointed at the carcass and said, in O'odham, he says to her: *Good dog, good flavor. I saved you half.*"

Mondy noted Kevin's smirk. "You know, kid," he said, "you need to gain a better appreciation of myth. One of these days you'll regret being such a smart ass."

When Mondy had fallen asleep again, Kevin spotted the Suburbans parked high on the ridge. He could only see the tops of them, though it appeared that no one had yet emerged. He wondered if the occupants had left during Mondy's story or sometime he wasn't looking.

Then the driver's side door of the front Suburban opened and a man stepped out. After a moment, the back driver's-side door opened and another man, shorter and wearing a baseball cap, emerged, and just after him what appeared to be a girl with blond hair. Kevin could see only her head and, over a mile away, could determine nothing about her face. Still, he knew with certainty that he was looking at Amanda Monahan.

He punched Mondy hard in the thigh, and Mondy woke with a

start and clutched at his leg. "Fuck, man," he said.

"Amanda," Kevin said. "Those motherfuckers have her."

They rode north, found the Jeep trail at the foot of the canyon, and saw the tracks made from heavy-duty truck tires. After half a mile they broke from the road and took an easy ridge that rose more directly to where they'd last seen the vehicles. The deer path they rode angled through a bank of scrub oak and buck brush and ended at a shelf-like flat just below a limestone sheaf of rim rock, where they dismounted and rested in the shade of a juniper. Dunk, as it turned out, trailed easily behind Kevin's mule, Sally, tethered with a length of cotton rope by his hackamore. Dunk sidled along, jug-headed and content, with Bonny at his feet. The little dog flared off the trail only occasionally now, and Kevin had only to say her name in a speaking voice to bring her back to heel.

Neither had spoken since they left the water tank, and Mondy finally looked over at Kevin. "I wish I'd seen her."

"I wish you had, too."

"Well, trust your gut, man," Mondy said. "I think I trust it better than you do."

"I don't know," Kevin said. "Here we are going on what I thought I saw, and we probably have twenty people out looking for us."

"Looking for you, anyway."

"Maybe we should go back to the corrals."

"Corrals are a long way. We wouldn't get there till after dark now. Besides, probably nobody's at the corrals. Probably out looking for us."

"I'm sure they left someone there," Kevin said. "O.D. maybe."

The ridge opposite them was a thicket of oak and juniper and various wild grasses, and impulsively the two hunters raised their glasses to look, knowing the lee shade in such a place was a perfect spot for game. In the canyon bottom between the ridges, an easy hillock dotted with oaks and broom grass swelled like a belly between two ravines. When Kevin glanced down at it he saw the five turkeys immediately, their heads bobbing in and out of the grama grass where they fed in a clearing some two-hundred yards down canyon.

"Check 'em out," Kevin said, pointing. He realized he was salivating.

"Oh yeah," Mondy said, sighting them in his binoculars. "Man, I could take one from here with that .308."

"No," Kevin said.

"Why not?"

"Too much noise."

"I'm hungry, man."

"Me, too," Kevin said. "I'm not sure I could eat right now, though."

Mondy, behind him, was silent a moment. "Me either," he admitted.

Kevin shook his head. "I think we should get up there, man. Think about food later." He turned to Mondy, who looked scared.

Mondy nodded, looked up toward the ridges. "I think maybe you're right."

When they reached the clearing where they'd last seen the vehicles, it was late afternoon. In the shade of two tall boulders, Almond Joy candy wrappers, quart-sized storage baggies, and Pepsi cans lay scattered about. Without word or ceremony, Mondy dismounted and crushed the soda cans with the heel of his boot, picking them up and shaking the remnant fluid from them. He walked back to Turk and put the crushed cans in the side satchels, then looked up at Kevin.

"I think these are smugglers," he said. "And I think they're real bad boys."

"Same here," Kevin said.

"I was holding out hope they were hunters or birdwatchers, fancy-assed vaqueros or some shit. But people like that don't usually leave trash."

"*Verdad,*" Kevin said.

"I was thinking you might be hallucinating about the girl and all, but I don't think so now. *Preocupado. ¿Tú?*"

"*También,*" said Kevin. "*Más que preocupado.*"

"Me, too, man," Mondy said, his left hand resting on the horn of Turk's saddle. "I'm scared, too." He rubbed his big stomach. "I can feel it right here—like a tugging. Man, I know they got her."

Kevin nodded. "I know it the same."

"Why do you think they took her?"

"I don't know," Kevin said. Sally shifted under him—he hadn't thought until now of relieving her for a time of his weight. He dismounted, his feet bricklike for lack of blood, then walked back and untied Dunk. He had discovered that Dunk did well ground-tied: anytime they stopped, Kevin dropped tether and the mule stood as though the rope were deep-staked to that very patch of ground. "Maybe she saw something she shouldn't have, but who knows."

Mondy walked back to the boulders and bent, picking up the rest of the trash, bunching it into his hand and stuffing it into his fanny pack. "You're not going to help me, are you?"

"Thought you were doing okay by yourself."

Mondy sighed and zipped the pack. "I thought you'd get better with age, but you haven't." He walked back to gentle old Turk, the horse resting a hind foot, his one eye drooped in half-sleep. Mondy put his hands up on the tree of the saddle. "You know, kid," he said. "This could get bad."

Kevin nodded. "How much ammo *you* got?"

"Two boxes. Man, I wish I'd thought to bring that Cobra radio."

"You couldn't get anybody right now."

"You don't think?" Mondy looked down at his feet, shook his head. "Man I'm scared."

"You've said that."

"I know," Mondy said. "But I just wanted to make sure you knew it."

They took the Jeep trail ascending the ridge and in half an hour crested the brushy top, where they discovered to their dismay that the road forked, both routes bearing heavy-duty tire tracks. Neither boy spoke, arriving at similar dilemmas and inevitabilities. The canyons were in shadow now—in less than an hour it would be full dark on an almost moonless night.

"I don't think those trucks would have split up," Mondy said.

"Why not?"

"What would it profit them?"

"I don't know," Kevin admitted.

Mondy pointed to the fork that appeared to run to the northwest, winding up a broom-grass littered slope and disappearing at the top. "I'm pretty sure this road goes close to those corrals we started at the other day. I think we should take it."

Kevin shook his head. "I don't know. Why would they take a long winding route like this when they could get there on a straight road?"

Mondy shrugged. "I don't know either."

Kevin pointed at the east-going fork. "This looks like it may drop down toward those ranches north of Janos—as good a place as any to run dope across. We know there's no house to the west. Maybe we'll be able to find a phone if we go this way, get some help. Either that or go down to that highway they're working on and try to find someone."

Mondy shook his head. "The highway's a couple of miles from here. By the time we got down there and found someone, we might as well go back to the corrals for help. We may find nobody at either place."

"Agreed."

"Best bet is to go either east to the old man's ranch—maybe he has a phone—or west, back to the corrals."

Mondy fished in his pants' pocket and pulled out a quarter. He was smiling and Kevin knew why. The fatalism argument was as old as their friendship.

"Either way's a guess," Mondy said.

Kevin shook his head. "Jesus, Mondy, just when you win a good point, you have to go and overstate your case again. Just digging the coin out would have been enough."

But Mondy would not be denied his moment. "I sure wish I had time to stomp your ass for being such a little shit. You're the reason we're here in the first place." The coin balanced on his thumb and forefinger, he smiled at Kevin. "Heads we go west, tails we go east. Best three out of five wins."

"'Wins,'" Kevin mocked. "As opposed to 'loses'?"

They rode two miles east, topping the ridge that overlooked a small meadow amid the jack pine and junipers. In it, the house and outbuildings of a small ranch lay scattered in a hundred-meter square. The basin was in shadow, and a faint tail of smoke rose from the chimney of the main house, little more than a twenty-by-twenty raw-wood clapboard shed. West of the house stood a Ford tractor with two flat back tires, its rusting visceral parts scattered about in a ten-foot circle. A hundred feet behind the house stood two small stalls and holding pens, fenced of cedar branches and barbed wire. In one lingered three skinny steers, in the other a buckskin gelding just flush with his winter coat.

They barely had a chance to take in the scene before a vehicle grumbled to a start close by. A flatbed, dual-wheeled '59 Ford started from its place beside the tack and hay crib and crept up the road toward them. The mounts shifted nervously, and Bonny affected her low growl. Whoever was driving shifted into second and kept it whining in that gear as the truck slowly closed the two-hundred meters between them. The Ford was the kind of colorless that came only of long use and weather. It bore six bald tires and no side rails and both headlights had been long since smashed out.

As it pulled up beside them their mounts shied slightly. In the cab was an Indian man, most certainly of Sonoran fount by his features. He was perhaps in his early to mid-fifties, his long gray hair loose around his shoulders. He rolled down his window and spat on the ground and eyed both of them too long before climbing out, heedless to Bonny who backed up, barked a spate of fierce yaps, then tentatively sniffed at his boots.

"*Ya ta he*, Armando Luna," the older man said, and he and Mondy laughed.

Kevin was always surprised at Mondy's transformation around his people. Even his laughter changed, becoming lower and more guttural. The older man had not acknowledged Kevin, and stood still, small and reed-like in threadbare indigo denim, unflappable in the evening chill. Kevin could see little of his raw-boned features in the dusk, though he could smell him—a pungent collusion of wood smoke and axle grease.

Mondy climbed off Turk. Smiling, he stepped up to the older man and extended his hand. "*¿Cómo le va, señor Conchillo?*" he said.

"*Como le va*, my ass," the man came back, though he shook the other's hand. "The way you little shits used to harass me, I shouldn't even let you drink my good whiskey or eat my *albódigas* tonight. I should just shoot your asses where you stand."

Mondy, his hand still in the older man's grasp, tilted his head slightly and clicked his tongue, an O'odham gesture of deference, shame, and humility.

The man looked at Kevin then. "*¿Qué ondas, chamaco? ¿Cómo te va?*"

"*Bien señor. ¿A usted?*" Kevin was mystified as to how this man had guessed he spoke Spanish, for his Scotch blood showed more than the Basque.

"*Bien*," the older man answered back. He glanced between the two, his face suddenly clouding. "Well, come on, goddamn it. Get those animals unsaddled and corralled," he said, gesturing impatiently toward the house. "That whiskey ain't gonna get drunk with us standing around out here."

Nineteen

Conchillo opened his door before Kevin had a chance to knock. He looked all of his eighty-odd years as he stood inside his doorway, the thin yellow glow of porch light falling uneasily on his features. From the kitchen, Kevin could smell coffee, and the fat cat rubbed at the old man's ankles. Conchillo said nothing, but moved back a step and gestured Kevin inside. The place looked like it had been cleaned up, the smell of Lysol still on the air.

"I figured you'd be here sooner," the old man said.

Kevin was feeling the after effects of the alcohol, his mouth dry, a throbbing just behind his nose. "I hadn't told you I was coming," he said. "I'm not even sure why I'm here."

Conchillo shrugged. "You think maybe I can help you. I knew you'd show up."

"Well, can you?"

The old man shrugged again, squinted at him. "You look like shit," he said.

Kevin looked about the small living room. "Can I sit down?"

"You'd better."

Kevin eased down on the couch and Conchillo moved off to the kitchen where Kevin heard him fumbling around in the cabinets. The obese cat jumped up onto Kevin's lap, and purred as he ran his hand over its belly.

The old man returned with two large coffee mugs, one of which he sat on the side table. Both mugs of coffee had been spiked with a heavy dose of whiskey—Kevin could smell it.

Conchillo nodded at the mug on the table. "You need to drink that and get some sleep, so you can be ready."

"Ready for what?"

"For today." The old man backed up toward an easy chair in the corner of the room and sat down. "It's gonna be kind of rough. You'll need rest."

Kevin picked up the coffee mug and smelled it. "Jesus. How much whiskey did you put in this?"

"Enough," Conchillo said. "Just drink it, and get some sleep."

"What do you mean about 'today'?"

"We're finding *Himdag*."

"*Himdag*," Kevin said. "I've heard of it."

"You'll see," Conchillo assured. "It's something I figured out to help get rid of things that are fucking you up. You need to finish what you started." With effort, he raised himself from the chair. Not even five in the morning and he was fully dressed, a brown wool shirt, jeans and hiking boots.

Kevin took a sip of the foamy head of the coffee. The effervescence of whiskey rose in his sinuses.

Conchillo made his way toward the kitchen. "You'll need your sleep. We have a lot of work to do."

Kevin looked down into the coffee mug as Conchillo rattled around in his pantry. There was the distinct sense he was making ready to go somewhere, perhaps a picnic or hike, though Kevin wondered how such an ancient creature could do anything like that without help. He considered asking the old man for more specifics, how he knew Kevin would come back, but he was too tired. Resigned.

Conchillo shuffled back into the living room with a bulging daypack, laid it on the easy chair.

"You going somewhere?" Kevin asked.

"We," the old man said. "You and me are going somewhere."

Kevin's mug was drawn down to about half. He lifted it to his lips but could barely drink for exhaustion. His head weighed a hundred pounds, and all he could consider at the moment was lying down on the dingy brown cushions.

He woke to find a note on the coffee table in the old man's penciled scrawl: *Be back around noon.* The plastic Walmart clock over the kitchen entryway read just before ten a.m. The cat was purring at his ankles, and he kicked it away and found the floor with his feet.

When he'd gotten himself collected, he glanced at the clock. He had almost two hours before the old man returned. Enough time to get to the library and look for the archives the woman at the consulate's office had told him about. Why he'd planned to keep some cryptic appointment with Benny Conchillo, he knew not. He'd exhausted every other possibility, he supposed. And the old man seemed sure of himself. It couldn't hurt to see out what he had planned.

132

Susan Murray sat at the circulation desk when he arrived, and she was taken aback when he walked through the doors. Kevin hadn't realized how he must look and smell at this point. She tapped on her computer, looking up over the monitor at him occasionally and trying to hide her concern for his appearance.

"Okay," she said finally, peering into the screen. "We do have state and county police documents from fall of '76." She looked up at him. "I'll have to open up for you. County archives are in the building next door. Also," she said, tilting her chin a bit, "I'm not sure about the legality of this."

"A favor for an old friend?"

"If we're caught, I'll roll over on you," she quipped. "They won't even have to torture me much."

"Thank you."

"Had that eye looked at?"

"No," Kevin forced a chuckle. "Now that it's opened up a little, I can see out of it. So I figure it's mending. I got it from a fist in the face, so I'm pretty sure I can practice reasonable prevention."

"The official rumor report says you hit your face on the edge of a table." Susan shrugged. "Small town. What can I say. Heard you were the only one who landed a glove."

"Wow," Kevin said. "I wish I remembered. Sounds like I was pretty fierce."

Susan laughed, genuinely tickled at the remark.

She wrangled her keys from a drawer behind the front desk and they walked out into the painful mid-morning sun. The parking lot of the Presbyterian church down the street was brimming with cars and the easiness of a normal Sunday morning rode on the air. Susan ambled down the walk slightly ahead of him, tempted, Kevin could tell, to glance back over her shoulder. No doubt, his situation was curious at the very least.

She fumbled with the key and the deadbolt lock on the industrial steel door, opening it to the dark interior of the ugly little modular building. She snapped on the light and made a sweeping gesture with her arm, as though inviting him into King Tut's tomb. The little room was stark, inhabited wall-to-wall by basic bookshelves filled with cardboard boxes and file folders.

"Man," Kevin said.

"All the musty secrets of Cochise County," Susan said. "Welcome to the sepulcher."

"It's kind of depressing," Kevin admitted.

"Oh, believe me, you have no idea."

Though the state files were fairly well organized, it took Kevin a good quarter hour to find what he was looking for. He located state and county police reports for November of '76, but found nothing in the files for that specific Sunday afternoon until he opened a dust-layered lady's shoe box he'd glossed over half a dozen times.

Inside was a stack of papers—state police and sheriff's reports on the incident. When he read the heading, written in the Pica font of an old electric typewriter, the skin on his face and arms tingled. **Incident Report: Compiled Documents for Shootings: 11/12/76**

The document was perhaps three-hundred pages thick, and Kevin leafed through it like a text book the night before a college mid-term, reading headings and random phrases. Names rose out of the page as in his nightmares. Benny Conchillo was among those interviewed, his report a little under two pages. "The old bastard was there—or claims he was," Kevin said aloud. More than once he stopped a moment to gather himself and rub his temples or his stomach. His belly rumbled, so upset he was sure a couple of times he would have to step outside and find a hidden corner to throw up in.

Russ Billman's name came up the most—he had, as deputy sheriff, written a report of his own and had been interviewed by Customs. Russell Billman. Kevin wondered if he was still alive. He would be over eighty years old now, and the way Kevin remembered the man used to drink, Russ would probably have a faulty memory at best.

Kevin read through Billman's three-page somewhat pedestrian report and found only surface and cursory information, for the deputy had been over two-hundred yards from the incident when it was at its most heated. He had reported: "I drove to where I heard the shots but I immediately was taking fire so had to take cover behind the left front tire of my vehicle. A couple of times I fired my shotgun but was out of range to be of any help."

Kevin leafed forward, feeling like the reporter in *Citizen Kane*.

He imagined a funnel of light falling on the cryptic document as he searched out "Rosebud." He was at once stopped by a name toward the end of the stack. For several heartbeats, he stared at the letters: **Interview with Kevin McNally.** He opened to the first page and read: *Kevin McNally, age 17, reports...* He looked up toward the bookshelves, unable to read on. It was as though he'd met himself coming and going. Before him was the horrified testament of a boy who no longer existed.

"Shit," he said.

Kevin looked at his watch. Almost noon. Clearly, he hadn't the time to read all of it, though he doubted it could provide what he was hunting for, whatever that might be. He flipped through the stack, considering the names of witnesses, and then carefully removed the few pages of Conchillo's, Billman's, and his own accounts out of the sheaf. Like a B-movie thief, he checked over his shoulder, lifted his shirt, and tucked the pages in his waistband. A moment of guilt shadowed by as he thought of Susan, the steward responsible for keeping these papers. The thing had been in a shoe box, for Christ's sake, and probably hadn't been looked at for over thirty years, and they bore no greater calling, he supposed, than the one he had for them. If the cosmos moved with any kind of order, that stack of papers had been left there for him to find—on this very day, at this very hour.

As he pushed the remaining pages together in a neat stack and returned them to their shoe box, he considered the names of witnesses who had not given their account. Most disturbing were those.

Twenty

The shack at Conchillo's ranch was warm, warmer than Kevin ever remembered his own house for all its size and opulence—hundreds of square feet of saltillo tile were pretty but cold to the feet on winter mornings. He sat next to Mondy on the ragged couch and eyed his jigger glass, which Mr. Conchillo had filled for the third time with whiskey from a plastic half-gallon bottle whose paper label had long since peeled off. They'd chased the whiskey with cans of warm Coors so old they were tin rather than aluminum. Right away, Kevin had asked Conchillo if he had a phone—*No*—if he had seen any vehicles pass through the place, and again Conchillo shook his head. "No," he told them, "but I heard one—old Chamo, on his way to throw salt block."

Kevin glanced over at Mondy, whom he could tell felt rather smug about being right, then looked around the shack hoping for space enough to spend the night. To ride anywhere at the moment seemed futile. And the alcohol in him and the comfort of a warm room made him second guess whether he'd seen the girl at all that afternoon. Likely she was back at her house, listening to music or writing in her diary or something.

Three fat, blond female Labradors slept by the woodstove. Bonny, after the requisite butt-sniffing, happily among them. The shack was one room with raw wood walls and no kitchen or bathroom or phone, and as the whiskey leached him, Kevin didn't even ask before he stepped out to pee and walked back in, stuffing in his shirt tail. In one corner of the shack stood a musty, stained cot with a Navy wool blanket and in the other a small Coleman camp stove. The only ornament was a little shrine against the west wall consisting of a candle-strewn plain wood table beneath a framed retablo of the Virgin of Guadalupe. On the opposite wall were two old black and white photographs, group pictures of some twenty-five unsmiling O'odham in peasant white standing shoulder to shoulder, presumably Conchillo's family.

As the whiskey and ancient Coors took hold of him, Conchillo became more outspoken. He told long stories and gestured with his hands, moving them, palms bared, in opposing circles, an idiosyncratic sort of oral punctuation, as he spoke. At one point, he became especially adamant, explaining why he'd moved from the res in Arizona back to his property in Mexico, blaming the U.S. government for everything from the drought to the crazy lights he saw in the sky after a bender. When he went out to pee, Mondy and Kevin sat in silence for a minute until Kevin was no longer able to resist.

He nodded toward the door and fought down a smile. "Mean old bastard," he said.

Mondy shook his head. "One of these days you'll come to regret being such a dick—maybe not today, maybe not tomorrow, but soon…"

"Oh please," Kevin broke in, "spare me. Jesus, Mondy, you're embarrassing." One of Mondy's especially appalling habits was to inadvertently quote movies. For Kevin it was like the sound of screeching tires or someone scratching a chalkboard.

After his fourth whiskey, Kevin told Conchillo about Mandi and the smugglers. The older man seemed suddenly alert, narrowing his eyes to concentrate on Kevin's account of what he'd seen that day. Conchillo didn't seem to doubt the story in the least. He held forth a plan of attack: "We can get down there early, *chamaco*, and head them off. Get the jump on 'em."

"You believe me, then?" Kevin said. "You think it is true."

The older man nodded slowly. "Yes," he said. "I wish I wasn't drunk or I would do something now. But tomorrow we got to get those vatos. Get some help if we can."

The warm air of the shack grew rife with the smell of the cilantro-and-chile-spiced meat in the *albondigas*, and Kevin's stomach turned itself inside out with hunger. But Conchillo had grown bellicose and made no mention of eating as he put oaths on the smugglers and talked of how he could take them all with his .30-30. As he ranted, he smacked the back of one hand against the palm of the other and whistled through his teeth.

"*Andale Pues*," he'd say, throwing his hand in the air. "If I had headlights on my truck we'd go there right now. Choot it out with those *cabroncitos*."

"*Cálmese usted, hombre*," Mondy said, patting the older man gently on the shoulder. Mondy was feeling his whiskey, too. "We'll get 'em tomorrow." He smoked the last of his cigarettes, squinting at it between his fingers as he savored every puff.

Conchillo had been amiable but hardly focused enough to deliver a coherent answer to any of Kevin's questions, though he was determined this time.

"Please, Mr. Conchillo," he said. "Is it possible to drive east to Janos?"

The older man looked at him, finally, sucked in a long breath and, head wavering slightly, struggled to process the question behind his red-rimmed eyes. He ran a sobering palm down the side of his face. "No," he said. "Goddamn road's washed out to Janos."

"*¿Los corrales?*" Mondy asked, pointing toward the west.

"Hell yes," Conchillo said, popping his knuckles against his palm and whistling through his teeth. He aimed a finger like pointing the barrel of a gun. "We'll go down there tomorrow and choot it out with those *vatos.*" He aimed his imagined rifle, crimped his left eye and made shooting sounds: *peyoo, peyoo...* He lowered the gun and looked at Kevin.

"If I can get over that bad spot with my truck. We'll trailer your mounts." He nodded his head reassuringly. "We'll choot with those *pinchi rucos.* We'll take 'em, too."

After a while, Kevin gave up asking questions of Conchillo and the older man and Mondy lapsed into the O'odham tongue.

Kevin walked over to the two-by-twelve plank on blocks that served as a counter and picked up one of the several mismatched bowls and a spoon. From the Dutch oven on the Coleman stove, he ladled up the *albóndigas*, not shy about how many meatballs he took, walked back to his chair and ate from the bowl in his lap. The stew was as good as its smell had promised, the garlic, cumin, and green chiles conspiring in a richness that filled one's head to the brow. He looked up to find both men looking on him gleamy-eyed and sentimental, the way a drunk in his cups might gaze upon his own children.

"What?" Kevin asked, "*¿Por qué me miras?*"

With some effort, Conchillo rose from his chair and listed toward the counter, under which he fumbled around behind the stacked cans of food, finally pulling out a folded paper grocery bag. He walked back to his place and, with a groaning effort, lowered himself to the floor, sitting Indian-style. He turned the bag label-side down then produced the stub of a pencil whittled to a writing point. Conchillo began drawing, starting with a circle, about twelve inches in diameter, and Kevin recognized the rendered image as *I'itoi*, The Man in the Maze, a significant symbol of the O'odham. The image was a relatively simple one, a labyrinth inside a circle, and some manner of human figure inside, though usually the figure was not in the maze but at the port, poised to enter.

Kevin looked at Mondy and spoke in English: "How is it when you fuckers get drunk you always want to talk about *I'itoi*?"

But Mondy just smiled as though Kevin had not spoken, and Conchillo continued his drawing, which had turned out to be a surprisingly fair rendition, the alleys of the maze intricate enough that one would struggle to pencil a clear passage to its center. Kevin found it odd the older man had drawn it with the stick figure already inside. Conchillo spoke to Kevin in Spanish: *Listen to me, joven.* He ran his hand over the sketch as though what elixirs it offered might come of being roughed, then traced his index finger around the edge of the labyrinth. Inside the maze, midway to the center, the stick-figure man stood about the size of a person's thumb. Conchillo tapped a knuckle against it and looked at Kevin.

Listen to me, boy. This is you, and you are part way through your ordeal to manhood. It is very important that you know this, and hear me well. Once you have begun the journey, you cannot climb clear of it until it is finished—for it is your fate, and yours, particularly, is a treacherous one. You will have help in finding your way, but you will not know when that help comes. It will come always on four legs but in various forms: sometimes an oddly colored or misplaced animal, perhaps a red-coated wolf or an elk in low desert, maybe a goat with the antlers of a deer or a cougar of pure white. Whichever, this animal will lead you. Always, before one finds the center, he encounters great danger, and here he will be tested.

Conchillo tapped a knuckle at the maze's center, then held up a closed fist, fingers out, to Kevin. *Very soon you will touch the center of who you are—and when you do you will either be alive, or you will be dead. You have no recourse now but to keep walking forward and to be ready.*

Twenty-One

Twelve miles northwest of Conchillo's ranch, Yolanda Monahan lit a cigarette. She hadn't smoked in over ten years, but tonight she was working on her third. The sting of the smoke in her lungs felt good against the whiskey that warmed the bottom of her empty stomach. Teresa McNally, across from her, sat back in her chair laughing and leaned forward again, elbows set, peering into her glass. The two women had covered a universe of subjects in the hour and a half they'd talked. Their Spanish came in rapid-fire phrases and shut out everyone else in the room to their conversation.

"God," Yole said, into her drink, "I'm all prayed out, Tere."

"Me too," said the other. "It's time to praise the Lord and pass the ammunition."

The women burst out laughing. They sat at a custom-made breakfast nook of rough-hewn ash that allowed a stunning view of the west-slope canyon cuts of the Peloncillos. The Monahan ranch had stood above a dry wash west of the mountains for better than a century, renovated too many times over the generations to count. It was warm Western chic with Mexican tile, Santa Fe-style antler mounts, and many Navajo and Hopi handcrafts—Kachina dolls of every size and sort, hand-woven rugs and blankets. In contrast to the homey clutter, the lines of the place were clean, the interior recently re-plastered and new doors and windows hung. The Monahans were not poor, though they had always been modest and humble in their ways.

Tom and Glen sat with O.D. and his wife, Olivia, in the living room. None of them spoke but a few words of Spanish but felt no resentment at the worried mothers' private talk. Every so often, the group in the living room broke into a burst of hard laughter at a typical O.D. quip, and Teresa felt a quick brush of anger, although she and Yole had laughed plenty that night. It seemed somehow appropriate for the mothers, a salve for the grief.

The two women in the kitchen had gone silent, each fearful of catching the other's eye across the little table and again losing to the tears. *Suck it up, woman*, Teresa told herself. Russ Billman had assured them before they split up that he would try to arrange for a chopper and three hounds he knew were good, and as many search volunteers as he could pull together, but it had been little comfort to the women, both of whom held an unvoiced fear of what those measures might find. After a moment, Olivia Hallot stepped in for another round of beers, but she closed the refrigerator and walked up to the table, resting a comforting hand on each woman's back.

"It's gonna be alright, guys," she said. "They're here somewhere and I know they're okay." Teresa and Yole looked up at her, smiled, nodded slightly, acknowledging the gesture of kindness. Oli stood five-nine, a big auburn-haired woman, thick at shoulder and hip. She was half Navajo, and a suggestion of those features showed under certain light and in a particular expression.

Olivia opened the fridge and gathered an armload of Miller beers, then paused in the doorway and looked back. "You guys did good today," she said.

And they had.

That morning, the women and their husbands, along with Russ Billman, crossed a state line—but that violation made little difference to anyone but young Si Banks. He'd stayed on the Arizona side all day, riding the line back and forth three times between the main road and Mexico at the cost of little more than a sunburn, saddle-sore rear end, and a half-scoop of extra grain for a worn out horse. By 2:00 p.m., O.D.'s vigil had succumbed to an afternoon nap and the remaining five searchers started up the tapering slope of a long east-going ridge cut along its spine with an easy, beat-to-powder cow trail. From a tangle of cattle and equine tracks, they'd guessed and followed the shoed prints of what looked to be horse and mule straight east. The group stood resting on the trail some five miles into New Mexico.

John Monahan took off his hat and mopped his brow with his sleeve. His wife suspected what was coming. "We start back now," John offered. "Be half an hour before full dark when we hit the trucks."

"I don't care about that," Yolanda said at once.

"I do," Russ said.

Teresa raised her chin. "Ever had a kid lost, Russ?" Though he didn't know it now, the words would sting into the night as he tried to find sleep in a lonely bed.

"No ma'am," he said without irony. "But I'm already wide of my jurisdiction here, and your all's safety is on my head legally no matter who says what."

"You know," Tom said, "our flashlights would get us through an hour in the dark. We probably could afford another forty-five minutes on this ridge. I think Kevin could have worked either of these two easy slopes to the crest. We should split, ride both these ridges, then meet at the top, see what we can, and head back."

They all agreed the plan was workable, but there was some difficulty deciding who would ride which route. Both women and Russ liked the south ridge because they could see into Mexico from it. John and Tom thought the north slope more likely for the prominent tracks; the problem was neither man wanted to split from his wife—no matter if their parting would be under an hour. Teresa finally told her husband she didn't care what he thought and that she would go her own way, while all others in the party looked off into the distance, embarrassed.

John and Tom had the easier go of it, as the trail on the north ridge widened and they saw nothing to keep their attention. In just over a quarter hour, they found the top where the ridges converged. They dismounted and glassed into the folds of vulcanized, chaparral-flecked mountains. They figured it would be another fifteen to twenty minutes before the rest would find them.

After only a few seconds, John said, "I got something."

"Where?" Tom asked.

Half a mile down canyon on a shelf-like flat, a man rode a dun-colored horse. He wore a cowboy hat and was alone and both men felt a sudden tug of disappointment as they realized he was no one they were searching for.

"That's old Walt Miller," John said. "He must be checking around the edges of his place. He didn't never get this far east, not usually, anyway."

"He's seen us," Tom said. Miller had reined his horse straight for the ridge.

The men kept their tones flat as though it were any other day and situation, and neither grudged the other this, for things were hard enough. They grew hopeful as Walt Miller approached. One of them had to say it. It was John.

"Maybe he's seen something."

Miller was lean and gray-haired and his clean-shaven face bore hard-angled Germanic features. He climbed off the mare with a groan and a confident grin as he stepped up to Monahan, now standing, as though he'd seen him only an hour ago. The men shook hands all around, and Miller nodded toward the north. "Think she'll be another dry one this year?"

John nodded slightly. "May be," he said. "A few good storms help us out."

"Reckon we'll get 'em?"

"Reckon not," John said, and the three men chuckled.

Miller asked, "You fellas hear about the Mexican patrol that was huntin' down gringos?"

Despite themselves, John and Tom politely shook their heads.

"Well, these Mexican soldiers, like I say, was walking along hunting gringos when this guy, this gringo, pops up from behind a rock. *Hey you damn Mexcans,* he says to 'em. So the *capitan* he sends a damn detail down to take care of this smart-mouthed gringo. Well, the six or seven soldiers in this detail jumps behind the rock and the rest can hear the shouting and shooting, but the damn detail never comes back. So the captain says to himself, what the hell, and sends down another detail. More shooting, and then these don't come back, so he sends another and another until nobody's left but him. Finally, the old captain calls up the sand to go look behind the rock for himself. When he gets down there, he finds the bodies of his men scattered all about, but one of them is still alive, see. So the captain walks up to the guy, and the guy's barely able to speak. And he looks up at his CO and says *Capitan, Capitan, it was a trick—they was two of them.*"

Tom and John both laughed politely at a joke that wasn't funny the first time they'd heard it.

"*Capitan, Capitan,*" the old rancher repeated. "*They was two of them.*" And all chuckled again.

John said, "Hey Walter, we're out here trying to hunt up two kids. My Mandi and this fellow's boy kind of got away from us yesterday."

Miller looked to the ground and scratched at the dirt with the toe of his boot, finally realizing, perhaps, that John Monahan was five miles into the wrong state.

"I'll be damned," Miller said. "And you think they come this far past the line."

"That old black cat's back in the country," Tom explained.

"You guys was chasing Pete, huh? I wish somebody'd finally get that old bastard. He killed three of my bull calves last year."

"Well," John said. "We think those kids got on to him and chased him into your part of the country here or down into Mexico."

"Damn sure could be," Miller said, spitting between his boots, thumbs hitched into the front pockets of his jeans. Then he appeared to have made up his mind the visit was over and climbed back on his horse. "Tell you what," he said in parting. "I'll damn sure keep an eye open for them."

When Miller had left, Tom and John waited another hour for the rest to show. After thirty minutes they were hopeful, after forty-five worried, and when the hour was up, they went looking. They found them low in the canyon, on the north side of the south ridge. On first spotting them, both men pulled their rifles from saddle scabbards— the rest of their party had gained two more people, both Hispanic men. But Russ raised both arms and shouted, "Don't! Hold up, you guys."

Closer, they saw the two strangers' hands were bound behind their backs and both women appeared unharmed, standing beside their respective mounts. When they'd closed the distance, Tom and John scabbarded their arms, dismounted, and eyed the two strangers, who stood handcuffed and bound at the elbows with a cotton rope some ten feet away.

"What the hell?" Tom said.

"*¿Podemos sentarnos?*" asked one of the bound Mexicans, but his query went ignored.

"*Necesitamos agua,*" said the other. He sounded more desperate.

"*Cállense,*" Yolanda said to both of them.

John Monahan looked at his wife. "What in the hell is this about?"

It was then that they noticed the fresh red gash on Russ's left cheek. It was about an inch and a half long and looked something like a closed eye. Russ touched at the skin just below the wound and winced slightly, then gestured toward the two bound Mexicans. "That kid in the blue jacket did it," he said, "with the butt end of a pistol."

Just after they'd split, Russ had glassed up something unusual in the bottom of the canyon. Through the binoculars, it appeared to be a duffle bag or backpack of some sort, and while he had seen such items before left by migrants, this was notable because the bag seemed new and not weather-beaten, as usually was the case. The thing appeared full of something. He'd tried to make the women stay while he went down to look, but they would have none of it.

When they'd neared the bottom, Russ insisted that the women stay up slope some twenty yards while he went to check the object. It turned out to be a backpack, brand new, and even before he opened it, he knew what was inside for the shape of its cargo and the sweet smell. That's when all went black and a cold pain shot from his cheek to the back of his head. When he came around a few seconds later, he thought he'd taken a bullet—but realized he was in too much pain to be dead.

Both women had already piled their mounts through the brush and down to the wash. Yolanda had crossed on her gelding and Teresa stayed this side, flanking the two Mexicans who, in desperate flight, were crashing down the wash the best they could afoot, having unloaded backpacks and drinking water, everything but their pistols. Teresa beat them to the bend in the creek bed and pulled up her bay mare thirty yards ahead of them. She drew her .243 from its scabbard and hopped off her horse, aiming the rifle as if at a target a mile away. "*Alto...Abajo!*" she shouted. For some reason, neither man challenged but stood there stunned—dumbfounded—until Yolanda, now behind them, chambered a shell in her .270 and both men went to their knees, still holding their guns.

Russ, hatless and holding his bleeding face, had made his way to the scene. "Don't kill 'em," he said to the women.

"Why not?" Yolanda asked.

"Just don't pull that trigger, Yole. You neither, Teresa."

Teresa's teal-colored eyes were wide and her jaw set, her fedora-like Stetson cocked forward on her brow, her feet planted apart. "I'd like one good reason why not," she said.

"*Suelten las armas,*" Russ said to the two men. Neither seemed to hear him. From behind them, Russ could tell both men were quite young, in their early twenties, with thick dark hair and typically wide

Indio shoulders. "*Suéltenlas*," he said more firmly. Finally, the one on the left, perhaps the younger, turned his head slowly to the other, who returned the look and the both of them carefully laid their pistols, both cheap Saturday-night specials, in the sand of the wash.

Russ, silent and struggling to endure the throbbing in his face, cuffed the men quickly and pulled them to their feet as the women, unwavering, held them at gunpoint. Russ was at a loss. Should he reproach them for putting themselves in danger? Trot off the usual things he would say to a partner in a bust? Thank them for maybe saving his life? Instead he said nothing, gathered up the two cheap pistols, and led the boys back to their backpacks full of high-grade pot.

They'd had little time to discuss the situation, and the decision had been a quick one. The four parents would ride back through the mountains, the way they'd come, to the trucks. If they moved fast, it would be only about an hour dark when they arrived, but everyone had flashlights, and Thomas had thought to bring an extra set of batteries. If they were careful, and lucky, none of the mounts would wind up with a broken leg or cut up from barbed wire. And, as they had all day, they would periodically call out the names of the two lost kids.

Russ would take the smugglers through the lower hills to the main road some two miles north, where he could probably radio someone from the Hidalgo County sheriff's department. He granny-knotted a twenty-foot length of cotton rope where the two Mexicans were joined at the elbow, then dallied the other end to his saddle horn. He had the two walk ahead of him, directing them through the easiest route back to the road. The two heavy backpacks were awkwardly roped to his horse's rump behind the saddle. It had taken them over an hour, but just before 5:00 p.m. the two smugglers sat resting and bound on the gully brow of the Guadalupe Trail county road and Russ was on his radio. And, for an hour out of one afternoon, anyway, a little luck came to Russ Billman, a man for whom good fortune had been a stranger a long time.

The first person he heard on the radio was Joanne Roberts, the dispatcher at the Hidalgo sheriff's central office. He'd known the girl's father for twenty years. At first she'd been officious, but when she realized she was talking to Russ Billman, her tone softened. "Russ! My god," she said. "I was still in high school the last time I saw you." She asked after Becky, his oldest daughter and her high school friend, and Russ, of course, reciprocated, asking about her people. Could she put him through to her father? Sure. No problem. He was off-duty now but would love to hear from an old friend.

George Roberts answered his radio immediately on hearing Russ's voice, perhaps for the two-thousandth time, over the speaker. "Come back, Deputy Billman."

"Hey George," Russ said. "Got a favor. A big one."

"*Dígame*, mister," George said. "Just say it, and it's done."

It was well after dark before George Roberts and his daughter Joanne arrived from Animus. Russ watched the headlights of the two vehicles as they coursed their way through the mountainous convolutions of the Guadalupe Trail. He was grateful to his old friend and partner. It was at least a two hour drive to the spot he and the two Mexicans sat. The perps, both asleep now, snored loudly, not terribly dangerous young men the way Russ had figured them, but they had made a mistake and would do well-deserved time.

As the vehicles came within a few hundred yards, Russ waved his flashlight.

The two pickup trucks pulled off to the shoulder, one of them an older Dodge with a single-horse trailer in tow. Joanne Roberts left her headlights on, and Russ got a clear look at her as she strode up to him. She had been a lanky, rawboned girl and had turned out to be a fine-looking woman. Long dark hair pulled back to reveal an unembellished beauty, she wore Wrangler jeans, a cotton sweater, and hiking boots.

"Hey there big guy," she said as she hugged him.

"Wow," Russ said. "You've grown up."

Joanne put her hands on his shoulders, cocked her head, squinted at the cut on his cheek.

Russ pointed to the boys. "Kid on the left," he explained. "Hit me with a cheap pistol."

George walked up and stood behind his daughter, flipboard in hand, ready of long habit to do the paperwork needed in a call. He had aged, gotten fatter. Though a big man and former athlete like Russ, he hadn't the penchant for keeping himself in shape.

"What the hell are you doing arresting our New Mexico criminals," he said. "You're supposed to be busting Arizona punks. These here are mine. Besides that," he pointed to Russ's face, "they're beating the crap out of you, anyway."

Russ walked up and extended his hand. "You're too fat and lazy to write a parking ticket, let alone chase dope runners."

George shook his hand, then affectionately put the crook of his arm around Russ's neck. "I suppose you're right. Say, you still look good for an old man," he said, gently tightening his grip. He stepped up to the Mexicans, now awake and sitting up. In Spanish, he asked why such fine young men as they seemed to be would want to make bad things happen to themselves. The boys looked at the ground, shamefaced. George poked at one of the backpacks with the toe of his boot.

"Hell, man," he said. That's a lot of pot."

"Good stuff, too," Russ said, "by the smell of it."

George pointed at the Dodge with the trailer. "I'll pick that up at that big shindig we have at the college in December. You'll find a warm twelve-pack of the cheapest beer I could find in the cab, too. On me."

Russ's relationship with George predated his journey through the twelve-step program and failed attempts at recovery, though Russ was grateful at the gesture nonetheless. He felt the tightening in his belly that came when his body chemistry called out for alcohol.

"I thank you much."

"I thank you," George came back. "I'm getting credit for a hell of a good bust here."

"For that truck and trailer, and a good night's sleep, I'll trade you out any time," Russ said, and felt his old friend's good-hearted grin through the darkness.

And now, three hours later, as Russ tried to find sleep after a long day whose events had pushed his emotional pains aside, his heart yielded to a dawning truth—Rachael was not coming back to him. For months, he had entertained the fantasy that he would wake in the night to her tentative footfalls, that she would slip off her clothes and slide into bed next to him, that the next morning the long nights of despair, the deepening loneliness, the hapless prospect of the twenty or so years left in his life (if he were lucky), would all be erased.

But again Rachael had not come, and Russ was left alone with his thoughts. He had his kids to live for—and of course the old devil drink that had gotten him here in the first place—but those two elements worked at cross purposes. His children tended to visit less when he was drinking. Their message was a good and wise one—if he would quit, they'd become a bigger part of his life. He'd learned in his fifty years that tradeoffs—about things that mattered, anyway—were hard as well as inevitable.

He thought about his relationship with Teresa McNally eight years before. God, she was a beautiful woman, far more attractive than Rachael, but Russ had realized from the first that theirs was a short-term hitching. He could feel it on her when he held her—that distance, an expression on her face when she looked at her kids that would never be directed at him. It was an atmosphere she wore about her person that was almost palpable, born of the dozen years she had built a life with another man. Russ remembered for an illuminated moment that ten-year-old kid, the boy, the oldest, who never left her side. He was a quiet, smart kid, and anyone who looked at him could see he would get by in life—more than get by.

No, Teresa, he thought. *I've never had a kid lost or in danger, but I know what pain is. That drag-footed devil is no stranger to me.*

Some twenty miles east, four worried parents tried to find rest. The Hallots and McNallys had taken up the offer to sleep in the ranch bunkhouse—a misnomer, really, for the place was eight-hundred square feet with two bedrooms, one and a half baths, and a full kitchen, more of a semi-fancy guesthouse.

Teresa McNally, despite how much she had drunk, had not yet closed her eyes. She noted how a person in grief did not remember the whole of the lost loved one, but bits and pieces, like television sound bites.

This held true for all four parents. Glen recalled how Mandi shook the first time she'd gotten on a bucking calf. He'd leaned over the shoot and told her this was just practice, that she'd gotten the feel for rigging up, and there would be no shame in quitting now—she could go the whole ride next time. But the twelve-year-old shook her head stubbornly. When the gate opened she'd only lasted four of eight seconds, but her father was proud. And tonight he'd wondered how someone with such courage could not yet be alive.

Yolanda, beside him, recalled Mandi's love for a hairless doll when she was five. When the family's new lab puppy chewed it up, dismembering it, the child grieved for a week. After that, though, Mandi seemed to harden, never mentioning the doll or wanting another. Strange, the things one remembers about a person.

Tom McNally had been the first among the parents to fall asleep, perhaps because of his confidence in his son's abilities. Kevin had always shown an uncanny wherewithal as an outdoorsman. Even at ten years old, when he started hunting with his father, he had an almost primal sense of the cardinal directions, a built-in accuracy in judging distances, and a natural eye with any sort of weapon. The boy was a month shy of eighteen, but his father held more faith in his survival abilities than those of most men he knew.

Kevin's mother, though, the only one yet awake, had not thought about Kevin's skill in the outdoors, but, strangely, his penchant for words, spoken and written language. He was four when she'd first sensed it, as the boy, when friends or family would visit, often broke from his play with other children to listen in on the conversations of the adults gathered in living room or kitchen. He would sit discretely in a corner, looking back and forth between the conversing grownups. One evening, when Teresa held the women's church group at their house, the child crawled onto the couch next to his mother and sat, apparently contented, through the entire meeting.

This gathering included some dozen ladies, and the topic was drunk driving laws, as one woman had lost her husband in such an accident a few years before. Consensus had it that a letter should be written to the state congressman or senator, and everyone agreed that Teresa should be its author.

"Easily done," she said. "I can have it sent by Monday."

Later that evening, she found her four-year-old son in his bedroom. He was doodling in his coloring book with a green crayon, and repeating aloud the phrase, *easily done, easily done, easily done . . .*

Twenty-Two

When the patrol car pulled out behind him, Kevin dismissed the thought that he'd violated any traffic law. He'd left the library in a calm fashion, easing out into the sparse Sunday noon traffic, even clicking on his turn signal. He felt the alcohol, residual under his skin, but certainly he was not drunk, driving well within the speed limit and safely in his lane. Another glance in his rearview mirror showed the cop behind him, closer now, within twenty feet of his bumper. When the lights flashed on, their unnerving flicks of blue and red, he had a moment's doubt those lights were meant for him.

Kevin lowered his window, but the young officer asked him to step out of the car before he could speak a word. Instinctively, he took the papers he'd stolen out of his waist band and tucked them under his seat before opening the driver's side door. The cop, M. Rosales by his name tag, glanced at Kevin's driver's license before handing it back to him.

"Dr. McNally, do you know why I pulled you over today?"

Kevin crossed his arms, leaned against his car. "Enlighten me."

The cop took a step back. "Sir," he said, "I'd like you to step away from your vehicle."

Kevin tipped away from the car, glanced back as though it may be contaminated. "How'd you know to call me doctor?"

The young officer could not have been more than thirty, his bullet-proof vest giving the trunk of his upper body more apparent heft, and he ignored the question. His collar radio crackled, a staticy voice at the other end. He tipped his head, answered back in some code. "Sir," he said. "Please place your hands on the top of the vehicle."

"I thought you said I couldn't touch it."

"Sir," the young cop said, his eyes softening a bit as his confidence blanched. "Please do as I ask."

Kevin had waited in the holding cell almost half an hour now, the plastic wrist binding too tight. The charge had been DUI, but he hadn't even been given a field sobriety test. In the room-length, two-way mirror stood a personage he could not bear to look at. The jeans and T-shirt he wore had not been washed in days, his hair grease-tangled and bed-flattened, his black eye yellowed at the edges and spreading past the cheekbone. When two men in plain clothes came in, Kevin was standing in front of the security camera contemplating whether he should scream at it or try to kick something over the lens like he'd seen people in movies do. One of the cops, older and thin with a tangle of gray hair that needed a trim, held a wireless phone. The other, perhaps in his late thirties, already sported a sizable dough-nut belly that obscured the top of his khaki Dockers.

"Good afternoon, Dr. McNally," the younger one said.

"I'd like my breathalyzer test now," Kevin said, as though ordering a drink at a restaurant.

The older man held up the phone. "We thought you might want to call someone later."

"Well, thank you," Kevin said. "Your hospitality amazes."

The cops looked at each other, then back at him, unsure how to take the comment.

"As does your reputation for honesty, integrity, and generally running a tight ship."

The cops' faces clouded, and the younger one stiffened with anger.

The phone, obviously, was a peace offering. Kevin shook his head, and looked at the ceiling. For a moment he thought he might cry. "You can't hold me here. You didn't give me a field sobriety test, so you have no probable cause."

"So we've got a proper lawyer here, huh?" the younger one said.

Kevin glared at him, the second time in two days he'd wanted to knock the shit out of someone. He glanced at the older cop. "I see you all have a whiz kid in your midst."

"I'm getting a little sick of this, George," the young man said to his colleague.

"Settle down, Derrick," the older cop said. He looked at Kevin. "We'd just like to have a talk, Dr. McNally."

"Well," Kevin said. "I appreciate your being so polite about it. "

The older cop hung his head in exasperation. The younger one wanted to beat on him with a night stick.

"I wouldn't have blown over the legal limit when you pulled me over. I damn sure won't now."

"Well," the older cop—George—said, friendly, as though chatting with an acquaintance he'd run into. "You'd be surprised how little it takes." His glasses were the next-to-invisible type, which Kevin hadn't noticed he wore until now.

Kevin looked down at his feet, wishing like hell his hands were free. He looked up at the cops. "Let me think about that." He lowered his brow in mock contemplation. "Seems a little like—I don't know— bullshit? I guess?"

George jerked his head, surprised at Kevin's temerity. His diplomacy was false, his condescension infuriating. "The officer smelled alcohol on your breath. You were acting erratic, and quite frankly you look homeless. I think we're helping you out here. I could get that restraint off you. We could have a talk, and you could make a phone call. Go on about your day."

"Hum," Kevin said. "Let me think about that again." He looked at the floor, sniffed the air, then looked back up at the cops. "Nope—still bullshit."

The cops looked at each other again. "Dr. McNally," the younger one, Derrick, said. "We'd like to be able to take off the wrist binds and sit, have a discussion."

These cops were desperate. It crackled on the air between them. He looked toward the pitiful little table, its four mismatched folding chairs. "This isn't about drunk driving," he said. He'd figured it out the moment he spoke the words, and he could feel his heartbeat now.

"We'd like to talk," George said.

"You have to test my blood alcohol," Kevin said. "If I'm under the legal limit, you have to let me go."

Derrick looked at his watch and smiled. "We have forty-five minutes—legally."

"What do you guys want?"

"To find some things out," George said. "Perhaps come to some kind of agreement—or understanding, at least."

Kevin felt faint, his mouth dry and head pounding. "My God. You guys are talking about the shootings at the Escrobarra."

Derrick took a step toward him. "This doesn't need to be about the violation of any law," he said, indicating the wrist bindings.

"Yeah," Kevin said, "it's about extortion."

George let out a breath, looked at his watch. "Derrick," he said, "what are the criteria for assault charges again? Seems to me there was a call a couple nights ago about a guy beating the shit out of Lester Johns. We probably have enough to make an arrest."

Derrick pulled one of the folding chairs away from the table, sat down. "Dr. McNally, we have the legal ability to keep you here, but we'd really like to be civil about this."

Kevin could see the name on his chest tag: Derrick Waylon. The name buzzed in the back of his head. It had emerged soon after the incident, and periodically in the three decades since. He shut his eyes tight, searched out a context, but it was hidden, as behind the blind spot from a camera flash.

"Waylon," he said, finally. "That name…"

"We wanted to talk to you about my father," Derrick said. "Philip Waylon."

"Yes," Kevin said. "Philip Waylon. I've heard that name, but…I'm not even sure who that is."

Derrick stood from his chair and took a quick step toward Kevin. George grabbed him by the shoulder.

"Easy," he said. "Easy, Derrick."

Derrick's chest was heaving, eyes reddened, fists tight. "Don't know who he was, motherfucker?"

"Derrick," the older cop barked. "Get your shit together, goddamn it. He might not remember."

Derrick glared at Kevin, shook his head, and walked to the wall where he leaned, palms down, breathing hard.

"My apologies, Dr. McNally," George said. "Derrick's father, Philip, was killed thirty-two years ago."

"I'm sorry," Kevin said, and meant it. "I'm sorry, Derrick."

The young cop, still facing the wall, shook his head.

"Russ Billman," Kevin said suddenly.

"What about him," George said.

Derrick turned from the wall.

"I'd consider talking to him." Kevin arched his back, flexed his shoulders. The wrist binding was becoming intolerable. "Is he still alive?"

"Yeah," George said, "but he retired from the county a long time ago."

"Well," Kevin said, "if you could get him down here, I'd talk to him—alone."

George looked toward Derrick. "Wasn't he up in Flagstaff at that AA thing?"

"He's back, I'm pretty sure," Derrick said. "I saw him and Rachael a couple days ago at Safeway."

"Call him." The older cop seemed to have made up his mind. "If he doesn't answer, get a hold of Rachael, find out where he is." He stood from the table, stepped up to Kevin and deftly released the wrist binds. He gestured toward the phone. "You can call someone if you like, but they'll have to wait. Or," he said, "I'd be happy to give you a ride back to your car whenever you're finished talking to Russ."

"Thanks," Kevin rubbed his wrists, his skin impressed with the ribs on the plastic ties. "I guess."

The older man placed the wireless phone on the table, and Kevin glanced at his name tag: George Meeker. "Go ahead and make a call, if you like," George said.

Kevin picked up the phone and dialed a 411 search, asked for Ben Conchillo in Douglas. When Conchillo answered, Kevin stammered a moment before he was able to explain his situation. He sensed, though, that Conchillo already knew about the arrest. He said they would talk about it later.

"It doesn't matter if it's dark out when we do it," the old man said. "It might be better that way."

"I may have to bow out, in that case," Kevin told him.

"Bull*shit*!" Conchillo said on the other end. "I'll send someone to get you."

"No," Kevin said. "One of the cops said he'd give me a ride."

"Okay," the old man said, "but if you don't come back, I'll go hunting for you."

"They're trying to save themselves embarrassment," Russ said. "They jack off all day and don't have anything better to worry over. Pisses me off."

Kevin sat across the table from Russ who, though still a big man, had lost some mass in his older years. He looked good, though, in his new cotton shirt and Wranglers, not a day over seventy, commendable considering how many years he'd spent drinking himself into a stupor. When the two cops had walked him into the room, Kevin recognized him at once. His demeanor, though, was now more benign, that of a kindly, churchgoing cowboy. The square shoulders had rounded, the angles of his face grown softer. He bore a thirty-two-year-old scar, two inches long, across his left cheek. Kevin's skin tingled at the sight of it. When they shook hands, Russ grabbed both of his. "God, you look like the ghost of old Thomas," he said.

"They probably can hear you, Russ," Kevin pointed out.

"I don't give a shit," the old man said. He looked up at the security camera. "Do you hear that, Meeker? I don't give a rat's ass."

"You have any idea what they want from me?" Kevin asked.

"Yeah," Russ nodded. "I know damn well what they want from you. They don't want you to go to the press with anything you remember about Philip Waylon."

"Why's that?"

This gave Russ pause. He squinted at Kevin. "What *do* you remember?"

"Not much."

Russ struggled to stand, pushing up on the table. Kevin rose, rounded the table and took his arm, intent on helping him.

"No, goddamnit," the old man said. "I can get up."

"Fine," Kevin said, removing his grip on Russ's upper arm. "Where are you going?"

"I'm going to get those bastards to turn off their hardware." He looked at Kevin. "We need to talk private about this. Off the damn record."

Russ came back into the holding cell as though on a mission. He sat down across from Kevin then looked over his shoulder and around the room. "I hope those bastards aren't lying about the cameras and shit. I told them to turn it off."

"What the hell is this about?" Kevin asked.

"It's about Philip Waylon," Russ said.

"They told me he'd been killed."

Russ looked at him, studying his face. "I wasn't right there the whole time, so I can't say what happened from my own seeing."

Kevin leaned back in his chair. "I don't get it," he said.

"Waylon wasn't working with the good guys." Russ jerked his head toward the two-way mirror. "That little bastard in there was spoilt rotten on the dirty money his daddy made. If it was his daddy at all, rumor has it." Russ looked up at the two-way. "Hear that, Derrick," he said loudly. "If he *was* your daddy..."

Kevin narrowed his eyes, a flash of memory flickering forth like old footage.

"That's why they don't want you talkin', Kev," Russ said. "The feds and state police jimmied the report way back when to make it look like he was on the up and up in the deal, that he'd been out on routine rounds and got caught up in the thing. Hell, the son of a bitch didn't even have a uniform on."

Kevin felt fixed in place, the room slowly turning. "Why are they so interested in me?"

"You were there. You were the one closest to the whole thing. Anybody else around is dead or paid off not to talk. That was the word, anyway."

"How did Waylon die?"

Russ's face hollowed. "Not for me to say."

"Why not?"

"I's two hundred yards away, hiding under my damn truck. I don't have much trade with any gossip I heard, nor memory neither."

Kevin wished he had a cigarette. "You got a smoke, by any chance?"

"Copenhagen," Russ said, reaching for his back pocket.

"That's okay," Kevin said, waving off the offer. Several moments of silence passed. "I'm working on piecing things together for myself," he said, finally.

Russ's face softened. "I'm sorry you still have to suffer this."

"Me, too. How's Emma?"

"Oh, she's good," Russ said. "Up in Phoenix. Three kids, all grown."

Kevin nodded. Em was the only one of Russ's kids he remembered, or he would have asked after the others. "Who all'd they pay off?"

Russ closed his eyes, a sort of wince. "Again, not for me to say."

"We're talking about people close to me here, Russ."

Russ leaned forward, fixed a look on him. "All I know is old gossip." He pointed toward the two-way mirror. "You think those chicken-shit bastards are going to tell you anything?"

Kevin leaned back. He wanted a drink. "How about whiskey. You got any of that?"

Russ smiled. "It's times like this I wish I did. Going on twenty-five years now."

"Good for you," Kevin said.

"Well," Russ leaned back, appearing to have reached some resolution. "Let's go tell those little pricks you're not gonna tattle on 'em."

Kevin glanced up at the camera, a reflex really, and wondered how many years it had hung in that corner, what secrets it had captured behind its dead, unerring eye.

Twenty-Three

Just after five o'clock they came into view of the camp, the two boys just ahead of her and Amanda riding Dunk, the mule tired and thirsty and anxious. With her own cotton rope, Amanda's hands had been tied to the saddle horn. Her fingers had stiffened at the joints and ached terribly, though pain came second to her fear. The boy called Chingo held the mule's reins while the other, Billy, stepped up to the men at the camp fire. Amanda so wished to get off the mule but didn't dare speak or even move but to breathe. She waited for her next orders, listening discreetly to the men's conversation, and even in her terror and fatigue called up the sense to hide the fact that she spoke Spanish as well as any of them.

"It is without good reason," the older man said for the second time. He was about her father's age, perhaps a couple years younger. "You are idiots."

"It was chance," Billy explained. "She walked straight to us. Did you want us to kill her without permission?"

The man shook his head, glanced up at Amanda, then back at the campfire. "Get her off, Chingo," he said to the white boy.

Chingo reached up and touched her elbow. "Get off," he said in English.

She pulled her right foot out of the stirrup and wheeled her leg over the saddle horn and mule's head, then slid, gently as she could, to the ground, the bones in her feet shooting with pain for lack of blood. Something told her not to look directly at any of them.

"Come here," the graying man said in English.

Chingo pushed her from behind. "What are you, retarded, bitch? Do what he says."

Amanda took five short steps and stood within six feet of the man. Still, she would not look up at him.

"What are you doing on my land?" the man asked in English.

The question confused her. She knew well these men were smugglers. The ruse—that he might be a rancher and these punks his *vaqueros*—was ridiculous.

Chingo popped her so hard on the ear that the blow almost took her to the ground. "Answer, goddamn it."

But she could call up no reply, for the ringing in her right ear.

"Don't hit," the older man said in Spanish, like a father scolding his quarrelsome children. He motioned the girl to step closer, and she complied. Gently, he brushed back an errant strand of her honey-colored hair. "Why are you on my property, pretty girl?" he asked.

"Hunting," she said. It was the first time she had spoken in over two hours.

"Well, you are trespassing."

The man's voice was smooth, like quality chocolate.

"How much Spanish do you understand?" Another man, one she had not yet noticed, asked the question in Spanish. He was big, stocky like football players she'd known.

Amanda squinted at him. Her ruse had worked. The big man glanced at the graying man and nodded, seeming satisfied that she had not understood.

The graying man lifted her chin. "Listen to me," he said. "How long do you want to live?"

Amanda chose not to dignify this with an answer. The graying man smiled, and the grin seemed genuine. He was handsome and reminded the girl of her eighth-grade science teacher, Mr. Renaldi.

"If you want to live," he said, "you'll need to play nice."

Amanda's throat tightened and she looked at the ground, but the man again, with a gentle index finger, lifted her chin. He touched his fingertips to her cheek and ran his thumb along her lips. Amanda felt she would vomit.

The man squinted at her, the same way her father did when he wanted to be taken seriously. "Tonight I'm going to untie your hands, but in return you have to be nice. Do you understand?"

Amanda looked down again, and again the man lifted her chin, less gently this time. "Do you understand me?"

The girl, unable to speak, nodded her head.

He was cupping her chin now, and, as if caressing the muzzle of a dog, ran his fingers down the length of her jaw. "I'll make it nice for you," he said. "I promise."

The fifteen-year-old girl had contemplated sex very little in her short life. She'd kissed several boys passionately and even succumbed to heavy petting once, but actual sex lay only in the realm of remotest possibility. Bashful thoughts of the act were always attended by elaborate fantasy—long courtships, presents, and promises leading up to one special night.

The man's face clouded, his gaze fixed on something over her shoulder, and he moved quickly away from her. "Get it!" he enjoined in Spanish.

In a moment, all seven men were running the same direction, chasing Dunk, who, untied, had decided to flee and was now at a solid gallop north.

"Run, Dunk," Amanda shouted. "Run, baby."

The white boy, Chingo, who still held the mini 14, was ahead of the rest. He came to a stop, raised the rifle awkwardly. It was obvious he had never fired one before. He aimed for less than a second, popping off six quick rounds, the bullets whizzing into the empty dusk. Dunk, unharmed, mended his pace to a slow lope and disappeared into the thicket.

The men stood twenty yards from camp, each of them chasing his breath. The boy, Billy, was the first of them to speak. "Sorry, Ise. He just took off."

Ise looked over at the stocky one. "What do you think, J.C. You know farm animals."

J.C. shook his head. "We'd better go find him—he'll go back to where he started."

"Ralph," Ise said, between breaths.

A boy Amanda had not noticed before stepped up closer, awaiting orders. In his faded green shirt and jeans, he seemed the quietest and least excitable of the five boys.

Ise looked at him. "Take Chingo's rifle. Go find it and kill it. Try to use one shot."

Amanda ran toward the men, her bound hands now seeming almost a normal condition. "No," she said. "Please no."

"Why didn't you fucking tie her to a tree?" Billy said to Chingo.

"She ain't going nowhere, man," Chingo answered. "Don't worry about it."

Amanda walked up to the graying man, Ise, the leader. "Don't kill Dunk. Please, Ise."

The others laughed at her spunk for calling him by his name. But he was listening now, and the girl used the opportunity. "He wants water," she said. "He's headed for that tank about a mile to the northwest. No way anybody can see him, and he can't jump the border fence, anyway." She nodded toward Billy and Chingo. "They restrung the wire after we crossed."

Ise was bent over with hands on knees, still chasing his breath. He looked over at J.C. "What do you think?"

The other man, at a loss, shrugged.

"It's almost dark," Amanda added. "It wouldn't be worth your time."

"Oh, we've got a smart little bitch now," Chingo said.

"Shut up," Ise shot back. He looked at the girl. "You make a good point." He looked around at the six other men and addressed them in Spanish. "My plan has not changed. Tomorrow we go to the meeting place we had planned, but we will need to leave earlier because we'll have to take a different route, a longer one."

One of the boys, who seemed to be the youngest, kicked at the dirt and shook his head. His hair had been shaved to stubble, and he looked as though he considered himself the toughest among them.

"*Andale*," Ise came back fiercely, his expression suddenly soured. He aimed his glare directly at young Paco. "Are you crying little boy? I don't comfort *llorones*, I just shoot them. You know what I'm telling you?"

Paco did not look up.

"Billy!" Ise barked, and quickly Billy stepped up. He still carried the carbine. Ise took the rifle from him and chambered a shell, then aimed at the complainer, seventeen-year-old Paco. "You boys watch and learn," he said. "This is how my employees are terminated."

Terrified, Paco raised his hands. All the bad-boy posturing cultivated in the last few years had vanished. He was ten years old again.

"*Por favor, Ise*," his older brother, Miguel, pleaded. "*No dispares*"

But Ise ignored him. He had not taken his eyes off Paco. "Look down at the ground," he told the boy in English.

His chin twitching, Paco was close to tears.

"Look down at the ground, I said."

The boy shook so badly now he seemed scarcely able to stand, but after a moment he did as he was told. And now the sobs came, head bent down and hands still shoulder high.

Ise went back to Spanish. "Does that look like a good grave site? That dirt under your shoes?"

Paco shook his head.

"If you complain again, the ground you're standing on is where your brother will bury you. Do you understand?"

The boy nodded.

Ise raised the rifle, clicked on the safety, and handed it back to Billy. "Look up at me now, *chamaco,*" he said gently. "You're a good kid, but you need to learn you can bleed. *Bueno?*"

The boy nodded. "*Bueno,*" he said quietly.

"Okay," Ise said, as though a school-yard squabble had just been settled with a handshake. "No more beer tonight, *chamacos.* You guys will need your sleep."

Ise felt more relaxed now that things had settled. The others all in bed now, he and J.C. sat talking by the fire embers. Everyone had eaten a little more before retiring, and Billy had even managed to feed the girl a few bites of steak before she finally shook her head. Ise could see that the boy was soft on her. Before slipping off to bed in the canvas tent where the other four boys slept, Billy had put his jacket over the girl's shoulders. When he and Chingo had returned to camp earlier, the mule and mounted blonde girl in tow, Ise had come very close to shooting the little *gabacha* right out of the saddle without ceremony. But something had stopped him. She was young, though the whore a few days before had been young, too. It was something else. Ise Leon was a born saver, forever putting coffee grounds in potted plants, reluctant to throw out the daily newspaper, fastidiously storing away any item that might be of later use; this girl, he sensed, was one of those items.

"I'll make him kill her if the time comes," Ise said quietly to J.C.

The girl, her back against the trunk of the sycamore she was tied to, was long asleep and well out of earshot.

"Shit, Ise, I don't want to hear about that."

"I don't want to either, J.C., but you can't ignore a mess."

They fell quiet. J.C. held a Corona he'd been nursing. He nodded toward the sleeping girl.

"What about tonight?"

"I'll cut her hands loose, zip her up in that big sleeping bag with me. She couldn't get out without waking me up."

J.C. nodded. "Well, man, if you can make her like you, she might be less likely to talk."

"No," Ise said. "I don't want to mess with her. I just want to make her think it's a possibility. Let it work on her. She's too young, anyway. Probably still a virgin. I'd be better off just to make her warm and comfortable."

J.C. took a sip of his beer, breathed through his teeth and shook his head. "Man, Ise, I don't want to have to put her down."

"I don't either. But I've done a lot of things I didn't want to do." Ise stood up. "We'll decide tomorrow."

Amanda woke next morning to the sound of men's voices in a heated debate. She ran her palms over her sore wrists and moved the joints to work the ache out. Her head rested on a pillow and the sleeping bag was warm and her stomach iced as she remembered the nightmare she'd woken into rather than out of.

"Goddamnit," one of the men said, perhaps for the tenth time. She could not put a face to the voice—that of a mature man, most likely Anglo.

"I can't believe this, Ise," he said. "I drive up here thinking everything is cool. Then this shit."

"We'll make the drop, man."

The men, speaking in low tones, were just outside the tent.

"You don't think somebody's looking for her?" the Anglo man said.

"What can they do when she's down here?"

"All kinds of shit. This is a kid, man. They'll have dogs and a chopper. It'll be a fucking mess. I think we need to bail."

There was a long silence. Ise finally spoke. "We back out now and we wait four months. And when did you say you fuckers were doing that big sting. We may not even be able unload this shit if you guys bust enough people."

The Anglo man sighed. "Shit, Ise. What do we do with her?"

"Let me worry about that. Think about it, Phil. The money. You can fucking quit this shit. Go to Kentucky and raise your horses. Never think about it again."

Amanda began to inventory her situation. She thought of ripping a hole in the back of the tent and trying to make a break for it. But her better sense, finally, had vetoed the idea as she realized she would run no more than ten steps before someone shot her in the back. She finally rose, noting that she was fully clothed, and poked her head out of the front flap of the tent.

Ise and the other man sat in the canvas chairs a few feet away. Both men jerked their heads toward her, and Ise put his hands on the chair arms as though readying himself to rise. The big man with him squinted hard at her. He was balding, big bellied and wore wire-framed glasses. "Do you know her?" Ise asked him.

The balding man shook his head.

"Have you ever seen this man before?" Ise asked Amanda.

Though the answer was no, for a moment the girl could not respond. The man was so typical, so physically average, she might have seen him a thousand times, his face never impressing itself in her memory. Finally, though, Amanda shook her head.

"Good," Ise said, and his tone sounded genuine. "That bodes well for you, *mija*."

Half an hour later, the party of nine people, separated into two vehicles, drove west on a rutted dirt road. Though the cargo and weight of the passengers had been divided roughly equally between the two Suburbans, still they sagged at their bumpers. Amanda sat in the back seat of the lead truck between the skinniest of the two boys, Paco and Miguel, whom she'd gathered were brothers. Neither boy had spoken a word to her. Each boy pressed himself as close to his respective door as possible and each looked out his window as though fascinated by the countryside.

Ise drove and cussed at every rock and rut in the rough trail. J.C. sat in the passenger's seat. Like the boys, the two men spoke neither to her nor each other. Her secret understanding of the Spanish language, though, had pulled together enough information that she had a rough idea of the smuggler's plan. Around midday they stopped for lunch at the crest of a tall saddle. The two older men sat in the shade of a large boulder eating burritos as the younger men played around, eating and throwing empty soda cans at each other until Ise told them to stop. At one point Billy walked to the lead Suburban and helped her out so she could stretch her legs. Amanda noted the mess they'd left, that they made no effort to clean it up. Her father would have been sorely tempted to shoot them on that alone. After thirty minutes, they loaded up again and began to drive the rough road.

Whatever their business, it would not happen today. They would make camp again tonight, as Amanda understood, in a well hidden canyon close to the border then make their transaction the next morning, for their connection, Rudy Chacon, couldn't arrive before 10:30. She'd overheard Ise and J.C. earlier that morning, and sensed, only with the briefest and most fleeting moment of hope, that she had one more day to live. But already her memory was calling up the prayers she'd learned years before at Bible camp. She would spend the day memorizing those prayers, so when the time came she could give them voice.

Twenty-Four

Conchillo's flatbed was stuck and the situation was not improving. Again, he jammed it into first and gunned it, the spinning, stationary tires flinging rocks and dirt, the truck inching evermore down the slope, away from the road. They'd unhitched the horse trailer before attempting the loose, rocky incline, and on Conchillo's second attempt to scale the hill, Kevin and Mondy had unloaded their mounts and saddled up. The old truck on its bald tires would not make it, and they had long since decided the corrals were no more than a two- to three-hour ride from where they stood.

"*Hay Jodido*," Conchillo cursed. He punched the gas, but the tires only sunk deeper into the loose dirt and rocks on the hillside.

"*Córtale*" Kevin shouted to him. *Shut it off!* He felt agitated, his head ringing from the whiskey the night before.

Mondy rode back to the ranch for the Handyman jack, which Conchillo could remember he kept in one of four different places. By the time Mondy had traveled the mile both ways, managed to find the jack and return, it was almost 7:30 a.m. It took half an hour, some cedar limbs, half a dozen flat, skillet-sized rocks, and a spate of profanities before the old flatbed was finally freed from where it had foundered on the hillside and turned toward home.

"No, no," Conchillo told them. "You go on ahead. I'll get back and saddle up old Lastima, catch up with you guys later. You'll need some help chooting it out with those vatos up there, jovenes. I have a feeling, anyway. I'll be there with my .30-30."

In their side satchels, Mondy and Kevin each carried a plastic baggy bulging with the old man's deer jerky and rock-hard biscuits, both canteens were full, mounts fed and watered, and Bonny had feasted on one of the dozen rabbits Conchillo had drying in the meat shed. Conchillo's less-than-reliable watch read just after 8:00 a.m., and before he ground the old Ford to a smoky, clattering start, he promised he would see them again sometime before dark. Kevin and Mondy smiled at each other, shook their heads as he drove back down the hill.

They headed west on the trail and for a long while neither one of them spoke. They had agreed they would not break from the road, which kept a fairly consistent altitude of oak, juniper, and pinion ridges whose south-facing aspects broke into clearings of grama and ladder back grass and Mexican broom. They rode almost an hour and found good shade on the lee side of a brushy ridge. The juniper grove they sat in stood at a precipice, a limestone cliff of about fifteen feet, so that as they breakfasted on jerky, the cuts and contours of the Peloncillos stretched out before them some ten miles to the northwest. Occasionally, they'd seen a Border Patrol chopper working the border several miles to the north and knew it was possibly searching for them, though the craft was just a tiny dot in the horizon, far too distant to signal.

Mondy raised his glasses, looking out at the farthest ridges. "Man," he said. "I don't think I recognize any of those hillsides."

"We're a long way from where we started," Kevin said. He tipped up his chin, gesturing due north. "That's the peak above Guadalupe, way up there. That chopper's flown over it twice."

"That's the peak? It looks different from this angle. So small."

"I'm pretty sure that's it."

Mondy lowered his glasses. "We're a fair distance from home, kid. No way those border patrols will see us before they go home."

"I know," Kevin said. "I wish we'd thought to bring some flares."

Mondy shook his head. "Man, they've got to be looking for us, or at least you and Mandi, anyway. They're gonna keep looking."

"Well," Kevin said, "judging from that high peak, we're about two miles or so into Mexico. I'm not sure they can cross the border to look for us, but I don't really know. And, hell, we're not even sure if that's Mandi with those guys, anyway. She may be at home eating breakfast right now."

"I think it's her," Mondy said. "I know your tone when you're sure. You had that tone yesterday." Mondy reached into the baggie on his lap and fished out a piece of jerky the width and length of a man's hand. "Shit," he said, "smartest kid in school, class of '77. Good looking, smart, white rich kids like you two. They should have called out the national guard by now."

"They might be getting pretty shook up. I'm not even officially missing until twenty-four hours passes."

Mondy chewed his jerky, swallowed. "It's been more than that," he said.

Kevin chose to ignore this. "I'm number eleven in a class of one-eighty-six. Big deal."

"I was number forty-one in a class of fifty."

"I thought you said you dropped out."

"I did, but I always knew my standing."

"I'd bet you didn't even know the number of kids in your class, let alone your standing."

Mondy bit off another piece of jerky. "Just shows you how much you don't know about me—how precise I am in ways."

"Have I told you today how full of shit you are?"

"Not yet."

"Consider it said."

They'd stopped for a midmorning rest when Kevin saw it. The spot was just a semblance of black at first, a hunkered form just below the skyline of a saddle a half-mile to the north. Mondy had been asleep some ten minutes, in which time Kevin had mounted his Zeiss on the tripod hoping to find a helicopter or signal flares somewhere in the northern distance. He looked at the black spot so long that his eyes blurred, making the object, whatever it was, appear to move. He pulled back and rubbed his eyes a moment, gave it another few seconds before he looked again. It was still in the same place, but the warming rays of the morning sun pulsed across the thing at that distance, caused it to appear in motion. *Nothing*, he thought. *Just a dark-colored rock or tree stump.*

Kevin lay back, put his head on his linked hands. He had slept maybe an hour or two last night, and the idea of a nap seemed inviting. He and Mondy had decided they would easily arrive at the corrals by the afternoon. Depending on how the traveling fared, and who may be looking for them, they may very well be home eating a good meal before sunset. Kevin held out the same hope for Amanda, that she would be with them at the table, laughing off a soon-to-be forgotten two-day debacle. His guts, though, told him otherwise. The smugglers were somewhere up ahead of them, moving the same direction, and an encounter with them was very likely.

He sat back up, intending to reposition himself on his side to sleep, and took a last look at the black spot on the ridge.

It had moved—decidedly, the object was twenty feet up slope. Kevin sat back, rubbed his eyes, looked again. The object was inarguably in motion, its long broadside form shaded just below the crest of the saddle.

Kevin woke his friend. "Pete," he said.

"You sure?"

"I'm sure."

They reached a canyon bottom two ridges north and still Mondy questioned his friend's perceptions, and even more Kevin's judgment for breaking from the trail. Mondy had tried to find the big cat in his own binoculars, but they were not strong enough. And when he'd borrowed Kevin's, he found them out of adjustment for his eyes and by that time Pete, or whatever it was, had moved on over the slope.

"We need to get back to the road," Mondy finally said. Even the animals seemed consternate, old Turk snuffling and stamping his feet, and Dunk and Sally reluctant to scale the next incline. Bonny, a few feet away, had sniffed at a spot of ground a few moments then looked up at them and whimpered.

"I just want to top that saddle," Kevin said. "Take a quick look at the other side. We can cut back to the road afterward."

"What if we can't?" Mondy said. "Then we have to backtrack and lose another hour and a half."

Mondy was right. To try to traverse unknown ridges horseback, especially in rough chaparral country, was foolish. Given their situation, going back to the road would have been their best option. Lingering with both of them was the conversation—in reflection almost surreal amid the haze-like effects of the alcohol—with Conchillo. *This animal will lead you.*

For the first time since Mondy had known him, Kevin's intuition had trumped reason. Mondy Luna knew it was a moment to relish, but the situation was pushing in at the edges, tightening vice-like around them. To figure this whole thing might turn out all right, with no harm done, was wishful thinking. But of course in the end the kid won. *Just one more ridge*, Kevin had pleaded, *a quick look, see if Bonny picks up the scent, then we get back on the road to home.* A twenty-dollar bet lay on the crest of that saddle. If Bonny hackled up, went crazy, was on for the chase, they would assume they'd come in old Pete's wake and Kevin would go home the richer man.

Twenty-Five

The wind out of the south had picked up, and they rode into the sun. Random, diffuse images appeared—movement, as in the edge of vision, people shouting, the adrenal sting in his belly. Then something fully formed: the heeler dog trotting beside them, the clomping of hooves, the blaze of sweat down the middle of Mondy's back as he rode ahead. What Kevin recalled most from this moment—visceral and urgent—was fear, the need to make haste, but to where and to what he couldn't tell. Often, his shouting to the dog was so vivid—*Bonny! Bonny!*—he could hear his own young voice, puny and impotent, as it echoed off the rocks behind him. And Mondy raising his hand to quiet him before the bullets whipped the air like hornets and popped the brush and rocks beyond.

Bonny, get back here. Bonny!

He felt a slight pressure on his thigh, a bumping, and he opened his eyes to see the old man's knuckles rapping lightly, like someone tapping on a door. He was aware now of the truck's rattling as its tires rumbled over the dirt road, the final bit of sunlight slanting through the back windshield on his neck. He shook himself.

"There's coffee in the thermos at your feet," Conchillo said, his stick-like arms seeming to barely manage the steering wheel.

Kevin looked down. On his lap were the papers he had lifted from the county archives, and he recalled willingly climbing into the truck with a man too old to drive. He shook his head in reproach, a bit of clarity about how much he'd short circuited lately, and remembered reading over the papers in his lap before he must have drifted off. He reached around to the floorboard, found the thermos.

"You talk loud in your sleep," the old man said. "It almost woke me up."

Kevin shook himself again, unscrewed the cap on the coffee. "Woke you up?" he said. "Shit, you're driving."

The old man chuckled. "Well," he said. "I reckon I am. Laugh, it's a good joke." He was quiet a moment, smiling. "You're right, *vato*. You don't have much of a sense of humor."

Kevin looked out the front windshield, the Perilla hills within a few miles, the Peloncillos beyond. They'd just passed Mormon wash and were veering up the long curve of road that cut through a mesquite and creosote *bajada* then out onto the Bernardino Valley, the same route Kevin had taken the day before. "Okay," he said. "Can you tell me again what the hell we're doing out here?"

"For the *Himdag*," the old man said. "Like I told you. You'll see."

Kevin poured a measure of coffee in the thermos cap. "You should let me drive."

"No," Conchillo glanced up at the rearview mirror. "That cop behind us might bust you again for drunk driving."

Kevin twisted to look out the back windshield. A half mile behind them, throwing up dust, was what appeared to be a truck or SUV. "That's a cop?"

"A sheriff's vehicle. That *cabron* followed us all the way out of Douglas."

"What the hell," Kevin said.

"It's from that Philip Waylon bullshit, I'm pretty sure," the old man said.

Kevin looked at him. "You knew about that?"

The old man nodded. "I wish I didn't."

Derrick Waylon was a city cop. Why would the county have any concern? "I don't get why the sheriff's deputy would follow us."

The old man shrugged. "My theory, for what it's worth, is that Russ Billman sent someone to make sure no one fucks with us."

Kevin laid his head back on the seat and watched the country change as they ascended. The sense of resignation, that he was no longer in control, was comforting. He was in it for the ride, and someone else, albeit a man brittle as kindling, was driving. Kevin sipped his coffee and resisted the impulse to question old Benny about his interpretation of *Himdag*, the desert peoples' way of life. It was a generalized O'odham term meant to overlay anything that had to do with prosperity, strength, wellbeing. *I could use a dose of that right now*, Kevin mused.

Just after they'd passed the Slaughter Ranch road, the old man clicked on his blinker and pulled over. He cut the engine and put both hands on the wheel, peering into the rearview mirror. The sun had just set, and nocturnal insects sounded through the open windows.

"What's up?" Kevin asked.

"Waiting for that cop," Conchillo said.

The cruiser, a Dodge SUV, slowed and pulled over behind them. Conchillo's hands had not loosed their grip on the steering wheel and his eyes stayed fixed on the side rearview. The passenger's-side door of the cruiser opened and Russ Billman himself struggled out. He grabbed the side frames of the door and pawed the ground with his boot, cussing at the driver, who'd tried to help him. Eventually, he emerged from the vehicle and came crunching up the gravel road toward them. When he reached the truck, he put his hands on the driver's side window frame, pretending he wasn't using it to hold himself upright. He looked inside, nodded a greeting at Kevin, then at the old man. He looked up the road as though to survey its worthiness. "Nice evening," he said.

Kevin and Conchillo nodded.

"I radioed Border Patrol, and this area is pretty clean right now." Russ poked his hand toward the southeast. "There's a two-man up at the mouth of Baker and another three teams in Cottonwood near the New Mexico border. Apparently it's been pretty quiet the last couple of nights. I think you guys are okay. Damn drug shit. Worse than ever, I suppose."

Kevin leaned over. "Is that the deal, Russ? You're concerned for us?"

"Well," Russ said, "that and I wanted to let your mom and sister know your whereabouts for sure. Kinda wanted to confirm you were in this vehicle."

"They called you?" Kevin asked with a rustle of irritation.

"Well," Russ said. He leaned his arms on the window frame, looked groundward, scraped a foot in the dirt. "They been worried as hell, and your mom was smart enough not to call the city police."

Kevin was a teenager before it had finally occurred to him that Russ and his mother had had a romantic involvement when he was ten. As a child that age, in the midst of emotional trauma, he'd formed a defense mechanism to shield from any such notion. Russ Billman was a towering hero figure of his childhood, come to help around the farm in his father's absence. For the few months that his parents had separated, Russ had been a proxy father to him, and Kevin was touched at the worry he sensed behind the stoic eighty-year-old eyes even now.

175

"Thanks, Russ," he said. "I appreciate it."

The old deputy nodded, looked up the road again. "Damn city police are just dirty as hell in all this. Damn thing's so tangled up you can't separate bad from good no more. They scare hell out of me—more than the dope runners themselves, I suppose."

"We're just taking a drive here, Russ," Conchillo said. "I got my .30-30 behind the seat in case anybody gives us trouble."

Kevin caught Russ's eye and they exchanged a smile. "You and that damn .30-30," the deputy said. Russ slapped the window frame lightly. "Well, I suppose this thing you guys are up to is important, whatever it is." He looked at Kevin, smiled. "I'll tell your mama you're in good hands."

"I thank you for it," Kevin said.

Russ looked at Conchillo. "Why don't you let him drive," he said, gesturing at Kevin. "You're ninety years old, you crazy old shit."

"I'm eighty-seven," Conchillo said. "According to my driver's license, anyway. You want to see it?"

Russ shook his head and glanced at Kevin, who shrugged.

"I tried," Kevin said.

Russ tongued the wad of Copenhagen out of his mouth and spit it on the ground. "Crazy old bastard," he said, then on stiff legs turned and made his way back to the cruiser, where the bemused young officer who'd been brow beaten into driving him waited patiently.

A good time to glass for deer, Kevin thought, an impulse he had not had in a long time. They were in the lower west hills of the Peloncillos, almost dark, and the canyons lay bedded in their shadows. The gas gauge on the old man's truck was broken and the needle lay below the E, but Conchillo had assured him more than once that he'd filled the tank that morning. It was no longer light enough to read the pages on his lap, though they had told him little. Reading his own account, however, had brought a clearer memory of his seventeen-year-old self. That Sunday afternoon was the most humbling day of his life, from cocky kid to scared little boy, and that's the persona the state police got, their questions answered with "I don't know," and "I couldn't tell." The shock of such an event on one so young was understandable, and Kevin, for the briefest of moments, his head lulling on the back of the seat as the truck rumbled forth, entertained the idea of forgiving himself.

The old man nudged his shoulder to offer him something wrapped in a paper napkin. "Take one."

Kevin opened the napkin to find a stack of oatmeal cookies. Gladly, he lifted one from the stack and ate it in two bites, chased it down with coffee. They drove on, Kevin leaning back against the seat, trying to doze. "That was a good cookie," he said. "Tasted kind of different, like it's got cumin in it or something."

"A gram of *peyote*," the old man said. "Gives a pretty good flavor. Earthy."

"Funny," Kevin said. "See, I do have a sense of humor."

Conchillo shrugged. "Don't freak out when you start feeling it."

Kevin looked at him. "You can't be serious."

Conchillo stared straight ahead.

"You *are* serious. God damn, you old son of a bitch. Pull over."

"Why?"

"I'm going to puke it out."

"Won't do any good," the old man said. "It's already in your system. Besides that, you'll probably puke, anyway, in a few minutes."

Kevin looked back, then out the side window. "Jesus Christ," he said. He'd shifted into a surging minor panic, a flight-or-fight impulse that prompted him to imagine jumping from the moving vehicle. His gut churned with what felt a touch like hunger, contradicted by nausea, and a warm buzz emanated from his center up toward somewhere between his ears. "You've just given me an illegal substance, and we're being followed by a cop."

"He turned around," Conchillo said. He smiled. "Besides, I'm American Indian. It's legal for me. Religious purposes."

"So this is supposed to be a religious experience."

The old man looked at him, his face iron. "You're goddamn right it is."

By the time they reached the mouth of Baker Canyon, the last stains of faded light that hung in the west were singing themselves off to bed, a multi-part harmony in the manner of African villagers. *Koomla Koooomlaaaa....* Kevin asked Conchillo more than once if he could hear it. "My God," he said, "it's so beautiful."

"No," Conchillo said. "But I've heard them singing before."

The mountain silhouettes either side of them seemed happy, like porpoises flanking a cruising boat. And infused in everything—the mountains by turns spectacularly rugged and maternal, breast like, the mesquite, the mountain birch and desert willow, the arroyos choked with smooth stones—was an amber hum, as though nature herself were keening them home, a boy and his father in from a long and mysterious journey. Conchillo turned onto the Guadalupe Canyon road and it seemed to open up for them, a welcoming and generous host.

"Wow," Kevin said. "Midway in life's journey, I found myself in a dark, dark wood…"

The old man looked at him. "White people are crazy," he said.

"It's Dante," Kevin said. "The bastard was Italian—but crazy as they come."

Conchillo shrugged. "*Hijuela Madre.*'" he said. "Here we go."

"Shit," Kevin said, as he gazed out at the country side, "this is better than shrooms and acid put together."

"It's not dope," the old man said firmly. "I don't do that shit."

Kevin looked out onto the dusk air, alive and electric, the varying contours of the never-ending, mythical hills. "Right," he said. "Not dope. Wherefore do we travel good Pangloss, worthy Sancho Panza?"

The old man looked at him like he'd grown horns.

"I know," Kevin said, "a strange mixture of references."

Conchillo shook his head. "*Hijuela Madre.*"

Kevin leaned out the window, shouted, "For Heav'n hides nothing from thy view Nor the deep Tract of Hell, too…" He pulled back in and looked over at Conchillo. "That's Milton—kind of. Now there was a white boy. Crazy, too, and blind to boot."

Again, Conchillo shook his head. In shadow now, his twisted hank of gray hair, his hands still firmly on the wheel, the old Indian cut a rather noble, if pat, figure. "This is gonna be harder than I thought."

Twenty-Six

At dawn on the second morning of their search, O.D. Hallot had again been stationed at his post by the corrals, and he was just as happy for it. The ice chest in the back of his truck held a quart Tupperware container of Teresa McNally's *carne machaca*, six tortillas, and a twelve-pack of Coors. It was just light enough to read, and he sat in a foldout chair, a hundred pages deep into a novel whose title he'd already forgotten, written by some woman whose last name he could not pronounce. A blurb on the jacket declared the book yet another proof that she was "the most brilliant and resonating voice of the American West," and O.D. was getting even bigger laughs out of this crock of shit than he had with the wolf novel. When he finished a chapter that ended with, "and the grinding gravel roads wired grid-like across grassy plains of western lands...", he chuckled, whispered *bullshit* and tossed the tome on the dirt between his feet.

He looked up toward the southeast to where the tapering end of the Erscrobarra played out into Mexico and just below it at the low ridge where he had last seen the riders. He contemplated rolling himself a burrito. He philosophized some on an ethical tenet, the one that prevented him from cracking a beer this early in the day, and found it to be erroneous. So many of people's practices, beliefs, aesthetic tastes were just so much bullshit. That people weren't supposed to be fat, for example—where was the ethical iron in that imperative, where the philosophic root? Truth was, there wasn't any. The world just made shit like that up according to the fashion of the day. A man sometimes has a big gut, that's all.

And O.D. was owner of a dandy. Kevin McNally's first encounter with his bare gut had been, at Kevin's young age, mildly frightening. At an elk camp in the pinion-juniper country near Happyjack, at a Dutch oven filled with cold soapy water, O.D. had made himself a whore's bath one afternoon, and hummed the flat notes of some made-up tune as he ragged off armpits, chest, and neck—then, with a pinky finger, dug at his navel, an aperture the diameter of a nickel. Kevin, twelve at the time, could not take his eyes from the hump of bare flesh—large enough, it seemed, to chamber a curled-up five-year-old—rumpled, yellow, and quaking, appearing attached as an afterthought. It served as an enviable rest for beer bottle, dinner plate, or wife's head in the late evening hours. Like the curve of Quasimodo's back or Groucho's cigar, O.D.'s gut was a character prop no one who knew him could imagine him without.

So significant a monument was it that his acquaintances became nonplused a few years before when O.D. found a diet in *Journal* magazine (O.D. was a closet reader of popular women's rags) and lost thirty pounds. Speculation ran for a time that he was sick, though it was soon enough discovered the reduced size of his stomach had been deliberate. O.D. was a line supervisor for Bell Telephone Company, and his appalled coworkers were so undone by his weight loss, they took turns bringing brownies, doughnuts, and home-baked pies into the office until O.D.'s midsection had been properly augmented and order to the universe at last restored.

O.D. decided a *machaca* burrito and two beers were not only in order but appropriate to start the long day's vigil. He had to be able to steady his nerves and concentrate, and food and beer were the best way to do just that. He and the others were now, for the third day, searching for two kids who'd been missing forty-eight hours. Neither child was inclined to be a runaway, and while Kevin bore a thick vain of bullheadedness, one or the other or both should have contacted someone by now. What had kept them from it O.D. did not want to think about.

Russ Billman had arranged to have area search and rescue fly out one of their choppers but had gotten a call earlier in the morning that no bird was available, as the several not in use were down for routine maintenance. State police had been contacted and by Monday would be weighing in on the search.

The situation with these two kids had become more serious, and everyone involved understood they weren't just dealing with errant teenagers on a joyride. The fact that Armando Luna had not yet returned disturbed as well. Something bad had happened and Russ had made that clear to the sheriff, who arranged for the feds to send a border patrol chopper out to the area that morning. All of this would surely draw the news media, especially as the border situation the last few years had pressure cooked to a crisis point.

Late the previous evening, Russ had radioed in for more help from the sheriff's department, and the county had appointed, along with Simon Banks, two other young deputies who had specialized in rescue missions in the service. The deputies had camped in the search area in order to get an early start, and Russ had assigned them the eight-mile stretch of the Peloncillos between Baker Canyon and Guadalupe trail, which they would cover on county horses. It was as good a bet as any, an area of the mountains where no one had thought to look and an appropriate day's task for the three competent young officers. Russ and the four parents had started from the corrals at daybreak and headed straight south, and trotting ahead of their horses were a pair of county-owned sister bloodhounds named Juice and Tick. Any scent trail would likely be dulled by now, but the dogs were good ones and it was worth a try.

The parents, Russ, O.D., and even the three young deputies, all understood the plan, though none of them had spoken it, and as the mounted party of five disappeared behind a rise, O.D. knew they would be in Mexico within the hour as he listened to the shouted names of the two children, now familiar as a mantra. Russ had gone without uniform and the five riders, for all intents, appeared to be a group of *vaqueros* gathering cattle. Were they caught by any Mexican official, armed as they were, a foot south of the border fence, the consequences were dangerous and vastly unpredictable: they could be fined, jailed, robbed, forced to walk back home, each scenario born out in the recent history of that area.

"*Does the pope shit in the woods?*" was one of O.D.'s favorite comebacks to stupid questions. On a turkey hunt three years before, Kevin had dubbed him Pope O.D. when Thomas had had to stop the truck on Highway 40 so O.D., roll of t.p. in hand, could cross the barbed wire fence and walk conspicuously into the woods.

Why these biological needs came on at such inconvenient times was yet another item on O.D. Hallot's slate of quandaries to consider. Perhaps it was the second *machaca* burrito, but O.D. soon found himself in search of the nearest bar ditch. With a balled up handful of paper towel and a quart canteen for washing up, O.D. could not be accused of being unsanitary. As he finished his business and hitched up his pants, he surveyed the area, a shady arroyo—a good place for a nap later if need arose.

He walked a few yards down the wash and came to a set of boot prints whose gender he was sure he could identify. O.D., if anything, was a student of scatology, and he stood certain at the moment he was looking at the site where a woman had squatted to pee, the unmistakable urinal trajectory putting the center of the now-dried puddle just back of the heel marks. A few feet ahead, at the base of a small mesquite, was a small piece of what looked like white paper.

It turned out to be the cellophane glue guard for a deer tag, the directions for tagging the animal, pictures included, printed on the back. The tag itself had been peeled off and the glue guard appeared to have been exposed at least a day or two to the sun as it was similar in color to a newspaper left in the yard for a day.

O.D. held the thing to the light. Any Arizona game tag must be signed by its owner to be a legal document, and turning the slip of paper several angles, O.D. found what he had hoped not to. Pressed into the paper from a ball-point pen was the pretty character of a girl's careful signature: Amanda Monahan. Passionate as most ranching people were about discarded trash, Amanda had likely stuffed the glue guard in one of her pockets after tagging the harvested deer. How and why this bit of trash was on the ground, O.D. couldn't say. But the thing was definitely a disturbing find. Where the girl had gone from here was now the question.

A few paces further down the wash, O.D. found the sure signs of a struggle, the ground torn up by several pairs of boot prints, two of them men's—even a few droplets of blood; to whom they belonged O.D. was loath to think.

Teresa had insisted on bringing an extra horse, her mare Trixy. The filly was twenty-six months old and a little rough, and everyone who rode her, even Teresa, had difficulty with the horse, who regularly fought her bit and bunched up as though to buck.

O.D. was glad now they'd brought the mare, wild or not. He'd never been on the back of anything he couldn't handle. He only hoped, though, the filly was stout enough to hold his considerable weight. She'd seemed amiable as he saddled her, and now he put his left foot in the stirrup, testing the cinch, and bore down with about half his weight. The horse seemed strong enough, but that wasn't what really bothered him.

He felt something bad had happened to the girl, and if that were true, she may not have survived the ordeal any more than a few hours. The little Cobra radios everyone carried didn't have the reach to find any of the Billman party, which he had tried nonetheless, without success.

Half an hour before, the green and white Border Patrol chopper Russ had asked for rumbled in. And the damn thing had been noisy. He'd heard it approaching ten miles to the west, the machine first a dot in the sky, then with its fast, arrow-like progression becoming more the form he'd been expecting. The craft flew straight to the corrals and slowed then dipped some thirty feet as though in greeting to O.D., then hovered some hundred feet to the north. O.D. waved at it, and it lifted and just as quickly resumed its course, droning in the distance as the agents searched the border from Guadalupe Canyon to Cloverdale just beyond the New Mexico line.

He'd not heard the helicopter now for some time and wondered if the government had put up their search for the day. Had he seen the bird, he would have hailed the thing by firing one of the six signal flares Russ had given him. Though he suspected, even if he had been able to flag down the agents, it would have done little good. One or more of the missing were in Mexico, and he wasn't sure if the chopper had permission to cross the border.

After several tries, O.D. managed to radio Simon Banks and the two deputies who were somewhere south of Outlaw Mountain, half a day's ride, at least, back to the corrals. O.D. didn't even tell them of the situation, only that he'd radioed to check their location and nothing more, knowing that young Si Banks would have advised him to stay put and wait for an officer.

And O.D. had no intentions of staying put. He felt sure of what had happened to Mandi, and maybe Kevin, and following the wash several hundred yards on the skittish mare was confirmation enough— three clear sets of boot prints, then a little later prints he felt sure belonged to the girl's mule, Dunk. The pang in O.D.'s middle told him he might very soon find the half-buried body or bodies, though the signs showed that Kevin might not have been part of this. Even still, the two burritos and beer were reminding him of their presence in his belly.

O.D. rode the wash until just after 9:30 a.m. when the prints trailed out as the three people and the mule had at some point climbed clear, though after a few minutes of careful searching, O.D. could not determine where. He marked the spot in his mind where he'd last seen the prints—at a slight bend in the wash beside a big white rock, though he wasn't about to give up on the trail. He would make the ten-minute ride back to the truck, see if anyone had returned, try another call with the radio, then he would pack food, water, a bedroll, and extra ammo. Time, he knew, was an urgent factor in this business. He could cover a considerable distance before dark and could perhaps find where they had camped or left in a vehicle or—God forbid—where they had abandoned the remains.

No one was around when O.D. returned to the trucks. He checked batteries and packed his radios and flashlight, then left a note under the driver's-side wiper of Russ's GMC: *Mandi and maybe Kevin taken by bad people I suspect. Prints in wash to the west headed straight south, so I've gone after them. Will try to radio.*

O.D. had just hefted his rear end into the mare's small saddle when he heard a vehicle on the county road. He could tell after a moment that the thing had turned onto the trail leading to the corral, and in a few minutes a Hidalgo county sheriff's vehicle, a Dodge pickup four-by-four, pulled up with a rusted-out, single-horse trailer in tow. A small dark-haired man stepped out, smiled and nodded a greeting at O.D.

"That's a hell of a nice-looking little horse," he said.

"Yeah," O.D. said, glancing down toward the mare's flanks. He felt sure he had never seen this man before. "She's not mine, though—and it's a good thing, cantankerous little bitch that she is."

"I can see she's got it in her," the little man said. "Good-looking horse, though."

The stranger had stepped up within a few feet of O.D. He walked with the kind of limp of a man who wore a prosthetic leg and was clad in a denim shirt and pants and wore slate-gray cap with "OMEGA

FARM IMPLEMENTS" in red letters across the crown. He tipped the cap in a friendly gesture to the back of his head, folded his arms and surveyed the mare.

The little man's neglected, burry dark hair bunched out from underneath his hat in contrast to the candle-wax color of his skin. He tipped his weight slightly forward as to signal the end of his horse inspection. "Yep," he said. "Nice-looking filly."

"O.D Hallot." O.D. extended his hand and the little man shook it.

"Harold Placer—they call me Hal."

"You with the sheriff's department, Hal?" O.D. asked, gesturing at the truck.

"I am," the little man said, "but not today. Today I'm a volunteer."

O.D. didn't know which direction to aim the conversation.

The little man spoke up. "I'm a friend of Russ Billman's."

Noting Placer's stature, O.D. doubted he and Russ had been teammates in football.

"We fought in Korea together," Placer explained. "May through April, fifty and fifty-one. Rich kid like Billman does a stint in a war overseas—noteworthy."

O.D. took a moment to get his mind around the relationships. "So you know old George Roberts, then."

"Oh, yes sir. Lieutenant Roberts' my brother for life and now my boss. Three of us spent twelve months in that frozen shit hole—none of us old enough to shave yet."

Placer ran his hand gently, expertly down the horse's neck. "I'm here about those lost kids," he said, not looking up. "George was gonna come, but he got hung up. I came in his stead." The little man's eyes tracked the horse's head and snout, like a veterinarian looking for signs and symptoms. "I'm off the clock. I'll go wherever—do whatever it takes." He looked up at O.D. "I'm here to help."

They'd ridden a quarter hour in silent mutual understanding that they were looking for a dead body. O.D. had shown the little deputy the site in question, and Placer agreed—there'd been a struggle, someone hurt.

The deputy's slight frame sat atop Buck, the big, hammer-headed, red-roan gelding, and looked for all the world a child at play on daddy's plough horse. When Placer had unloaded the saddled horse, O.D. could not believe that such an animal had fit into the beat-up little trailer. Even stranger was his weaponry—he carried a nine-millimeter, fixed-sight semi-automatic about the size of a man's hand and, of all things, a compound bow he kept in a homemade saddle scabbard.

When they came to the place in the wash were O.D. had lost the trail, Placer easily picked it up again. The prints played out and reappeared, became lost amid a tangle of other tracks. Uncannily, the deputy was able to relocate the trail. When they arrived at the border fence, the two men removed fence tools from side saddles and went about the work of taking down and restringing strands of barbed wire as though they had discussed the job at length previously.

About mid-day, Placer pointed out a grove of cottonwoods and sycamores in the flats half a mile southeast. "There we go," he said. "I bet we find signs of a camp."

The tire tracks at the site looked to be those of two vehicles, and the spent coals of the fire were still slightly warm to the touch. Placer snapped on his flashlight, scanning the ground around them. O.D. had all morning been impressed at the guy's using a light in the middle of the day. Placer nodded toward a flat space. "Tent was set up right over there."

"How'd you learn all this shit?" O.D. finally asked, the last two hours spent in silent amazement of Placer's tracking skills.

"I's a tracker in Korea," the deputy said flatly. "Followed Korean soldiers all the way back to China." He limped over past the fire coals and went to one knee still scanning the ground with his light.

"Is that where you lost your leg?" O.D. asked. "Over in Korea?"

"No," Placer said with a chuckle. "Lost that in a mining accident." He glanced up at O.D., smiled. "Damnedest thing, huh?"

Placer shined his light about. "I wonder where they're headed."

"Who's to tell," O.D. said. "But I bet we can catch them before dark." He walked over to see what the deputy had fixed his light on.

"I know one thing," Placer said, pointing out the small footprint held in the beam. "Same size-five Red Wing boot made this print and the one in the wash a couple miles back. Bet a hundred dollars they were made by that little girl."

"I wouldn't take any part of that bet." O.D. thought a moment.

"How do you know that's the same boot track?"

Placer pointed to an area toward the bottom of the print. "She's got a little chunk of heel knocked off the edge, 'bout the size of a thumbnail. I noticed it when you first showed me the prints by the corrals."

"Well I'll be a sorry son of a bitch. What do we do?"

"Keep after 'em. They've gone where they've gone. One thing's sure, though. She was alive when they stayed here a couple nights ago." Placer lifted his hat and scratched at his ratty dark hair. "Maybe we could try getting a hold of the Mexican Federal Police."

"Shit," O.D. said. "Don't hold your breath. I wouldn't count on those bastards to help us out."

"Well," the deputy said. "I got some connections down here. Might be something we can do."

O.D. walked to his horse and dug through the saddlebags—lunch time. He promptly made himself three burritos with the left-over *machaca*, careful to save enough to offer Placer as a courtesy. The deputy, seated on a stump, apparently concurred on lunch and had just opened a can of sardines, which sharpened the air. He politely waved off O.D.'s offer.

"No thanks," he said, pointing at the can of sardines. "These are enough for me." Placer looked at his watch. "Ten minutes for lunch?"

Ten minutes later, O.D. tried the radios. No luck. For a passing moment, O.D. regretted leaving his post, for his job had been to keep search volunteers and news media apprised. They had the note on John Monahan's truck, at least, and O.D. wasn't sure how much help even thirty or forty other people would be, anyway. Certainly, the news of two missing kids had spread after this much time, and that kind of news always made for good headlines. It wouldn't take long for the circus to arrive, and O.D. decided he was better off not part of it for now. He was more useful sneaking down into Mexico with this little expert tracker, who turned out to be full of surprises.

They mounted up and followed the tire tracks. As they rode, they chatted, discussing everything from dogs to law enforcement to hunting to Placer's choice of weaponry. At one point, the deputy mentioned his days in college after he was out of the Army.

"College?" O.D. said, vexed by yet another incongruity. "What'd you study?"

"Well," the deputy said. "I eventually ended up with a Ph.D. in Education. Teach some night classes at Hidalgo Community."

"Well I'll be go-to-hell," O.D. said. "I'm out here hunting down bad guys with a damn sardine-eating college professor. Who carries a stick with a string for protection. Wonders never cease." O.D. laid a hand on his belly, the other reining his horse. "Wonders never cease."

Twenty-Seven

Kevin was spooked. The dark around the truck, he'd told the old man several times, was getting heavier, as though pressurized, smashing down the light the vehicle and the people in it emitted. They'd bounced past the Magoffin ranch, where Kevin was almost too shaken up to get out and open the gate, though he'd done it, and as the truck passed through the opening, the stay posts lighted by the head lamps, he'd felt as though he'd accomplished one of the list of tasks on a heroic journey. He was by turns exhilarated and terrified, and he had no idea which of those feelings would come next. The last few minutes they'd driven in silence, and when Kevin became too anxious to go on, he begged the old man to stop the truck. Conchillo halted the vehicle immediately and cut the engine.

"Turn off the lights," Kevin told him.

The old man snapped them off and they were cloaked in pitch.

"Can you hear that?" Kevin asked.

"No," Conchillo said. "But you should listen to them."

Kevin's breathing was heavy and he was sweating. "They're singing," he said. "But different from before."

"Can you hear what they're saying?"

Kevin shook his head, the dark palpable, seeming to move with the properties of a living organism. He listened more, shook his head. "They're gone now."

Conchillo started the truck, snapped on the lights. "Listen for them, *mijo*." Kevin could hear his breathing, deeper, more pronounced. "We were meant to come here this night, this hour *mijo*."

They wound around the squat hill just east of the ranch house and began to climb into Styx Canyon toward the Escrobarra. The old man had locked the hubs on the truck and it groaned over loose stones and craters in the road. Kevin peered out into the night, the thin cloud cover obscuring the stars. It was as though he could see, as on a movie screen, the contours of the Escrobarra just ahead. The voices came again, taking on a sort of dreamlike form, and he felt bits of his life as though they moved through his veins.

He stands a distance south of the house, the bedding his mother had

189

put up on the clothesline rising in the breeze, her leghorn hens, having quit their pen and abandoned the coop, peck the dirt in scattered pairs and threes. The wind is easy on his neck and feels good under his shirt and his twelve-year-old arms are covered with dust from playing in the barn with his cousin Jeremy, who laughs and bolts from the tool shed and ducks behind the chicken coop.

In ten skipping steps, Kevin moves toward the coop, dips his shoulder, tucks and rolls where he's up again, his back to the clap-board wall like a movie desperado, the Sundance Kid hemmed in from all sides. He poses, the pellet pistol in his right hand. "Fill your hand," he shouts.

In the cast of the moment, Kevin forgets his pistol is cocked and loaded. Jeremy rounds the corner, Kevin levels at him and pulls the trigger, shocked that the gun has fired, at the whiz and smack of the projectile entering his cousin's skin. His first thought is the weight of his father's disapproval, the code in which he'd been so long steeped—that guns and foolery, even pellet guns, are never mixed.

All sense of play disappears and the moment draws out several beats in the afternoon light. His cousin stands frozen like a soldier on a land mine. Jeremy puts his fingers to his chest as though feeling for a mosquito bite, a look of terror and betrayal in his eyes.

Kevin steps up to him close enough to touch. Jeremy drops his gun in the dirt. Kevin does the same. The CO2 pistols had come as a boxed pair, a Christmas gift. One of the molting hens dumbly taps the dirt a few feet away. The bed sheets flap on the line in the yard.

Kevin raises his cousin's T-shirt to find the red eyelet a few inches below the nipple, a tear of blood pushing forth and down the boy's rib cage.

"Don't touch it," Jeremy says.

Kevin's throat is too bound up to speak. His impulse is to take the hurt boy to the house, his mind racing. Would he die before an adult could get him to town?

Jeremy moves his other hand to the wound and puts his fingers on either side of the tiny hole, pushing at the edges.

"Shit, Jeremy," Kevin says.

His cousin gives him a look, works his fingers around the hole, and in a moment the flattened lead pellet emerges, dropping to the ground.

"Hit a rib," Jeremy says. "We won't tell."

"It's bleeding."

His cousin looks up at him, and his eyes harden. "We're not telling. Indian swear."

The boys stare and each other several seconds. "Okay," Kevin says, nods. "Indian swear."

Conchillo parked. Kevin tried to lift the door handle, but his arms seemed to work like rubber bands, and when finally he was able to step from the truck, the ground under his feet felt foreign, and his legs seemed to move of their own volition under him. The night was alive with sounds, as though he'd stepped though a vortex into another world. A meadowlark called, its rising and descending trill played for him in particular, a pair of coyotes yipped in the distance, and a bank of cloud cover slid to the east, leaving a portal of delicate stars. Never had they looked so crisp, so alive and distinctive.

"Stay right there," the old man said from the other side of the truck.

"Thought I'd jog around the block," Kevin said.

Conchillo snapped on the flashlight, lifting items from the truck bed. He laid the light on one of the bed walls and adjusted the arm straps of the daypack under the beam.

"You need some help?"

The old man didn't answer. In the trapped light, Kevin could see his arthritic hands struggling with the pack. "I think you're past helping anybody but you right now," Conchillo said.

"It's your doing, you old crow," Kevin said. "You tricked me."

"It's the best thing I could think of," the old man said sincerely.

"Do you have any whiskey in that pack?"

"No," Conchillo said. "It would corrupt your visions. They need to be pure."

They set off, breaking trail by the flashlight beam, Kevin having managed to convince the old man to let him carry the pack. The darkness, rich and alive, felt comforting now, like a buffer against whatever may come. The possibilities seemed galaxies wide and the rough ground conveyed easily under foot, Kevin's perception of his physical, mental, and emotional state capricious and slave to whim.

Their footfalls gained a rhythm, and Kevin was sure the old man could feel it himself. The crickets and birds fell into time, and Kevin wanted to sing but he could think of no songs. The voices came again, not in words but in hums and chants, and the old man fell in with them, singing as he moved slowly up the trail ahead. His voice rose from just above a whisper to a keen that bladed into the night, the other voices seeming to shape themselves around his lead. And Kevin understood, now, the singing was not for him to do, only to follow. It was his, only, to follow, and he did not think about the direction they were going or where they would stop. He moved inside the voices.

Twenty-Eight

Armando Luna could not reason out what he was seeing through his glasses. So out-of-place was the image that for several minutes he could not speak his discovery to Kevin. By the time they'd reached the base of the ridge, they'd had to short-rope Bonny to the mule's saddle horn, so crazed was she by the scent she'd encountered. She'd strained and bit at the rope, tried to shake loose her collar, and they felt sure they had located Pete's trail again. They'd found a good ridge to glass from and had tied the dog to an oak sapling a few feet away, but her whimpering anxiety made it hard for Mondy to concentrate.

The thing was less than a hundred yards away, in the wash at the base of the canyon, which was probably why Kevin had not yet seen it, not having bothered to look that close. Mondy pulled away his binoculars, gave his eyes a few seconds rest, then looked again. The white in the image was irrefutable, but the object that took form in and around that white, though it seemed definite, was so out-of-place it had again and again given Mondy pause.

"Kevin," he said, finally. "I see something weird down there."

"Another moose?"

"No. Jesus. Just look," Mondy said. He directed Kevin to the thing.

"Shit," Kevin said. "It's a baby."

"Not a dead one, I hope."

"No. I saw it move its leg."

Indeed, a baby, perhaps two or three months old, lay in only a disposable diaper, asleep on its stomach, its bed apparently a folded blanket or canvas tarp.

"There's a guy," Mondy said suddenly. Sure enough, a man had stood up not ten feet from the infant. In a moment the canyon bottom was alive with people, ten or more, all apparently waking from a mid-morning nap in the cool sandy bottom of the arroyo. One of them shouted, "*Mira el caballo.*"

"Well," Kevin said. "They've seen your horse."

"Your horse," Mondy corrected.

"*Necesitamos ayuda,*" shouted an unfamiliar voice—we need help. Mondy and Kevin said nothing, each looking through his glasses trying to count the number of warm bodies. They could see fourteen.

"What do you think?" Kevin asked finally.

"I was just about to ask you the same," Mondy said.

"They just look like a group of wets."

"True, but if they have any kind of contraband with them, they're dangerous."

"But they have a baby."

"That doesn't mean shit," Mondy pointed out.

In the end, though, they found themselves riding to the bottom of the canyon. As it turned out, there were fourteen in all, twelve of them men, ranging in age from seventeen to sixty, plus the infant and its mother. Her name was Ursula Maria, and she was more or less the leader and spokesperson of the group.

Sitting in a clump of broom grass, she did not rise, as did the men, when Kevin and Mondy rode down to them. One of the younger fellows, perhaps eighteen, whose black hair had been cut sloppily in the shape of a bowl, brought her the child, whom she promptly began to nurse. She was a striking woman, older in many ways than she appeared, perhaps twenty-one or -two. Over her head she had tied a wet blue bandana against the sun, and her sorrel-colored hair spilled out of it about her shoulders. She unhitched the top two buttons of her light cotton jacket, lifted the khaki T-shirt and quickly delivered an ivory-colored breast to the child.

"Bring me the blanket," she said to the boy in an accent from deep down, perhaps Oaxaca or even further. "He feels cold." She had not taken her eyes from the two strangers, and she waited a long time before she spoke to them.

"We need your help," she said to Mondy, probably because he was the older of the two.

"What can we do?" Mondy asked.

Though one could see in her expression she had long before determined the answer to that question, the woman told her story from the beginning:

The men with her were her brothers, cousins, in-laws, and cousins of cousins. They had left a month before from Puerto Angel and had traveled through the gut of Mexico mostly on foot, the baby with them the whole way. The party had left home, as she put it, on the shoulders of a promise—a promise made by the father of her child. His name was Leandro Cruz and he was the finest brick mason in southern Oaxaca. Cruz had sent a letter six months before describing the beauty and wealth of America, saying he worked a job which paid more than fifty dollars a day. A month later, Cruz sent another letter saying he was contracted to build a small motel in a place called Colorado and he needed a crew.

The girl gestured at the men sitting silently behind her. "I bring him his crew. Two days ago I injured my ankle and could not walk. I told these imbeciles to leave me food and continue ahead, but they refused, and here we wait—almost out of food. It is only by God's grace that we have a spring nearby."

Now, finally, the young woman was ready with the answer to Mondy's question. She plucked the now-sleeping child from her breast and handed it back to the boy, who seemed always in attendance to her. She pointed at Dunk. "That brown mule," she said, "seems little use to you." She let the comment settle with them a moment. "Mules have better meat than most people think."

When Kevin spoke, the woman seemed surprised, perhaps by the Spanish, perhaps for the temerity of one so young to speak at all. "If this mule belonged to me, I would help slaughter and butcher it and with your grace share a meal of it with you. But it is not my mule."

The woman nodded, apparently satisfied with his answer. "¿De dónde eres?," she asked Kevin. "The tongue is Spanish, no?"

"My mother is Basque," Kevin said.

Again the woman nodded.

"How long have you been without food?"

The woman held up two fingers, then pointed at one of the men, an older fellow whose white hair fell in tangles out of the Yankees baseball cap he wore. "We have no gun," the woman said, "but Eduardo here brings me wild onions and cactus heart and we have some dried mango and jabanero chiles. They gave me the last few bites of our jerky, but still I'm going dry. By tomorrow, perhaps, I will be able to walk, but I'm not sure if the baby will survive."

Kevin walked back to Turk and then Sally, removing the biscuits and jerky from the saddlebags. Slowly, he approached the woman and handed her the plastic baggies, her presence so strong he almost obeyed the impulse to bow.

She looked down at the baggies, examining their contents, then looked up at Kevin in gratitude. "A thousand thanks," she said. Closer to her, Kevin could see she was no more than three or four years his senior.

And the men behind her murmured: *muchísimas gracias, muy amable.*

Kevin pointed a finger downward and made a circle in the air to indicate the whole group. "That is enough for everyone to take off the pain in the stomach," he said, "but my friend and I have good rifles. We will find noon dinner and the next few meals."

Just over the ridge to the south, Kevin and Mondy pushed up a doe and fawn from a shallow cut, but Kevin could not find them in his scope before they disappeared down the wash. Ten minutes later, though, they startled a herd of six javelina from their bed. All but blind, the little pigs, when frightened, will run no more than a few feet if unsure what has threatened them.

Two from this group stopped and froze just a few feet away, and Mondy had started to draw out his rifle when Kevin stopped him, indicating the .22 pistol in his belt. Mondy nodded: less noise. Kevin climbed off Sally and moved ten steps away so not to spook the mounts. He raised the pistol, and with a pop dropped the largest of the two pigs. The other snorted, bristled up and trotted a few yards up the hill. Still, the animal was no more than thirty yards, and Kevin easily took it as well.

Both hogs were mature, perhaps forty to fifty pounds apiece, and when Kevin and Mondy brought them back to the arroyo, the Mexicans were very pleased. Immediately, Ursula and her young attendant set about butchering the meat, and emphatically waved off any help Mondy or Kevin tried to give. But old Eduardo whistled through his teeth to Kevin and pointed to his pack, from which he produced a combi-tool, a digging implement often used in firefighting, with an eight-inch pick on one side and a spade on the other, which when folded out measured a little under two feet. As with most migrants, these bore sparse belongings, none having any more than two sets of clothes and the same pair of shoes he walked out his door with. The garments were cheap Mexican off-brand, the clothing of the poor, the seams of pants splitting with no more than a month's use, shirts long since bereft of buttons, and the soles of shoes duct-taped to the frame.

"You can help me dig the fire pit," Eduardo said to Kevin.

As Kevin and Eduardo spelled each other on the digging, the older man told his version of their coming north. He also knew the trail Kevin and Mondy had broken from, as he and his party had walked it several miles before breaking from it themselves. Eduardo assured Kevin that the road looped back north, that catching it again was an easy ride from where they stood, and that the boy and his O'odham companion had probably saved themselves an hour, perhaps two.

"Our first guide was stupid and a coward," the older man said. "I and three others hired him in Morelos in a small cantina. He was a boy little more than your age, a big talker, and we hired him for 150,000 pesos. That decision we soon came to regret.

"For the first hundred miles or so the boy found us a ride in the back of a fruit truck. We traveled through Mexico City. Most of us had not been to the city before, and we smiled and laughed and made jokes about the sizes our living rooms and swimming pools would one day be in America.

"We were just south of Pachua when," Eduardo snapped his fingers, "we saw the lights of the federal police flashing behind us. As it turned out, they had no issue with the many passengers in the back. They simply fined the driver for the lack of the proper licensing for hauling fruits and vegetables. Still, our young guide insisted we get off the truck. After he had paid off the driver, we walked for twenty, perhaps thirty kilometers through the jungle at the side of the road.

"Finally, the boy—our guide—stopped us, pointing to a far chain of mountains, perhaps fifty kilometers north. 'Just the other side of those hills is your land of riches, the United States.' Then he left us. What a liar. We made it to those hills and the ones after that and the ones after—all jungle, mosquitoes, snakes, rats this big..." Eduardo held his hand at his elbow to indicate the length of his arm. "Two of the men with us contracted dysentery and died a few kilometers before we reached San Luis Potosi. We buried them under small stick crosses. What else could we do?

"Somewhere in that long, desolate stretch in Zacatecas, good fortune landed on us: two long hairs from America—how do you call them—'hippies', a man and a woman, driving in an old school bus, picked us up off the side of the highway. They drove us all the way to Ciudad Jimenez, and they would have taken us farther but that they had to turn for Santa Barbara, on their way to a place in the Sierra Madre Occidental. They fed us, gave us food for the trip, the American woman cried to leave the baby.

"In a little town just south of Chihuahua City—Meoqui—we contracted our second *coyote*. This man we did not meet in a tavern but in someone's home, where our inquiries had directed us. He seemed better than the last—he was older, more credible, dressed nicely. For his services he required 250,000 pesos—one pays more for quality, no?"

At this, old Eduardo paused and took a long silence. Kevin had dug with no help for a long time now, but he didn't mind. The pit was close to being big enough to roast both hogs, and Kevin felt no compunction about finishing the job up himself.

"Of course," Eduardo continued, "as is the case with such tragedies—we were wrong again. To be sure, this guide obtained us rides, mostly by truck. One time he packed all fourteen of us into a Jeep-like vehicle. This *pollero* took us all the way to a place ten miles north of Janos—just over here to the east. From there we were again on foot, and all of us sensed we did not have far to travel. There hung an uneasy mood about our group—for we had not joked, or hardly even spoken, for thousands of kilometers. And even our guide—I will not speak his name—was entwined in this mood.

"Then, just a few days ago—a week, I think—it happened. We had just taken lunch in a shady arroyo when our guide pulled out a gun, a little pistol that he had carried with him the whole time. Between us we had perhaps two, maybe three hundred thousand pesos—he took it all.

"After that, he told we men to move away a few yards. He took Ursula over by a big rock." Eduardo looked away then, up canyon toward the climbing sun. Kevin could see that images he did not want to speak played through his mind. "We wanted to look away but would not for the dread that he might bring more harm to her. Through the whole ordeal, I could see her lips saying, *Be calm. Do nothing.*

"When he had finished, somehow Ursula's little cousin, Peto—the boy with the strange hair cut—had sneaked through the bushes and got the advantage on him—gun and all—and managed to slam him in the head with a rock and stun him. As it turned out, the gun had only three cartridges and did not even work well. Sometimes it fired, sometimes it did not, and the bullets only wounded the pollero. How we dealt him after that, I care not to say. We got back our money, but what happened to Ursula—*that* can never be restored. The last few nights, I have been comforted to sleep by the memory of that *coyote's* screaming before he slowly went silent."

Some smaller parts of the hogs were ready to eat just after noon. Eduardo had spiced them with the baked jabaneros and salt he'd ground from chips off a cow lick. Kevin had never before encountered people so hungry.

All had shown restraint as the hogs were cooking, but as soon as Ursula had torn off the first length of flesh from one of the hams, the men with her descended quickly on the designated meat, each coming away with steaming double handfuls so hot it burned blisters into their palms. And for a long while Kevin and Mondy had stayed away, and finally after repeated entreaties from all they each took a serving. When everyone was sated, a whole untouched hog remained and yet several pounds of meat on the first.

The afternoon sun pleasantly warm on their backs, Kevin and Mondy saddled up. One of the baggies that had held the jerky was now filled with hog meat and they had taken water from the spring for their canteens. Most of the party of *Mojados* had woken from their naps and milled about, gathering up personal items and breaking camp, such as it was.

The Mexicans would travel straight north, following the high, rocky peak of Outlaw Mountain as a marker that would lead them to the sparsely populated valley and they would be safe from robbers and border patrol. Ursula had in her jacket pocket a crude map of Colorado, the proximity of Boulder and the area where her man was probably working, which Kevin had sketched for her. She had held the rough pencil drawing delicately in her palm and peered down at it as though into an oracle.

"*Gracias,*" she had said to Kevin. "*Gracias.*"

Kevin had been sitting no more than an arm's length from her and had a sudden sheepish yearning, an urge as she sat in the shade of a spring-side sycamore, to gather her in his arms. When she caught him looking at her, she smiled knowingly. She had about her, wrapped like a shawl, a sense of certainty and prowess, and Kevin knew she would find her way and live well and be happy. He was glad for it.

When he had pulled tight the cinch on the mule's saddle and mounted up, he noticed Ursula staring at him, some foregone intent clearly in her expression. She handed off the child to her cousin and walked up to Sally, where she stood with her arms folded, squinting up at him. Her silences were at least as unnerving as those of the Monahan family.

"You are very young," she said. "I will pray you travel with God's blessing."

"I am always careful."

"Still—I have the rosary, and I will pray for you."

Though he had been tempted all morning, Kevin had not told anyone about Mandi and the smugglers and now he was grateful for it. This poor woman had enough to fret about.

"*Ven te*," Ursula said, motioning him to lean down. An order.

Kevin bent toward her, expecting a kiss on the cheek, but instead she slipped something over his head. A small chain on which hung a *milagro*, a pendant the size of a nickel. Relieved into the zinc plate was the profile of a saint. He stared down at the coin in his palm, trying to decide which of the many saints it was.

She answered for him. *Es el santo de los niños, San Miguel.*

No soy un niño, Kevin said, a touch offended.

Eres un niño, she came back. *Por poco tiempo, pues*, for a short time, at least.

They stared at each other a long moment.

Ven te, Ursula gestured again. Kevin bent down again and she took his hand, squeezing it harder than any female ever had, and cupping the back of his head with the other hand, she kissed him hard on the lips.

Her mouth tasted like the meat of some unnamed melon, and Kevin wanted to kiss her again and longer, but he didn't. For years to come, in dreams, when drunk, or in reverie, her face arrived before him. Again and again he would bend down for that same sweet kiss.

Twenty-Nine

Some eighteen hours earlier, another day had ended for Amanda Monahan, and the only emotion she felt was a numbing sense of resignation. Why Ise had not yet killed her she didn't know. A dozen times during that afternoon she had thought the moment had finally arrived—as they had broken camp, stopped and parked the vehicles for lunch, or walked out to a rise to survey the area. She'd expected Ise to draw his nine millimeter, put it to the back of her head, and bring the darkness. Each time, though—her hands still bound, her ankles hobbled, mouth duct taped from nose to bottom of her chin—she had been spirited back to one of the two vehicles.

It was deep evening now, and the men had decided to put up for the night. They parked in a high shallow canyon that Amanda recognized. She'd been there several times as a young child when she and her father had helped a family friend, a Mexican rancher named Beto Garcia, find a few of his wayward cattle. Under the happier circumstance of riding through this valley with her dad and Beto, she'd always thought the place pretty. The little depression, which ran right along the border fence, was perhaps a quarter mile long and wide, pocked with clumps of bear grass and a few lone juniper and mesquites but otherwise resembled a meadow, the Jeep trail they'd ridden up on winding quaintly through it. The place took on a different look now that she might die there.

The men had talked little through the day, but now as they gathered firewood for a rough camp, they were less reticent. The boy, Billy, who had more or less attached himself to her, led her from the Chevy out to a bundle of broom grass where she could sit in relative comfort. *What a gentleman*, she would have said, had her mouth not been duct taped. She had not made a sound in twelve hours.

She watched as three of the boys with armloads of fall wood strode up to a bare patch of ground. As the evening drew into dusk, an edge on the air spoke winter. Not only had the boys not brought jackets but they all wore T-shirts and jersey-type tank tops resembling those of professional sports teams. Intent on a little warmth, they had a tall fire ablaze within ten minutes. And as they stood warming their hands, occasionally one would glance sheepishly in Amanda's direction. It was likely one of them would be tasked with killing her. Most of the day, they'd heard a chopper to the north and felt almost certain it was searching for the girl. When its monotonous sound finally droned off and disappeared into the west, all of them had been relieved.

Amanda was some twenty-five feet from the group, though she could feel the warmth of the fire touching the edges of her face. All five of the younger men sat close together around the fire, four of them avoiding looking her direction. But Chingo stared straight at her, sometimes for whole minutes, the way a poised housecat might stare at a bird. Soon J.C. nodded her direction and looked at Billy, now sitting on his haunches on the other side of the fire.

"Better go get her," J.C. said to the boy, who rose immediately and walked out to the bundle of grass where the girl sat. He took her under an arm and helped her to stand then walked her over to the fire with the others.

Philip Waylon glanced up at her, then looked at Ise. "This is insane, Leon."

"Does that mean you'll do the business?" Ise shot back.

The big man was silent.

Ise held out his hands in a "who cares" fashion, a signature gesture, Amanda had come to learn, when he was exasperated. "Because, Phil, the business has to be done."

"You know, Ise," he said. "I wasn't the one stupid enough to take her."

Ise stepped up to him then, plucked his nine millimeter from the shoulder holster and handed it over butt-first to Phil, who still squatted by the fire.

The big man only stared up at the gun.

"Go ahead," Ise said. "Cap her."

Still, Phil only stared.

Ise stepped away from Phil and walked up to Billy, who, now sitting on the ground, would not look up at him. "Come on, man" Ise said. "You're it, and you know it."

"What about me?" Chingo spoke up.

"Not your job," Ise said to him. "It's Billy's. Come on, Billy." He pushed the gun to him. "Take it."

But Billy would not look up, only stared into the fire.

Amanda was almost overpowered by the impulse, hobbled though she was, to turn and run. But terror gave way to reason. Her ranch-girl sense knew the running mouse only provoked the cat. Her chances were better waiting it out.

The moment lingered on, Billy staring at the ground, Ise holding out the pistol within a foot of the boy's fire-lit face. Finally, Ise holstered the gun. "You're a bunch of fucking pussies," he charged. "*Quieren dinero, quieren carros suaves, quieren comprar joyas para las mujeres.* But you don't want to think about what all that shit costs." He pointed at the girl. "Sometimes it costs a hell of a lot."

Later, Ise walked over to her with an open can and a spoon.

"You've got to be hungry," he said to her. "I'll take off the tape and feed you, but you need to be quiet."

Mandi shook her head, jerked it side to side and worked her duct-taped jaw in order to plead with him, and despite her effort to stop them, she felt the tears come. Her heart thumped now that he was close, a natural panic, flight-or-fight impulse she could no longer quell, even in her exhaustion.

"I understand," Ise said. "I would struggle against those ropes, too. It might help you to know your side of this is clean. You are in no way to blame. I don't have to tell you how much I regret this." He looked at her a few seconds and pointed skyward. "The stars have it this way, though. It's just how it works out, *mija.*"

And now they were walking out into the darkness, the beam of Ise's flashlight thrown out a few feet ahead, the other men left by the fire in an ugly tell-tale silence, not even a whisper. For the last day and a half, Amanda had thought herself calm and ready, but the sobs came from a deep place in her chest, despite her will to push them back. Isedro Leon was silent, allowing the sobs to come, allotting the girl a reasonable amount of time to fully realize what was happening to her.

"*Lo siento,*" he said to her. "It means 'I'm sorry', but it's a little different in Spanish."

At first the light was just a spec to the northwest. Then it widened into a hazy bubble. Initially, she thought it another party with a flashlight, but then she heard the unmistakable drone of an engine, and it took a moment for her realize: *headlights.*

Some seconds before, they had stopped and Ise had turned off the flashlight. Amanda heard him snap open his knife case, then the click of the blade. Ise, in a single, quick movement, was down on his knees behind her and inside one second had cut the cotton hobble rope.

"Run back to camp," he told her. "Fast."

Surprisingly, they were less than a hundred yards from the fire. As she ran, Amanda could hear the blades of the shovels striking dirt and made out the shadows of the men as they worked the implements furiously to kill the fire. She fell twice as she ran, plunging face first into the grass and dirt, both times Ise pulling her to her feet and enjoining in a whispzer, "Run, goddamnit." The girl could feel her right cheek had been badly scraped, even through the duct tape, and registered the sting of the flecks of gravel imbedded in her skin.

When they arrived at the fire, all the men were bent, hands on knees, chasing their breaths. Mandi stood, her head tilted down, feeling the blood drip like tears from her face. The fire almost stifled, two of the boys, brothers Paco and Miguel, stomped at the remaining coals until all evidence of the fire was covered in the darkness of a partial-mooned night.

"Where is it?" Ise finally whispered.

And it was Chingo who answered. "The lights disappeared behind a rise over there and never came out."

"Quiet for a minute," Ise said. And everyone stood silent, listening. No engine sounds.

"He must have parked," J.C. whispered. "We should take off."

"No," Ise said. "We'll wait them out. How far away do you think they are?"

"A quarter mile," J.C. said. "Four-hundred yards, maybe."

"They'll be able to hear us if we talk above a whisper," Ise said. "They'll damn sure hear if we turn over an engine."

"I think that road may be on the Arizona side. It could be Chacon," Phil said.

"No way," Ise said. "Chacon told me tomorrow and with a horse trailer."

"It looked like that rig had a trailer," Juan Carlos said.

They were silent now, all of them seated beside the doused fire and realizing the cold night air on their skin. Amanda was shivering but was so relieved she could now stretch her legs she hardly noticed the chill. Ise finally spoke.

"I don't think they're going to leave."

"I thought I smelled smoke," Phil said. "I think they made a fire."

Another silence. "J.C.," Ise said finally, though Juan Carlos already knew and was pulling himself from the ground.

"I'll go check them out."

He and Ise went to the vehicles, gathering up sleeping bags and blankets, water, and two of the Mini 14 rifles. Without speaking, the men laid out bedrolls for a cold camp, then J.C. picked up one of the rifles from where he had carefully laid them on a blanket. He opened the breech, and with his fingers checked to make sure the weapon was loaded.

"I'll go with you," Billy said just above a whisper.

"None of you stupid fuckers is going with me," J.C. came back at once. "Any more than one of us would make too much noise."

J.C. was surprised when he'd walked no more than three hundred yards before encountering the border fence. They had been closer than they thought. He was glad now he'd resisted the temptation to bring a flashlight because almost surely now he'd have used it as he struggled, at 250 pounds, to climb the four strands of barbed wire. When he caught the cuff of his pants on the bottom wire he repressed the impulse to cry out in frustration, for the alien vehicle was just over a small brush-covered knoll within a hundred yards.

When he came close to cresting the rise, he strapped the rifle over his back and began quietly to crawl. Finally, he could see them, and though their fire was small, J.C. recognized the uniforms at once. The three sheriff's deputies appeared to have just finished supper, their empty food cans strewn about their canvas, aluminum-frame camp chairs. They were all young, none over twenty-five, probably part of the search and rescue effort for the missing girl. Parked nearby were a dual-wheeled Ford truck and a stock trailer. Just beyond it three horses had been tied to a mesquite. Now that J.C. lay still, he could feel the cold on the air, and found himself shivering and sweating at once.

One of the men stood, and Juan Carlos tucked his head. Through the stalks of grass, he could see the deputy pick up his spent food tin and look in J.C.'s direction. "Did you guys hear something over there?"

"Probably a damn cow," one of the others said. "Old man Magoffin's got a shit load of cows around here." The young man was spooning the bottom remains of what appeared to be a tuna can. "So Russ caught those two little fuckers in New Mexico today."

One of the other cops, who under the glow of a lantern was just rolling out his sleeping bag, turned to answer. "I told you," he said. "The two ladies with us caught them."

"Bullshit," the other came back. "You're just protecting Billman so he doesn't have to explain the bust to the suits."

"I was there, Jones. Those kids' mothers had them facedown when he got there."

The young deputy eating had finished and put aside the empty can. "Well," he said. "Sounds like bullshit to me."

"Believe what you want." The cop with the bedroll tilted his wristwatch under the light. "It's past midnight. We start early."

The third deputy was digging his things out of the truck cab. "Where from?"

"That ridge about two miles down the road."

"Then why the hell did we camp here?" said the seated cop.

"Because it's a nice place to camp," answered the one with the bedroll.

After the deputies had doused their light, J.C. waited most of half an hour. It seemed longer. He could hear the pulse of his heart between his ears and sweated though the air was no warmer than thirty degrees. Even after lights-out, the cops continued talking, their conversation drifting in hushed tones on the cool night air. At one point a deputy mentioned something about both kids probably being dead. As the conversation finally died, J.C. made his exit.

"Why didn't you cap them?" Chingo asked for the third time. The first two times, his question had brought no response. For warmth, sleeping bags had been rolled out in two close rows of four over the dirt-covered coals. The men were lying and sitting on their respective bedrolls and Amanda lay on her side—hands still bound and duct tape now feeling almost a part of her natural face—some fifteen feet from them, her right ankle tied to the base of a small buck bush, and one of the men's sleeping bags thrown over her.

J.C. finally answered the kid. "I thought about it," he said, "but it wouldn't have been smart."

"Damn stupid, in fact," Ise said. "Blow away three cops—when we don't have to. They'd hunt us all the way down to Tierra del Fuego."

"Maybe we should just take off," J.C. suggested. "Those guys might not give a shit about anything they hear south of the fence."

"Yes, they would," Ise said. "If they're looking for a lost kid, they won't let anything slide."

"You're sure they were county?" Phil asked J.C.

"Absolutely," Juan Carlos said, exasperated. "You guys need to keep your voices down. Phil, I got busted by the sheriffs once. I know what their fucking uniforms look like."

"Then for sure," Phil said, "they're out here looking for that girl. They'll have fifty people in search and rescue. The state police will be involved by Monday. And what you said about that other kid makes me nervous as hell. If there are two lost kids we're really fucked."

When Juan Carlos had come back and told the others he'd heard a boy was missing as well, they naturally queried Amanda. Ise had asked her three times if she was sure she knew nothing about another lost kid. Each time she had shaken her head.

"I say, when those guys leave tomorrow," Phil said, "we lay low for an hour then draw out of this deal."

"We could do that," Ise said calmly. "But I know Rudy Chacon, and he's not very patient. If we don't hook up tomorrow, he won't give us another chance. Within a month he can line up with a score this big or bigger."

A long silence walked by as Ise allowed the notion to settle with all the men. Phil and J.C. stood to become millionaires, and Ise had agreed to triple the boys' salaries because of all the trouble.

"If it doesn't get done now," Ise said, "it won't get done—not now, and maybe not ever. Not for this kind of money, anyway. Opportunities like this are rare. Fools and cowards usually won't take them." Ise's voice hardened then, like a grammar-school teacher driving home a tough lesson to a group of refractory students. "If you want the good things man, I mean the big stuff, you've got to pay big and you've got to take risks."

When Amanda woke she could feel dawn on the air. A breeze had picked up out of the east and the grackles and titmice were just beginning to flutter their wings in the tree branches.

The scraping noise seemed part of her dreaming at first, but when she opened her eyes to the familiar dark shapes of her nightmare, she could still hear it: *scratch, scratch, scratch*, coming from behind her. Slowly, she turned her head to find the hunched form of a man. She recognized Chingo at once, his deep oniony body odor, the dome of his shaved head, as he sat within arm's reach, the glint of a knife blade catching starlight as he scraped it across a smooth, fist-sized stone.

"That's your new alarm clock," he said, just above a whisper.

Then he put down the stone, closed the short distance, and rolled her to her back, pinning her shoulders to the ground with his palms. He brought over his right knee and straddled her thighs, then laid the edge of the knife blade just under her left ear.

"You make one fucking noise and you're dead." His breath made her gag.

He scooted off her legs, unbuttoned her pants and yanked them to her ankles. He cut the hobble loop tied tightly around her left pant leg and boot but could not pull the pants over the stiff leather of the Red Wing. Frustrated, he took his knife to the pants and within thirty seconds had them cut in half. He pulled one half of her jeans, boot and all, over her foot.

He patted her on the hip. "Lift your ass," he whispered. "Lift it." When she complied, he pulled clear her underwear. Amanda clamped her legs tight.

"Open them," Chingo said.

Even threatened with death, she could not will herself to relax those muscles.

"Open them," the boy enjoined, "or I turn you over and do you another way."

She spread her knees two feet apart, the dirt and sharp grass stalks jabbing at the backs of her naked thighs.

"More," he said.

She complied, the cold air intruding the space between her legs. Snow angel, she thought for an absurd moment. The boy loosed his pants.

She squirmed and curled away, and he pushed her back down, back into a long-forgotten dentist's chair, terrified and trapped. She was twelve at the time, and the root canal had been inevitable. She had walked trembling into the waiting room. Once in the chair, though— the spotlamp bearing down on her, the middle-aged, bespectacled man who smelled slightly of oily cologne and hummed blithely as he readied his row of evil-looking instruments—she willed herself to another place, a niche in her consciousness, away from invasion of a private space, away from the trauma, a place where the pain seemed not part of her but a distant happening, where she could empathize with the plight of some other soul without feeling it herself. And now again she was at that place. It could have been five minutes; it could have been an hour.

Not a snow angel, she knew now, but a cricket, crushed underfoot, another cowbird for the stalking cat. She hurt down there, could smell her own blood. Now she knew: nothing was so precious it couldn't be torn, or ground, or butchered, or chipped for kindling—all food for the fire, and no more. It was a simple choice: to endure, to suffer, or to end—dark nothingness. Were it not for her mother, she would choose the latter, and it was that thought—her mother—that made her lift her head.

The men were up now, and tense. They moved little and they eyed the rise to the northwest, on the other side of which the three deputies' loud, jocular voices could be heard as they broke camp. The men noticed her, naked and shivering violently, and J.C. stepped quietly over to her with a blanket, Billy just behind him.

"Damn, she's all blue," Billy said. "Will she make it?"

"Don't know." J.C. knelt down, looked away as he looped her underwear over her ankles and slid them up to her hips. "Butt up," he said to the girl, wincing at the traces of blood on the insides of her thighs. He pulled up her underwear, secured them, then dropped a blanket over her.

"Who the hell did this?" Billy asked.

J.C. turned down the corners of his mouth. "I know who did it."

Ise suddenly turned to the group and raised a hand. Everyone froze. Over the rise, the engine of a large vehicle ground to a start, then the squeak of a trailer and the crunching of gravel under heavy-duty tires.

"Everybody down," Ise hissed. "Flat."

As they lay prone, they watched the sheriff's truck nose out from behind the rise, then clear completely as it slowly moved westward on the main road.

"Don't look back," J.C. said to the moving vehicle. "Don't you fuckers look behind you."

When the vehicle had moved out and the drone of the engine died away, the mood among the men lightened. Ise held up his fist and said yes, like a bowler who'd just made a strike, and a couple of the boys celebrated with whistles and momentary applause.

"*Andale pues,*" Ise said. "Get the shit in the cars and let's move."

"What about her?"

J.C.'s question brought their activity to a stop. Ise walked up to where his partner stood over the shivering child, who, though blanketed, had not regained her normal color, her face a light blue and lips almost lavender. Ise knelt, reached under the blanket to feel the girl's chest. It was cool.

"She's hypothermic," he said.

"What should we do?"

Ise looked to the west. "I'm still nervous about this shit with the sheriffs, man. We'll put her in the Chevy and figure out what to do with her later."

They wrapped the blanket tightly around her, and, J.C. taking her under the arms and Ise at her knees, negotiated the girl's limp body into the back seat of the vehicle.

"Fuck, man," Chingo said. "There ain't any room for us."

J.C. walked to the front of the vehicle and picked up the rifle he'd leaned against the grill, then walked up to the boy as though about to hand him the carbine. He held the weapon to his chest like a guard at attention, then quickly brought the butt of the rifle across the side of the boy's head. Chingo went straight to the ground.

For several seconds, the kid did not move. When he groaned and rolled to his side J.C. kicked him hard in the stomach. Chingo gasped silently, unable to breathe.

Juan Carlos pointed the gun skyward, chambered a shell, and brought the weapon down, the end of the barrel two inches from Chingo's right temple. "My daughter, Ysena, is fourteen," J.C. said. "You won't get the chance to rape her."

"Jesus, J.C.," Phil shouted. "What the hell are you doing?"

"Don't kill him." Ise still leaned, arms folded, against the Chevy.

Finger on the trigger, J.C. stared down at the kid in silence before lifting his rifle and backing out the round.

Chingo spit a mouthful of blood on the ground beside his head. "*Espera, pinche guey*. Just watch, you fat motherfucker. One of these days when you're not looking—*pow*, and your lard ass is dead."

Though the impulse to leave was strong, Ise pointed out that the meeting time with Chacon was between four and five o'clock. It behooved them to lay low and quiet until about noon. The next several hours were tense, and no more than a few words passed between the men. They started the engine to the Chevy and turned up the heater and the girl, still sleeping, began to regain color. The thought of killing her as she lay shivering was unthinkable, even to Isedro Leon.

They had driven the semblance of Jeep trail west for ten minutes when one of the boys, Miguel, spotted the horses on the ridge behind them. He, Billy, Paco, Chingo, Ralph and J.C. were packed in the Chevy as the others in the GMC led the way, so when they stopped, those in the vehicle ahead did not notice right away.

"Right there," Miguel told J.C., who had turned and trained his binoculars through the back windshield. "Right almost at the top of the hill."

"Okay," J.C. said, squinting through the glasses. "It's just some horses. Two are mules, I think." The three animals were at least four hundred yards behind them. All appeared to be saddled, but no riders were in sight. "It's gathering time for ranchers," J.C. offered. "They're probably just rounding up cows, but we'll keep an eye out for them."

When those in the GMC ahead noticed their party in tow had stopped, they did the same and waited, though no longer than a moment, not long enough to raise any kind of concern. But the sound of the chopper, after they'd gone another mile, stopped them dead. All eight windows in both vehicles opened and everyone strained to listen.

The chopper was getting closer, the whirr of its blades slicing the air. Ise emerged from the GMC and trotted back to the Chevy.

"Get out," he said to J.C. "Phil says it sounds like a *Migra* bird— I've got an idea."

By the time the helicopter arrived, cruising fifty knots at two-hundred feet, the three men had donned chore jackets and duckbilled caps. They leaned two rifles against the grill of the GMC and spread a blanket, tossed a couple of opened daypacks on top. The men, for all the world, looked like a trio of Mexican hunters stopping for a late lunch. It was likely Phil knew the occupants of the bird, so when the green and white chopper pattered overhead—the rest of the party holding their breath in the Suburban—they had a shot, perhaps a fifty-fifty chance, of not raising suspicions.

The men waved, and the chopper blinked its white runner lights in return, then moved east and out of sight. Everyone in the party considered the ruse a success. The three men hurried about, wadding up blanket and backpacks and throwing them in the vehicle. They had a little time, at least.

The hook-up point was about three miles west where the road dropped into an arroyo and a four-by-four could cut into the wash, drive a few hundred feet, and park. In the brushy ravine, vehicles were hidden from view both on the ground and in the air. The last time Isedro Leon had used this particular place was several years before. It was a hard spot to get to, and there always stood the risk of being caught, but a relatively large group of packers could mule their con-traband through the wash and hike undetected the half mile to the border.

This was by far the most dangerous drop operation Ise had ever been involved with. J.C. knew this as well, and both of them worked hard not to let it show to the others. Ise was sick with the fact that he needed all the mules. Under any other circumstances, he would have already killed two of them, and for sure he would take out the white kid and probably one of the others after the business was done.

The biggest and most regrettable hitch, though, was the girl. Her color had come back, and she was sitting up in the back seat, still bleeding from the crotch, her underwear now soaked through. Ise had not yet decided how and when to deal with her, but the decision, he knew, had to be made quickly.

Thirty

The fire was warm on Kevin's face. The voices had begun to die away, but Conchillo was still singing.

They had come to a place where the ground leveled out, where the voices were strong, and Kevin, tired, his legs seemingly unable to bear his weight, tried to sit, but the old man had told him to remain standing. Conchillo raised his chin to the star light south of them and sang louder to the voices, mingling such that they no longer sounded human. Kevin tried to cover his ears, but the old man slapped down his hands, pointing himself to the southeast and singing his answers. They began to quiet, the voices and Conchillo along with them. Kevin folded his legs to sit in the dirt, and the old man, still singing softly, went to his knees and began to build the small fire of the special twigs and grasses he'd drawn from the pack.

When the twigs in the fire began to snap, Conchillo told him to look into the flames. "And don't turn away, *mijo.*"

Kevin shook his head. "No," he said. "I'm tired." He had not realized until he tried to speak that he was sobbing.

But the old man, lost again in his singing, did not respond. The flame light caught the contours of his face and his voice rose, keening, and he looked skyward.

Kevin looked at the fire and realized everything was inside him—the singing, the darkness, the stars, the call of the birds, the flames opening a space of light. And the space of light was himself—all his thoughts, and all that he was or ever will be was alive in the flames.

The old man had quit his singing and was speaking to him. First the words made no sense, then they began to form into discernible shapes on the air, and as he realized those shapes he could hear the old man's voice in his head. *Don't be afraid*, he said. *You are safe from these figures.* The shapes came clearer.

First, movement through the flickering light, then muscles working as something stalked along among the cedars on the hillside. Then Old Pete, *El Sombro*, in full form emerged from the thicket into the light, his shining black coat almost touchable. The big cat stopped, ears perked at the scent he'd found on the air, then he lowered his head and drifted on around the hillside. The old man was there beside Kevin.

Follow him, mijo, Conchillo enjoined. *Push away the fear and follow him.*

And so he moved around the hillside after the cat, the ground a cushion of air under his feet, and as he followed he heard the old man's words in his head.

A long time ago, when the world was not yet finished, the darkness came down over the water and their bellies rubbed together in coupling. The sound they made was like animals drinking at the water's edge.

The wind blew strong, and from the tiny space between the darkness and water a child emerged, born of their coupling. He was called First Born. First Born saw the world was not finished, so he got help from the termites and they decided a shape for the world. It would be round. So First Born sat at the bank of the water. He prayed a long time, and this is the song he sang:

> *I ask you Earth Medicine Man to finish the earth.*
> *Come near and put your hand to it.*
> *Come near and give it shape.*
> *Come near and leave the marks of your touch.*

And so, First Born finished the world. Still, he had not made the animals and plants and rocks and mountains.

Also, there was no sun or moon, always dark. The living things didn't like the darkness, so they asked First Born to make light. That way the living things could see each other and be happy together.

"All right," he said to them. "You will name this thing that sheds light."

And so they said, "Its name will be Sun."

So First Born pulled a ball of fire from his mouth and placed it in the sky.

Then the living things said, "Who will keep Sun company? Who will be his mate?"

With help from Medicine Man, First Born chose a stone from the ar-

royo. He placed it in the sky opposite Sun, on the other side of the world, and said, "We will call her Moon. She and Sun will long for each other across the world. They will only touch at special times." And so he set the world and all things in it on this same round path of the stars and Sun and Moon.

First Born watered the earth with fluid from his body, and when he saw the trees and grass move with the wind he was happy, so he said, "There will be plenty of deer and prickly pears and onions and you will always live well."

In this way, First Born prepared the earth for us. Then he went away.

The sky came down and touched the earth, and the first one born of their coupling was I'itoi, our Elder Brother.

The sky met the earth again, and Coyote came forth.

The sky met the earth again, and Buzzard came forth.

Elder Brother, Earth Medicine Man, and Coyote began their work of completing the world, each creating things different from the other. Medicine Man and Coyote gave shape and movement to land and water, to bush and tree. Elder Brother brought forth people out of clay and gave them the sun's red light on the hills in the evening, and so the people knew beauty. And the Desert People knew this as their home, and there they stayed.

Elder Brother, I'itoi, told them to remain in this land, which is the center of all things. He told them that he was the spirit of goodness who watches over them. But he pointed at Buzzard, who rode high in the sky. He warned the people that he, too, would be here always, as long as the moon and sun.

And it is in this way the world has always moved.

Kevin followed the old cat for miles, and from the high ridge, he could see him slowly moving through a wide flat into the shadows.

There was a feeling of completion in this, as though he had run a long race. The air around him felt open, and there was nowhere he was afraid to go. The cedar flat lay in shadow now, and the big cat was gone, and from far away he could hear the old man singing, calling him back.

The singing grew louder, and his limbs felt heavy again and he opened his eyes to see the fire embers, Conchillo on the other side of them. The old man's arms were wrapped around his knees and he was shivering. The night air was raw, and Kevin turned his head, stretching his neck, stiffened for cold.

"*Ya ta he,*" the old man said. "*Bienvenido.*" He laughed.

Kevin smiled. *Welcome back* was an appropriate greeting.

"It's cold, old man," he said to Conchillo. "You should stoke that fire."

"Where did you go?" Conchillo asked.

Kevin shook his head. "I'm not sure," he said.

The old man gestured at the fire embers. "*Pon mas.* Put more wood if you want."

Kevin rose and gathered a few twigs, laid them over the coals and blew on them. In a moment, new flames rose.

"How do you feel?" Conchillo asked.

The effects of the peyote had *waned,* though he still felt a buzzing in his ears. "I don't know," Kevin said honestly.

Conchillo put his hands out, warming them on the fire.

"It must be late," Kevin said.

The old man glanced up at the stars, nodded. "Pretty late."

They stared into the fire. "I feel like I've been somewhere," Kevin said. "But I don't know where."

Conchillo nodded, as though to a story he'd heard before. "You will," he said. He smiled. "If I was Navajo, we'd do a sweat right now."

"I could use a sauna," Kevin said. He lifted his arm, smelled. "Definitely a bath."

"No doubt," the old man said. They laughed, fell silent.

"I'm driving back," Kevin said.

"I know."

Another silence. Kevin stood, helped the old man to his feet. "I remember now," he said.

"I know."

As they made their way back down canyon toward the truck, Kevin thought about Ursula and his first good kiss. He knew she was alive, he could feel it, and her son grown and strong. A whisper of sadness moved through him, the understanding that he would never again have such a kiss. It was a sendoff, the last sweet thing before he would walk into the hell that was the remainder of that day.

Conchillo moved slowly ahead of him, the beam of flashlight leading them down the trail. The old man sang softly, and Kevin was caught by a cold, thirty-year-old wind blowing out of the south.

Thirty-One

Kevin, on Sally, had broken trail, and he and Mondy were anxious to get to the corrals and back home. They'd bottomed out in a particularly steep canyon and rested there. Dunk pushed up next to Sally, and Turk snuffled, shifting his feet. Bonny had nosed off into the brush somewhere, but Kevin knew, as always, she would come back soon enough. All the animals were tired and hungry and wanted to get home.

When they gained the top of the ridge, they cut a cattle trail that angled for a high saddle to the northwest. From this vantage point, they saw, at the base of the ridge, the road they had been looking for, which old Eduardo had confidently told them was there. Kevin had felt the strength in the old man's character and the words he spoke. Still, he was worried and tired and scared—and ready for whatever was to come.

They had ridden the road just a few minutes—Bonny trotting contentedly ahead of them, the three equine, heads hanging, settled into a molly trot—when they heard vehicles perhaps a half mile behind them. Quickly, they made for the oaks, thicker on the left side of the road, and hid from view. As the two vehicles slowly passed, they saw snatches of black steel between branches and knew these were the vehicles from the day before. Their detour and stay-over with the bracero camp had put them on a shorter route, so that now they'd come out ahead of the vehicles.

When engine sounds faded, Mondy and Kevin climbed the nearest hill for a better view. At a small clearing about two-thirds up, they dismounted and watched the vehicles through their glasses. The vehicles had gone some three hundred yards when the one in the rear stopped, its brake lights as unnerving as an alarm bell.

"Shit," Kevin said. "Do you think they see us?"

"I don't think they can see *us*," Mondy said, "not hidden in this juniper. But I bet they see the horses."

The thrum of Kevin's heart would not allow him to hold his glasses steady. "What do we do?"

"We wait," Mondy said. "We don't panic."

Kevin counted his heartbeats. After twenty, the vehicles began to move slowly down the road, disappearing into the trees.

They decided to stay on the ridge, which ran parallel to the road for at least a mile. Though they ran a risk of being seen on higher ground, they needed the vantage point. Once they'd struck a game trail along the crest, they lifted to a lope until they could again hear the drone of the vehicles, then they moved downslope until the brush opened up to a clear view of the two Suburbans. They dismounted and, through binoculars, watched as the vehicles—a Chevy and a GMC, directly below them—passed from view.

"Could you see in the windows?" Mondy asked.

"No," Kevin said, "they're too damn dark."

They didn't speak for a moment.

"We still don't know if they have her," Kevin pointed out.

"What does your down-deep tell you?"

"My down-deep says the girl I saw by those trucks yesterday was Amanda."

"I'll go with your down-deep," Mondy said.

Through the space between the oak trees they could see the Arizona side of the mountains lumbering off to the north. Kevin put up his glasses, looked for a moment, brought them down.

"We're pretty close to those corrals we started out at the other day."

"How do you know?"

Kevin pointed north. "See the red bluffs about three miles away?"

"Yes."

"That's the south-east side of Outlaw. Your screwy friend from the res was right. We're within two or three miles."

"Why would they be headed that way? There'll be a shit load of people looking for you—maybe Mandi."

"I don't know," Kevin said. "Maybe they couldn't change their contact point."

They'd regained the top of the ridge and had ridden just a few minutes when they heard the helicopter. A distant, low thumping at first, almost dismissible, but within seconds it became distinct and there remained little doubt that the craft was getting closer. Kevin and Mondy swung off their mounts and jogged to a large clearing. They shed their jackets to wave like flags. Mondy opened his fanny pack, drew out an empty Pepsi can, cut it in half to use its inner lining as reflector signal.

When the Border Patrol chopper finally came into view, it was a good half mile north. Wave though they did, the chopper only dipped behind a distant rise then banked north, apparently headed back for Sulfur Springs valley.

They continued along the game trail for a quarter mile when they heard gunfire. It was perhaps a mile away and came in rapid, sputtering volleys—thirty to forty rounds fired inside two minutes. Not hunters, not target shooters—this was a battle. They decided to take the road and hurried down the ridge, bringing their mounts to a gallop on the Jeep trail. They had reached a silent agreement. They could not sit idle, or run away, or even go to this thing at a saunter.

Bonny, the mules, and horse seemed to have tapped some deep store of saved energy as they stretched themselves into full run. The road rounded a small rise and they saw—two hundred yards to the north—a county vehicle and stock trailer, all four doors of the pickup's king cab hanging open.

Mondy pulled Turk to a stop, and eyed the inert vehicle.

"That's a sheriff's truck," Kevin said.

They broke from the road and made straight for the truck, coming upon a barbed-wire fence.

Mondy climbed off Turk, dug a fence tool from a sidesaddle, and snapped the top wire.

"That's a federal offense right there," Kevin said. "Cutting down an international border."

Mondy snapped the remaining three wires. "We don't have time to fuck with taking it down and putting it back up."

Kevin resisted the temptation to hector his friend for stating the obvious. A bad feeling had gripped him and when they reached the sheriff's truck he found out why.

The two dead men lay about six feet apart, faces down. Kevin could tell by the shapes of their bodies, their hairstyles, that both deputies were young, little older than he. When Mondy got off his horse, Kevin could not will himself to do the same. He watched as his friend took the pulse of each man, though the exit wounds in both bodies spoke little hope of life.

Mondy shook his head. "They should be alive."

"Did you not dream this?" Kevin asked.

"No," Mondy said. "I'm glad I didn't."

One of the deputies lay a few feet from the driver's side door. He apparently had died quickly, shot when he climbed out of the truck, and he bore two exit wounds in the center of his back. One of the bullets had probably severed his spine and he seemed to have died without a struggle. Not true, however, for the other young man.

This boy had been thirty feet from the truck when he took the first bullet through his stomach. The second and third shots had struck him in the back, probably as he had turned to run, just below the rib cage. After finally covering the thirty feet back to the truck, he had crumpled beside his already dead colleague. The ground around him was scarred with his struggle—his boots had cut the dirt and he'd dug small pits in the road with his fingernails in the perhaps fifteen minutes it had taken him to finally expire. The smell of his excrement, as one bullet had passed through his large intestine, was undeniable, perverse.

Kevin almost asked Mondy to turn the bodies over, then thought better of it. He did not want to see the faces and was almost certain, and glad for it, he did not know either man. Both officers had been stripped of weapons and radios and the short band in the truck had been smashed to bits with some kind of implement, perhaps an ax or shovel. The keys had been taken and all four tires slashed.

As they examined the scene, three horses clumped around and snuffled nervously in the stock trailer, and though the trailer was pocked with several bullet holes, none of the animals, amazingly, had been hit. Mondy backed the horses out and they agreed to leave the animals to free range to find a water tank on their own. All three were fine Appaloosa stock, and they would be easy enough to catch when the time arrived.

Kevin and Mondy walked the fifty yards to the border fence and found two sets of heavy-duty tire tracks on the other side.

"Those guys in the Suburbans shot from right here," Mondy said. "The deputies must have seen them on the road over there. So they drove up to this fence close range and took 'em by surprise. God they got a lot of fire power. Must have been eight or ten guns fired. And those two guys back there never shot a round."

"They're damn sure desperate," Kevin said. He felt about to vomit, and tried to train his mind off his stomach.

"Must have a lot at stake. Big money."

Kevin said what they were both thinking. "I hope Amanda's okay."

They were quiet. "We could look for her here," Mondy finally said.

Kevin shook his head. "I've thought of that. If she's left somewhere in this brush it's already too late."

Though they'd considered saddling the fresher, more rested county horses, Mondy and Kevin determined they were better off on the mounts they'd grown accustomed to the last few days. They decided to stay on the Arizona side, and as soon as they stepped on to the county road they cut a blood trail, a dozen half-dollar-sized drops that quit at the opposite shoulder.

"A third guy," Mondy said.

They came into sight of Simon Banks' body within a few seconds. The young deputy had staggered from the road and, for some odd reason—perhaps addled for loss of blood—had tried to climb a barbed-wire fence a few yards from the shoulder. A small caliber bullet had taken him in the soft flesh just under his jaw and had exited below the chin. The round had apparently nicked his jugular and he was able to walk eighty yards before he finally bled out, and now the young deputy—his jacket sleeves caught in the barbs—hung, arms splayed, from the fence.

Kevin and Mondy stood on either side of the body. Kevin wanted to lift Banks' corpse from the wires, but Mondy admonished him not to—they were looking at a crime scene and it would contaminate forensics to touch anything. But Kevin had made up his mind. He could not leave a young man he knew in such an undignified attitude.

Banks' body felt heavier than he had looked in life. Kevin and Mondy pulled his jacket sleeves from the barbs and leaned him to the ground on his back. His arms had stiffened at the elbows and would not lay flat, so with his clouded eyes turned slightly upward and his fingers curled, he looked to be making some grotesque plea to the heavens. Kevin went to his knees, held his belly and rocked back and forth, trying not to vomit. He began to sob instead, harder than he had since he was ten years old. Mondy laid a hand on his shoulder, and Kevin swatted it away. "Don't touch me." Mondy stood silent as Kevin wept. When he'd recovered himself, he took a deep breath, and Mondy helped him to his feet. They looked at the road, where it cut across the ridge and down toward the west.

"This is real," Kevin said.

Mondy nodded. "Yes. This is real."

Thirty-Two

Kevin felt a hundred pounds lighter, having showered and slept. The old man had worried that he would be uncomfortable on the couch, but Kevin was so tired and strung out that he could have easily passed out on the floor. He'd called the Gilberts when he and Conchillo had gotten back earlier that morning to let his mother and sister know his whereabouts, and now he sat at the old man's kitchen table drinking his raunchy coffee, the stack of papers from the county archives in front of him. The old man was determined to cook breakfast, and he stood at the stove, his curses mingling with the smell of burnt pancakes.

"Looks like it's gonna be just eggs and toast, *mijo*."

At Conchillo's behest, Kevin had phoned Russ Billman, who would be over shortly. Talking with Russ seemed the appropriate resolution to all of this, though the old deputy may have a limited or inaccurate account of his side of things. Kevin, nonetheless, had given him directions to Conchillo's place. As he perused the police reports, he was reminded of how poorly cops tended to write. They either erred on the side of over-officiousness, sounding like a mawkish Joe Friday, loading the report with so many facts and details that the gist of the narrative was smothered—or they were Spartan and inarticulate, leaving unanswered questions.

A Toyota compact pulled up about 10:30 a.m., Rachael Martinez driving and Russ in the passenger's seat. Through the yellowed pane of the old man's front-room window, Kevin caught her profile as she leaned to kiss the old man goodbye.

"Jesus H Christ, Benny," Russ said. "You call this coffee?" The old man had poured him a cup from the saucepan.

"It's all I got," Conchillo said.

Russ eyed the papers in front of Kevin. "You steal those?"

Kevin glanced up at him. "They're on loan."

Russ jerked his head. "Well," he said. "I'd arrest you for possession of state property if I still had the authority."

Kevin flipped through the pages. He could feel Russ studying him.

"They don't tell you much, do they?" Russ said.

Kevin shook his head. "No, they don't."

Both men leaned back in their chairs, looked at each other. "Even if I could remember everything that happened," Russ said. "Even if you could relive the whole thing, right here, right now, you'd still have questions—doubts."

"I know."

"Another thing," Russ said. "Derrick Waylon is hell bent right now."

"To do what?" Kevin asked.

"He's working on an arrest warrant for you. Assault."

Kevin groaned. "Shit, Russ, I've got to teach on Wednesday."

Russ waved his hand. "He won't do anything," he assured. "But you do have to talk to him, Kev."

"And what the hell am I supposed to say."

"Just talk to him. See where you go from there."

Russ flipped through the papers, muttering occasionally, cursing under his breath, at one point chuckling softly. Finished, he pushed the documents back into a stack. "Looks like nobody knew too much about this whole thing."

Kevin nodded.

Russ looked across the table at Conchillo, dirty breakfast plates between them. "Got any more of that crappy coffee?"

Conchillo pointed to the kitchen. "You can get your old ass up and get it yourself."

"I'll get it," Kevin said. When he returned with the coffee, Russ took a sip and winced.

"This shit's worse than what they give you at AA meetings." He looked at Kevin. "Best I can do," he said, "is tell you what I remember and what I heard."

Russ stared off toward the corner of the room, lost in some thought—not a happy one, by the look on his face. Focusing in on the two men at the table with him, he said, "This is what I know."

Thirty-Three

A morning of miscommunication and fiasco had put Russ at his destination hours later than intended. The two dozen search and rescue volunteers and a TV news truck from Tucson had confused his directions from the night before. They had agreed to meet him at seven a.m. at the Monahan ranch, but they had instead taken the wrong road and ended up in the front yard of a perplexed rancher, six miles north of the Monahan place. Russ had driven up and down Geronimo Trail half the morning trying to locate them, but finally gave up and headed for the corrals where he expected to meet both sets of parents and the Hallots.

Upon finally reaching his destination, he found the place vacant. The parents and Olivia Hallot, despite his telling them to wait, had left to continue the search on their own, leaving two bitch bloodhounds, lent out by the county the day before, baying in their kennels. Russ poked around the corrals and parked vehicles for several minutes before he found O.D.'s note. The stitches on his cheek itched and the wound throbbed beneath so that he had difficulty drawing his thoughts together. He figured the parents and Olivia Hallot had followed the two sets of horse tracks, made by the McNally's mare and the horse of the driver of the New Mexico truck, down the wash that ran south.

The deputy walked back to his truck and clicked the receiver on his short band, surprised to hear Si Banks' voice booming back at him.

"That you, Russ?"

"Hey, Si. My twenty's at those corrals from yesterday. What about you?"

"A few miles east of there. We camped last night after Dan called us."

The three young deputies had ridden the trail fifteen miles both ways that day, calling the lost kids' names until hoarse, and had seen nothing. The young deputy explained, however, that he'd gotten a broken transmission from O.D. Hallot earlier that morning.

"What'd he say?" Russ asked the boy.

"Don't know," Banks said. "I lost him."

"Well, get over here quick," Russ said, eyeing the note bearing O.D.'s scrawl. "I've got a new lead."

"Roger that," said the young man, whose voice Russ was never to hear again.

Russ learned later that the parents and Olivia Hallot had ridden southeast, following the sets of tracks for about an hour.

Just after eight a.m. they'd ridden over a lone, small creosote-covered hill in the flats south of the Escrobarra trail and glassed the long rugged vista below. Thomas suggested he and John make a short jaunt, about an hour's ride, around a gentle hill to the southeast, saying even more of the Mexico part of the range could be seen from there. The three women had disagreed with the plan.

"I think we're going the wrong way," Teresa said.

"Why do you say that?" Thomas asked. "I'm pretty sure those are Trixy's prints we've followed."

"I'm *not* sure," she said. "And even if O.D. went this way, it doesn't necessarily mean Amanda and Kevin are still in this area. I'm for going back to the corrals."

Finally, it was Olivia Hallot's argument that was the most convincing: the tracks they had followed were not necessarily those of Teresa's mare, since the ground in the area had been cut with those of so many other equine. They had now searched going on two days and it only made sense to get outside help. Certainly, law officers and the volunteers would be at the corrals sometime that morning. In the end, though, John convinced the group to make a short excursion east and circle back to the corrals along a road he knew ran beside the border fence.

They rode well into the morning, by turns cutting back to the north and then to the south. All were exhausted and heartsick and feeling grim when they heard the shots about a mile and a half ahead, close to the border. Dozens of rounds fired within a minute did not suggest hunters, or any kind of recreational shooters, for that matter.

John Monahan pointed slightly northeast, to the bare side of a long sloping ridge. "There's a good trail over the low side of that ridge. Other side's a road that runs alongside the border fence. We can be there in twenty minutes."

At the corrals, three miles northwest, Russ climbed behind the wheel of his truck and decided it was a warm enough day to roll down his window. The shots were far enough to the east to seem a mere series of soft poppings. The sound did, however, get his attention. He stepped out of the truck and cocked an ear, certain now it was gunfire.

Thirty-Four

O.D. and Harold Placer found a rise high enough to see where the shooting had come from. After a half-day tracking venture which had taken them in a circle, they found themselves on a Jeep road. Placer was sure the two vehicles whose tire tracks they'd supposedly followed all morning were heading for this particular piece of road. O.D., though, was skeptical. Placer had spent all day looking down at what O.D. thought to be regular old rocks and dirt, and just as O.D. was beginning to suspect Placer was a bit of a bull shitter they heard the gunfire.

They'd immediately spotted the parked vehicle a mile or so to the east, and after examining it through binoculars, determined that two or more of its doors stood open. They kept an eye on the county truck some ten minutes, but no one returned to claim it. When the low grind of vehicle engines emerged several canyons to the east, Placer touched O.D.'s shoulder. "Listen up," he said. "There's our perps."

"Yeah," O.D. came back, "and they could be quail hunters, too."

"Quail hunters shoot shotguns. That was rifle and pistol fire."

"Close as I could tell," O.D. allowed. "But my hearing ain't so good anymore."

"Well, mine is."

The two black Suburbans came into view a mile west, their drivers horsing them up a steep incline, then dropping over to the lee side of the ridge.

Placer nodded down to the ground on which they sat. "They're right on this road here."

"It seems."

Placer tucked his binoculars into his shirt and surveyed the area. "We need to find high ground."

A few minutes later, they sat in a low mahogany and cholla-littered saddle overlooking the road where the Suburbans would soon pass by. They'd tied off their horses out of view on the other side of the rise. Slowly, the two vehicles, as though the machines themselves were attempting to sneak, passed then disappeared under a canopy of oak branches then reappeared, ascending a rise a quarter mile west. Soon after the vehicles had gone over, the engine sounds ceased perhaps a half mile from the original corrals were everything had begun.

"They've parked. I'll bet they're getting their packs and making their run now," Placer said. "If we got a chance to help that girl we need to get going."

The ridge they were on had little cover, but they rode it out to the point at which it converged with the small broom-grass swells where they'd last seen the vehicles. Just as they bottomed out, before climbing the rise the road cut through, they heard more gunfire. This series, though, was not as frantic as the last and came in intermittent volleys, like the sound of Fourth of July fireworks.

When they topped out, the two vehicles were much closer than anticipated—within a hundred-fifty yards. It was movement, not men, they saw first. One of the several men stood, rifle aimed, and fired a rapid eight shots toward the northwest. Some of the other weapons were aimed at Placer and O.D. "They've seen us," Placer said. "Get down and find cover."

Even in battle, an uninitiated soldier will often take a few seconds to recognize he is in danger. In that time, a bullet from even a small-caliber weapon has long since found its path. By the time O.D. realized they were being shot at, Harold Placer had already been hit.

A moment before the bullet found its mark, perhaps a sixteenth of a second, there had been a sharp pop on the air, as the projectile broke the sound barrier. It sounded as though the little man had perhaps popped his big gelding on the rear with the reins—but a twenty-two caliber bullet had already exited through his back and tumbled into the brush behind them.

Placer had climbed off his horse and walked back into the mahogany thicket as though, it seemed to O.D., to take a leak. In the midst of his bewilderment, O.D. realized the sonic clap and buzz-whistle noises he was hearing were bullets flying past, the reports from the rifles following shortly behind.

By the time he and Placer had dropped from the shooters' view, and O.D. had climbed off Trixy, the little mare had been hit in the chest. She stood trembling, rocked back and forth for a moment before her haunches began to quiver and her hind end settled slowly to the ground and she collapsed altogether.

O.D. stepped over to the spot where Placer lay. The little man held his right hand over his chest like a school child reciting the Pledge of Allegiance. The front wound was not immediately visible, but the exit hole had pumped a puddle of blood that had spread under the deputy and past his shoulders. O.D.'s first impulse was to cover the wound, and from his front pocket he pulled a wadded paper towel he'd stuck in there earlier that day. But the gesture seemed futile when he looked down at the little man's face.

Placer's stare was aimed blankly skyward. He worked his jaw as though to chew up the gristle in the air and then was dead.

"Gonna be okay, Harold," O.D. said. "You stay down. It'll be okay."

Trixy lay on her left side, the butt of O.D.'s .308 poking out of the saddle scabbard. On his big belly, O.D. crawled to the dead horse faster than most twenty-year-olds could have. He pulled out the rifle, unbuttoned the side pack and removed a box of shells. Across the horse's still-warm shoulder, he laid the rifle, putting his crosshairs on the first man he found in the scope. Some hundred-and-thirty yards away, the man lay prone, what appeared to be a carbine rifle resting over his large backpack. The others, eight of them, lay scattered about a twenty-yard perimeter in much the same attitude. They were all aiming to the northwest, apparently no longer considering O.D. and Placer a threat. O.D. could not make out what they shot at now. Firing intermittently, none of them noticed one of their party had been shot as O.D. touched off on him.

When the bullet struck him in the chest, the man jerked slightly and lay still, the others still firing at the yet unidentified target. O.D. chambered another round and took aim at a second man, when he finally saw what the smugglers were shooting at.

Several hundred yards north, on the road just the other side of the border fence, Russ Billman's county vehicle flashed in and out of the mesquite and ranger sage, weaving to a stop in clear view of the assailing smugglers. O.D. adjusted his rifle scope to twelve power and watched as Russ, apparently unhurt, piled out of the driver's-side door and took cover behind the front end of his truck. More shots, two fired from different weapons, about two seconds apart.

These rounds, however, were not fired by O.D., Russ, or the smugglers, and seemed to have originated several hundred yards to the east. The two bullets careened over O.D. and hit in the brush twenty yards below the rise where the Suburbans were parked. O.D. would learn later that his wife Olivia, Teresa McNally, and Yolanda Monahan had been behind him on a ridge high enough to see the entire exchange and had in desperation lobbed bullets from their rifles at the assailants. Olivia, as she later told federal investigators, could at one point, within the field of her binoculars, see O.D., smugglers, Russ, Mondy, Kevin, and Amanda Monahan all at once.

O.D., of course, did not yet know this and was intent on determining Russ's next move. The deputy emerged from behind the truck and returned three quick rounds from his county issue shotgun, a weapon manifestly inadequate for the task at hand.

The smugglers answered with a volley of shots then waited for the deputy to raise his head again.

"Russ," O.D. muttered. "Keep your ass down. You can't do no good."

O.D. had just leveled down on the second man again when a thought struck him. He reached for his belt and plucked from it the little Cobra radio. He clicked the receiver button to call, waited several seconds, then clicked it again, more desperately this time.

"Come on, Russ, answer up," he said. "Answer up if you know what's good for you."

Thirty-Five

Kevin had agreed to go with Russ and Conchillo to Douglas police headquarters, but regretted it as soon as they arrived. Like a cat about to suffer some wrongdoing at the hands of children, he'd sensed malice afoot. Russ, in the passenger's seat, had glanced back several times at Conchillo on the drive over, and Kevin could feel some sort of trap tightening around him. By the time they pulled up in front of the building, he'd tried to turn around several times and had been talked out of it. In the parking lot, Kevin refused to get out of the car. When he spotted his sister's Honda Accord a few cars down, he knew he shouldn't have come.

They were admitted behind the glassed front counter into one of the interview rooms, where Kevin wasn't terribly surprised to see his mother, sister, and Olivia seated at a conference table. Derrick Waylon stood at a window.

The police station had once been the El Paso railroad depot, active from before the turn of the Twentieth Century until the mid-1960's. Kevin thought its dignity had been considerably sullied when, six years before, the city had restored the structure into the police headquarters and jail, as though a makeover would somehow cover a lack of integrity in the Douglas police force.

"Shit," Kevin said. "This *felt* like a damn setup."

George Meeker walked into the room from a side door and flopped a file folder into the middle of the table. No one spoke. Kevin moved to the head of the eight-foot table. The room was considerably spiffier than the one he'd been held in, framed certificates and watercolor landscapes arranged on the walls. No visible security cameras.

"I could sure use some coffee," he said. "And to know what the hell all this is about."

"I'll go get coffee," Olivia said.

"Hold on," George said, raising his hand. "Someone's bringing coffee. It'd be nice if everyone just stuck around." He walked to the center of the room, looked at Kevin. "I arranged for us all to meet here this morning." He contemplated his shoes, head down, hands on his hips. "This is a delicate matter, and there's been a lot of confusion," he said finally, looking up. "I don't want it discussed in a public forum."

Kevin chuckled. "You guys wouldn't want to damage your reputation."

Both cops glared at him, Derrick looking from the window to stare a hole in the side of Kevin's head.

George threw up his hands in exasperation. "Look," he said, pulling a chair out from the table and sitting. "This is a police matter, yes. And no. I would rather no one went to the press—but it's also personal." He looked down at his hands on the table. "This happened a long time ago. There were no TV cameras and only one officer," he gestured toward Russ, "to have a record of what happened. We have fragmented memories. Fear. Guilt. And that's about it. Derrick here is ready to hear some unpleasant things. Neither of us, nor the local authorities, wants this to go public. Still, it's time to draw things out into the open."

Police radios and voices in the throes of their day-to-day routines could be heard from adjoining rooms. George nodded toward Derrick, who still sulked by the window. "This young man is a friend of mine, and he suffers for this, believe me."

"Well, he's not the only one," Teresa said.

"Okay," George said. "Derrick, I'm going to go ahead and tell them."

Derrick's shoulders tightened, and he did not look away from the window.

George stared at the file folder on the table. "Until yesterday," he said, "Officer Waylon here did not know about his father's activities in November of 1976 or his involvement in any illegal activity prior. That was the first time he'd ever heard of it—a hell of a blow." Meeker looked around the room, checking expressions. "Any kind of real cover up preceded me and this administration and the one before and the administration before that." He looked at Kevin. "Go to the press if you want. Shout it from the rooftops, I can't do anything about that— but I'm here today for another reason."

"So," Kevin interrupted. "What is the purpose of this? Gifts and well wishes?"

"Kevin," Tracy scolded from across the table.

George let out a breath. "I don't know," he said. "A purging of sorts, I guess. Too much confusion and innuendo going around. You are some of the people still alive who were there at the time of those shootings." The cop put his hands flat on the table. "I'm risking my career here, but this has gone on long enough. I think we should get our heads and our memories together and exhume this thing and figure out, as close as we can tell, what happened that day."

Teresa held up her hand, looked across the table at her son. "Kevin?" she asked.

"I'm okay," he assured her.

Teresa looked at George. "This has been hard."

The cop nodded. "No offense, but anybody can tell that by looking at him," he said, gesturing Kevin's way. "He's lucky to be a free man right now."

"It pisses me off," Russ broke in, "that you hold any law over this boy's head, George. That guy the other night didn't press charges for assault. And you guys picking up Kevin on DUI was bullshit."

George held up a hand. "I know, Russ. I stand corrected. Kevin's extortion charge was close to accurate. Like I say, this is a risk for me. I do it for friendship, and for the sake of the truth, I guess."

Kevin was skeptical, though he worked not to let his doubts show. After the strange ceremony last night, he felt much more relaxed in this business. He looked over at Conchillo, sitting stony-faced beside the equally stoic Olivia. The old man had not said a word, and his rock-like expression signaled disapproval, but the fact that he was here, that he'd been involved in arranging this meeting, suggested otherwise.

"What's the folder for?" Tracy asked.

George picked up the folder. "This is an FBI document on the incident." He looked at Kevin. "It wasn't in the reports you stole from the archives."

Russ moved in his chair, and George looked at him. "A misdemeanor at most, Russ. No worries."

"Phil Waylon was a federal agent," George said. "The Bureau, under these particular circumstances, did an investigation."

"Whose testimony?" Kevin asked.

George looked at him. "From some of you in here, though you all were pumped by so many entities for information it's probably just a blur." The cop placed the folder back on the table. "And from a couple of people not at this table today."

"Like who?" Kevin asked.

George looked at his watch. "I'm not disposed to say who," he said, "but one or both said they might be here later."

"The feds never talked to me," Russ broke in.

"Yes they did, Russ," George said. "You just don't remember."

Kevin felt panicked. Quickly, he moved his chair back.

"Kevin," his mother said.

"I want to know *who else* is coming today." Kevin stood, and the room went silent. He looked at George, then at his mother.

Teresa looked down into her lap.

"I've told my mother," Kevin said. "I'm not ready to see anyone else who was there."

"Honey," Teresa said. "You've got to sometime."

"Listen," George broke in. "I don't even know if they're coming yet. Dr. McNally, please relax."

Kevin remained standing.

Derrick Waylon turned to face him, his chest inflated, fists clenched.

"I'd like to know what your malfunction is, boy wonder." Kevin said to him.

Waylon took a step toward Kevin, and George stood. "Derrick," he barked. The younger officer froze, and George shook his head. "I swear to God, both of you. If this doesn't stop, I'm having you both stripped down buck naked and thrown into a cell together."

The comment put a crack in Conchillo's stony expression, and the old man smiled. "It's a good joke," he said. "Laugh."

Russ smiled. Tracy covered her mouth to hide her giggling. And in a moment everyone, including Kevin and Derrick, gave in to an embarrassed chuckling.

"*Siéntate, mijo,*" Conchillo told him. "*Cálmate.*"

"You, too, Derrick," George said. "Come sit down."

Kevin sat. "Anybody got a deck of cards," he said. "I don't know why, but I'm kind of in the mood for some strip poker."

Everyone laughed a bit too heartily. Reluctantly, Derrick took a chair beside Russ.

George waited for the chuckling to calm. "I have a kind of plan for today." He looked about the table. "I thought we could give each person their time to speak—a few minutes at least, uninterrupted. That way we're not talking over each other, cross-remembering. Everyone has a chance to give their side of things. That is, if they want to. No one *has* to say *anything*, obviously."

"Quakers, I guess," Kevin quipped.

"I'll start," Olivia said suddenly. She looked at Teresa. "I may need your help."

Teresa nodded, and Tracy reached over and took her hand.

"None of us have really talked about this since it happened," she said. "I'll do the best I can."

Thirty-Six

Olivia and O.D. Hallot never had a moment's doubt they would see this thing out to its end. Though both of their boys, eleven and thirteen, were safely at home with Olivia's sister, Kevin had been like one of their own children. If Tom and Teresa, their best friends, were in any kind of trouble, the Hallots owned that trouble too.

They set out on the second morning of the search with the four parents, O.D. stationed at the holding corrals and Olivia staying with the search party. It was about 2:00 in the afternoon and the mounted searchers had come to the road just south of the border fence and were making their way west. It was John who pointed out the two black Suburbans picking their way up the road. They quickly determined that to follow them directly on the same road would put the party out of sight of the two suspicious vehicles, so they made for higher ground, luckily finding a ridge trail that kept the Suburbans, for the most part, within visibility. After riding a quarter mile, they stopped at an outcropping of granite to glass. As the others watched to the west, Olivia glanced east, noting, about a half-mile away, the Arizona side of the fence and the stopped county truck, its doors standing open.

"Looks like Si Banks' rig," John said. "I wonder what those guys are up to."

"No telling," Teresa said.

"Hey, look at this." Yolanda Monahan's voice was tight, urgent. "Look at them, the one toward the middle."

They trained their glasses back to the Suburbans, whose occupants, a thousand yards away, had emerged. The people, perhaps ten of them, looked like slow-moving specks.

"That's Amanda," Yolanda said. She was shaken, crying.

"No way to tell," John said.

"Goddamn it," Yolanda came back. "I know my child. That's her."

John looked up the ridge and pointed to another lip of granite outcropping. "Either way," he said, "we need to get closer. Let's get to that rim rock there."

Riding horses any distance in rough terrain with no clear trail is dangerous—the party had, at a hard lope, ascended the better part of the low-pitched ridge when Yole's mare snapped a front leg. When the horse plunged forward, Yolanda managed to tuck and roll, unharmed, into a patch of grass. The mare, now on her side, thrashed and screamed in distress.

"John." Yolanda was up on her knees.

John ran to his wife. "You okay?"

But Yolanda was fixed on the suffering animal, now making a futile attempt to raise itself. "Chica," she called to her.

John went back to his horse, pulling his rifle from the saddle scabbard. The shooting to the west, from the direction of the black vehicles, came intermittent and spoke urgency. "Turn away," he told his wife.

"No."

"Turn away, Yole."

"No, goddamn you."

John, in three strides, stepped up to the horse and put the muzzle to her ear. Surprisingly, the animal did not move, seeming to resign itself to fate.

Yolanda spoke to her. "It's alright, honey. It's alright."

When John shot, the horse's muscles constricted, its hind legs, as though on a bicycle, pedaling a moment. John climbed back on his horse, and Yolanda followed, swinging up behind her husband without taking her eyes off the dead mare. All of them hoped that no one from down below had noticed the shot.

At the second point of rocks, they were perhaps seven hundred yards from the parked Suburbans. Though they could hear the fired shots, it took several moments to find through their glasses the vehicle's occupants, who were lying scattered on the ground a short distance to the right. None of them appeared to be Amanda Monahan.

They spotted Russ Billman's truck and then Russ himself taking cover behind the vehicle, the circumstance more solid support for Yolanda's earlier suspicion. John and Thomas spoke under their breath to each other and the three women watched through their glasses down canyon. When Yolanda heard her husband say, "…and if we can get to that bald rise down there…" she turned and said, "No way. No fucking way."

"It's the only way we can do any good," Thomas came back.

"If you go, we go," Teresa said.

"No sense all of us picking our way down there," John said. "Five of us would be in plain sight of those guys for a few hundred yards."

"Then none of us goes," Yolanda said.

"I think Amanda's down there," John said.

"I know she is," the girl's mother said.

Despite the objections, the decision had been made. John and Thomas mounted up and edged their horses down slope, the women quiet, no farewells. When the two men dropped into the trees at the base of the ridge, Yole and Teresa wept quietly. Olivia had not taken down her glasses—she had seen something that brought a crossways feeling of both distress and relief.

In the middle of the two-hundred yards of space between the shooters and Russ's truck, three equine appeared, two mules and a horse, the last of which Olivia felt sure was the McNally's one-eyed gelding, Turk. Two male figures emerged momentarily from the brush and ran behind a clump of boulders a short distance away. Kevin and Mondy.

Now that the two were hidden behind the rocks, Olivia doubted what she had seen and remained silent. Then Kevin, clearly Kevin McNally, stood and fired his rifle, ducking back down after less than a second. And it came together then—the assailants were not only firing at Russ but also at the two boys, all of them pinned down by the shooters.

Two of the assailants were standing, rapidly firing their weapons. Prone on the ground beside one of the backpacks lay a person, apparently female, apparently blonde, though she could not be sure at such a distance.

"Yole—Teresa," she said. "You guys need to take a look at this."

Thirty-Seven

Russ Billman had done two tours of duty in Korea, and he assured the people around the table that he knew well what it felt like "to have bullets flying around you." But on that long-ago afternoon, he told them, he suspected his guard was down. The moment the first bullet struck the bed of his pickup, Russ did not suspect he was being shot at. Ironically, he was focused on the gunfire he'd heard earlier, knowing those shots had come from at least a quarter mile farther down the road. He'd driven the road for only a half mile when the strange popping noise occurred, and he'd thought it an errant pebble thrown into the wheel well from the tread of a back tire. But when the second bullet arrived, striking the hood of the truck, he came to a rapid understanding of the situation.

It had taken him a few seconds to come to a full stop, and by this time he could see the two black vehicles just south of the border fence. The bullets now struck sporadically against the side of the pickup, one of them punching through the passenger's-side window. Russ, moving more quickly than he had in a very long time, grabbed his shotgun and sat breathing heavily against the front tire of the Dodge. The bullets stopped whizzing past, and he began checked himself—as far as he could tell he had not been hit. He dabbed a finger at the wound on his face, for it still throbbed. Otherwise, he was untouched.

More rounds hit the truck, and Russ's first emotion was anger, having not felt this mad since battles in Korea. He stood, pumping three furious rounds from the shotgun at his attackers, then went quickly back to his cover behind the vehicle's front end.

"Shit, Russ." He looked down in his lap at the shotgun, whose optimum range was maybe twenty feet. "What the hell do you think you're doing?"

A clicking noise came from the Cobra radio on his belt. Russ was reluctant to take a hand off his weapon in order answer it, but when the clicking came again he unclipped the radio.

"Come back?"

"Russ. It's O.D. Keep your ass down."

"O.D." Russ was relieved. "What's your twenty?"

"That little rise about a couple hundred yards south of them Mexicans."

"You're in Mexico?"

"Fucking A I'm in Mexico."

"What are you doing?"

"Shooting the shit out of dope runners—what the hell do you think I'm doing? Keep your head down. I'm behind them guys and can take a good part of them before they figure out who's shooting."

"You'll need some help."

"That'd be nice," O.D. said. "But you can't do no good with that damn shot gun, and my only other help is dead."

"Who's dead?"

"I'll tell you about it later."

"Roger that."

"Well, it's been a nice chat, Russ, but if you'll excuse me," O.D.'s radio crackled a bit. "I was right in the middle of shooting Mexicans."

"I don't think all of them are Mexicans." Russ had gotten a look at the men and was sure he knew one of them, a border patrolman named Waylon.

"Well, dope runners," O.D. came back. "Whatever the hell they are—they need shot, and that's what I'm busy doing."

Thirty-Eight

Russ's story had made him emotional and he worked to keep the tears back. He shook his head and tried to steady his breathing. Derrick poured him some water from a pitcher on the table, and the old man lifted the glass to his mouth, determined not to look up at his audience.

"I'm not finished," he said. "I got more I need to tell." He put the water cup down. "I'm glad some of the others aren't here." He looked at Teresa, then at Kevin. "I know some stuff, details, situations, I guess, that the rest of you don't. From the investigation I was naturally involved with, things people'd told me. Tom and I talked about this sometimes before he died. One night I remember in particular when we were drinking at the Red Barn. Must a been three or four hours, just us two talkin' low at a table by the window feeling desperate and helpless. And *drunk*. Jesus, I never seen old Tom so wasted before. I'm just glad—someone's not here, cause it would be hard for them to hear how some things went down."

Tom and John left their wives and Olivia and made their way to within three-hundred yards of the shooters but could not see them for the brush. They descended the open ridge, luckily undetected, and lingered behind a wall of mesquite and ranger sage that stood between them and the fray. Shouting and intermittent rifle fire rose muffled from the west, and they dismounted in order to pick their way to a nearby clearing for a clean view. This, of course, would mean they were visible to be shot at. Thomas was especially anxious as he was certain he'd heard his son's voice in the distance, but because the words were shouted in Spanish, he couldn't be sure. His radio clicked several times as someone tried to call him.

A shell chambered, rifles in the crooks of their elbows, they picked their way through the brush. That John broke trail had been an unspoken conclusion, perhaps because he'd ranched this country so long and was a natural point man. When the two black vehicles came into sight, they were barely visible, obscured by branches and tall grass. Things had been quiet the last few minutes and the shooters were nowhere to be seen. Thomas tapped John on the back. They stopped, went down on their haunches to whisper.

"We'd better crawl from here," Thomas said.

John cocked back his hat, scratched at his hairline. "No," he said, shaking his head. "I want to move faster than that."

They stood again and crept along some twenty feet when several bullets crackled through the brush. The two men went flat to their bellies and six more shots whizzed by, striking the leaves and branches of the mesquites in front of them.

"I don't think they can see us now," Thomas said.

"They know where the hell we are, though." John raised his head, his chin just a few inches from the ground, and surveyed the area. "Over to the left it's thicker. I say we break for that."

"They'll see the movement through the brush."

"But they already know we're here. Pretty soon someone'll come for us."

Thomas nodded. "Agreed."

"On three," John said, but before he'd reached that number both men were on their feet and running. The shots came, more abundantly this time, perhaps a dozen or more. Bullets zipped into the grass and dirt around them. They stopped finally at a shallow ravine banked by several mature juniper trees. Thomas went to his knees, John bent over, hands on his thighs, both men chasing breath, and Thomas noticed the blood.

It had settled and spread on the back of John's pant leg and dripped out by the heel of his boot.

"You're hit," Thomas said.

"What?"

"You're hit." The blood was coming fast. "Pants down," Thomas said.

John bent and yanked his Wranglers to his knees. "Jesus," he said. "I didn't even know it."

The bullet had entered his inner thigh, about three inches below his crotch, and had exited in a quarter-sized hole just below the buttock. The blood ran like a partially open faucet. Thomas had already pulled off his belt.

"What are you doing?"

"Tourniquet," Thomas said. "You'll bleed out if I don't."

"Holy God," John said.

Thomas had just situated the belt above the wound when a bullet, passing within a few inches of his head, hit the rocks on the other side of the wash. Both men hit the ground. They heard people moving toward them, then shots that seemed to originate from the low rise to the south.

Thomas' radio crackled again, and O.D.'s voice emitted from it, but he was too busy, too scared, as he bound the belt as tightly as he could around John's thigh. John looked drowsy, weak.

"Can you run, you think?" Thomas asked. "Can you get up?"

John shook his head.

"They'll be here in a minute." Thomas nodded toward the arroyo. "I'll move down this wash a few feet, then up the bank. I want to get to them before they get to us, try to get a jump on them." Tom tapped the barrel of John's Mini 14. "You be ready."

John nodded, though he did not look altogether cognizant.

More shouting from the brush. One of the voices, Thomas was sure, was Mondy's.

Thomas had run down the wash perhaps fifteen steps when he heard John shout: *Sonofabitch.* He had never heard this particular oath applied in such a tone, invoking not anger or fear but, strangely, shame. The shots came. First one. Then a second.

Thirty-Nine

An hour and a half earlier, the three young deputies had spotted the two black Suburbans, which appeared quite suddenly and seemed benign enough, parked as they were just a few feet on the other side of the fence. Between the three men, there'd been some argument earlier as to what the fence represented. Ken and Jonesy thought it the border, while Si Banks, proud of how well he knew the area, insisted it was a cross fence for one of old Magoffin's bull pastures. Perhaps because he was the senior of the group, Banks' claim was accepted. So when they rounded the bend, encountering the two parked vehicles, they assumed they'd run across a party of American deer hunters.

Jonesy stopped the car. "Let's ask those guys if they've seen anything."

"I don't think they're there," Ken said. The windows were heavily tinted and the vehicles appeared to be vacant.

"There's a guy," Jonesy said, pointing.

A big white man in his forties had stepped out of the Dodge. He wore a camouflage shirt and cap and was corroboration for Banks' opinion. The man stood by the open passenger's-side door. He waved, almost shyly—not so much to flag them down as to acknowledge their passing.

"I want to talk to that guy," Jonesy said. "Maybe he knows something."

"Don't," Si said. A strange feeling iced the bottom of his stomach.

"Why?" Jones asked.

"I don't know."

"I'll go with you." Ken opened the passenger's-side door.

"I think we should move on," Banks said.

"Shit, Si," Jonesy came back, "we need to follow whatever lead we can."

Ken had already stepped out and moved around the front of the truck. Jonesy opened his door and walked a few yards toward the black vehicles just on the other side of the disputed fence.

"Hullo, sir," Jonesy said to the man.

The man only gave a nod and waved again, but the gesture seemed too shy, too nervous for the context. The other men climbed out of the black vehicles, calm and unhurried. One of the men rested a rifle, a carbine, over the hood of the Ford.

Perhaps because of the young deputies' long search that morning, poor Simon being the butt of the others' jokes the last fifteen hours, they didn't recognize the danger, dumbfounded even as the first bullet struck Jonesy in the gut.

Everything moved quickly. Jones turned, his hand over his midsection. "It burns," he said, the look on his face almost comic, a combination of surprise and horror, like that of a two-year-old who, having been warned, has just touched a hot oven. He began walking back to the truck, his feet falling too heavily, almost stomping the ground as he approached. The second and third bullets exited through his chest; he pitched slightly forward and went down with a thud in the dirt.

Ken, just two steps from the fallen Jones, drew his pistol. When the first bullet had passed through his chest, he spread his arms, emitting an annoyed "Ahhhh!" like a man who'd just spilled coffee in his lap. The second bullet put him on the ground like a dropped stone.

The driver's-side windows had been shattered, and Simon Banks opened the back passenger's door of the king cab. He felt dizzy, and his neck burned as if stung by a bee. Staggering, he focused on the fence off the north shoulder of the road and began to move in that direction. On the other side, he felt, lay safety, peace, and the kind of comfort one can only have in dreams.

Forty

Russ Billman's most salient regret, of course, was the deaths of those three young officers. For a long time, he'd packed the blame, prompted into a two-year, guilt-infused drinking binge. In that time, he'd threatened to quit the county several times, always persuaded to stay by the then-sheriff, Ron Jessum. Sometimes he'd been sober through the work day, but more and more often he'd kept a pint of Fleischmann's vodka under the seat of his cruiser, usually finishing it by noon. He bottomed out, in AA terms, one evening when, drunk, he ran off the road on the way home, totaling a county vehicle against a rocky embankment and leaving without a scratch on his body. He'd not taken a drink since.

Russ looked up at Kevin from across the table. "I still think about that kid, so gung-ho. He was a good officer, like the other two." The old man shook his head, clinched his jaw to stave back the emotion. "I don't know why it waddn't me that day, why I'm sitting in this room here pulling breath and they're all gone."

Kevin started to speak, but no words came. Teresa blew her nose, and Olivia stood, moved around to the table. She kissed Teresa on the cheek and hugged her.

Russ sat back in his chair and glanced toward Conchillo beside him. "Benny, you haven't said anything," he pointed out.

Conchillo raised his chin at Kevin. "I'm waiting for him."

"No," Kevin said, his heart thrumming. "I..." his throat caught. "I'm the one who started the whole fucking mess."

"You did not," Olivia said. "A seventeen-year-old boy did."

The aptness of her comment registered with everyone in the room. Kevin looked over at Derrick, who, hands folded quietly on the table, had not uttered a word. "Some things are clearer to me," he said. "Derrick, I'm not sure how much I can help you here." He shook his head. "I hadn't expected to talk about this in front of so many people."

The others in the room seemed unmoved. Kevin knew he could no longer retreat, though he was doubtful he could be as stoic as the others in his telling. "Okay," he said. " 'The readiness is all,' I suppose."

It was Bonny who gave them away, though Kevin credited the little dog's courage. He'd thought a moment about tethering her to his saddle horn as he had before, but he'd altogether forgotten. After leaving Si Banks' body, they followed the road half a mile before breaking from it.

"I think staying on the road will put us too much in the open," Mondy said. "That damn chopper went home—we need to look out for ourselves." Kevin, though scared and silent, was in agreement. Shortly after parting from the road, they came to a section of downed border fence. It appeared to have been pushed over by a vehicle perhaps a month before, probably by drug- or people-traffickers. They paid no thoughts or words to the fact as they crossed into Mexico and rode a sandy wash that angled west.

Soon, they climbed out of the arroyo and topped over a rocky butte. There stood the two Suburbans in plain sight about fifty yards to the southwest. Eight men with heavy backpacks, Amanda Monahan in the middle of the group and naked from the waist down but for her underwear and boots, had just stepped out and were moving quickly north. Seconds passed, Mondy and Kevin silent, all four animals standing dead still, ears cupped forward.

They had not been seen. Bonny, at Dunk's feet, stood alert, her eyes fixed on the blonde-haired girl she knew to be her master. The dog did not bark, and in a moment she lowered her head and bolted. Kevin could not call back the words, any more than a fired bullet: "Bonny! Get back here! Bonny!"

In seconds, Bonny arrived, biting furiously at the legs of the man closest to Amanda, who to this point had been holding a gun to the girl's head. Another man, further to the rear of the group, drew a pistol, stepped up to the fighting dog, and shot. Bonny went down, struggling, as though caught in a trap, against her injury. The second shot pushed her to the ground and she lay still.

Mandi's shrill screams had a certain pitch Kevin would always remember—not so much terrorized but angry, frenzied, suicidal. The men had spotted Kevin and Mondy. In the months to come, Kevin, in his recollection of the episode, was to confuse the circumstances of the ensuing actions.

The .22 pistol was in his hand now, though he could not recall having drawn it. Sally had bunched up as though to buck and was pivoting in a tight circle. When she stopped momentarily, he pointed the pistol the general direction of the group and fired half a dozen shots—with no effect, apparently, as the nine people stood unmoved as stones. What left him sleepless many nights was the fact that one of his reckless bullets may have easily hit Amanda, who stood in the middle of them.

Kevin lost his reins, and they dangled in the grass as he groped the saddle horn for them. Bullets blasted by, some of them just missing his body, a few crashing into the rocks and dirt behind him. In a moment, Mondy had the reins and the three animals were running—back toward the knoll over which they had come. But they were much too open, bullets swarming the air around them. They made for a bank of brush to the left and dropped into a shallow wash.

Kevin was most keenly aware of the shouting at first, and in his scrambled panic could understand the words, though, strangely, could not distinguish them as Spanish or English. Coming from one of the men by the vehicles, the voice had the resonance of maturity. *¿Quiénes son ustedes?* it asked for the third time. Who are you guys?

Kevin and Mondy sat in the sand of the wash, backs against the bank toward the shooters. Mondy turned and put his hands on Kevin's chest and Kevin could smell his sour breath.

"*¿Estás herido?*" Mondy asked. Are you hit? He ran his hands over Kevin's neck, shoulders, thighs.

Kevin held out his hands and, for some reason, looked into his palms. He felt as though he had come out of a long sleep. "*Creo que no,*" he said.

A few yards down the arroyo, the three animals, unhurt, clomped in the sand, snuffling at the tufts of love grass along the bank. This, when the pieces of the story were later put together, was the designated miracle: twenty-odd shots fired from rifles at two men and three big animals at just under fifty yards, and not one bullet touching flesh. The news media, when they and twenty-six search and rescue volunteers found their way to the scene just before nightfall, would spin this into a small measure of journalistic gold.

"Who the hell are you?" the man's voice shouted again.

Mondy sat up from the bank, turned, and on his knees shouted,

"We only want the girl!"

"What girl?" the voice came back.

Mondy raised his head again. "*¿Quiénes son ustedes?*"

"*Federales,*" one of the men said, which brought chuckling from the other men at the vehicles.

"*¿Tienen visas?*"

"*Visas,*" the voice said. "*No necesitamos pinches visas.*"

The joke was funny, though beyond the referential reach of anyone but Armando Luna and its deliverer. Kevin was puzzled at Mondy's smile.

"What?' he asked.

Mondy shook his head. "Nothing."

Again they heard the man's voice, more hushed this time: "Go around. Go around—over there."

Mondy looked at Kevin. "I think some of them are coming over here."

The only voice they could hear now was Amanda Monahan's, muffled, weeping, unintelligible.

Some hundred feet to the north, just outside of the arroyo, stood several waist-high boulders. Twenty yards up the wash, the bank dipped low enough for them to clear. Between that point and the shelter of the rocks was forty feet of clearing.

"Let's go for those rocks," Mondy said. He picked up his rifle from where it lay on the bank and slung it by the strap over his shoulder.

They had stuffed their pockets with ammunition, though Kevin realized at this moment he had left his rifle in the scabbard on Sally's saddle. He looked down the wash at the animals. All three, exhausted, dosed in the shade of a desert willow. Kevin looked at Mondy. "I need to get my .270." And easily enough, as though it were any other day or circumstance, Kevin strode up to the mule, removed his rifle and walked back to where Mondy crouched behind the bank.

"Fuck," Mondy said to him, real anger in his voice. "You've got to be more careful, man. Keep your fucking head down."

They looked up the wash at the low point in the bank.

"On three?" Mondy asked.

"Fuck that," Kevin said and took off running.

Kevin had no immediate memory of running through the clearing between the embankment and the rocks. Piecing it together later, he would realized they had so surprised their assailants, the shooters only had time to fire two, perhaps three errant shots at the moving targets.

Hunched behind the boulders now, Kevin and Mondy stared a moment at each other, struggling to absorb the reality of their situation. They were startled at two quick rifle shots, the bullets striking futilely against the protective boulders.

"*Alto fuego*," came the older man's voice. *Stop shooting.*

Mondy smiled. "They can waste all the ammo they want on these rocks."

"No kidding," Kevin said. He felt clarity now, even a bolt of confidence.

"*Oye, chamaco*," the older man shouted. "Hey, kid!"

Kevin was incredulous that the man had called to him. "*¿Mande?*" he responded.

"We all fell in love with your girlfriend, man."

Kevin took a beat or two to process the statement. "Fuck you," he shouted back.

Mondy put a finger to his lips. "Don't talk to him," he whispered. "The guy's fucking with your head."

The man laughed—loudly, his mirth seeming genuine. None of the others but Amanda had made any sound at all. "The trouble is, though," the man went on, "she can't decide which one of us she likes best. You know, she thinks all of us are good lovers, man, but she can't choose. We're all kinda jealous, so I guess I'll just have to cap her."

Kevin stood and, without aiming, fired his rifle. Mondy put a finger through Kevin's belt loop and drew him immediately back down.

"Jesus, Kevin. He's trying to draw you out. Don't be stupid."

Kevin was chasing his breath and could feel the thrum of his heart. "We can't just sit here," he said.

Suddenly, with no provocation from Mondy or Kevin, the shooters were clamoring among themselves, their voices low and unclear. Finally, a man whom they had not heard before raised his voice. "On the hill, man. Up on the saddle." More shots now, but no bullets struck the rocks.

"Where are they, Ise?" another man shouted. With no trace of

Latin accent, he sounded Anglo—a mature man. "Shit, man, they got Chingo."

Mondy and Kevin were perplexed. Mondy cupped his hands to his ears. "They aren't shooting at us, man."

"Who, then?"

"Somebody looking for us, probably."

The voices of the shooters rose to shouting. The voice of the Anglo man repeated: *There's two behind us. In the brush. Somebody needs to go after them.* Then more shooting. Again, no bullets struck the rocks. After some minutes of audible chaos, all went unnervingly silent. Then, more shots. Strangely, the bullets arrived a moment before the reports and struck nowhere near Kevin and Mondy.

The men by the vehicles were shouting again.

Mondy pointed toward the ridge. "That shooter's on the hill behind them. Gotta be somebody looking for us."

Kevin nodded his agreement.

"I say we wait it out right here," Mondy said. "We got good cover and we got help now."

"Really?" Kevin said. "I was considering a short nature hike."

Mondy shook his head. "No place for that bullshit now," he said.

Kevin nodded. "Sorry."

More rifle fire from the hill to the south. More shouting.

"Somebody's hitting them pretty good," Mondy said. "Maybe your dad or somebody."

"Somebody," Kevin said. "Maybe Russ Billman."

"No," Mondy said. "I'm pretty sure Billman's on Guadalupe Road behind us, other side of the border. I was him I'd be hiding under that county truck. Gotta be someone else. Maybe one of the Monahans."

More shots now, frequent and coming from all directions, the men by the vehicles shouting exclamations, profanity, and orders to one another. "Get her! Get her!" one of them said amid the fray.

Mondy and Kevin, with the simultaneity of raising their binoculars on a hunt, peeked a moment over the rocks. The brief picture which impressed itself, snapshot-like, behind their eyes, was that of the distraught blonde-haired girl, all but naked and cradling the dead dog, walking their direction.

And then the voice of the Anglo man. "Shoot her, goddamnit.

Somebody put her down."

"We got to do something," Mondy said. "When I take off, you get up and shoot all four shots as fast as you can—away from Mandi. Shoot right at those black trucks. Try to get your crosshairs on them. It'll be close enough to probably keep those guys down."

And then Mondy was gone and Kevin stood and fired. The shooting from all directions had been so tumultuous that Kevin could scarcely hear the report of his own weapon. He was down again now and could feel the pulse of his heart in his throat.

"Mondy!" he screamed.

He heard, in the distance, his name shouted, though the voice was not Armando Luna's but O.D. Hallot's. "Kevin. Keep down."

Behind the rocks, Kevin worked through the images printed in his brain: Mondy, head lowered and without a weapon, sprinting toward the girl, who staggered in plain sight through a clearing in the brush. And then, like the Rapture had suddenly come, both had vanished from sight, Mondy having pushed the girl to the ground.

"Mondy!" Kevin screamed again. He heard sobbing now along with obtuse syllables. To remain behind the rocks was all but unbearable.

Kevin found out much later that his father was within two-hundred feet of him. Thomas had left the dry wash, assuming John Monahan dead. When he'd heard the shots that took Monahan's life, he'd doubled back, surprising the attackers, both of whom stood over Monahan's body. They were boys no older than twenty, one Hispanic, one Anglo. Thomas had gone to one knee, steadying himself on an embankment, thirty feet away. He downed the Anglo boy first, as his rifle was held at ready, the bullet striking the boy's cheekbone and exiting through the back of his head. The second boy looked on in surprise as Thomas took careful aim, shooting him in the chest, just above the sternum.

Thomas could hear his son shouting and moved in that direction. The black Suburbans were parked between him and Kevin, and when he heard footsteps approaching from the direction of the vehicles, he took cover behind a cedar tree. In a moment, a heavy-set Hispanic man, Juan Carlos Rascon, came into view. When J.C. had passed where Thomas lay hidden, Thomas rose and stepped out of the mesquites. J.C. froze, raised his hands, arms spread, and dropped his weapon.

"I have three kids," he said to the man behind him.

"So do I," Thomas said. He stepped up behind J.C., put the muzzle of the Dan Wesson to the base of his skull and fired. The big man fell backward, his head thumping the toe of Thomas's boot before he could move away.

Kevin shouted again. Thomas was tempted to shout back but thought better of it. He ducked down and moved toward the vehicles, toward the sound of his son's voice. When he was twenty yards from the Suburbans, Ise moved into view. He stood between the vehicles, breathing heavily.

Thomas took aim, shot, but hit to the right, striking the vehicle in the side panel. Ise, standing in plain sight, bent down and picked up a rifle, a Mini 14, checked the magazine to discover it empty. Thomas shot again, missed again, and the man took cover behind the vehicle on the left.

"T-o-o-o-om," O.D. shouted from the rise.

"Talk to me," Thomas shouted back.

"You missed him."

"Well I know that, goddamnit. Where the hell'd he go?"

"He's hiding behind the truck. There's two left. I can't get a clear shot at neither of them."

Tom moved to the back of the truck on the left. He could hear the man breathing on the other side and positioned himself behind the left rear wheel for better cover. The man moved about, probably looking for ammunition.

"Are you a reasonable man?" Ise asked.

For a moment, Thomas did not answer. "Not right now," he said, finally.

The man rustled about again, then a click, a lock-blade knife, he was sure, being opened.

"We could talk," Ise said.

"Not much to talk about," Tom said. Quietly, Thomas lowered himself to the ground. The truck was high clearance and he could see the lower half of the man hunkered down on the other side. He wore bell-bottom pants and patent-leather zippered boots, a wide belt with an H buckle. Tom moved to a prone position, put the front sight of the pistol at the base of the belt buckle and squeezed the trigger. The undercarriage of the vehicle muffled the pop of the pistol, and the man groaned and fell straight backward.

"You hit him," O.D. shouted.

Staying low, Tom crept around to the front of the truck and found the man, convulsing in pain, flat on his back.

The man looked up at him, a questioning expression around his eyes.

"You won't make it," Thomas said. "We're a long way from any town, and you're just gonna hurt for a long time."

The man nodded.

"Turn your head to the side," Thomas said.

The man complied.

Thomas opened the Dan Wesson to check the ammo. Two shells left. He clicked the cylinder back into the frame, cocked it, put the muzzle a foot from the man's right ear and pulled the trigger.

Two more shots, again from the hillside to the south, sounded. Then came two pistol shots—more shouting now, and Kevin was sure he heard his father's voice. Then O.D. Hallot's. They were calling to each other.

"He's the last one." O.D.'s voice, clearly.

"Where the hell is he?" his father shouted back.

Then O.D., faintly, from the hillside to the south. "He's in the brush—twenty yards ahead of you."

"Is he hit?" Thomas shouted.

"Yes," O.D. came back, the word very annunciated. "But he's got a gun."

Kevin walked out from behind the boulders. No more than one hundred feet to the south stood his father, holding his Dan Wesson revolver at ready, like a cop, in both hands.

"Dad?"

"Kevin? Get down, goddamnit!"

"Dad?"

Then O.D. from the ridge: "He's moving, Tom!"

In the mesquite thicket twenty feet before him, closer to himself than to his father, Kevin noticed—as though this figure had grown out of the dirt—a man crawling like a baby on hands and knees toward him. The grotesque spectacle leaving him a little undone, Kevin simply stood there. The man was big, Anglo, balding. Except for the camouflage shirt he wore, he had the same soft, benign look of many of Kevin's teachers over the years. Only this man was bleeding badly from the neck, and in his right hand he held a pistol, which clumped along the ground as he crawled.

"Shoot him, Kevin!" came O.D.'s voice from the ridge.

But Kevin couldn't absorb the words.

"Shoot him!" O.D. shouted again.

Fifteen feet from him now, the man came to a stop, pulled himself up and sat slowly back on his knees. He pointed the gun at Kevin, then pinched his face and shook the weapon as a man would a watch that had stopped. With the butt of his other hand, he banged on it—once, twice.

"Shoot him, Kevin!" came his father's voice.

Kevin brought his rifle around, the butt along his right hip, the muzzle pointed at the man's chest. He found out later that neither O.D. nor his father could fire at the man without endangering him.

When Kevin pulled the trigger, the firing pin clicked. He jacked back the action of the .270, hammered down the bolt and took careful aim, though the man was only fifteen feet from him. Another click. It took him a moment to realize no shells were chambering.

The man raised his pistol and pointed it at Kevin, but in a moment the man was face down in the dirt, the gun shot and smack of the bullet hitting him in the head seeming to play out in reverse. Kevin looked down at his rifle, thinking perhaps his struggle had found a stray shell in the magazine. He looked up to see his father, pistol still at the ready, approaching him, the fallen man between them.

"Hold on, Kevin," he said. "Just stay right there." Thomas stood over the body of the balding man, whose head was bleeding out onto the ground. "Are you alright?" his father said. "Kevin, are you okay?"

Forty-One

George and Derrick had left the room, and the latter's raised voice could be heard just outside the door. The older cop was trying to calm the younger. Kevin's mother and sister had moved around the table to him, and he could not stop crying. He shook his head as they tried to comfort him. Kevin sat back in his seat and his mother put her arms about his head. Olivia stood nearby, though she had a sense of what her parameters were, what distance to keep from the scene.

The two old men had not moved from their places, and sat staring across the table at each other. George came back into the room alone and Conchillo looked up at him. "Bring that boy back in here. There's something I need to tell him."

The older cop left and returned ten minutes later with an armload of sodas and Derrick Waylon in tow. Emotions had settled, and everyone had taken their original seats. Kevin and Derrick would not look up at the others. Conchillo opened a Pepsi and took a drink. He looked directly at Derrick. "Young man, I have to say this thing to you, and it won't be easy for either of us."

Derrick looked up from the table at the old Indian.

"When I heard the shooting over to the west," the old man began, "I ran Lastima, my old gelding, almost to death." He looked up at Russ. "After he wouldn't go no more, I ran through the brush a long way on foot."

Russ nodded. "You were pretty scratched up," he conceded.

"I ran over to Russ's truck, and he'd just come out from behind it and was walking toward the other vehicles. I called to him, and he waited for me. I'd met him once or twice—in bars around the area—but didn't know him other than that, did I Russ?"

Russ shook his head.

Conchillo leaned back, and with his eyes closed, gave his version of the incident.

He'd left his house on horseback soon after the boys had gone and took the Jeep trail west, when he encountered a group of migrant workers who told him the direction Kevin and Mondy had gone.

"Russ and me walked up when most everything was over," he said.

They could see Kevin with his rifle about fifty yards south, and the other man, Waylon, close to him. "When I saw the man raise his gun to Kevin, I went down to one knee, aimed my .30-30. In Iwo Jima, I was nineteen years old. I killed a lot of men at fifty yards."

Derrick was shaken, the set of his shoulders tense, and he would not look up.

"I'm sorry, young man," Conchillo said. "I'm not proud to tell you that." He glanced over at Russ. "We haven't talked about it since all the damn police interviews. Russ and I pretty much kept it to ourselves. And from this time on, I won't talk about it more."

"I checked Philip Waylon's pistol," Russ said. "The gun was no longer jammed. He had a round in the chamber when he aimed it at Kevin."

Kevin's mother and sister were sitting on either side of him now, his mother gripping his right hand. The events that followed that day on the Escrobarra had come in a series of dreamlike episodes. He recalled pulling away from his father, who had a grip on his upper arm. "Kevin, stay close. This area might still be hot."

He could hear the men's footsteps behind him as he moved up to Amanda Monahan, who sat in the dirt in her underwear as though she were playing jacks. He sat down and they faced each other, the dead dog across her lap, Mondy prostrate between them, his arms folded under his chest.

"Hi, Kevin," she said, as though they'd passed each other in the breezeway at school. She was rocking back and forth as though the dog were a child.

"Hi, Mandi." Kevin looked down at his friend but could not see his face. His feet were within Kevin's reach and he grabbed the heel of a boot and shook it, but he found himself unable to say the name.

"He's tired," the girl said. "He pushed me onto the ground."

Kevin leaned forward and put his hand on the middle of Mondy's back, came away with his palm covered with blood, wiped it on his jeans, grabbed the boot again. "Hey, man," he said, shaking him as though to rouse him from a night of drafts at the Red Barn. "*Levántate*," and then again, "*Levántate.*"

The time was 4:00 p.m. on what had been a beautiful, unseasonably temperate day. The lucid blue, cloudless sky had in the last half hour turned amber, and now a luminous silver where the sun had just dropped behind the cut edges of a rugged horizon which, on this low knoll where it had ended, could be seen all around. The heavy wind had quieted, and a light breeze spirited out of the south, and the last of the late fall light came at such a slant to throw cool shadows on the north aspects of the hillsides. A red-tailed hawk, just a spec in the east, kited on the wind and all had become quiet, the way the land seems to rest, to let itself heal, in the wake of a violent storm.

Mondy Luna was now two minutes dead, and Kevin looked up to focus on the three men standing over him who had been trying to gain the distracted boy's attention.

It was Russ, perhaps because of the authority of the uniform, whom Kevin heard first: "Come on, son. Move away from him."

Then Kevin was aware of his father's hand gripping his shoulder, gently pushing him to scoot backward a few feet. Russ held a canvas tarp, which he laid blanket-like over Mondy. Kevin scooted a foot toward the tarp and placed his hand on Mondy's covered back. He looked up at the deputy.

"He's warm," Kevin said, as though to question the need for such a covering.

"It's okay, Kevin," the girl assured.

Amanda sat cross-legged, the dead dog in her lap, and Kevin noticed the blood on the crotch of her underwear. Thomas McNally knelt down beside his son.

In minutes, the three women would arrive on the scene. They would go immediately to respective loved ones—Olivia wrapping her arms around O.D.'s waist and smiling into his face, almost as though greeting an old school chum rather than her husband, Teresa McNally falling on her son, squeezing him so hard Kevin would feel compelled to push her away—*Christ, Mother, you're hurting my neck*—Yolanda Monahan sobbing over her violated daughter, Thomas McNally unable to draw up the nerve to tell the woman her husband lay dead in a ravine not a hundred yards away. In an hour, forty-odd people would arrive at once, their lights and equipment, their questions and wide-eyed clamoring, many of them the lost search volunteers, many from the various news media. Several reporters would press everyone present for comments, though all but Russ Billman, out of the burden of his office, would decline, the two distraught teenagers having been taken to one of the vehicles, locked inside to be sequestered from the aggressive news people.

But in the interim few minutes, the several on the scene fell into an eerie meditation, quietly taking in the verity of the circumstance, each wishing in some part of his or her brain to climb free of this dream. It would be a long three decades, though, before any of them would begin to cut themselves loose from the trauma.

Kevin could not bring himself to remove his hand from the canvas tarp, as though the still-warm body under it brought some manner of comfort, and his father beside him spoke to the tarp as though the lump of flesh beneath it might somehow spring to life.

"Indian," Thomas McNally said, the words too loud, as though spoken to someone at a distance. "I owe you, Indian." He put his hand on his son's and squeezed. Kevin squeezed back—more affection than had passed between them in many years.

"You hear what I'm telling you, Indian?" Thomas said. "Do you hear what I'm trying to say?"

Forty-Two

George Meeker had looked the document over the night before and had a pretty good idea of how the shootings went down, but the testimony of people at the table that afternoon added another dimension to the episode. After everyone who had wanted to had spoken, he opened the folder in front of him.

"Some of this was put together by various law enforcement agencies," he said. "There's also testimony from Thomas McNally as well as Amanda and Yolanda Monahan." George looked around the room, stopped on Kevin. "If you want to read this privately, I would understand, Dr. McNally."

"No," Kevin said. "It's not really a private matter now."

George looked at Derrick Waylon. "Are you alright?"

The young cop nodded.

George looked around the table. "How's everyone else holding out?"

"I could use a shot of whiskey," Conchillo said.

Laughter all around. George even smiled amicably down at the paperwork in front of him. "I'll just read aloud some key parts of this, try to summarize. I don't think anyone here wants to hear police-report writing."

It would take federal, state and county investigators from both countries almost a week to untangle the network of events and legal implications that ended in so much bloodshed. Along with the sheriff's department, FBI and DPS agents, *Federales* from Hermosillo sorted through the evidence of a crime scene that spanned a square mile. Authorities recovered three-hundred-sixty-five pounds of uncut cocaine and almost two hundred pounds of pure heroin, worth about twelve million dollars on the street. In all, fourteen people had been killed and one wounded.

The three young deputies—Simon Banks, Kenneth Jones, and Dan Jenkins—had been the first casualties, all of them dying from bullet wounds from the same kind of .22 caliber rifle. They had been killed just a few yards north of the border when, apparently, the perpetrators, just south of the line, became nervous at their presence. This transpired around 1:30 p.m., a mile east of where the final and incident-defining fire fight had occurred.

Just over half an hour later, the smugglers—whose respective legal paper trails in the days to come would confirm their identities—had decided on a crossing point. The perpetrators had lingered a few moments before embarking after they heard the sound of Russell Billman's vehicle, which they perhaps determined to be their smuggling connection. At this point, they had been surprised by Armando Luna and Kevin McNally, whom they fired upon. They were surprised a few minutes later by O.D. Hallot and Harold Placer, on whom they also fired. Hidalgo County Sherriff's Deputy Harold James Placer became the fourth victim, shot to death with a Mini 14 about two hundred yards into Mexico.

The next casualty was Billy Rojas, dying seconds after being struck in the upper chest by a single bullet from O.D. Hallot's rifle. Soon after, John Monahan was shot. He was found in a shallow drainage about seventy-five meters south of the border fence. He had, in all, suffered six bullet wounds fired by at least two perpetrators, Justin "Chingo" Echardt and Ralph Garcia, both of whom lay dead within a few feet of Monahan's body, and both having been killed by .35 caliber bullets fired at close range from Thomas McNally's Dan Wesson revolver.

The remaining five perpetrators had become confused, two of them, brothers Paco and Miguel Hernandez, standing with rifles held when O.D. Hallot fired, hitting Miguel low in the abdomen. When the boy doubled over, his brother Paco approached him and was struck immediately by another of Hallot's bullets, which entered his upper scapula and exited just below his right collarbone. Paco Hernandez expired within minutes, while Miguel lingered several hours, and was finally pronounced dead at the scene at 6:45 p.m., just before the helicopter medical transport arrived.

Juan Carlos Rascon was found thirty meters south of the two Suburbans. Thomas McNally, having just shot two in the party, and having heard Rascon's approaching footsteps, surprised Rascon after hiding behind a cedar tree. J.C. died from a single wound to the head from McNally's pistol.

The remaining two perpetrators, Isedro Leon and Philip Waylon, had taken cover behind the two vehicles. Waylon had been struck in the neck. Forensics ballistics experts determined the wound had probably been caused by a ricocheted bullet from Kevin McNally's .270. Injured, Waylon had moved into a nearby cluster of ranger sage to hide. Waylon was reported to have been shot and finally killed with a single bullet from Kevin McNally's .270 when he emerged from the brush; however, the report was later amended to show the shot was fired from a thirty caliber rifle owned by Benjamin Conchillo.

Leon, out of ammo for his nine-millimeter and having no other firearm available, remained alone at the vehicle until surprised by the armed Thomas McNally who had come up behind him. The official report read that after McNally had wounded Leon, he ordered him to sit and link his hands behind his head. Leon drew a hunting knife from his belt, whereby McNally fired his weapon, striking Leon once in the head, killing him immediately.

Thomas McNally and O.D. Hallot were extradited to Mexico on charges of illegally crossing international borders and seven counts of negligent homicide. Though the ordeal for both men became a grueling two-year extension of this nightmare, they were eventually given suspended sentences for the illegal crossing; the seven homicides were ruled justifiable by way of reasonable self-defense.

Armando Luna, the last of the victims, had been struck in the chest by three bullets—one from a twenty-two caliber rifle, two from a nine-millimeter pistol fired by Isedro Leon. Luna died almost immediately.

The room they were situated in was on the second floor, and outside the police station afternoon traffic sounds rose to meet the open windows—rush hour, such as it was, in Douglas. The angled sunlight softened the corners of the room and an easy feeling settled around those gathered at the table. It was as though a forecasted storm had passed and the world had clattered back to life.

After George finished reading, no one spoke for a long while. The cop rose and walked to the window, and Teresa backed out her chair. Everyone made ready to leave. Kevin's cell phone broke the silence. The name on the caller ID read "Jessica."

"Well," Russ said. "Who wants you now?"

Kevin smiled. "My girlfriend," he said.

Amicable laughter all around.

Kevin looked up to find Derrick Waylon smiling at him. "Well, answer it, fool—before she hangs up on you."

Kevin picked up the phone, clicked it open as he walked out of the room. "Hi, darling," he said.

Epilogue

They pulled into the visitor's parking area a few minutes after 7:00 a.m., and Kevin noted how much things had changed over the years. The Forest Service had built a trim camping area, laying concrete slabs for recreation vehicles, erecting cinder-block grills, picnic tables and bear-proof trash bins, strategically arranged to accommodate some fifty or so nature appreciators. The mood had been light on the hour-long drive up to the mouth of Guadalupe Canyon. Kevin and the three women had eaten doughnuts, sipped Starbucks coffee, joked and laughed. Rachael Martinez had driven out behind them, transporting the two old men to the site. Rachael had agreed that she, Russ and Benny would stay at the campground while the others hiked up the ridge to release O.D.'s ashes. Later, they would all enjoy the rest of the afternoon together in the shady oak canyon.

The majesty of the high desert, on this clear morning, seemed familiar as a relative. The pink hues of the rocky outcroppings, the brush-choked canyons, the sharpened relief of October sky seemed to welcome this spirit of mirth. When they stepped out of Tracy's van, Kevin, Styrofoam cup in hand, walked a few paces toward the trailhead and paused. It wasn't wonder, really, but an old familiar sense of humility that he'd worn so easily as a kid when standing in the palm of this canyon, confronted by these mountains which had stood here long before him and would remain long after. And he was surprised by the tickle of a memory that came so suddenly and without warning he found himself lost in it—he as a boy of fifteen and Armando Luna climbing down Rustler's Ridge on the Escrobarra after a long day's hunt, stopping midway down, amazed to see the sun setting in the west and a rice-paper moon climbing a blue sky in the east.

Kevin was lifted from his reverie by the sound of a vehicle, a blue Ford pickup, pulling into the campground parking lot. A woman stepped out of the driver's side, and even at a distance Kevin recognized her at once. Amanda Monahan was more beautiful now than she had been as a girl. Her hair had darkened to a sandy brown and her features had settled nicely into womanhood. From the passenger's side of the pickup emerged her mother, Yolanda, and a boy, about thirteen, who by his square frame and blond hair Kevin knew to be Amanda's son.

The women fell into rounds of hugs and chatter as Kevin, coffee grown cold in his hand, and the boy stood un-introduced and awkward to the side. Yolanda finally turned to Kevin, and they looked at each other wordlessly for a moment. What had been salt-and-pepper brown hair was now pure gray and hung in a braid, the way she always wore it, down to the back belt loop of her jeans. Her eyes loaded up, she took a step toward Kevin, and they hugged a few moments, long enough for the others to grow uncomfortable and silently register the somber occasion of their gathering. When Amanda and Kevin finally greeted, they fell shy as teenagers, only shaking hands and hardly looking each other in the eye, for they had not seen each other since Kevin's high school graduation. Amanda introduced her son, Michael, her youngest child of three. Kevin shook the boy's hand and looked again at Amanda.

"You look good," she said to him.

Kevin shook his head. "You look way good," he said, and Amanda laughed self-consciously. She pulled at the sleeves of her denim shirt and looked down toward her feet. Even dressed so simply, in denim and hiking boots, she was stunning.

"I didn't know you were coming," Kevin said.

"I didn't either—until about two hours ago. My mother talked me into it."

Kevin looked off at the trees that lined the campground. "It's been rough for me, too," he said, finally.

Amanda nodded. "My psychiatrist says this may help."

Kevin drew a long breath. "Not much has. For me, anyway."

"Me, too."

As they made ready for their hike, the group fell into a more comfortable rapport, Kevin and Amanda catching up after so many years. She had attended the University of Arizona for three years until she met and married a young man from Montana who was attending law school there. She had lived in Tucson ever since, raising her three children, her husband first a public defender and later in his career a member of several successful law firms. Amanda told Kevin how much she admired and worshiped her mother who, by herself, had run the ranch since John's death.

The party of seven started up the Mormon Ridge trail. Kevin began to recognize the old familiar route up the Escrobarra, and he harbored a little buzz of pride that no such pantywaist trail existed for him thirty years ago. To the southeast, the slope he and Mondy routinely climbed was still a tangle of catclaw brush and snaggle-toothed rim rock, and he wondered at how he and his companion had managed such a rugged hillside. After another quarter mile, Olivia Hallot pointed out through an opening in the Emory oak and junipers the nape of the ridge, beyond which lay the slated canyon.

O.D.'s ashes, though he was emaciated at death, weighed seven or eight pounds, and Olivia insisted on lugging the box in her daypack, summarily waving away Kevin's several offers to spell her. They would reach the canyon half an hour later and the ocotillo in the bottom would be just past bloom. The women had planned a picnic and they lunched on hard salami and Swiss cheese, French rolls, two bottles of good red wine. They lingered about, finding the shade of a mature oak on a granite shelf that overlooked the Peloncillos spreading out toward the northwest and the grass-covered Bernardino valley beyond that.

Kevin and Amanda sat close together under the oak, no longer uncomfortable in each other's presence but now bound in a mutually remembered terror. The others, and even the boy, sat apart from them, giving them the needed time and space.

Each of them in the party, in his or her own time, glanced down to the west at where the border fence cut the shallow chain of sage-and bear-grass-covered hillocks where it had finally ended. No one spoke of it or even acknowledged the place.

The time had come, though no one had prompted it, all simply knew. Kevin and Michael were charged with finding a place to scatter the ashes. They walked two hundred yards up the ridge and came to a limestone outcropping, below which the canyon dropped severely away before them. They could see the full measure of it, side-to-side and end-to-end.

"Whoa!" the boy said. "I don't want to fall off in there."

When the women caught up, everyone agreed this was the place. Unceremoniously, Olivia dropped the backpack from her shoulder and opened it, removing a wood box about a foot wide and long. As though she had rehearsed this procedure, she took her Leatherman tool from her belt, backed out the screws holding the top and removed the plastic bag of gray ashes. She untied the bag and carried it to the precipice of the rock ledge, and she didn't hesitate a second before turning the bag and letting the ashes flutter to the canyon's bottom, the finer sediments collecting in a small cloud of dust that drifted, spirit-like, up canyon on the north-going wind.

"So long, Tubby," she said. It had been a pet name she'd often used for him.

Amanda and Yolanda were both seated, arms wrapped around each other, both women in tears. Amanda was especially beside herself. "Daddy," she said, not so much to call him forth, but as though she'd been surprised by his voice on the phone. "Daddy, where are you?" Her son stood a few feet behind them, at a loss to help.

Kevin did not speak, nor could he, his throat feeling as though held in a vice. His mother and sister put their arms about him. He had not known his mother to weep so in a very long time. The presence of Armando Luna, he felt, surged through him like electricity, and for a long while, an hour at least, none in the party spoke, nor did any one of them look another in the eye.

On the way back down the ridge, Kevin fell apace beside Yolanda Monahan.

"You ever see old Pete anymore?"

"Pete?" she said, laughing. "That old varmint's long dead of old age. I see one of his sons around, though."

"You ever go after him?"

Yole laughed again. "Lord no," she said. "I sold the hounds long ago. Truth be told, though, John never wanted to hurt that old cat. Never even took a shot at him, despite rumor."

Kevin nodded. "Not surprised," he said. "I've felt it myself."

It would be a long time before Kevin McNally returned to that ridge, though he caught himself thinking often of the place and at times even dreamt of it. In the dream, he walked along the nape of an easy, tapering slope, the valley floor spreading below him, the mountains beyond arching in a chain of contoured blue into the distance. When he stopped to rest, he sat down in a thatch of sweet-smelling broom grass, a soft breeze touching his skin. When he spoke, he listened for the wind, and on it the voice of an old friend always answered.

Acknowledgements

To the following people whose help and encouragement was invaluable, I give grateful and heartfelt acknowledgements: Robert Houston, my former teacher, for a great endorsement; Jennifer Carrell, Jonathan Evison, Charlie Quimby, and Andy Nettell for their wonderful initial reviews.

I am indebted also to Cappy Hansen for the first read and suggestions on a very rough book, Beth Colburn for encouragement and suggestions, Leslie Clark for her keen eye, Guillermo Retana for cleaning up the Spanish, Robbie Pock for her brilliant help with the hard stuff, and Mark Litwicki for one last look. Finally, thanks to Bob and Ann Hastings for their generosity with their cabin in the woods.

Special thanks to Mark Bailey for his faith in this book and to Kirsten Allen, my editor, for her help in fine tuning my story and for "talking me off the ledge"—more times than I care to name.

ABOUT JAY TREIBER

Jay Treiber holds an MFA from the University of Montana, where he studied under writers William Kittredge and Earl Ganz. His poems and short stories have appeared in various literary journals, such as *The Chattahoochee Review, Farmer's Market,* and *The Fiddlehead.* He makes his home in Bisbee, Arizona, and teaches creative writing and English composition at nearby Cochise College.

ABOUT TORREY HOUSE PRESS

The economy is a wholly owned subsidiary of the environment, not the other way around.
—Senator Gaylord Nelson, founder of Earth Day

Love of the land inspires Torrey House Press and the books we publish. From literature and the environment and Western Lit to topical nonfiction about land related issues and ideas, we strive to increase appreciation for the importance of natural landscape through the power of pen and story. Through our *2% to the West* program, Torrey House Press donates two percent of sales to not-for-profit environmental organizations and funds a scholarship for up-and-coming writers at colleges throughout the West.

Torrey House Press
www.torreyhouse.com
Visit our website for reading group discussion guides, author interviews, and more.